CW01426055

IN DREAMS

By Darren Frey

ISBN: 9798858753278
ASIN: B0C3T6QSM9

TABLE OF CONTENTS

Foreword and Dedication

What could I say that was not already said in *Psychonautic*? What took years of life experiences to come full circle, the writing allowed me to release much of the trauma I picked up along the way. They say, "We cannot heal until we feel." I could not have written such a story a decade ago, but that is because my part in the story was not yet complete. The universe still had many hard lessons to teach me. Now, the parallel journeys of Darren Frey and Julian Frost continue. *Psychonautic* was about digesting and letting go. As Julian wrote his story, I wrote mine. *In Dreams* is about moving forward and welcoming change—embracing the great unknown. *Psychonautic* was a labor of pain, but *In Dreams* was a labor of love: my gift to you.

Along the journey thus far, I have had lots of help from some amazing people. I would like to thank Aila Nate for producing another breathtaking piece of cover art. To my editor, Dagan Boyd, who stepped in at exactly the right time, understood my vision, and put her absolute all into this, I thank you from the bottom of my heart. To my beta readers: Jennifer Foulk, Elizabeth Krenek, and Carrie Ann Musselman, I thank you for offering your eyes, ears, time, and support. I couldn't have done it this way without you.

To my friend, Autumn Cornett, you have read this book front and back; combed this thing more than the desert in "Spaceballs." You have volunteered far more of your time than I could ever ask. Your passion for the characters and the story has inspired me. I thank you for all the great ideas, support, and for allowing me to drive you absolutely insane! You have been wonderful, and I thank you for being exactly who you are!

Not so long ago, I had a phone conversation with an old friend—someone I grew up with. He enlightened me to something I had not really thought about. He noted that I seem the happiest and most focused when I am either working on a project or talking about writing. Even if it is something I am frustrated with, if it is writing-related, my passion shows. He was right.

Late last year and earlier this year, I had issues with relocating. I lost friendships. I lost faith in myself. It was not until my phone rang that morning—my old friend on the other end—that I was reminded of my place and power. I was reminded of what my words and actions are truly capable of when I practice self-love. We are all capable of self-love. We must all nurture our inner child. Thank you, Nathan Adkins; not just for the phone call, but for that reminder, and for the truth I needed to hear. I love you, brother.

Dr. Timothy Leary famously said, "Think for yourself and question authority." In many ways, *In Dreams* will beg you to do the same. You will be presented with many ideas—new and old. You will encounter cultures with abstract beliefs, not all of them fictional. These are simply that: beliefs and concepts, created by man—no more or less worthy than you. Though I do write from my own head and heart, I ask you to read and consider with the same.

Not only do I want to tell an entertaining story, but I also want to encourage and enlighten. But primarily, I want to show you it is okay to not agree with me or anyone, but to know for yourself. Like my lovely vampires, I bleed red, just like you. To be human is to be free, cooperative, and passionate, but individualistic. Ask yourself this question, "What am I passionate about, and how could that benefit myself and others?" If you have not reached a conclusion by the end, start over, and see what you might have missed. Who knows, you could just inspire yourself into creating something positive! Wouldn't that be nice?

Chapter One

Julian's heart stumbled when he opened his eyes, finding himself not where he'd fallen asleep but somewhere else—somewhere dark, damp, and far from home. Inert with fear and uncertainty, it was not until drawing his first conscious breath of musky air, a heartening wisp of sweet vanilla followed. "Violet?!" His nocturnal gaze rapidly adjusting to the obscure environment, a shadowy figure emerged.

"Violet?" The shape, looming over him, said nothing. Instead, a gentle, feminine hand took his and pulled him from the hard, rocky surface he'd lain upon. "Where are we?" The figure turned away, leading Julian through a narrow, cave-like setting, faint, natural strands of light reflecting off the moisture along the dilapidated walls.

Just ahead, an exit appeared, giving way to such a sight. A brilliant green mist danced amongst the stars and a mighty full moon glowed in the backdrop. Beneath the phenomena, Julian gained a better view of not just a surrounding winter forest, but the petite figure in a white dress. It was the same dress Violet wore at their wedding. Still gripping his hand, she peered over her narrow shoulder, her face cloaked beneath a veil of thick, dark hair.

"Is it really you?"

She offered a single nod and released his hand, turning towards a series of giant snowy evergreens. Violet's extended white train slithered behind her, and Julian followed. The only sounds were that of snow crunching beneath their feet and the rhythmic heartbeat growing in his ears. Ahead, frosted boulders of many sizes circled a natural spring, its sparkling water mirroring the green aura above. "Violet? Look at me."

She spun slowly in Julian's direction, her head bowed. With both hands, she steadily reached behind her back and unzipped the dress. It landed in a crumpled pile at her feet. Gawking upon his beloved's unclothed body for the first time, Julian's heart couldn't help fluttering in awe for such beauty.

Violet's hair, draping her breasts and resting over her flat stomach, rose and fell with every breath she took. Just below her waistline, her trembling thighs clenched tightly, safeguarding her femininity. Awkwardly, she stepped away from the pile of fabric. She ambled backward to the water, stopping once her lower half was entirely submerged. From there, she raised a hand to her bridegroom—provocatively curling her index finger—urging him to join her.

Despite the polar climate, the cold had no effect on him. Until then, Julian hadn't even noticed, nor what he was wearing: the white tuxedo and shoes from the wedding. After removing everything, he advanced until his feet met the warm liquid. Three steps farther, the water tickled his navel. He now stood less than a foot from his beautiful bride, still a silent dark shadow, hiding beneath her hair.

He extended both hands, and Violet took them. Fingers interlocked, he nervously muttered, "I love you." With their wet, naked bodies now closer, two erect nipples brushing his chest, Julian closed his eyes, preparing to kiss her until "Nights in White Satin" filled his ears, overcoming the moment entirely. Both of his eyes burst open, finding he was no longer in the spring or his lover's arms. He was in their bedroom, lying on Violet's hammock, marinating in a film of his own sweat.

From the small wooden end table separating the hammock from the bed, Julian's cellphone rang, the Moody Blues song he and Violet had danced to on his last birthday playing as the ringtone. "No!" he cried, discovering it was only a dream. He rubbed his somber eyes and picked up the phone. *Tara Stillwater* flashed across the screen as the caller. His heart sank instantly. Reluctant and unsure what to say, he took a deep breath and swallowed a lump before answering. "Hello?"

"Julian, it's Tara!" a frantic Appalachian twang declared. "Have you seen or talked to Daryl since last night?!"

"No, why?"

"I don't know where he's at! I've been calling his phone all day, but he ain't answering. He was supposed to come to Mommy's last night after he left your place, but he never showed. You got any idea where he is?"

"No, I—I don't," Julian scrambled, guiltily peering across the room at the motionless, dark mass on the bed.

"Well, I don't know what to do. I've called everyone he knows, but nobody's seen him. I even tried calling you this morning. You didn't answer, so I came over and knocked on your door. I reckon you and your wife were asleep."

"Yeah, and ..." Julian sighed. "I—I don't know what to tell you."

"I'm scared! You know it's not like him to just disappear. Between that and everything that's been all over the news, I'm freaking out!"

"The news?" Disoriented and still shaken from the dream, he asked, "What do you mean?"

"You don't know? A bunch of people died, and Times Square nearly burned to the ground last night. There was some helicopter crash. It's really messed up, but right now all I care about is finding my husband. The girls and I are out looking for him. If you happen to see or hear anything, please tell him to call me. I don't know what else to do."

"I will, but I'm sure there's an explanation."

Following a frustrated sigh, Tara whined, "All right, thanks." She snorted again, tearfully concluding with, "Bye."

"Bye," Julian repeated, feeling every bit as lost as he imagined her to be. He ended the call and checked the time on his phone: *4:33 p.m. EST.*

He stood from the hammock and flipped on the light, gaining a better view of his friend. Sprawled out across the bed, the burly bear of a man appeared comfortable. His breathing was steady, but his chin, chest, and a large surrounding portion of the white bedsheet were all covered in dried brown vomit from his transition.

Julian headed towards the closed bedroom door and cracked it open. He scanned for any signs of light upstairs. When he saw nothing, he entered the hall, also listening for Anna or Bernard in one of the other bedrooms. The only noise came from the television nobody ever turned off. He walked softly to the basement bathroom, beyond the hall, passing a small kitchen and living room area that Violet and Xavier often used when awake during daylight hours.

After retrieving a wet washcloth, Julian returned to the bedroom. He gently cleaned Daryl's face and chest and removed what remained of his bloody, bullet-ridden, striped shirt. Then he struggled to pull the dirty bedsheet out from under him without yanking him out of bed.

Making more noise than he'd like, he cringed when a sleepy voice groaned through the wall. "It's okay, Bern. I think Julian was just checking on his friend. Go back to sleep, love."

After cleaning Daryl, Julian switched off the light and returned to the hammock. Restless, he faced the ceiling, all along reliving the horrific tragedy as if it were happening again in real-time. The concentrated panic in Violet's brown almond eyes—deadlocked on his; it was all he needed. *Violet,* he wailed in silence, focused on a sparkling tear as it dripped from the corner of her eye and splashed against his cheek.

From behind, Christopher Cauldwell emerged, his exposed teeth clenched and his golden-brown mane blowing in the wind. The militant savagely clawed a handful of Violet's auburn hair, whipping her head back. He raised a fat, glimmering blade to her tender throat. Julian cupped his hands over his eyes, begging the torture to end, but the vision endured, forcing him to repeat the sadistic nightmare of watching his flower's precious flesh sawed through like a melon. In a grotesque, lukewarm gush, her crucial nectar rained from the gash, baptizing her lover as it did. The sickly-sweet gore seeping down his throat, Julian gabbled, "Stop!"

Upon the desperate appeal, his cerebral assault fell silent. Pulling himself back into the present darkness of his bedroom, he yanked his hands away from his eyes and moved one to his heart. Following a series of deep, quivering breaths, he told himself, *It's okay*, but it was a lie. He knew it wasn't okay, nor would it ever be again—at least, not in this lifetime.

Muffled sound drifting down from the television upstairs, the latest news report drew his attention away from the vividly obscene memory. It was a morsel he took to like a ravenous parasite. "… the president arrived back in Washington at twelve p.m.," a deep male voice relayed. "He has reportedly been debriefed on the situation and is expected to give a speech later this evening, addressing the nation regarding last night's tragedy.

"Currently, firefighters and rescuers are still working to battle the blazes and attempting to rescue and aid survivors. The death toll now stands at nine-hundred-sixty-seven people. Over two thousand are confirmed injured, and one-hundred-forty-six people are still reported missing. We now go live to New York correspondent, Sierra Montgomery. Sierra?"

"Thanks, Tom. I am standing here in Brooklyn as the entirety of Manhattan Island has been evacuated. Except for police, firefighters, and rescue teams, no one is being let in, for the time being. The scene across the East River is bleak, to say the least. Though only one building collapsed, four others surrounding Times Square caught fire and were in danger of collapsing as well.

"From the information I have received, most of the fires have been extinguished. Firefighters are still working hard to battle the remaining blazes, and rescuers are searching just as hard for survivors. I was told the nine-story building that collapsed hosted residential condominiums, and it is believed that many people are still trapped in the rubble. Whether they are dead or alive has yet to be determined, but officials are still unclear regarding what exactly happened to cause such a tragedy to unfold.

"We have here with us an eyewitness who was in the crowd last night, enjoying the New Year's Eve festivities, when the Black Hawk helicopter initially crashed, killing everyone inside. It was then the detached propeller and helicopter itself fell onto the crowd." There was a brief pause before the reporter asked, "Sir, can you please tell us your name?"

"Matt O'Brian."

"And Mister O'Brian, can you tell us what you saw?"

"At midnight, just as the ball was dropping to ring in the new decade, I saw a helicopter flying overhead. Suddenly, it spun out of control and crashed into one of the tall buildings. Before I knew it, the propeller came flying towards the crowd."

"And Mister O'Brian, how far were you from the propeller when it fell?"

"I was only about fifty feet away. It all happened so fast, and it was so surreal. At first, I thought it was staged, like a publicity stunt or something, until I saw the blood. That is when the propeller came twirling towards me."

"Then what happened, sir?"

"I jumped out of the way, but it hit a sweet young woman I previously spoke with. She was here from Washington state." He loudly sighed. "She was split in half right in front of me."

"Oh my God," the reporter groaned. There was another brief pause before she moved on. "We have someone else here who was also in the crowd. Ma'am, could you tell us your name, and what you saw?"

"Stephanie Ingle, and I saw a Black Hawk helicopter crash into a building. After that, the propeller hit the crowd. I thought it was an act—you know, like a publicity stunt, but then I saw the blood."

Moving on, the reporter said, "And you, sir, can you tell us your name, and what you saw?"

"My name is Andrew Rhodes. After the helicopter crashed and fell off the side of the building, it exploded onto the crowd. Then a naked man crawled out of the wreckage, and—"

"Back to you, Tom," Sierra blurted, cutting the man off mid-sentence.

"Damn," Julian grunted. He grew rigid with goosebumps, hearing such things—things he was responsible for.

"Thank you, Sierra. We will continue round-the-clock coverage of this tragedy and keep you up to date on any new developments as they become available," the newsman said as Julian's attention drifted to the door squeaking open in the next room over. Three soft knocks on his door followed.

"Julian, it's Anna. May I come in?"

"Yes."

The door opened slowly, and the overhead light came on again, momentarily stinging Julian's eyes. He blinked a couple of times before fixating on Anna's. Tragic rings, as red as the frizzy, unkempt mess atop her head, circled both. Her simple burgundy dress from the wedding was wrinkled and torn, but it was all she'd brought with her. "Did you hear that shite?" she asked.

Sitting up in the hammock, Julian said, "I did. At least they cut that last one off before he could say anything else. The way the first two just repeated themselves, it sounds like they're trying to keep as much covered up as they can."

"That's a good thing. But it has me wondering what they might already know. Everyone laughed at Christopher Cauldwell before, but someone might've believed him, especially now."

"Do you think someone's on to us?"

"Probably not us, but someone doesn't want to create panic." Turning her eyes towards Daryl, she asked, "How's he?"

"He seems to be okay. He did throw up at some point. I cleaned him the best I could."

"Has he been awake yet?"

"No."

"When he wakes, he'll have to feed."

Julian sighed. "That's what I'm worried about."

"What do you mean, love?"

"Daryl's not going to be happy as a vampire. He's a proud man, and he's got a family to support. It's really going to mess him up. I even tried to confide in him last summer—everything that happened at Leviticus—but he didn't believe me. He thought I was making it all up."

"There's nothing we can do about that now. He'll believe it when he wakes up. He was shot, and should've died, but through Hell Belle's death, Daryl was saved."

Hearing that name brought Julian to tears again. "I miss her so much," he said. "I would give my life to bring her back—her and Xavier. Neither of them deserved to die, and Daryl was innocent. He was only here because he's my friend. What's he supposed to do now?"

"I don't know."

"His wife, Tara, called. She's worried about him. She said she came over here earlier."

"So, that's who was knocking on the door," Anna groused. "Don't worry. We locked his truck in the garage, so it would be out of sight."

"Thanks." Julian sat near Daryl on the edge of the bed. "I'm so worried about how he—" The door squeaked open again, cutting him off.

A goateed, groggy-eyed face beneath a bald, pink scalp appeared. "Would you shut the hell up?" he snapped. "I'm trying to sleep!"

"Oh, get over it," Anna griped. "We've got things to discuss."

Entering the room, Bernard yawned while stretching his arms above his head. His raised, buttoned, blue shirt exposed a sunken navel at the center of a flat, hairless, baby-smooth stomach. "What the fuck is so important?"

"In case you haven't noticed, my wife and Xavier are dead," Julian said. "My best friend was turned against his will. Times Square is in shambles, and I don't know what we're supposed to do now. Someone was talking about me on TV. It's only a matter of time before videos or pictures start surfacing, and our faces are seen."

Bernard smirked. "It's not our problem. Once it gets dark, which should be any minute now, Anna and I are getting the hell out of here."

"Excuse me?!" Anna protested. "We ain't going nowhere. Julian and Daryl need us."

"They're not our problem, my love."

"Why would you say that? This is our coven."

"What coven? Everyone is dead. There is no more coven!"

"Look, I don't know what we're supposed to do. All I know is last night was utter chaos. We lost a mentor and the sweetest—"

"—a mentor?!" Bernard chuckled briefly. "Is that really what you're calling him after all this time?"

"Yeah, it is. What else would I call him?"

"Considering your past and his, I don't know what you'd call that slimy twit."

"Really, Bern? You're going to throw that in my face again, here and now? Please, don't. I love you. I married you. Doesn't that tell you anything?"

"I don't know, does it? You've wept all day for him. Are you loyal to me or a ghost?"

"My heart is yours. But I am also loyal to this coven."

"Bah! I said there is no more coven!"

"But there is! Xavier's blood flows through Julian's veins. So does Hell Belle's—in his, and Daryl's. We can't just abandon them. It takes two to make and keep a coven."

Bernard shrugged his shoulders and turned his nose up. "I don't give a shit about either of them. Julian's soft, and Daryl wouldn't even know how to care for himself."

"That's why we've got to teach them."

"I don't have to do shit!"

"After everything Xavier did for you, saving you from Eustice and giving us a home, this is how you'd honor his memory?" Bernard said nothing. "Would you rather be back in Austria … back in that cage and serving that monster like a dog before we rescued you?"

"Why, you fucking whore!" Bernard flipped in rage, angrily stomping forward while raising a fist.

Before he could act, Julian instinctively found himself caught between a charging ram and its target. Even his grief could not prevent him from momentarily seeing his own father's face overlapping the present danger. "You think I'm going to let you hit a woman?!" he roared, slapping Bernard's hand away. "I spent my childhood watching my mother get beat on, and I'll be damned if I'm going to let you lay a hand on your wife!"

Bernard stopped in motion. He snickered and turned away, appearing to collect himself before doubling back, taking a lightning-quick, closed-fist swing. Julian knew to duck. He then rose with a fist of his own, connecting with Bernard's nose, dropping him to the hardwood floor. Julian growled, "Don't even think about trying that shit again!"

Wide-eyed, dazed, and holding his nose, Bernard fumed at his attacker, then at his wife. "Fuck you both! If you want to stay here with these two, 'my love,' then by all means, stay here, you fucking whore."

Julian yelled, "You call her a 'whore' again, I'm going to hurt you again. I don't need your shit! Do you understand?!"

"Fine," Bernard pouted. Back on his feet, he released his nose, uncovering a moist red smudge he wiped away with his fingertips and spread down his blue shirt like he was buttering toast. "I'm leaving," he said, turning to the door, bounding for the stairs leading up to the living room.

"Bern, please!" Anna ran after him while Julian rolled his eyes at the gesture. "Please, don't leave! I love you!"

"No, you don't. You love him! You always have and you always will." Fearing Bernard might try to strike Anna again, Julian bolted up the stairs into the dark living room, lit only by the television.

"Bern, wait!" Anna cried from outside the opened kitchen door, her desperate voice cracking. "Please, come back! Don't leave me—not you too!"

Chapter Two

Her drab upper half lying broken over the far end of the dining room table, drowning in tears, and insisting she be left alone, Anna suffered. While noting her sorrow from the open-adjacent kitchen, Julian took one of only four remaining IV bags from the freezer. Then he let her be—dragging his bare feet through the living room, the granite floor's cold touch revealing little to his senses.

At the other end, he sat on the curved, black leather sofa. Minding his own grief and weary of the reports, he picked up the remote and flipped through the channels. No matter where he settled, it was all the same: fire, death, and chaos. Finally, he dropped the remote and sighed, knowing he could not escape the hell he'd co-created.

At the top of the hour, the tall grandfather clock chimed from the corner of the room. He could no longer hold it in. Warm, salty beads spat from his eyes as he remembered that fateful July 4th night when Violet returned. At the stroke of nine, she had burst through his window and saved the day like a superhero. *What I wouldn't give to turn back time and bring you back—both of you*, he thought, remembering it wasn't just his lover he lost, but a father too.

"I could sure use your wisdom right now," he mumbled, visualizing Xavier's face and empty eye socket, as plain as day. He sighed again and wiped away the tears with the back of his hand, his thoughts drifting to the dream of Violet standing before him, naked and vulnerable.

Even with his distaste for the news coverage, Julian turned his attention back to the television, in search of a new distraction. Facing his sins failed in comparison to the heartache he held for his slain bride. Still, his gut electrified with dread of what the president might say during the upcoming speech. Sure enough, as the chimes of the grandfather clock concluded, a live feed of the Oval Office appeared on the ninety-six-inch flatscreen, mounted on the rough, gray stone wall above the dormant fireplace.

Wearing a black suit and tie, a thin, elderly man entered from camera left. His head bowed, exposing a crown full of unkempt white hair, the frail old man slowly shuffled to a brown desk emblazoned with the Presidential Seal. Between his sickly pale hue and the dark rings bordering his woebegone eyes, he appeared exhausted and mortified. After clearing his throat, the president placed his palms and elbows atop the desk.

He inhaled a deep breath and said, "Good evening, my fellow Americans. I come to you tonight not as your leader, but as a man, humbled and heartbroken by last night's tragedy in New York." The president cleared his throat again. "First and foremost, I want to assure you, the great people of this nation: last night's occurrence was not motivated by international terrorists. It was a domestic incident in which a Black Hawk helicopter was hijacked from the United States Navy by a disgraced militant and his company. They acted of their own accord. Though the men's names are not being released at this time, their bodies have all been identified, as well as everyone else involved in the anomaly."

Julian snorted, whispering, "Bullshit," under his breath.

"I want to assure you all—as fire and rescue teams are still clearing and searching Times Square—the situation is under control. I also want to urge everyone not to believe the fabricated stories, pictures, and videos surfacing on the internet of men flying and crawling out of the wreckage. It is all fake news, and while it is currently unclear how the helicopter crashed, this was no act of God or supernatural occurrence."

"… like hell!" Anna squawked from behind. Julian looked over his shoulder, finding her watching from the entry separating the kitchen from the living room, some twenty feet away. In the forefront, her dark, featureless silhouette eclipsed the sharp, fluorescent backdrop. At her side, an IV bag dangled in her closed fist, its contents glowing as vibrant as the bushy mop hanging off her head.

"Are you all right?" he asked, his eyes following her to the opposite end of the sofa—the spot Violet once claimed as hers.

"I will be."

"I'm not sorry for hitting him, but I am sorry that he took off. You didn't deserve that."

"It's not your fault. Mine and Bern's marriage was falling apart before it began. He's been throwing my past in my face for ages." Anna's shoulders sank and her head fell forward, her red strands now curtaining her gloomy face. "I knew it was only a matter of time before he left me."

"Where do you think he went?"

"That's just it. I don't know. We were all he had. Bern's got no one else."

Julian watched Anna's pale, shaky hand lift the clear IV tube to her pink lips and drink. Finding his own bag thawed, he also took a sip. Then he asked, "What now?"

"We have to make sure Daryl's going to be okay. After that, we need more blood. There are only two bags left, and he'll need them both."

Julian took another drink before returning his attention to the president's speech. "… I ask everyone to remain calm. There is no reason for alarm. Everyone involved in last night's tragedy perished in the fires. As search and rescue teams continue finding and aiding survivors, I only ask that you keep them in your thoughts and prayers. We shall overcome this tragedy together as one nation under God."

"How much do you think they know?" Julian asked.

"I don't know. He says everyone was accounted for, but you, me, and Bern know that's shite."

"Cauldwell and his men are all dead. I saw Bishop die, and Xavier—" Julian paused, trying to keep his tears at bay. "I—I can't believe he's gone."

"He was a good man. The best man." She raised her head and brushed her hair aside, her chafed, pink eyes meeting Julian's. "Once, I thought we'd be together forever. That is such a complicated word for our kind, I suppose: 'forever.'"

Julian snickered at such a patronizing idea. "I thought Violet and I would be together forever too. What kind of God would give me such a life, then dangle her in front of me like that—giving me hope—just to snatch it all away? What kind of God would do that to anyone?"

"The same God who created us: a cruel, narcissistic overlord and puppeteer." Anna's cold reply instantly brought Julian back to tears. She added, "Hell Belle and Xavier may no longer be with us in the physical world, but they are both still with you in your heart and dreams. You drank their blood. Not even death can separate you now. As for Xavier and me—we never shared our blood. All I have left now are memories." She closed her eyes and tried to smile.

"So, Bernard was right; you were in love with Xavier?"

Her puffy lids opened, releasing the dam of dew drops upon each freckled cheek. "I will always love him. I know it's not fair to my husband, but I can't help it."

"Last year in New York, Bernard threw all that in his face about sleeping with his sisters. I recall Xavier telling him that was a one-time thing."

"It was."

"Then why is he so upset about it now? Wasn't that over two-hundred years ago?"

"Bern was always jealous. He knew what Xavier and I did; everyone knew, but no one alive knows our true secret now but me."

"What do you mean?"

"Long before the night, he, I, and our sisters went mental, Xavier and I were lovers."

"If you loved him, why'd you marry Bernard?"

Anna took another drink from her bag. When the tube fell from her lips, she licked away the remnants. "It's complicated. The way Bern came into my life and the way I came back into Xavier's … it's just life. Things happen, and sometimes it's not always what you want. I do love Bern, though. I would have never married him if I hadn't. I made a mistake by not telling him the truth when I should have. That's on me. But after all these years and the hell he's raised over what he does know, nobody must ever learn about the history between me and Xavier because Bern must never know."

Perplexed, Julian asked, "Why are you telling me this?"

"Well, I guess it's because this is a—"

—*Thud!*

"What the hell was that?!" Julian yelped.

Anna leapt to her feet, shouting, "It came from downstairs!" Julian dropped his IV bag and gave chase. In the basement, at his and Violet's bedroom, Anna reached the open doorway first. "Oh, bugger!"

"What is it?!" Julian barked before entering the room and seeing it for himself. Beside the bed, atop the hardwood floor, Daryl lay twitching on his back. "Is he all right?"

Anna gently lifted the big man and placed him back on the bed. "I think so," she said.

Julian watched him wiggle his toes as if he were trying to get comfortable. Though his eyes were shut and he appeared unconscious, Daryl groaned, "Yeah, I know he is."

Julian sat on the edge of the bed, whispering, "Daryl? Can you hear me?"

"I think he's dreaming," Anna said.

"Can you hear me, Daryl? Who are you talking to?"

"Yeah," Daryl's grumbles continued. "I'll tell him—you left it in the library."

"The library?" Anna asked. "What's he talking about?"

"I don't know. There's a library upstairs, but who's he talking to?" He looked from Daryl to Anna, wondering, *Is it Violet?* "Should I go up there and look around?"

"Go on; but along your way, could you take one of the other bags out of the freezer so it can thaw? Daryl should wake soon."

Julian nodded. His hand over Daryl's, he whispered, "I am so sorry," in his ear. He stood and headed towards the door, his heart pounding and mind racing over what he could find upstairs and what it might do to him once he did.

Chapter Three

A smooth wooden staircase led Julian from the living room towards the second floor; all the way, his restless mind bubbling with curiosity. *What the hell is happening? Is any of this real?* His destination the library, he didn't even know what he was looking for, but in his heart, he knew Violet wanted him to find it.

The stairs landed in the corner of the spacious game room, its baby-blue carpet the same shade as Julian's eyes. When he turned to face the other end, he caught a chill. It wasn't the metal folding table and two matching chairs, nor the antique wooden chessboard and all its hand-carved pieces arranged atop it, either.

Behind such sentiment, hanging on the wall to the left of a white cubby shelf that was full of other old toys and board games, Xavier's favorite painting stared Julian in the face. The elder's young sister, Sibilla, was a spitting image of him. With a mouth half full of baby teeth, the long-jawed little girl smiled brightly. Clutching her wooden toy knight between a pair of infant hands, her thick headful of soured milky strands blew wild in the old portrait's backdrop. Having never before noticed the finer similarities between the two, using his old eyes, Julian continued, his focus returning to why he was there: his immaculate bride.

After rounding the corner and reaching the library, he opened the door and flipped on the light. All at once, he was taken aback by the powerful aroma of the old books. He'd whiffed them many times before, and always loved the smell, but this was different. It was the first time he'd visited the room as a heightened vampire. For that, he nearly gagged on the pungency.

He scanned the walls, all lined with tall wooden shelves full of either law and business books, once belonging to his uncle

George, or Xavier's large cache of various bindings he'd collected over the centuries. In the middle of the room sat a large brown desk that just two months earlier, had been delivered from New York along with his and Violet's other belongings.

Atop the desk, a small but thick, old blue book with a worn spine and edges caught Julian's attention. Though he could not recollect the circumstances, he knew he'd seen it before. He approached the desk and sat on the black office chair behind it. Further examining the hardback, he discovered a folded piece of notebook paper poking out from between two of the pages near the end. *Is this it?* he wondered. *Is this what I'm supposed to be looking for?*

He opened it, turning to the page with the folded paper, gasping with recognition of his own sloppy handwriting. *Happy Valentine's Day, Violet!* was scribbled in black ink above the childish outline of a heart. A single tear rolled down Julian's cheek as he opened the card he'd made for his beloved just a month after they met.

His soft voice cracking, he read aloud, "Dear Violet, this has been one of the toughest, yet best months of my life, and I am so grateful to have spent it with you! I love you. Forever yours, Julian." A couple more tears fell before he wiped them away and set the card aside. For the split second it took his lips to rise, he flashed a smile when returning to the book, its open page decorated in Violet's superior calligraphy. For that split second, it was the closest to happy he'd been since hearing her vows. Chasing that high, he read her words to himself like they were holy scripture.

2/14/19
Dear Diary
    This last month has been hell! First, Eric was murdered. Now, according to the news tonight, William, too—on the same day Christopher Cauldwell was released from jail! It wasn't enough that

those fucking bastards took Eric from me. They also took the sweetest priest from such a lost world that was much better with him in it. The way everything happened between the brothers after Autumn died, and then finally reuniting at the club before Eric was killed; I am happy they are together again—hopefully with their mother and in a much better place.

All I've done here is mope and cry this whole time. Julian has been every bit as sweet and good to me as I always knew he would be. He's done everything in his power to make me feel loved, heard, and comfortable. I have lost count of all the times he's held me while I cry. Just like Eric once did, he wipes my tears, and he listens to me ramble about my feelings. It feels so good to be held again. I keep telling Julian he must be sick of holding me. He just smiles and says cuddling me is a pleasure. He likes the way I smell. I told him it's just cheap vanilla bean perfume, but he loves it. He doesn't smell so bad himself. He uses some kind of fruity-scented Old Spice. It suits him.

It is after midnight now, but yesterday was Valentine's Day. He made me the cutest homemade card. Nobody ever made me a Valentine before. He even gave me some freshly picked daisies. I feel like such a bitch, though. He's told me he loves me several times, and I don't know what to say. I do love him. After all that has happened since we met, I know without question I was right to follow my heart to Las Vegas. He is the man of my dreams, and I want to tell him everything, but all I can think about right now is my family.

This has all been such a huge burden on Julian. He's experienced so much misery in his life already. When I read his thoughts, I see his intentions. He really does love me. He loves me as much as he possibly could at this point in our relationship. That makes me happy. But I also see fear and confusion. He is not scared of me. He is scared I will leave him.

He's been abandoned so many times by so many people he loved and trusted that it has traumatized him. Now, he's just waiting for me to do the same, especially with Dad still missing. After we found out about William, we talked. Although it hurt him to say, he told me to follow my heart when I finally broke down and said I didn't feel right being here while Dad is still out there somewhere.

It isn't just that either. Now that Christopher Cauldwell is out of jail, he's going to come looking for us. If I am here, Julian is not safe. I cannot put him through that, no matter how many years I have longed for him. I don't want to be a bad person. It hurt Julian, telling me to follow my heart. He knows what it would mean. If I left, it would devastate him. I don't want to leave and possibly never come back ... not after all this, but what else can I do? If we really are meant to be, nothing can prevent it, right? God, if you can still hear me, see us all through this.

Violet

New moisture gathering in his eyes, Julian wailed, "I miss you so much." He took a moment to cry and then recover. While wiping his tears, a light bulb shattered in his brain. He remembered where he'd seen the old blue book. "Could it be?" he mumbled, flipping back a couple of pages until reaching a specific date.

1/13/19

Dear Diary

I killed her. I just killed Chloe! I had told her I made up my mind about Las Vegas. I had told her how beautiful of a person she was, and she would make another woman happy, but I wasn't her. I said we could still be friends ... but she became so angry with me. We were dancing together when I told her. She yelled at me and told me I was a stuck-up, privileged tease. I got so upset and caught in the moment that I also told her what I was and why we couldn't be together. At first, she laughed at me and thought it was an excuse. I proved myself by reading her thoughts aloud. She started screaming at me and said she was going to tell everyone about me.

I didn't want to do it, but Bernard overheard everything. He hated her more than anyone here. He said he was going to kill her if I didn't. He'd likely make her suffer. I did not want that. I followed her outside after she stormed off. When nobody was looking, I dragged her into the alley beside the building and I broke her neck. By then, the band had finished their set, and Bishop said he would get rid of her body. I can't believe this happened, Diary! It breaks my heart. I blame myself for being so careless with her.

I had to get out of there, so I flew back to Las Vegas a little earlier than I planned. Now I feel so confused and conflicted, as if perhaps God is already mocking or punishing me for my choice. I got in my car and found a random late-night café a few miles from the strip. I am sitting here watching a man who's just as miserable as I am. I love his jacket! It's a lot nicer than my old Ramones jacket. Like mine, it's black leather, but his has embroidered skulls circling the chest and back.

Oddly, he looks just like the man from my dreams. His body is the same shape, and his hair is brown but not quite as long. He is wearing glasses. I never saw his eyes and always wondered if something was wrong with them. Is God tricking me, or could that be him? Maybe I am just so hurt right now, I only want it to be him. He is alone, writing about his life on his computer. His ex-girlfriend did something horrible to him. He is so heartbroken, like me.

This was probably mean of me, but to humor myself, I played a Tom Petty song on the jukebox. I found it after hearing him thinking what he was typing. Apparently, his dumb ex-girlfriend thought Tom Petty was a racecar driver. He noticed, and I even saw him smile when it started playing. He's cute, and it would be nice to talk to someone feeling just as low as I am, whether that is "him" or not, but I am too distraught to converse with a stranger right now. If it is him, we will meet again—right, Diary?

It will be daylight soon anyway, and I need to get back to the Parliament. Later tonight, after dark, is when my Psychology of Dreams class starts. Maybe that will cheer me up. For now, I need to get out of here. I feel like I'm going to have a breakdown, and the last thing I need to do is draw even more attention to myself.

Violet

Though Julian wondered what she meant by "the man from her dreams," his suspicions were true. Violet's diary was the same book he'd watched her writing in at the diner in Las Vegas, the first time he'd ever laid eyes on something so precious. He flipped through the book, finding every page full but the last. He stopped at random near the end. The date was *4/21/19*. He remembered that day well. It was the day Tara Stillwater picked him up from the local jail after Christopher Cauldwell had said Violet's name on television the night before: leading to Julian's drunken outburst and arrest.

4/21/19

Dear Diary

I left Julian. I did it in such a cowardly way too. What was I thinking? I fucked up! I should have never left, not like that, but I felt so powerless there. I was going to tell him my plans once it got dark. His friend, Daryl, came over earlier in the day, and he went back over to his house with him. I should have waited for him to come home, but I got scared and took the easy way out.

I left him a Dear John letter. Real classy, huh, Diary? He is going to hate me for just leaving him like that, especially after all the times he did the same thing to Faith. He never told me that himself either. Now, he'll probably know I saw it. I said I wouldn't pry into his thoughts, but I couldn't help it. I hope he will forgive me.

I am in Alaska now. Dad's not here. I've been here a few nights. Everyone has been good to me like they always have been. Meanwhile, all I do is worry. Nobody here knows where Dad could be. I told Pana I was considering flying down to Peru to see if he was there. Pana gave me his blessing, but he wants some of the others to accompany me. I am scared to fly that far by myself, but I'd rather just go alone. I know this is Pana's coven, and what he says goes, but I am a big girl. I will sneak away when everyone is asleep if I must.

Violet

Chapter Four

*D*ing ... *dong* ... *ding* ... *dong*, the old grandfather clock bellowed from downstairs, its ghostly chimes haunting the otherwise desolate house. Shocked back to life, Julian sprung to his feet, gasping for air. *When did I fall asleep?* At a loss, he scanned the library until his anxious eyes found Violet's diary on the desk, opened to the last page he'd read.

While catching his breath and remembering where he was, a faint movement came whispering from the hallway. Facing the open door, he called, "Anna?" but nobody answered. He placed the homemade Valentine back in the old book as the rummaging moved towards the game room. "What the hell is she doing in there?" he mumbled along his way out of the library, down the hall, and back around the corner. "Anna, what are you—"

Before Julian could finish, the appearance of a man in a teenage body garbed in a black suit and tie had all but knocked the wind out of his timid young creation. Tied neatly behind his head, the elder's fine, pale strands rested just inches beneath the nape of his neck. A basic black eyepatch concealed his left socket. He sat alone before the chessboard, vacantly fixated on its pieces.

"Xavier?!" Julian cried.

With his one hazel eye, the man locked onto Julian's dumbfounded blues. He forced a smile, slowly expanding his colorless lips. The gap between them exposed several broken or missing teeth, the immortal now bearing even more resemblance to his sister on the wall behind him. "Hello, son."

Finding it difficult to reply, Julian cleared his throat and took a deep breath. "Is it really you?" he finally managed.

"It is," Xavier replied, offering a single bow of his head.

"What happened?"

"You were there. You already know."

"I mean, what happened after that building fell? I thought it killed you."

"As did I." He smirked. "But if it had, I would not be here now, would I?"

"I don't suppose so," Julian mumbled. Unable to resist, he extended his arms and stepped in for a well-received hug. His maker's loving touch quilted his tender being in the warmth of a father. "I am so glad you are okay!" he cheered. "You must tell me what happened."

"Have a seat," Xavier said, pointing at the empty chair. "Let us play."

"I am not in the mood for a game of chess," Julian snorted. His maker said nothing. The stern glare did it for him. Offering no further resistance, Julian obeyed his wishes, settling where directed.

"Chess is not just a game," Xavier continued. "It is a metaphor for life. Did you know that?" Julian shook his head. "We are all born pawns—the weakest players in the game—surrounded by forces that seek to control us." He moved one of his center white pawns two spaces forward.

Figuring he might as well play along, Julian gave in and moved one of his own stubby black pawns, repeating, "What happened after the building collapsed?"

Xavier made his next series of moves in silence. After wrapping two of his long, narrow fingers over one of his bishops, he said, "The bishop represents religion and the ensnaring of the mind." He then moved the piece several spaces forward, capturing a black rook.

Growing frustrated, Julian asked, "What does that have to do with anything?"

"You saw the news on your television … the way this so-called 'president' lied to everyone, yes?"

"Yeah, but what's that got to do with religion?" Julian asked, reaching for one of his knights.

"Ah, the knight! The knight represents the military and police who protect the people from protest and revolution." Unsure what Xavier was trying to say, Julian shrugged it off, moving the piece and claiming a pawn. In response, Xavier used one of his rooks to best Julian's knight. "The rook represents government and media. Think of the rook as a castle wall, shielding all within it from outside forces—or from truth, in some cases. This president's lies are the rook. His influence may also be seen as the bishop to a populace of feeble minds."

"The president lied about what really happened, but why?"

"If you led a country of timid, easily manipulated people and you did not want to frighten them, would you not have lied as well?"

"I guess," Julian breathed. "When the building collapsed, Anna grabbed me, and we all got out of there. I tried to get Bernard and her to look for you, but we all thought you were dead."

"And so did I," Xavier said, as if just to stop the pandering. "After taking two of those darts, falling so far—twice—and getting shot in the hand, my body was weak. I hadn't the strength to move away in time. I experienced the crushing weight of stone and metal bearing down on me just before I lost consciousness. A time later, I awoke in a barren field somewhere outside the city."

"How'd you get there?"

"I could not say. I was alone. The sun was quickly approaching. I returned to the city in time to seek refuge inside an old subway tunnel. Once darkness fell, I fled."

Looking over his shoulder towards the stairwell, Julian asked, "Have you seen Anna yet?"

"I have not. She is tending to Daryl in the basement, yes?" Julian nodded. "Why?"

His heart sank deeper than he thought possible. He didn't want to say it. He wasn't even sure if he could, but after clearing his throat and swallowing a lump, he forced himself. "Daryl was turned. He's one of us now."

Instantly deflating into the chair like a balloon, the elder moaned, "How?"

"Violet's blood leaked into his wounds. That is how."

Xavier gasped. "I never knew such a thing was possible. But now it makes sense."

"What?"

"Dajhri told me Violet would make a vampire. When I arrived here in September, I was expecting to find she had already turned you. Even Dajhri believed it. In all my years, I've never known the queen to be wrong." Under his breath, he added, "Yet, here we are."

"About that," Julian groaned. "I—I swallowed some of her blood too."

"I know," Xavier said, his sullen grimace offering little wonder. "You were covered in it." He sighed, turning back to the chessboard, and moving his queen. "That was the last thing I wanted."

"Why? Anna said Violet would be with me forever now."

"Exactly."

"And what is wrong with that? I love her. If I can't be with her like this, at least I can still be with her there. In fact, I—"

"—until the day you die!" Xavier shouted. "That is the only way you will ever be with her. Dreams are temporary, and we cannot control how long they last."

"Yeah, I found out."

"How so?"

"She already visited me. I dreamt we were in a cave. She led me out to a snowy forest with a spring nearby. I think we were in Alaska. It looked like the Northern Lights in the sky. I also just read something in her diary about Alaska."

"Her diary?" Xavier tipped his head inquisitively. "I never realized she kept one." He wiped a knuckle over his widened, uncovered eye. "What did it say?"

"She wrote about someone named Pana, and how they wouldn't let her go to Peru by herself, but she wanted to go alone."

"Ah yes—Pana," Xavier mumbled. "He was quite confounded by that."

"Who is he?"

"He is a close, long-time friend of mine and the leader of a large coven. He was also who I have acquired our blood from since Leviticus fell."

"Speaking of blood, we only have two bags left."

"I see." Xavier curled an index finger over his chin, turning back to the game again. Only a small handful of Julian's pieces remained. Xavier quickly cornered his opponent's king with one of his pawns, declaring "Check!" Though Julian still had no interest in playing, he moved his king and claimed the pawn, not wanting to disappoint the man he'd spent all night wishing back to life. "The king represents the elite of the world," Xavier said. "The king controls the entire game."

Struck by a sudden spark of determination, Julian found a clear shot across the board for one of his pawns. Nodding in approval, Xavier said, "Pretend for a moment you are that pawn. If you can overcome all the obstacles and make it across the board—'running the gauntlet'—per se, you will be transformed into the queen, who symbolizes God. The divine nature of the queen—or God—exists inside every pawn."

"But what does this have to do with life?" Julian asked, removing his hand from the game piece resting only one space from its goal.

"Abrahamic religions surrounded by militaries, governments, media—even kings and presidents—all want you to fear and worship the queen, rather than become it. The goal of chess and life is to transform yourself from the weakest player to the strongest by recognizing God as not outside you but within. Therefore, you control your destiny and make your own choices. No one can take that away from you. Never forget that." Xavier placed his hand atop his final knight, positioned just enough spaces away to make his move. As he foiled Julian's plan by taking the pawn, he snickered. "… however, nobody will ever simply just give it to you. You must take it yourself."

Julian shrugged again, saying, "I still don't understand. What does that have to do with—"

"—if you would quiet your mind and listen, you would understand."

"What the hell do you want from me?!" He smacked his fist against the edge of the table, rocking the few pieces left on the board. "My wife is dead! My best friend is a vampire! And I just gave up my mortality for nothing! I have so many questions, so many statements, and so many thoughts that I don't know where to begin! I mean no disrespect, but I don't give a fuck about your metaphors or a goddamn game of chess right now!"

Julian seethed, losing his breath and watching the world burn in his head. Xavier reached across the table, placing a hand over each of his devastated creation's. Calmly, he said, "What happened to Violet is a catastrophe, as is Daryl, but you chose this life. Do you not recall Violet and I imploring you to ponder, until knowing with absolute certainty, this is the life you wanted?" His ego cracking like an egg, Julian's shoulders sank, and his head fell forward. Xavier thoughtfully tightened his loving grip, adding, "Like pawns, we cannot go back. We can only move forward."

"So, what now? Where do we go from here?"

"Even if we had blood, staying here longer than necessary would not be wise. Now that you are among us, it will be safe to meet Pana and the others. But I must request something of you, first."

"What is it?"

"Do not tell anyone outside of this house about Daryl's transformation or that you ingested Violet's blood."

"Why not?"

"I cannot tell you that. I only need you to trust me."

Though Julian's nerves had begun to settle, a newfound anxiety now coursed through his veins like a lethal dose of adrenaline. "I don't understand why you can't just tell me," he squawked.

"I know, son. I truly wish I could say more—I do. One day you will understand everything. But for now, I must insist these matters remain within the coven."

Though pitiful, Xavier's broken visage remained sincere. Even clouded by such grief, Julian saw how deeply regretful delivering such a somber proclamation had to be. Nonetheless, he nervously brushed his fingertips through the back of his hair, saying, "You realize how weird and suspicious that sounds, right?"

"I do. But for certain reasons—mainly involving yours, Daryl's, and others' safety—only you, I, Daryl, Anna, and Bern—" Xavier paused, glancing towards the stairs. "—where is Bernard?"

"He's gone. He got pissed off because he wanted to leave, but Anna didn't want to leave me or Daryl behind. Bernard called Anna a whore—saying she was in love with you."

Xavier smirked. "Bernard was always jealous."

"He even tried to hit her, but I stepped in."

"You did?" For a brief second, Xavier grinned honestly, further revealing his mangled maw. "Look at you, stepping into your new power!"

"It was instinct," Julian said. "After he flew away, I spoke with Anna. She told me about you two." Julian watched Xavier show no emotion to the news. "That was when we heard Daryl fall out of bed in the basement. When we went to check on him, he was talking in his sleep."

"What did he say?"

"It was as if he was talking to Violet. He told her he would tell me to go to the library. That's why I came upstairs and how I found her diary."

"What did it say?"

"I only read a few pages, but it was mostly about how sad she was last year over missing you, me, and then losing Eric and William."

"Yes, she and Eric were very close," Xavier said, turning his attention back to the chess game and using the other rook to trap Julian's king. "That's checkmate, son."

"She also wrote about killing Chloe and how much it devastated her," he said, ignoring the game's outcome.

"I would imagine so. Aside from your cousin and his two friends, that was the only time she had ever killed anyone since her parents died all those years ago. Even that was not entirely her fault."

"Wait, what?!" Julian gasped, thinking Violet once said she accidentally killed a man while trying to have sex with him. Bewildered, he said, "She told me she—"

"—Julian!" Anna shouted from the dark. When he opened his eyes, he found himself no longer in the game room or his maker's presence but lying facing a white ceiling illuminated by the fixture in the center. From the right, Anna's dangling red hair tickled the back of his hand. Her own stormy eyes turned to sunny days when she saw him looking back at her. As if she'd just found a new reason to live, she happily wailed, "He's awake! Guys—Julian's finally awake!"

Chapter Five

Two sweet sniffs of the air were all it took to discern musty old books from the ethereal aroma he knew better than God: vanilla—but it wasn't just any vanilla; it was her vanilla. His senses returning, Julian's right hand fell to his side. The golden declaration Violet had placed on his finger the night before skidded along the webbed surface of her hammock. *How'd I get back here?* Then it hit him. "Where's Xavier?" he shouted, nearly falling to the floor while trying to stand.

"Xavier?" Anna asked from the side of the bed. Behind her, two white pillows sat sandwiched between the wooden headboard and Daryl's bare back. The big man lounged upright, fully conscious, and blankly staring forward into space.

"Where is Xavier?" Julian repeated, his eyes meeting Anna's. "I just saw him!"

Her bottom lip starting to quiver, she moaned, "Xavier's dead."

"No, he's not! I was just talking to him—upstairs!"

"Upstairs? Nah, you've been down here this whole time."

"What are you talking about? After Daryl fell out of bed and we came down here to help him, he was talking about the library. Then I went up there. Don't you remember?"

"What?! That never happened." Anna stood, her and Julian's shared bewilderment never breaking. "After you came down here early this morning, you never left the room. Bern and I cleaned up everything and put Daryl's truck in your garage. We—"

"—you already told me that, after I woke up. There was that whole thing with Bernard, and—"

"—what about me?" a deep murmur interrupted from the hallway. Julian cringed, hearing the Austrian timbre. He followed his ears to the open doorway. There, Bernard stood, gripping a full

38

IV bag and wearing the same blue shirt as before, minus the red smears from Julian's assault.

"Wait?!" Julian's eyes dashed from Bernard to Anna to Daryl, then back to Bernard, "Did I just dream that whole thing?"

Anna shrugged her boney shoulders. "I don't know what to tell you, love. As I said, you've been down here all along. Earlier, Bern and I were upstairs watching the president give a ridiculous speech about last night. Daryl never fell out of bed. He said nothing about a library either."

"But I dreamt it," Daryl croaked, finally breaking his silence. Everyone gave him their attention. Julian sat on the edge of the bed where Anna had. The nothingness in his old friend's eyes said he already knew his old life was over; his frail ego just hadn't caught up yet.

Hesitant, Julian forced himself to ask, "What did you dream about?"

Daryl hocked and cleared his throat. He turned slightly in Julian's direction, facing him. "Your wife ... I know it was a dream, but it was real. She was there with me. She told me things."

"She came to me too, also in a dream," Julian said.

"No," Daryl argued. "She said she tried, but she couldn't find—"

"—I woke up," Julian interrupted, wishing his truth were lies, wishing he could sleep forever. "You said Violet told you things. What did she tell you?"

"She told me everything ... that I'm a vampire." An abrupt, dry laugh escaped his chapped lips. For a moment, it was like his lifelong beliefs and the present reality were sinking in, preparing him for an epic battle of contradiction he wanted no part of. Finally, he asked, "What happened to me? I know I got shot. I know I should be dead. Not only am I alive, but I don't have a scratch on me. Why?"

Having no choice but to rip the Band-Aid, Julian said, "I really don't know how to say this in a way that won't sound crazy or impossible, but Violet was right." Watching the already pallid color of Daryl's troubled face drain with each devastating word, Julian hated himself, telling his best friend, "You are a vampire."

"That's not possible."

Stepping forward, Anna asked, "Why not? You said it yourself: you got shot and should have died. Yet here you are, completely untouched."

"How do I know that wasn't a part of the dream too? How do I know y'all didn't drug me or something?!"

"What are you talking about?" Julian asked.

"You're the one who was taking that *Ayahuasca* shit! How do I know you didn't give me something last night, and I hallucinated everything?"

"Really, Daryl? Do you really think I would do that to you?" Julian grunted. "Do you even remember eating or drinking anything?" Spitting each syllable, he barked, "Why the fuck would you even say that to me?!"

"Calm down," Anna said. "It is a lot to take in." To Daryl, she said, "I'm afraid everything happened the way you remember. Violet was killed. Her blood entered your wound. It healed you, but it also transformed you."

As if he heard nothing or just didn't care, Daryl asked, "Who the hell are you again?"

"That's my wife!" Bernard hissed from the door.

Anna shook her head, otherwise ignoring the outburst. "My name is Annabel, but everyone calls me Anna."

"And you're a vampire?" Anna nodded. Daryl looked at Julian. "You too, bub?" Julian also shook his head. "And now ... so, am I?"

"You are," Julian said. As if Daryl had waited his entire life to get the punchline of the greatest joke ever told, his fat cheeks suddenly exploded, releasing an almost exaggerated, unnatural fit of laughter. The maniacal outpour drowned the entire house for at least twenty seconds before it finally ended.

From the laughter, a disheartening wail of internal soul torture followed; its overlapping shades of anguish so desperate and shrill, only those with something to lose would understand. As if he had anything left to break, Julian's heart shattered further, beholding such a requiem. He watched on, wishing he knew how to console his friend, wishing he knew how to console himself. The gentle giant he once knew better than anyone, who never feared anything or showed the slightest hint of grief or weakness, was now crumbling to dust before his eyes.

When Daryl ran out of breath, he gagged, snorted, and cleared his throat. After a deep breath and wiping his eyes, he asked, "Where's my wife?"

"I imagine she's out looking for you," Julian said. "At least, she was in my dream."

"I got to go home!"

While scooting towards the side of the bed, Anna put her hand on Daryl's shoulder. "You're far too weak to go anywhere right now."

"I feel fine," he croaked, pushing the hand away.

Astonished by Daryl's ease and strength, Julian asked, "How? It took me a few days before I could even stand, and that was after a few feedings."

"Feedings?" Daryl asked, his round face wincing. "You mean, you drink blood?" Julian nodded. "That's fucking sick!"

Anna said, "I'm afraid blood and water are all you can ever consume again."

"Well, I ain't drinking no blood!"

"But you'll die."

"If I'm a vampire, ain't I dead already?"

"No, love. You are not dead. But I promise if you don't feed, you cannot survive."

"What about sunlight? Will that kill me too?"

"Yes," she said. Daryl shook his head in disbelief, snickering and still unable to fully grasp such severities. Bernard approached with the IV bag, handing it to his wife. She said, "This is not going to taste good, but—"

"—get the fuck away from me with that!" Daryl shouted. He swatted Anna's hand. "I told you, I ain't drinking no blood!" He looked at Julian, asking, "Did y'all kill somebody for that?"

"No. It was willingly donated," he said.

"I don't care. I ain't drinking it."

Anna gently cupped her hands over Daryl's cheeks, her deliberate eyes gently cradling his. Though his bulging forehead wrinkles implied confusion, he offered no qualms to the gesture. Julian watched on, hearing an uncomfortable sigh from Bernard. "Listen, Daryl, I know you're scared," Anna began. "It is entirely understandable, but this is serious. Nobody meant for this to happen. Julian loves you, and we love him." Still watching and listening, Julian heard Bernard sigh again.

"Just like him, you are one of us now," Anna continued. "Your maker was a good woman. She loved Julian with all her heart. Her spirit now lives within you, just like Julian's maker's lives inside of him." She peered at Julian, offering a half-cocked smile. Looking back at Daryl, she said, "You have a wife?"

He nodded, confirming, "I also got two girls."

"They need you. If you don't feed, you'll die, and your family will be without its head. I've been there before. You don't want your daughters to be without their father."

"What's it matter now?" Daryl moaned. "If I can't even go outside during the day, how am I supposed to work and take care of them?"

"Let me worry about that," Julian said. "You know I've got money now. You can have it. I don't want it anymore."

Daryl's eyes widened on Julian, his chest pumping harder. "I don't want your money," he said. "I don't want shit from you." Then to Anna and Bernard, he added, "Any of you!"

Julian's heart sank into a bottomless abyss. He would've cried, but his tears were depleted. "Please, let me help you," he said. "I feel like this is my fault."

"You're goddamn right it's your fault!" Daryl shouted, throwing out his right index finger. "You've ruined my life is what you did!" Julian wished he had the words, but even thinking hurt too much. Instead, he watched Daryl slide his legs off the side of the bed and stand with no help from anyone. "I'm going home. You freaks stay the fuck away from me!"

"Daryl, wait!" Anna squeaked. She held her free hand up to his chest, offering him the IV bag. "At least take this."

"No!"

"If you don't drink that before the next time you go to sleep, you'll never wake again."

"Then what?" he asked. "How am I supposed to find blood after that?"

"You can drink animal blood," she said. "You can also try to find someone willing to let you have some of theirs."

Daryl sighed and shook his head again but hesitantly took the bag. "Now get the fuck out of my way," he muttered, brushing past her and stomping towards the door.

Julian watched with amazement over how easily Daryl moved for how little time his body had to heal. Refusing to let things end so appallingly, he followed him out of the bedroom, down the hallway, and upstairs to the living room. "Wait!" he cried as Daryl reached the kitchen door, leading outside. "Wait, don't leave yet." Daryl kept going, never stopping or acknowledging Julian following close behind.

He growled, "Where the fuck's my truck?!" before grumbling, "Oh … I think she said it's in the garage." The brick, single-vehicle garage sat thirty feet away from the house, its white steel door pulled all the way down. Julian followed him past Violet's purple Firebird, parked where the truck once was. At the door, Daryl tried twisting the chrome handle, but it was locked. Appearing more frustrated, he twisted harder, tugging it until the entire door suddenly dislocated from its tracks. In a loud, screeching crash, the whole metal setup collapsed to the frozen earth.

In awe, Julian squealed, "Jesus Christ!"

With little effort, Daryl kicked the mass of twisted metal aside. "Who has my keys?" he asked.

"I do," Anna said, emerging from the house. Handing him the keychain, she said, "We won't stop you from leaving, love, but there's still so much you need to know."

Daryl ignored her, heading towards the driver's side of his basil green pickup. From beneath the carport, Bernard said, "Fuck this guy. Let Hell Belle teach him everything. It's not like she's got anything else to do for eternity."

Julian heard it. He wanted to punch him in the mouth. Instead, he tried reaching for Daryl, saying, "Please, brother. I—"

"—you should've just stayed in Las Vegas."

Julian softly quavered, "I'm sorry." He grasped Daryl's shoulder, trying to stop him and speak reason. Daryl pushed him away. The force behind the shove was minimal, but Julian went flying. Unable to catch his footing, he sprinted backwards, across the driveway, and over the side of the steep, snowy hill.

Round and round Julian tumbled. Though it ended quickly, every tree, rock, and blunt object cut, smashed, or gouged his unnatural flesh along the hundred-foot drop. At the bottom, he crashed into a small, naked oak tree at the edge of his grandfather

Johnny's backyard. It wasn't until stopping that he heard the snap. From his lower left leg, he experienced a pain unlike what he had the night before when thrown from the helicopter. That pain was blunt, and it all came at once. This was sharp, intense, and still growing. This pain had claws, pulsating throughout his entire body like icicles violently flaying his raw innards. "Fuck!" he screamed at the heavens.

Setting off a bomb of white powder in every direction, Anna landed by his side, whispering, "Shh—quiet." She wrapped her palm over his mouth, swaddling his agony. With each breath, Julian's exhales became more aggressive. Before she could assist him any further, a golden yellow light appeared outside Johnny's den door. The shoveled driveway and a portion of the yard illuminated, the porchlight's reach ended only feet short of the tree.

The door opened next, squeaking as it slowly did. A wrinkled, bald head emerged from the crack. "Julian?" Johnny squinted, panning back and forth in search of his grandson. "Julian?! Are you out here? Are you okay?"

Stewing in excruciating pain, Julian wished to be anywhere but there. He closed his eyes, madly focused on the most positive image he could: his precious flower's face, her beautiful brown almond eyes, her pillowed red lips smiling back at him, the way she spoke, the welcoming smell of her breath. For one eternal second, it was all he knew. But then, the roaring blast-off of Daryl's engine hitting warp speed down the mountain-hollow road drew him back to the reality he only wished he had the power of God to change.

By then, Johnny went back inside and turned off the light. Anna whispered, "Okay, come on." She gently took Julian in her arms, lifting him from the broken mess in which he lay. As the pain intensified, he shoved his rightmost knuckle between his teeth to bear down on if he needed to scream again. Before he could even give it another thought, Anna already had him back up the hill and inside the house. She carried his mangled, snow-covered remains into the living room and placed him softly on the sofa.

After Julian caught his breath, not wanting to look at his leg, he asked, "How bad is it?"

"Well …" Anna hesitated, trying not to cringe. "You might as well get comfortable, love. You're going to be here a little while."

Chapter Six

A full IV bag thawing on the coffee table, Julian lounged next to it, his left leg and foot lazing over a stack of black throw pillows. Waiting for his food and wounds to absolute, he sighed. "Why me?"

From Violet's end of the curved leather sofa, Anna asked, "Why you what?"

"Why any of this? Why survive so much just to find happiness and have it ripped away?"

"I told you once before; God is a cruel, narcissistic monster. He gives us what we want just long enough to feel something. Then He takes it away and basks in our grief."

Julian rolled his eyes, grumbling, "There is no God—and if there was: fuck Him." He took the IV bag from the glass tabletop once enough blood had thawed for a drink.

Anna said, "You know that's the last one, right?" Julian nodded. "How's your ankle?"

"It doesn't hurt anymore, but it's tingly—like a hot tub jet is blasting it with bubbles—if that makes sense." After a couple of sips from the IV tube, Julian finally grew brave enough to look down. Just below his rolled left blue-jean leg, a thick, bloated, pink ring of smooth epidermal tissue clasped his ankle like a shackle.

"It looks that way because it's healing so fast," Anna said. "Try to wiggle your toes."

Though a dull pain followed, Julian moved them all. "Should I try my whole foot?"

"I wouldn't yet. When I brought you in here, your foot was twisted most of the way around and barely hanging on. You're lucky it stayed intact enough to heal or else you'd probably have lost the whole thing."

"Daryl didn't even hardly push me. How'd he do it with such force, or tear down the garage door? How'd he do that?"

"I've been wondering that myself. I have never seen anyone heal so quickly, let alone show such feats of strength so early."

"What does that mean?"

"I don't know. Until last night, Bern and I'd never seen a fireproof vamp either. I knew Hell Belle never made a vamp or shared her blood with anyone, but I never imagined either of you would be so powerful, especially so soon."

Julian sucked down another cold drink, quivering at the foul, metallic taste. "In my dream, Xavier told me nobody outside this house should know I drank Violet's blood or that Daryl was turned."

"Why not?"

"He wouldn't tell me. He said I had to trust him."

"What else did he say?"

"He said he'd been getting our blood from someone named Pana, and—"

"—Pana?!" she chirped, a blend of surprise and curiosity livening her otherwise dismal tone.

"In my dream, I went to the library. I found Violet's diary there. That's where I first read his name. Then I found Xavier. He told me it was time we met."

"I suppose we could go to Alaska—but it's going to be a little awkward. I've not spoken to Pana since my wedding. I saw him a couple of years ago at Hell Belle's hundredth birthday party, but we didn't speak. He and my father don't see eye to eye. They're not enemies, but they certainly ain't friends either—at least, not anymore."

"But Xavier and Pana were close."

"But that's Xavier. He fancies everyone." Anna paused, masking her face with an open palm. "Well, at least he used to," she whimpered.

"About that … when we spoke, Xavier thought he was alive."

Anna jerked her hand away. "What do you mean?"

"He said he woke up in a field. After that, he hid in a subway tunnel until it got dark. Then he came here."

Anna's bottom lip quivered until falling open. As if it killed her to say it, she moaned, "He must not know he's dead." New tears seeping, she wiped them away with the back of her hand.

"Why wouldn't he know?"

"Even in dreams, sometimes dead vamps don't know they are dead. To them, the dream is every bit a part of reality as the waking life is to us. Since they are no longer living or dreaming, they go on existing from beyond as if they were still here. It doesn't always happen, but when it does, it can be difficult to convince them otherwise."

"That's awful!" Julian cried. "I wonder if Violet knows she's dead. I dreamt of her too. It was a dream within a dream. Later is when Daryl started talking in his sleep about her diary. You said the president gave a speech, right?" Anna nodded. "In my dream, I watched that speech. Is it possible I just heard it in my sleep and dreamt it?"

"It's possible."

"Then I wonder if Daryl really said that in his sleep, and I heard him in mine. What if Violet's diary is really up there?"

Already on her feet, Anna asked, "Want me to go check?"

From his crippled position, he said, "Could you? It might be on the desk." She nodded and disappeared beyond the sofa, her bare feet smacking against the granite floor on her way towards the stairs.

Julian swallowed another red gulp. He scowled and set the bag aside, focusing on the television. The eleven o'clock news was just warming up, opening with a live, aerial view of Times Square. All of the fires appeared extinguished. Surrounding the metropolitan holocaust, a wide array of ambulances, fire trucks, and police cruisers remained, their sirens collectively setting the night ablaze once more.

In the kitchen, the front door opened. Julian listened to Bernard's footsteps, growing louder as they passed into the living room, his footsteps echoing as he drew nearer. "Are you still watching that shit?" he asked.

"There's nothing else on."

"I don't like it. It reminds me we are responsible, and someone will eventually find out."

"Christopher Cauldwell was responsible, not us," Julian said.

"Does it matter? The kingdoms won't care."

In the most detached, dead-to-the-world tone, Julian said, "Neither do I."

"I fucking care, you little smartass! That shit's not—"

"—aww!" Anna gushed on her way down the stairs, splitting the tension in two. "That card was so cute and sweet."

"What card?"

"So, her diary really was up there?" Julian asked.

"What card?"

Anna came to the sofa and handed him a thick blue hardback—the same blue hardback from his dream. "There you go," she said, smiling down on him and showing her most favorable emotion yet.

Bernard growled, "What fucking card?!"

"Jesus, Bern!" Anna squawked. "It's a fucking Valentine's card Julian made for Hell Belle!" As if trying to diffuse the mood, she instantly changed her tone, playfully teasing, "How come you never did anything like that for me?"

He said, "That's child's play, my love. You know how I feel about you."

Bernard's footsteps advancing closer to the sofa, Anna asked, "Did you get the garage door put back up?"

"And I also locked Hell Belle's Firebird in there."

"Thanks," Julian muttered, his eyes never leaving the worn old book. He turned to the page with the card and gave the entry a second glance. Word for word, it was everything he read in his dream. He folded the flimsy notebook paper again, hoping to further tuck it away and keep it from getting torn or lost.

Each taking a seat at the other end of the sofa, Bernard asked his wife, "What now? You know we can't stay here."

"When you were outside, Julian and I were talking. Xavier came to him and said he needs to go see Pana."

"Pana?! What for?"

"Because we need blood," Anna said.

"But we can get that anywhere and from anyone."

Without thinking, Julian anxiously jerked his foot at Bernard's cold suggestion, kicking it away from the stack of pillows. To his surprise, he felt nothing. "Are you all right?" Anna asked. He nodded. To Bernard, she said, "If we go to Alaska, we won't have to kill anyone for it."

"I'm not killing anybody," Julian said.

Bernard chuckled. "You say that now. Just wait until the day finally comes when you have no other choice." His decree ended with a sneer every bit as grim as the unfortunate words he spoke. Even the microfibers on the back of Julian's neck all hurled in unison.

"Stop it, Bern! He's been through enough, and you're being a cunt!"

Tell me about it, Julian thought. He was still angry over the snide remark he had made outside about Violet. He wanted to tell him where to go and how to get there. Instead, "If Xavier said we should go to Alaska, that's where we should go," is what came out.

"I'd rather just go to Paris—but fine!" Bernard pouted. "If your ankle's healed, I am ready."

"How's it feeling?" Anna asked. Julian shook his foot by the ankle, feeling no aches or pains. He stood easily. "Very good," Anna said. "It's not going to be safe here, so it is hard to tell how long you might be away, all things considered. Go pack some clothes and anything else you may need."

Julian tested the waters, baby-stepping around the sofa and then picking up the pace towards the basement door. At the bottom of the steps, he froze. For the first time since his transition, a chill overcame him. It wasn't a temperate chill. It was a phantom chill. He couldn't see her, but he knew she was there, longing for him on a whole other frequency.

He put his right hand over his heart, its restless beat gaining traction. "Please," he whispered, his delicate treble breaking under the pressure. "Just let me die." As if a religious mantra; an epitaph, he repeated the desperate appeal until it became redundant.

***

Julian moped throughout the house, preparing to leave the home he and Violet were supposed to build together. Now wearing a matching black pair of jeans and shirt, he retrieved the green hiker's backpack he'd put away when they first arrived. Unsure what he might need, he threw in a couple changes of clothes. Then he returned to the living room, where the others waited.

On the coffee table sat Violet's diary. Beside it was what remained of Julian's IV bag and a short stack of hundred-dollar bills he'd taken from his and Xavier's safe. "Surely, I won't need this much, but I'd still rather have it and not need it," he said, sliding the wad into his billfold. Next he packed the diary, carefully zipping it away in a compartment of its own.

Sitting closer to the center of the table, Julian's red laptop caught his eye next. Just looking at it was a burden. For over a year he'd labored, pecking out his life story one key at a time. It was

Violet who had inspired him to finish and email it to forty-four publishers at once. It was Violet whose act of love had so eagerly hit the *Send* button before he could. But like all the others so far, he had no choice but to push the painful memory aside, leaving the device where it lay.

"Drink the rest of that before we go," Anna said, pointing at the IV bag. "Your ankle may have healed, but your body's endured much. We've also got a long way to go."

Julian picked up his dinner. Before drinking, he asked, "How long will it take to get there?"

"About an hour," she said. "Speaking of such, you flew on your own last night, yeah?" The blood-red tube hanging from between his puckered lips, Julian bowed to confirm. "I thought so. It may take a while before you can do it at will, but you'll get there eventually." Julian saw and even appreciated the encouragement, but he didn't care whether he ever flew or not. Even superpowers were trivial compared to the real prize at the end.

Once he emptied the pint-sized bag, Julian took his black leather jacket with embroidered skulls from a small wooden coat rack beside the grandfather clock. He slipped it on, followed by the backpack. He stuffed his cellphone charger into one of the jacket pockets, along with his wallet. Then he put on his black sneakers. Hanging on the walls around the living room, several multi-colored psychedelic paintings of spirals, mandalas, and fractals jumped out at him one last time. He looked away, unable to see anything but *her* in every vibrant image.

As if beyond his control, Julian's eyes wandered towards the fireplace. He squeezed them shut, hoping to avoid whatever he was meant to see, but it was inevitable. Violet's cheerful reaction when first discovering the tremendous stonework is what he saw. The once blissful memory played itself back in real time: his overhauled limbic system, the projector; his shaded optics, the screen.

There she was in her little black dress, skipping like a schoolgirl to the high hearth and flopping her tiny butt down on the makeshift bench. Julian giggled out loud. "You are so perfect," he declared, opening his eyes to find Anna and Bernard staring back. Bernard glared as though Julian had lost his marbles while Anna remained indifferent.

Shaking it off, he turned towards the kitchen, catching a passing glimpse of the red-and-yellow jukebox resting against the wall. Just above it hung the mounted purple Stratocaster, inked with the legendary words: "Stay groovy, Jimi Hendrix." He'd bought it for Violet when he wasn't even sure she would come back to him, but she did, at least for a while.

With that, "Nights in White Satin" overwhelmed the room, the inanimate jukebox's golden soundwaves rising from nowhere and crashing to nothing. For a second it was almost like she was holding him in her arms again, floating. Unable to resist, Julian's tears also rose to the occasion. After taking a moment to let the music end and accept the pain he was meant to endure, he forced himself back to the present, smacking his left jeans pocket. His cellphone took the impact. *Check! ... Keys?* He smacked his right pocket, producing a jingle. *Check!* "All right," he said. "Let's go."

Once outside in the driveway and beyond the carport, Anna said, "You can ride on Bern's back." Her husband sighed. Julian approached and put his arms over his shoulders.

"Try not to move much," Bernard insisted. To Anna, he said, "If we get separated, you know where to go, right?"

"Yeah. It's the northmost town in Alaska," she replied. "The top of the world ain't that hard to find."

Julian took a series of deep breaths, preparing for and dreading his longest flight yet. Bernard refused to wait, shooting to the sky without warning. *For fuck's sake, asshole!* Julian tightened his grip, having nearly lost it just before his pilot shifted northwest, picking up speed and giving no signs of making the trip easy on the widower.

Great! Over an hour of this shit, Julian thought, having nothing else but his own darkness to occupy. Like any other time he'd ridden on Violet or Xavier's backs, he shut his eyes but kept his head and guard up. *I wonder what would happen if I just let go. Sure, it would be a long way down, but what if I landed just right and got impaled by a tree? Would I survive? Would suicide matter?* He considered it, tempted by the sweet release of death and all its decadence, yet he remained fearful of what forcing it might or might not accomplish. *What if I just snapped this Nazi prick's neck and we both fell to our ends? I wonder if I'm strong enough to do it. Would it still be suicide if I attacked first, and he fought back, killing me in the process? I've already killed two people. What difference would one more make?* He cackled at his own absurdity. *Get it together! You've got an eternity of this. So, pack a lunch and strap yourself in. You did this! You gave up your mortal coil for something you can never have. Be proud of yourself. You earned it!*

The self-loathing continued, lasting for what could have been hours for all Julian knew. Neither time nor space held much water in his ocean of chaos, until a gut feeling opened his eyes. He nearly lost his breath over what approached. Eerie shades of pellucid green with occasional slivers of dull yellows and golds danced for all to behold. *The Northern Lights!* Remembering his dream, Julian wondered, *Could she be hiding somewhere beneath them?* Drawing closer, the Aurora expanded, eventually swallowing him whole.

Moments after entering the mist, Bernard slowed down and came to a stop in midair. Anna joined them only a second later. "Well, that didn't take as long as I thought," she said. Fat white flurries spat viciously from all directions. Though Julian imagined how severe the cold must be to humans, his only chill was rotting desire, which had no concern for the weather.

"We're here," Anna said, all three descending and touching down at once. "This is the Arctic Circle."

Chapter Seven

The vampires struggled on foot, making their way through the knee-high snow. Starting over half a mile away, they'd hoped the effort would camouflage their landing from any potential onlookers. Once reaching civilization, Julian faced multiple rows of houses and storage buildings, the frontmost tier stretching from east to west as far as he could see. Most structures radiating their own lights, the noble viridescence overshadowed everything above.

"So, this is Alaska?" Julian asked, scanning the harsh environment. He looked back in the direction from which they'd come. Aside from the foot trails that new snow hadn't already filled in, only white tundra and greenlit sky covered the otherwise barren canvas. "I thought there'd be trees."

"This is the Arctic Circle. Nothing like that grows this far north," Anna said. "The ocean is only a few kilometers ahead. Even that's frozen."

"And Violet liked coming here?" Anna shrugged in response. "I couldn't see this place appealing to her," he said.

"It can be quite peaceful. Lots of vamps come here for winter on account of its two months of darkness."

Bernard sped up, groaning, "Come on. This bullshit is falling hard, and I don't want to be out in it any longer than I have to be." They continued until they reached a narrow, snow-packed roadway. Broken-down, rusted remnants of cars, trucks, and other mechanisms lay scattered and abandoned along the sides. The harder ground now easier to maneuver, Bernard and Julian shook away all the loose powder clinging to their pants while Anna only had to kick her legs and brush the rim of her burgundy skirt.

Ahead, Bernard pointed in the direction of an old, single-story house with chipped, white-panel sidings. "That one?"

"Yeah, love. I think that's it."

Puzzled, Julian stared at the small dwelling, softly detailed in its surrounding ambience. It hadn't a single visible window, which was expected, but the meager size was not. "That doesn't look like the kind of place a vampire coven would live," he said.

Bernard snickered. "Were you expecting another Leviticus, or perhaps a dramatic castle on top of a mountain? This is life, kid, not a petty fairytale."

Fuck you, piece of ... remembering Anna could hear him, Julian quickly redirected his thoughts. He rolled his eyes, mumbling, "Yeah, stupid me," under his breath.

Centered at the front of the house, beneath a shallow connecting portico, a heavy metal door stood guard—hand-painted with overlapping shades of dry red drips. To the right eyes, it could be a sign. At the door, Anna said, "Let me do the talking." The others nodded. Using a closed fist, she banged three hard times, each echoing louder than the last. They waited several seconds, hearing nothing from inside. Anna knocked three more times using the same method, but still nothing happened.

Julian shrugged, griping, "Well?"

Anna repeated the same pattern. Two seconds after her third knock, she rapped two more times, softer but faster than the others. Finally, Julian heard movement beyond the door. When it squealed open, the round, wrinkled, elderly face of a woman emerged, native in appearance, and bearing a wildly unkempt scalp full of thin white hairs. Her silver-dollar eyes fixed on Anna, her accompanying smirk hinting at a joyous bewilderment.

The woman said nothing, so Anna spoke first. "Hello. We'd like to see Pana, please."

"Oh, hmm…" The old woman spoke softly. She looked everyone over before disappearing back inside the dark house, pushing the door shut all but an inch.

From beyond the crack, a raspy, masculine voice announced, "That was an old knock. Who are you? What do you want?"

"It's Annabel Gaunt, and—" The door flung all the way open, cutting her off. On the other side, next to the short woman stood a taller, sinewy man; shirtless, and toned. Like the woman, his skin was the color bronze. Atop his head, shorter dark hair gave way to a longer mullet tail, falling and disappearing beneath his tree-trunk neck and expansive shoulder line. His piercing, intimidating gleam led Julian to believe he was no stranger to conflict.

"Princess Annabel?!" the man gasped. He shot a quick glare at Bernard, but it was Julian he stared at the longest. Unsure why, he looked away, hoping the man would do the same. "It has been, what, seventy years, since we last spoke, Princess?"

"Indeed, it has."

"Why are you here now?" The man's wise old eyes hammered down on the redhead.

She released the longest, most heartbreakingly desperate exhale Julian ever heard. "May we come in?"

"Why?" he asked, shifting his gaze between all three. "Where is Xavier?"

"You ain't heard?"

"Heard what?"

Anna sighed again, momentarily closing her eyes. Julian watched, knowing she was doing everything in her power not to burst. When reopening them, she cried, "He's gone, Pana! We lost him last night. Violet too."

Her shrill sobs on display for anyone to hear, Bernard hissed, "Shut up," in her ear.

Julian shoved his palm into Bernard's shoulder. "Hey! Don't talk to her like that."

Before Bernard could react, Pana motioned them all forward. "Come in," he insisted. He and the woman moved aside for them to enter. Once everyone was in the pitch-black house, Pana closed the door. Even with Julian's new sight, he saw nothing until an overhead light flickered on. Having a much better view of Pana and the old woman, he saw their more detailed features. Pana was barefoot and only wearing a fire-orange pair of pants. Under the light, hints of silver sparkled in his otherwise blackish tresses.

The old woman, tightly wrapped in a peach cloak, slowly approached. Her sparkling, silver-dollar eyes aligned with Julian's. She smiled, pressing her feeble old hands over his cheeks. He looked at Anna in confusion. She offered nothing. Moving back to the woman, his gaze caught Pana's. He was also staring again.

"Say anything, child," the woman said.

Julian's heart beating in his ears, he gulped, "What?"

The woman smiled gently. Her touch was warm on his skin but cold in his bones. "What troubles you?" she asked, speaking just above a whisper.

"I—umm." Julian swallowed a lump. His soft voice full of shyness and sorrow, he said, "My world ended last night."

Her hands still gripping Julian's cheeks, the woman looked at Pana, distinctively bowing her head once. "Lusa," Pana interjected. The elder removed her hands and stepped away. "Go downstairs and tell the others: Princess Annabel is here." She smiled and bowed again—not so deliberately—at the Inupiaq's request.

"Don't call me 'princess,'" Anna said.

"Why not?" Pana asked.

Julian watched Lusa waddle across the room, heading towards the far-left corner. The room was mostly empty, appearing to make up the entirety or bulk of the dwelling. Various hand-paintings of brown and black tribal symbols and colorful red and yellow masks hung from the browning white walls. Two wooden rocking chairs and a torn, black leather sofa sat crookedly atop a dirty gray carpet. Lusa approached the wall. With both hands, she pushed a rectangular shield of drywall aside. A doorway-sized portion opened, leading into the darkness, where she disappeared.

"... I gave that life up decades ago," Anna said, drawing Julian's attention back to the conversation. "Just call me 'Anna.' Everyone else does."

Pana smirked. "I don't care what you call yourself. What happened to Xavier?" Once again, his domineering eyes landed on Julian. "And who are you?"

"His name is Julian," Anna said.

"Ah!" Pana chuckled. "So, you're the famous Julian Frost, I presume?" Julian looked away again, keeping his silence and finding the Alaskan's stare both frightening and intrusive. "I asked you a question, boy!"

Julian nearly jumped. "Y—yes, I am Julian Frost."

"Yeah, I've heard of you." Turning back to Anna, he said, "It was that soldier, wasn't it? He killed them both?"

"He and his men," she said, "but we got them all."

"You did, eh?"

Bernard stepped forward. "We did. You didn't hear?"

"No. I didn't. We don't get that kind of news all the way up here in Utqiaġvik as quickly as others down south do."

Anna stressed, "You don't understand! Times Square was torn apart last night. Hundreds of people are dead. As if that wasn't enough, it all happened on live television. Do you know how many people watch that every year?"

Pana's face turned sickly. "Come with me," he said, motioning everyone towards the hidden passage in the wall. "The others must know." With no questions asked, the trio followed. On the other side of the wall, an old wooden staircase led down. Pana was the first to descend, then Anna, Bernard, and after shaking an unsettling feeling of potentially being somewhere he didn't belong, Julian went too.

At the bottom, he watched Pana push open a white metal door, the brightness within overshadowing the dark. He stepped through first and held the door open for the others. Once they were all inside, he shut the door and locked it. Julian scanned the shallow concrete corridor with nothing but another door on the opposite end, closed and without a knob. He wondered, *What the hell is this?*

"It's safety, boy!" Pana said along his way to the door. He loudly banged in a specific rhythm. The door opened, a thick chatter erupting from the other side. "Isolation is not invisibility," he continued. "We take great pride in what we have here, and there's not one of us beyond this door who would not gladly kill or die to protect it for the rest of us."

"In other words, don't fuck it up," Bernard nagged.

Pana glared at the remark but said nothing. Instead, he motioned everyone forward again. Anna was the first to walk through. Along her way, Pana draped his weathered old hand over her shoulder. He said, "I truly am sorry, Annabel. Your brother was one of my oldest and dearest friends. Every one of us is grateful to him. They will all be devastated."

Anna wiped a new tear from her eye. "I appreciate that, Pana, but we don't want to make a spectacle. We came here because we need blood."

"We shall get to that later," he said, letting his hand slide away. "If what you say is true, first everyone must know what happened."

Anna continued through the doorway. Bernard went next. Despite all the macabre emotions and deathly desires Julian suffered throughout the evening, he was intrigued by the mystery of what lurked on the other side. The nostalgia had naturally taken him back to the night he first met Xavier in New York. As he stood outside his maker's apartment—*number 44*—with Violet by his side and his heart an upbeat drum circle, Julian had experienced the same fantastic sense of fear, self, and optimism then as he did now.

Just as he did on the night in question, he passed through the doorway, entering a much larger room, spanning at least fifty feet in diameter. On the other three sides, a closed metal door stood centered between two dark hallways, leading elsewhere. Waiting in the concrete bunker must have been twenty people or more. Men and women, ranging in age and appearance, stood gathered. Everyone stared in Julian's direction. Most were Indigenous Peoples, like Pana and Lusa. The few paler faces in the crowd wore more casual, everyday clothing, while most of the Inupiaq wore cloaks and furs of assorted colors and styles.

Julian, standing next to Anna, asked, "Is everyone here a vampire?"

"Yes," she said. "Most are native Inupiaq, though there are also a few Canadians and Northern Europeans here too."

Julian panned the crowd further. A soft female voice said, "That's Princess Annabel! What's she doing here?"

A deep, manly voice said, "Something must be wrong."

Pana stepped forward, silencing the crowd. "Yes, something is wrong. Annabel; her husband, Bernard Gaunt; and Xavier's blood child, Julian Frost, have brought devastating news." Turning towards Anna, he said, "Tell them what you told me."

Anna paused, appearing uncomfortable with her position. She smiled awkwardly, finally squeaking, "There was an accident last night, a bad one. It began in Virginia and ended in New York."

Though Julian was not the one speaking, the big moods blaring from the crowd affected him the same, creating tangible tension. His breathing intensified, and his head spun. It was panic, seducing his fragile nervous system. Like the void he'd always known, it opened wide to swallow whatever remained.

He locked his eyelids so tightly they hurt, focusing on the only sanctuary he had: his flower and all her perfections. When he saw light again, he was still beneath the microscope but feeling only his beloved's tender courage, vicariously holding him in her angelic arms.

From the gathering, a short, stout man came forward, nestled in a black cloak and hood. A long, thick, rusty-red beard grew wild from his hardened face and brushed his chest. In a low Nordic timbre, he asked, "What accident?"

Anna first looked at Pana, then her husband, each giving her a nod. She turned back to the cloaked man, took a short, reassuring breath, and said, "Xavier Van Abarrow and his daughter, Violet Troúton, were both killed last night." The crowd erupted, ripping and roaring uncontrollably.

"Quiet!" Pana yelled, raising both arms high above his head. Instantly, everyone obeyed him. "There's more," he said, taking a step back and allowing Anna the floor again.

"Where it first began, in Virginia, Violet was marrying Julian." She pointed at him when saying his name. "Xavier was officiating the wedding. Bernard and I were there too." Anna's vulnerability surfacing, she snorted and wiped her eyes. "It all happened so fast. First, Julian was shot with a tranquilizer. Then Violet and Xavier also got shot."

"… and I got shot too!" Bernard insisted.

The cloaked man asked, "Then what?"

Oh God, Julian dreaded. *Please, Anna, don't let Bernard say anything about Daryl. I told you, Xavier doesn't want—* He paused, remembering his thoughts traveled. Knowing he'd gone too far and could take nothing back, the panic returned. Imagining all eyes were on him, he stammered. Desperately in search of something, anything. *Shit! Umm … what the fuck am I supposed to think about?! Anna, help!*

"Are you all right, boy?" Pana asked, arriving at Julian's side and firmly letting his hand fall over his back.

Knowing Pana must have heard everything, he trembled. "No. I'm not."

Anna took Julian's hand. "It's okay, love."

Bernard resumed the story, saying, "After I got shot, Xavier told Anna to take me and go." Again, the crowd overlapped in irate bickering.

A thin, dark-haired woman, wrapped in a gray fur blanket, shouted, "You just left them all there?! How could you?"

"Xavier told me to!" Anna wailed, her agony only growing. She covered her face with both hands and quavered, "I don't know why he wanted me to leave him. I didn't want to! What would any of you do if Pana, your leader, told you to do the same?" Dismal beads of saltwater rolling down her rosy cheeks, she screamed, "I'm sorry!" Despite his own dejection, the cruel reality in Anna's broken voice floored Julian, attacking his empathy on all fronts.

Ignoring Anna's display of guilt and heartache, the cloaked man asked, "Where'd you go after that?"

Her hands fell to her sides. She said, "I took my husband up into the mountains, behind Julian's house, until he was able to move again. By the time we returned to Julian's, nobody was there."

Every eye in the room turned on Julian, sending a raging swarm of electric eels up his spine and into his brain. He swallowed another lump, just waiting for someone to ask, "Who did this?" It was the youthful, dark-haired indigenous woman wrapped in fur who obliged.

"His name was Christopher Cauldwell," Julian said.

"Was?" she asked. "He's dead?"

"He is now—him and his team of Seals." Julian grew tired of waiting to be asked one specific question after another and feeling judged for something neither he nor Anna could help. "That son of a bitch killed my Violet! He cut her head off right in front of me! I couldn't move! I couldn't save her! I couldn't even tell her goodbye or that I love her!

"All I could do was stare at her staring back at me, knowing she was … knowing she was going to die." By then, Julian had to stop. Sobbing so deeply, he could barely breathe, let alone speak. His body spasmed uncontrollably, having forced himself to relive the most horrifying nightmare of his life as if it hadn't already been playing on loop—reminding him just how real Hell was.

"At some point, they also mangled Xavier's face and shot Julian's friend, Daryl," Bernard offered.

Son of a bitch! Instantly abandoning his grief or its reason for existing, Julian burned red with the Hell he carried. "Shut up!" he growled. "Just shut the fuck up, you goddamn, cock-sucking, mother-fucking, neo-Nazi-looking, Adolf-Hitler-worshipping—"

"—woah!" Pana interjected, stepping between the two before Julian could hurt someone.

The gathering of vampires watching, some mumbling in confusion, Bernard laughed obnoxiously. "Excuse me?! Who the fuck do you think you are, talking to me that way, you little runt?"

Julian exploded towards him, but from behind, Anna threw her arms around his waist in a bearhug. All he could do was shout, "I said shut your fucking mouth! Do you ever shut up?! Do you think anybody cares about your little fucking commentaries you keep shitting out every chance you get?! Fuck you!"

While Pana blocked Bernard from charging, Anna spun Julian to face her. In a more empathetic tone, she whispered, "Calm the fuck down, love—you must." Julian's tense shoulders sank. "Breathe … breathe with me," she continued. He took slow, deep breaths with her while Pana escorted Bernard to one of the nearby hallways.

Another female in the crowd asked, "Who's Daryl?"

"Julian's best man," Anna replied. "They shot and killed him."

The same woman asked, "Then what happened?"

Julian nodded for Anna to release him. "I'm okay." To the woman, he said, "They shot me and Xavier with another tranquilizer dart. I blacked out. When I came to, He and I were both in their helicopter. They flew us over Times Square in New York City. Then they dropped us onto the crowd." Some of the vampires gasped. "There were thousands of people there for New Year's Eve. It was shown on live television. Before they dropped us, Cauldwell said he wanted everyone to know we are real. Nobody believed him before."

"My God!" a soft, feminine voice let slip from the crowd.

"I don't know how, but I survived the fall. We both did," he continued. "It was then Tony Bishop came from out of nowhere and helped us."

"Tony Bishop?!" the cloaked, bearded man asked, his change in pitch offering a hint of surprise. "The same Tony Bishop that killed Eric Grant?"

"Yes."

"Why was he there?"

"Unless it was just to celebrate, we don't know," Anna said.

"Then what?"

"Then we went after them," Julian said. "Bishop was shot and killed. The helicopter crashed and several people in the crowd were also killed. That's when Anna and Bernard caught up to us. Bernard killed the biggest part of the Seals. I got two of them, and Xavier—" He paused, trying not to weep again. He sucked it up and cleared his throat. "The building the helicopter originally crashed into collapsed. It fell on Xavier and Christopher Cauldwell. It killed them both. I would've also died if Anna hadn't saved me."

The cloaked man sighed. "And so … now the whole world knows of us?"

"Actually, that part's being covered up," Anna said. "Even the US president is denying that it happened."

"Why would he do that?" asked the woman in the blanket.

"We don't know, but it seems to be working in our favor—at least for the time being."

"I don't like this," the woman said. "Something's not right."

"Either way, what's done is done," Anna said, she and Julian watching Pana and Bernard return from the hallway.

"And, what, we're also supposed to just go on pretending like this never happened?" the woman argued. "Princess Annabel, how do you think your father's going to react?"

"First of all, don't call me 'princess.' I'm no princess. Just because Caanis is my father doesn't mean I claim to be royalty. I gave that life up when I left Paris, just like Xavier did." Though it was subtle, Bernard grunted upon Anna saying Xavier's name.

"Now then," Pana began, stepping between Julian and Bernard. "If the two of you can be civil, we won't have any problems." He looked at Julian first. "Agreed?"

"Agreed."

Pana asked the same of Bernard, but he tipped his chin rather than giving a verbal response. "Very well." He faced everyone. "This is a difficult time, and it might get harder if the truce is disrupted between the kingdoms. But what happened last night was none their fault," he stressed, individually pointing at Anna, Bernard, and Julian. "Please, treat our old friends and new ones alike with the same respect you showed Xavier."

With that, the crowd dispersed, leaving behind such melancholic tones in the air. The meeting room empty, Pana started towards one of the hallways, looking over his shoulder at the visitors behind him. "You need blood? Come with me. I want to show you something that might surprise you first."

Chapter Eight

Their quarters adjacent, Anna and Bernard were shown to one guest room, and Julian the other. After leaving his backpack, he rejoined them and Pana, outside the door. The coven leader began walking down the long hallway first, its smooth concrete brightly lit by overhead fluorescent tubes. He motioned the others to follow.

That was intense, Julian thought, still reeling over the earlier encounter. He was not just suffering the excruciation for himself and the ones he lost, but for Anna too. He didn't need supernatural abilities to know how devastated and guilt-ridden she was. The evidence was indented all over her poor, freckled face. A distinct shade of heartsick pink circled each bloodshot orb from all the tears she'd spilled. Not even vampiric healing could maintain her fair, natural complexion.

Bernard, having shown no empathy to his wife's needs thus far, asked, "What did you want to show us, Pana?"

"That is where I am taking you now," he said. They reached another hall. On the left, four white doors with red crosses lined the wall—three of them slightly cracked open, their rooms unoccupied. Ahead, a plate-glass window stood on the right. Beside it was a solid red door. That is where Pana stopped, his rough hand gripping the painted knob. Julian peered through the big window. Inside a small room, tall machines sat side-by-side: all shiny, chrome, and covered in buttons, dials, and connected cables. Julian had no clue what the machines did, but he assumed they had something to do with the full IV bags that a woman in a long white lab coat was placing inside a freezer. He recognized her as the sassy, dark-haired Inupiaq woman, wrapped in the fur blanket during the meeting.

Bernard asked, "What is all this?"

"It's progress," Pana said. "I know nothing of modern science, but Uki has spent many years studying around the world on how to create a healthier, safer, and more sustainable synthetic blood. Thanks to her, we have no need for hunting or relying on human donors. Our entire species could survive without ever having to puncture another vein again."

"Where's the fun in that?" Bernard chuckled alone. "But wouldn't getting it directly from the source be easier?"

Pana smirked. "Bernard, maybe this logic doesn't work for all our kind, but none of us want to hurt, kill, or feed from anyone here. We never have. Not only is it becoming more difficult to get away with, but we also need to evolve with the times and learn to coexist with humans. It is not their fault we are here, just like it is not our place to be their God."

"Pfft!" Bernard shrugged his nose up. "Humans wouldn't think twice about killing us."

"People also fear what they do not understand. If you were bathed in a culture who led you to believe we were all dangerous storybook creatures, how would you react—coming face to face with one of us—knowing what they assume?" Everyone looked at Bernard, but he said nothing.

Julian asked, "Is this the blood you were giving to Xavier and Violet?"

"It is."

Anna said, "I was wondering why it tasted a little different. Bern and I thought something was wrong with it. We almost didn't drink it."

"It certainly does take some getting used to," Pana chortled. "And though I do hate to admit it, there is no comparison between real and synthetic. Real blood just has that flavor and kick the synthetic lacks."

"That is so neat!" Anna squeaked, finally showing signs of life, less heartbroken.

Pana smiled. "We have your brother to thank for all this. When he saw what we were doing, he was overcome with joy. He even said Uki is more innovative than he could ever imagine himself to be." Uki turned in everyone's direction. Pana held up his hand. Uki lifted a finger.

Through the glass, Julian watched the woman remove her white coat, revealing a simple blue gown. She hung the coat on a rack near the door. Lying on a table next to it was the gray blanket she had worn at the meeting. She draped it over her shoulders before opening the door. Ignoring the others, she looked at Julian first, saying, "So, you're him, huh?"

Caught off guard, Julian croaked, "Who am I?"

"The one Violet wouldn't stop talking about while she was here this last time." She half-smiled. "I am so sorry for your loss, Julian."

"Thank you," he replied, unable to smile back.

To Anna, Uki said, "You, too. Your brother was such a wonderful man."

"He was," Anna mumbled.

"And I am sorry for yelling at you out there like that. Hearing everything at once was hard to take in. I know this is a challenging time for you, and the last thing I want is to make it even harder."

Anna said, "Thanks," in a careless, withdrawn tone.

"Uki, I was just telling them a little about your work," Pana said.

She bobbed her head. "Yeah. Thanks to modern technology and a few dozen college classes, I have learned it's quite easy to copy and produce red blood cells in such a way that provides us with all the essentials we need. If only the other more savage vampires would also be willing to adopt this technique, things could be so different. Unfortunately, Raz Ahrim and Taltosia are far more 'old school,' as they say. But we can hope that one day, they will change their minds."

Though Uki's appearance was younger than Julian's, he still sensed a more modern vibe and lingo from her than the others he'd encountered since arriving. Thankful for a new distraction, he indulged, asking, "How old are you?"

"I was twenty-two when I turned, but that was over a century ago." She giggled, adding. "I don't look too bad for a hundred-and-forty-four-year-old, do I?" Julian shivered when hearing the number. Unaware of his own dumbfounded expression, Uki's girlish smile disappeared. "What is it?" she asked.

"Nothing. It's just hearing that number: forty-four."

"What about it?"

"It means something to me."

"Now that you mention it, I believe Violet might have said something about that while she was here last."

"Really?!" Julian gushed from the heart, his body charging with life. "What else did she tell you?"

"Just this and that. Mostly girl talk. It was nice to hear her obsess over somebody besides Eric, like she used to."

"Wait, what?" Julian gasped. "What about Eric?" Moving from one to the other, he looked everyone directly in their eyes, but nobody answered. Nausea crept up, seizing his gut from nowhere and flooding the pit with toxic purple venom. He dared ask, "Was she in love with him?"

When Anna sighed, he braced himself. "She was, but—"

"What?!" Julian squawked. "She—she never told me. I—I thought sh—she only loved me."

"It's a long story, love," Anna said.

"I'm sorry," Uki moaned, her short face drooping. "I didn't mean to open a can of worms." She tried to pat Julian on the shoulder, but he pulled away.

"It is okay, my sweet daughter," Pana said. "The boy's grieving. Why don't we let you get back to work?" Her uneven eyes full of regret, Uki nodded. Then she silently returned to the lab, exchanging her blanket for the white coat. "Come," Pana said. "I will get you all blood from the other icebox."

Julian followed, trying not to think too deeply about Violet and Eric together, but the unsettling idea was force-feeding him anyway. The relentless, unlubricated grinding and churning of all his senses and nerves, the disturbing mental picture of the two aggressively fucking like rabid dogs, Violet screaming Eric's name in orgasmic pleasure; it was more than enough to make him puke.

Such indecent imagery provoked the same life-altering assault on his psyche as his discovery of Faith and Travis's affair—leading to his suicide attempt, four years earlier. He gagged, emitting a high squeal of dry heaves. Accompanying the barbaric hurling of nothing came a sharp puncture in his stomach. He winced and firmly grasped his abdomen, nearly losing his balance in the process.

"Are you all right?" Anna asked.

He caught his breath as the pain subsided. He nodded, and everyone continued. The hallway ended in the large meeting room. They crossed it, heading towards the opposite corridor. Like the hallway with the guest rooms, this one was lined with several closed white doors. Reaching the last one on the left, Pana opened it.

Inside, three tall black freezers sat against the back wall, near a sink and overhead cupboard. At the center of the kitchenette, two wooden picnic tables sat parallel. "Have a seat," Pana instructed. Anna and Bernard claimed one table, and Julian, the other. Pana took two clear, pint-sized IV bags from one of the freezers and gave them to Anna and Bernard. He took two more, giving one to Julian and keeping the other for himself. He sat opposite the widower, looking on with more compassion than before.

Julian's eyes scurried away, still finding Pana's demeanor intense. He looked at the thawed red pouch on the table in front of him. "Drink up!" Pana said.

Julian groaned, "I'm not hungry." He watched Anna and Bernard at the other table, both feeding from their bags, but he was too oblivious to do the same.

"Take it back to your room with you later, then," Pana said.

There was a moment of silence before Anna turned to their host, asking, "How long can we stay?"

"For as long as you would like—all three of you," Pana said, shifting his gaze among everyone. "But wouldn't Caanis want to see you now?"

"Don't you think that's going to be awkward?" she asked.

"You know him better than I do."

"It doesn't matter. He resents me."

"Your father is difficult, but I don't believe he has ill intent towards you or your brother." Julian watched Bernard pump his cheeks. "He loves his children, but he has demons."

Julian asked, "What do you mean?"

"It is no secret to those older than you that the king and I lost touch centuries ago. Since moving from Germany into the catacombs, he has wanted us to conform. I respect him and his position, but I will be damned if he thinks I will yield the leadership of my people, especially to someone whom most of them despise."

"Why did Caanis move L'abisme?"

"The short answer is war," Pana began, Anna nearly chuckling. "Long before L'abisme, there was Reinhardt. Reinhardt was the largest vampire kingdom in the world. Their numbers were nearly twice the combined current size of L'abisme, Taltosia, Raz

74

Ahrim, and even us. They were also the only kingdom to actually live inside a castle."

"What happened?"

"It was said the kingdom's founder and longtime ruler, Arvil Reinhardt, was assassinated by his own son: Aellin. Aellin was not only Arvil's natural son, but the heir to his throne. When Arvil died, Aellin's accuser, Caanis—who was also made by Arvil—revolted. The kingdom split. Half its people believed in Aellin's innocence while the other half, led by Caanis, believed otherwise."

"It wasn't just accusations," Anna said, the others lending her their eyes and ears. "There were so many vamps making vamps back then. The kingdom was rapidly growing. Aellin feared having so many of us in one place. He encouraged many vamps to venture out into the world and start covens of their own, but their loyalty was not yet his.

"Arvil detested his son's efforts. He forbade anyone to break away. Though Aellin obeyed the king's wishes, we all knew he grew bitter towards his father. Then the night Arvil died, it was Caanis who found his body." Anna's eyes briefly met those of her husband. "Xavier and I were both there, too, but we were each in separate parts of the castle when it happened. It was Aellin's dagger—once given to him by Arvil—that was found sticking from the old man's heart."

"How long ago was this?" Julian asked.

"Seventeen eighty-eight," she said. "It was during the French Revolution, right around the time they started using the catacombs to bury all the plague victims in Paris."

"So, until this war, you and Xavier lived in Germany?"

"Yes. We would've probably stayed there. But in a twist of irony, Arvil's assassination caused such turmoil, the split led to a long, bloody war that made its way into the public's eye. Lots of people died because of vamps fighting in the streets and even in the sky. We tried to get rid of everyone who we thought saw us, but hunters from Vatican City got involved."

Hunters? Julian gulped, remembering what Christopher Cauldwell had said about his family heritage. He shuddered, visualizing the medieval war hammer shoved into his and Violet's faces again.

"None of the other kingdoms got involved, but the war eventually ended," Anna continued. "As a result, we had to flee Germany. That's when we moved to the catacombs, declared Caanis our new king, and dubbed our home 'L'abisme' on account of our bone-ridden abyss."

"I thought Xavier was from Paris," Julian said. "He once told me he was born in eleven forty-four, and then he was turned by Caanis when he was seventeen."

"That's right," she said. "Caanis loved Paris long before we ever called it home. He visited often. It just so happened to be fate that he was there to find Xavier floating in the Seine River." She began to smile but quickly straightened her face when Bernard grunted loud enough for everyone to hear. "… it was also fate that Caanis visited the port city of Arbroath, in Scotland."

"Is that where you're from?" Julian asked.

Anna sucked in a drink, and said, "No, but that's where my old life ended and my new one began."

Though Julian never touched his IV bag, the other three had finished theirs. Bernard stretched his arms high above his head and forced a yawn. "It's getting late and I'm tired," he said.

"Yeah, I guess we ought to get some rest," Anna murmured, with little enthusiasm.

"Do you remember how to get back to your room?" Pana asked.

Bernard, rising from the table with Anna, said, "Yes."

Lifting his hand to wave them goodnight, Pana said, "Very well, then. I shall see you when you wake." Once the Gaunts exited the room, he turned his full attention to Julian. "Are you going to bed now too?"

"I'm not tired, but I don't want to keep you from anything you might need to do."

"Nonsense! I have all the time in the world."

Unsure what to say, Julian sat silent, staring at the tabletop's wood-grain lines, thinking, *What now?*

"I don't believe anyone else heard you earlier," Pana said. Julian tipped his head. "—when you grew upset, not wanting Bernard to tell anyone about your friend, Daryl." As if put on the spot, Julian struggled for words, trying to say something, anything, but nothing spewed from between his cold, gaping lips but hot air. "It's okay, boy. Your secret is safe." Pana reached across the table and patted the top of Julian's hand with his rough, leathery palm.

"You said nobody else heard me, but can't the others read minds?"

"Most of them can. That is what I find so remarkable. You have been a vampire for a week?" Julian nodded. "Have you read anyone's mind yet?"

"Daryl's—at mine and Violet's wedding."

"Then not only can you read minds, you might also block certain others from reading yours." He smiled. "It is a gift that must be trained to strengthen. Be proud, boy! It is rare to have both, especially so soon."

"About that," Julian began. "Why am I coming into my powers so quickly? Last night, I was in the helicopter when it crashed and exploded. I caught fire. My hair and clothes all burned completely off my body—even my shoes. The only thing left was my wedding ring and the ankh pendant Violet gave me, but the flames never affected me. Why?"

Throughout Julian's confession, Pana watched, his eyes growing wider and more bewildered as he learned each detail. "I never knew some of us could be fireproof," he said. "Then again, I never knew our kind could start fires with their emotions either." Julian shuddered, knowing exactly to whom Pana referred. "Violet's blood was strong. You already have gifts unlike those of any others. Daryl too."

"So, you know about Daryl?" Julian shook his head, thinking, S*o much for that idea.*

"I told you, it's okay. You don't know me, so there is no real way to convey this to you properly, but I am not your enemy. Xavier visits my dreams, too."

Julian's jaw fell towards the table, his mind racing with questions. The first to reach the finish was, "He doesn't know he's dead, does he?"

"He does not."

"How do we convince him? Anna told me he will perceive dreams as reality and assume he is alive."

"That is true. Trying to convince the damned they've moved on is far more difficult than you may think."

"Then what should I do, just validate him and act like it's not a dream at all?"

"Yes. You will need him as he is. I fear we've reached the beginning of something long, dark, and abominable. If you tell Xavier he's moved on, it may frighten his spirit into retreat. That means he may never come back to you. When he visited my slumber last night, he told me the onset of Dajhri's prophecy had come to fruition. I had no idea what it meant, nor that he was already expired. If that is true, you—and perhaps even I—will need him to remain in his natural state of being. Perhaps I could work with him, but it must not be forced."

"I understand. What about Violet, though?"

"What about her?"

"She came to me in my dream last night too. Her face was hidden beneath her hair, but she never said a word to me. It was as if she tried to give me our wedding night, but before I could even kiss her, that part ended, and I woke up. It was a dream within a dream."

"That's a tough one. Violet may know she is dead. I wouldn't know. Xavier said nothing about her. I would tread lightly for now. Her not talking to you and hiding her face makes me think she knows but may fear what you'll think."

"Then why did she try to make love to me?"

"I wouldn't know. She only just moved on. Give her time and be patient. She will come when she is ready."

"It was so strange. First, we were in a cave, but then she led me out into the open. The ground was covered in snow. There were tall trees everywhere, and the Northern Lights were in the sky." He watched Pana stroke his chin while he listened. "She led me out to a hot spring. It made me wonder if maybe the spring was something she'd seen up here. In her diary, she had previously written about coming here and how she was going to go to Peru."

"Ah, yes," Pana chuckled. "She disobeyed me, and while I do not like disobedience, the little fireball surprised me. I only wanted someone to go with her because I knew how much she hated flying that far alone. I wanted her to be safe. As for the hot spring, I do not recall ever seeing such a thing this far north, certainly not the trees. Those are farther south."

Again, the conversation grew silent. Julian had done a wonderful job of blocking what Uki said, but eventually he couldn't help revisiting the same ego-bruising analogy—everyone wallowing in each other but him. "Violet was faithful to you," Pana said, interrupting the pity party. "She was truly in love with you."

"Please, get out of my head."

"Then stop blaring such loud emotions, boy! All Violet talked about while she was here was you. She drove us crazy with it. What happened between her and Eric was long ago, and it is not what you believe. So, instead of jumping to conclusions, why not do your own research? You might be surprised."

Julian sighed. "What research?" Then it hit him: *Her diary!* He remembered putting it in his backpack. "I think I'm going to go to bed now," he said, all but leaping from the picnic table. Now full of excitement and yearning, he took the IV bag and said, "Thank you."

Pana smiled and bowed his head. "Assuming you remember how to get back to your room, have pleasant dreams, boy."

Chapter Nine

The overhead lighting hummed and fluttered when Julian hit the switch. Like everywhere else in the concrete bunker, the floor, walls, and ceiling of his modest guest room were dull and gray. Near the door sat a twin bed with a brown fur blanket and pillow on top. Wedged between the bed and wall, a small end table stood level with the mattress. At the other end of the room, a porcelain bathtub with connecting pipes and faucets took up the left corner. To its right, a white sink sat over an open linen cabinet full of folded washcloths and towels.

Above the sink, an oval mirror hung from a leather strap. Scanning the room, Julian caught his own reflection. He approached, taking the first hard look at himself since all hell broke loose. What he saw was a broken-down shell of a man. His slim, colorless lips hung like a sick old hound's, just begging to be taken behind the barn and put out of its misery. His brackish ocean blues were no less pitiful. The raw, red aftermath lining each socket wasn't as historically bound as Anna's but still too many shades of heartache for his liking.

He held up the IV bag, abhorring it through the mirror. "Look what you did to yourself," he taunted, hatefully snarling at his own parallel. "You stupid son of a bitch. You have ruined your entire life for nothing." He laughed at himself. "You really are a loser." He looked at the blood, thinking, *And now you're a fucking parasite too.*

After a long, depressing exhale, he tossed the bag across the room. He watched it land on the table, the hard smack triggering a random thought. *I wonder if Daryl drank his yet.* He took his phone from his pocket. The date and time read: *2:22 a.m. AKST. Jan 2, 2020.* "What time zone is that? What time is it in Virginia?"

He intended to send a text message but instead rolled his eyes upon discovering he had no signal. Figuring there was nothing to lose, he typed one anyway. *I just found out the blood we gave you is artificial and not from a human. I know it probably means nothing, but I am so sorry, brother. I am in Alaska now, but I will get back home to you as soon as I can. I will make sure you get all the artificial blood you will ever need. I promise. I love you, Daryl. Please, forgive me.* Unsure when or if he would get the message, Julian tapped *send* and put the phone back in his pocket.

He took off his jacket and tossed it on the floor by the end table. Beside it sat his backpack. He pulled it closer, his mind fixated on the old blue book, but once he started digging past his clothes, the idea of taking a hot bath first grew more tempting by the second, especially when uncovering an old bottle of body wash.

He went to the tub and turned one of the faucets. Water poured from the spout, splashing against the dry inner surface. He put his hand in the flow. The water was freezing but without the same effect it would have on a human. It wasn't cooling his skin either. It simply existed as an inconsequential discomfort. He turned it off before trying the other. After allowing it time to warm, he placed his hand in the flow again, finding the same result. He gave up, thinking, *Fuck it! What are you avoiding?*

He returned to the bed and took Violet's diary from his bag. Just holding it was enough for his heart to sound off, ticking louder every second he imagined his precious immortal coupling with another man, even if it was before they met. *Are you going to read it already or just keep sulking and trying to compare her to Faith?* Finally, he shook the fear and took a breath, telling himself, *Here goes nothing.* He opened it and started with the first page, reading to himself.

8/14/24

Dear Diary

Hello, Diary! You are mine now! My mommy bought you for me. She said I can tell you all my secrets and about my life, so I will start by telling you my name. I am Violet Cordelia Troúton, and I am seven years old. I live in Savannah, Georgia, but Mommy said my great, great grandparents and their entire family sailed here a hundred years ago from Amsterdam.

My favorite thing in the whole-wide world is church! Church was so much fun today! Mommy even let me sing with the choir. Our preacher said I have the voice of an angel and could maybe even be a star someday! It made me so happy! I was excited to come home and tell my daddy, but he was too busy with finishing the harvest. He grows peaches and oranges. I also think he was drinking. He is not nice when he drinks, and he smells bad too. My brothers and I were supposed to help pick peaches when we got home, but we just played around all day. I think that made him mad too. Now it is getting late and—

The entry ended abruptly. Julian turned the page and continued.

8/15/24

Dear Diary

My daddy hurt me really bad last night. It still hurts down there. Please, don't ever tell anyone, Diary. Mommy swore you wouldn't. Will you keep my secret?

Violet

Julian's gut churned. He remembered what Violet once told him about her real father. He rushed to the next page, hoping for the best, but dreading the worst.

4/4/44

Dear Diary

Well, hello there! It has been twenty years since I last wrote to you. My apologies, but sadly, I had forgotten you. When I was cleaning out my closet and packing for my big trip up north next week, I found you hiding at the bottom. Well, I have made it this far, Diary! I am turning 27 in one week and I discovered long ago there will never be any hope in finding what I want in Savannah.

I have been working on the plantation for years now. I have saved half of everything I've earned. One decade and thirty-five hundred dollars later, I can finally move out of Georgia and pursue my dream. In one week, I am moving to New York City! I am going to be an actress! Even my acting coach thinks I have what it takes. He said my look, exotic name, and talent will "put asses in seats." I am so excited to feel like life is finally moving forward! 1944 will be my year! Wish me luck!

Violet

Julian never knew, but when moving to Las Vegas, he took as much money as Violet had to New York. Unlike hers, his money was given to him by his grandfather, Johnny. *Synchronicity*, he thought, turning the page, and moving on.

4/11/44

Dear Diary

Happy birthday to me! I am on the bus now, getting ready to cross the South Carolina state line! I still have a long trip ahead of me, and I am scared shitless, but I am letting my heart lead the way! I can just see it now—my name in big, bold black letters on the same marquees as Carey Grant, Jean Arthur, and Clark Gable, to name a few. Just wait until all my old schoolmates back home see what I can do! I will show them all. It won't be long now that the whole world will know my name: Miss Violet Troúton

4/14/44

Dear Diary

The goddamn bus broke down near Richmond, and it took an extra day and a half to get here, but I am here now. My hotel room is right in the middle of Manhattan! The room stinks like cigars, and it is expensive, but it is nice otherwise. In the morning, I am going to start looking for an apartment. Then I'll get a job and go from there. I'll check back soon!

Violet

5/14/44

Dear Diary

I've only been in New York a month, and it is more stressful here than I thought it would be. I did find the cutest little studio apartment the day after I arrived though. It's really cheap too! Now, my address is on Bleecker Street, in the West Village. There's a stray mutt who lives in the alley out back. He's really sweet. I think he might be a terrier. I call him Rusty.

I got a job at a café just down the street. I also found an acting school to help with getting leads and better acquainted with the local scene, but I am not sure how much I will like it there. It's close, but also a little pricier than I expected. The instructor is an asshole! All the other female students are, too. I already want to quit. There is one nice boy there. His name is Nathan. Everyone is mean to him, too.

He told me there's a better acting school, where I could learn far more and at a much cheaper price, but it is on Staten Island. That's almost twenty miles and a long way for me to keep going back and forth. I would have to take a ferry. At least I can walk to this one. I can't give up now. I won't! I refuse to go back to

Georgia, unless it is to rub my success in everyone's faces. Well, it is time for work, so I will end things here for now.

Violet

7/26/44
Dear Diary

Sorry it's been a while. When I'm not working, I sleep. I quit acting school last week. Fuck them! The instructor called me a "dumb tomboy grandma." Some other rich bitch told me I would get more attention whoring myself to the sailors on short leave than I ever would as an actress. Fuck them all!

The ladies at the café have all been really nice to me, and as long as I have half a sandwich to toss him on my way to work, Rusty will give me all the stinky, garbage-flavored kisses I want, but I am already sick of this place. I don't get it, Diary. What did I do wrong? I followed my heart. Isn't that what you are supposed to do? Should I go check out that place on Staten Island? I've been thinking about it, but I don't know. I guess I'll figure it out.

Violet

9/4/44
Dear Diary

I just spent the last month trying to talk myself into going to look at the "acting school on Staten Island." There is no acting school on Staten Island. Nathan lied to me. It took me forever to get there and back. But it's okay, Diary. I realize now I was meant to be there after all. Tonight, I had an epiphany and a complete change of heart.

I was so mad when I got there, finding it wasn't an acting school. It was a theatre—a very nice one, actually: The St. George Theatre. I've been so wrapped up in life, I haven't even gotten to see one film since arriving in New York. I'd also forgotten, Carey Grant had a new one out. So, in my attempt to turn a bad night into a mediocre one, I bought a twenty-five cent ticket for "Arsenic and Old Lace."

I can't explain it, but it's like the movie killed whatever remaining aspirations I took across the harbor with me on the ferry. Ever since I was called a "dumb tomboy grandma," it has stuck. I was aware of my age when coming here. I knew it would be harder for me. I also knew better than to go directly to Hollywood and pretend I could compete with eighteen-year-olds. I didn't realize just how cutthroat the business would actually be, though. Back home, in Savannah, the scene was far less competitive and much friendlier.

"Arsenic and Old Lace" was originally a play. I think it's fairly new. I remember a few people talking about it in my old class, not long before I moved. Some, who were also players at the Savannah Theatre, wanted to perform it. So, naturally I was interested in seeing it, especially since Carey Grant was the lead. The dark humor was nice, but I didn't like how they kept comparing the antagonist to Boris Karloff, implying the character looked like Frankenstein's monster. Please! I laughed at that more than the parts I was supposed to laugh at—and some of those Teddy Roosevelt scenes had me busting a gut!

The actor who played the antagonist might not be the prettiest man, but even in makeup, he didn't look any different. I found nothing hideous about the character's appearance. It was like they had to keep verbally reminding us of who he was supposed to look like, rather than letting the audience draw their own conclusions.

It made me wonder, how pretentious and insulting is this to anyone's intelligence? Are we not allowed to think for ourselves? I know it's just a movie, but Jesus Christ on a bicycle! I can't explain it, but it was like the idea of pursuing a career in this malarky suddenly made me want to vomit! I know I was pissed and hurt, but sometimes maybe we need to get pissed and hurt to see things clearly. Maybe I should thank Nathan. Because of him I even got to see the Statue of Liberty from the ferry. I got a full-frontal view of her, and it was breathtaking. I wish I owned a camera.

Unfortunately, I have no idea what I'm supposed to do now. I guess I will just keep working at the café and see what happens. What else can I do? I can't go home. I can't go back and tell my parents after all this time—thinking I am some big deal and believing I would have everything I wanted—only to come here at 27 and discover it was a lie, and all for nothing but a failed dream!

Violet

Julian knew Violet's peers were mean to her, but to what extent, he had no idea. Moving on and trying not to conjure more tears, he turned the page.

10/19/44

Dear Diary

I only have a minute before heading off to work, but I just wanted to say, the ladies at the Corner Cup Café are the most amazing ever! They know how I've been feeling. Some of them even take me out for a drink occasionally. There's a little hole in the wall they found after the war started. I certainly don't drink to get drunk, but it is nice to knock one back every so often and forget about the war and those Nazi cunts, even if just for a while. It will take some time to sort myself out, but I am in New York fucking City! This is the place of dreams. I can just find another one, right? There is no need to give up on the future yet. For the first time since quitting acting school, I feel optimistic, and it actually feels good.

Violet

11/11/44

Dear Diary

　　Something wicked has become of me. I am not me anymore. According to the man who did it, I am not even human anymore. He said I am a vampire. He said I am immortal now. I still don't want to believe it. Who even could? But I cannot deny something very dark and satanic is living inside of me, and in the name of my God, Jesus Christ, I rebuke it.

　　It happened a couple of weeks ago. We were short-staffed at work. I was the only one there until closing. That is where I first met him. He said his name is Xavier. He said some things only I would know. I got so scared. I didn't know what he wanted, but when he finally left, I closed the shop early and tried to hurry home. Just outside of my apartment building, I was hit by a car. I would have died on the sidewalk if it wasn't for Xavier. He'd followed me. I don't know why.

　　He took me to someone else's apartment. That is where I have been ever since. I must have slept for a week. Xavier has been feeding me human blood. He says I cannot eat regular food anymore. I am so scared. Ms. Grant, the woman who lives here—and her two sons, Eric, and William—have been friendly, especially Eric. Xavier has been kind too, but I have no idea what his intentions are.

　　I am still very weak. Just writing this is taking all my strength, but I feel like it needs to be written. I have not been allowed to go outside. The windows are all boarded, and it stays so dark and stuffy in here. At some point, Xavier went to my apartment and brought my belongings here. I don't know how long he wants me to stay, but I want to go home. I just want my mommy, or at the very least, death. I would even settle for one of Rusty's stinky trash kisses—because this is monstrous and unholy. Please, God, wash me in the blood of the lamb, free me, and keep my wretched soul. Don't let me burn in Hell for something I had no control over. Please, God!

Violet

Julian was so shaken by the horrifying account that he lost his breath and dropped the book. He imagined his wilted and weary flower, every bit as miserable, desperate, and longing for death as he currently did. Thanks to even more drear, he had no choice but to curl up in a ball and cry into his pillow.

The salty tears burned his chafed sockets as they festered from each duct. His face buried, he continued wailing until the distinctly warm and loving pressure of an open palm lay gently against his back. He spun instantly, facing the direction of the touch. He saw nothing but the sink. In the mirror, above it, his deeply disturbed reflection stared back.

"Who's there?!" He listened, hearing only his shaky breath. "Violet?! Xavier?!" He waited, hoping for a sign. He looked up at the fluorescent light strip on the ceiling, begging it to flicker; but nothing. "If someone is there, can you knock on the wall?" Still, nothing. He tried again, asking, "Can you knock three times on the wall—like this?" He knocked three times against the concrete above his head.

In response, came, *Knock ... Knock ... Knock ...*

"My God!" he squeaked. "Violet?! Violet, is that you?!"

Faint laughter emerged from the wall. He listened closer. It was a man's laugh. "Bern! Stop it! Leave him alone. He's mourning, and you don't need to mock him for it!"

"Oh, fuck him!" Bernard shouted. "After that shit he pulled in front of everyone earlier, and then having Pana pull me away like that to scold and tell me not to talk about Daryl—fuck him! Fuck them both!"

"Don't you care that he's suffering?"

"And what about you—my love?'"

"What about me?"

"You have been mourning all goddamn day and night over that cock-less asshole!"

"So? He was my brother! And you know how much I loved Hell Belle. She was a sister and daughter."

"Cut the shit! I am not talking about Hell Belle. Don't be stupid. I bet if I had been the one who'd snuffed it, you would barely shed a tear."

"What the fuck, Bern? What are you saying? I love you! I'm the one who came and got Xavier to help me save you from Eustice! Don't you remember? After what he did to you, it took me so long to reach your soul, but I found it, and it was beautiful. I fell in love with you. What Xavier and I did was nothing, especially compared to what you and I once had. Doesn't that count for anything? You have no idea how much I want that back, but I can't help my past no more than you can.

"I am nine hundred forty-two years old, Bern! You're only two hundred nineteen. You can't expect someone to live that long and not do things with others. You already know I was supposed to be married when I was only sixteen and still a human. Just like then, what Xavier and I did was long before you and I ever met. With him, it was just a one-time thing. With you, it is forever—I swear, love."

When Anna finished pouring out her heart, Julian grew anxious over the silence that followed. The lovers' quarrel took him back to his dream. So heavily wrapped in the parts with Violet and Xavier, the rest had remained hazy in the backdrop until then. He'd forgotten about assaulting Bernard, and his wife's confession after. But now, he remembered everything.

In a more pleasant tone, Bernard finally said, "I'm sorry, my love. All this has been so much for me to take in. I don't want to be here. I don't feel comfortable."

"I don't either. We ain't got a choice right now, though. We couldn't stay in Virginia. I don't want to go home either. If there is one thing Father can't stand, it's revealing ourselves to humans. If he didn't already hate me before, I'm sure he does now."

"Your father does not hate you. In fact, I think we would be better off there than here or anywhere else in the world. Who would he protect if not his oldest daughter? If the king blames us, why can't we just tell him that Xavier, Julian, and Hell Belle were responsible? We might have been involved with Leviticus, but last night was not our fault. There's no reason we should have to pay the piper too."

Excuse me?! Julian nearly choked on the air. His facial muscles tensed, and he imagined bursting through the wall and forcing Bernard to say it to his face.

"Bern!" Anna squealed in a shrill tone of disbelief. "—the fuck's wrong with you?! How could you even suggest that? It wasn't Julian's fault—neither was it Xavier's, and certainly not Hell Belle's!"

"Maybe not directly, but Xavier made them a part of this when he fed them his blood."

"You are un-fucking-believable. You know that? I could put up with your offhand, smartass remarks before, but it's as if you're a whole other man now. I don't need this shite. I'm going to bed. By the time I wake up, you best have changed your attitude. You fuckin' hear me?!"

All fell silent beyond the wall. Throughout the exchange, Julian had dissected every word. In any logical scenario, he felt he should be scared of, or at least offended by Bernard's suggestion. However, on the off chance it could ultimately lead to his own execution, he would gladly say, "Yes! I did it! I did it all, and you should kill me now before I do it to you!" Then he could be with Violet. His overly eager body was nearly shaking at the idea. Any abstract method of murder—no matter how clean, grotesque, or biblical—could not possibly compare to an eternity of the soul torture he longed to escape.

His eyes returned to the mirror, finding the scowling mug of a less tolerant self staring back. "What the hell is wrong with you, Julian?" His question implied the spirit in the meat suit known as Julian Frost, and Julian Frost, the ego, had become two separate entities, engaged in a conversation of morality versus blatant stupidity. Demanding an answer from his subordinate, he asked, "Are you really going to give up that easy? ... Well, are you?!"

His empty belly growled like a starving dog, dousing the flames before he could set the world on fire. He shook it off and finally drank the blood he'd taken back to his room. Though it wasn't cold anymore, he still gagged on the unacquired taste. After finishing it, he scanned the blue diary on the bed, wanting to continue but now struggling to keep his eyes open. *Fuck it. I'll read more tomorrow.* He set the book on the end table. Then, he turned off the light and climbed into the bed.

He wrapped himself in the fur blanket, not too fond of its odd fish-like smell but enjoying the silence next door too much to care. *If I can hear through concrete, I wonder just how far my new ears can reach. When will I be able to fly like the others? What else can I do?*

Even with all the outlandish possibilities that would drive any ordinary person to addiction or worse, he drifted off to the only place he imagined happiness could still exist. But his slumber was short-lived. As quickly as he dozed, his eyes opened, finding himself wide awake again. Riding his second wind, he threw his hands up and sighed in frustration. "Now what?" he groaned. Restless and refusing to slice open another vein with the diary, he pulled away the blanket and got out of bed.

He put on his shoes and went out the door. He looked both ways down the hall, seeing nothing and hearing less before heading in the direction of the large room where everyone had previously met. Passing each door, he listened closely, not meaning to pry but curious if he could. Still, he heard nothing but himself. Entering the large room, he found an open door on the other side. It was the door he'd followed the others through from the gutted house upstairs.

Pana had stressed how important safety and security were to him and his people. The open door made no sense. "Umm—is this door supposed to be open?!" Julian shouted, hoping someone would hear and not bite his head off for waking them. He debated on whether he should close it himself. *Surely, it is open for a reason, but I can't see why they would just leave it open and unattended like that. Whatever! It's not my problem.* Refusing to let it become his problem, he turned back in the direction of his room.

"—Jul?" a familiar voice moaned. Like the Arctic above, Julian froze, experiencing a chilling wave of untouchable energy, ping-ponging from head to toe in a loop. "Jul?!" she wailed, calling the name like a long-lost ghost, in desperate search of her love once lost.

"I hear you!" Julian cried. "I hear you! Where are you?!" He tried with all his might to swivel and face the direction of *her* distinct southern drawl. "Violet?! I'm here! I'm here!" He struggled, hardening every muscle in his body to savagely throw himself at her, but it was like his body had turned to stone. "I can't move! Help me!"

Then came a soft whisper, so close to his ear, she could have kissed it. "Jul." He nearly jumped the height of his own body, landing hard on his rear in the same spot as the night she almost hit him with her car. Violet playfully giggled. "You just keep falling for me, don't you?" Her flirty banter was euphoric, an angel's lullaby, but even he knew it wasn't real. It was only a memory.

The fond recollection zapped him like an electrical current, shocking him back to life as the created monster he'd become. Gaining sudden control of his head, he spun it about in search of his flower, but she was not there. "Where are you? Please, show me. Don't be scared. I love you!" As if released by a mighty, unseen hand, preventing him from completing his quest, Julian instantly regained full control of his other muscles and their functions. He sprang to his feet and dashed for the open door, knowing his heart would lead the way.

He soared through the opening, across the corridor, and into the darkness. Then he made a beeline up the old wooden stairway, faster than his feet would normally allow.

"Jul? Where are you?"

At the top, he practically ripped away the thin piece of drywall that hid the secret passage from the rest of the house. "I am coming, Violet!" Rushing across the pitch-black room, Julian tripped and almost fell over a piece of furniture before reaching the front door, kicking it open, and disappearing into the night.

The snow had stopped falling, and the Aurora shone brighter than he remembered. "Jul!" Her voice echoed from afar, like she was moving in the same direction and at the same pace he was. Her tone grew more desperate, whining, "Jul! Why won't you come to me?!"

"I'm looking! Where are you?!"

"I'm here!"

Julian looked in all directions, only to find other buildings and their outside lights. "But where?" he screamed, his soft, cracking voice now every bit as lost and hopeless as hers. He then looked to the one place he'd ignored: the sky. Squinting his vampire eyes, he carefully inspected the misty green. Finally, he spotted a dark speck in the lean shape of a human female: fully nude, her thick, lumbar-length hair blowing wildly behind her in the breeze. The starlet shape hovered hundreds of feet above Julian's head. "Violet, I see you! I am down here—on the ground! Come to me!" He reached up as far as his extended hands allowed.

Violet remained in place, neither retreating nor advancing. "Where are you, Jul?! I am so scared!"

"I am down here! Look down! Violet, I'm here!" Julian fell to his knees, arms and fingers extended, still worshiping his goddess and tearfully screaming his prayers like they were swansongs. "Can't you hear me?! Violet! Fly down to me, please!"

He lost his breath while howling so intently. Before he could catch it and try again, the unforgiving Aurora and all it illuminated began a slow, agonizing fade to black, the growing void swallowing Violet's immaculate image with it. "No!" Julian cried, pounding his closed fists into the frozen white earth. "Please! Not yet!"

His eyelids cracked and he shot upright, finding himself back in bed, beneath the fishy fur blanket, and shaking with the fear of something even God couldn't create. It took a moment for his speedy breathing to hit the brakes and to regain control of his senses. Once he did, he growled, "Goddamn it! I can't fucking do this anymore!" He leapt out of bed and flipped on the light. "I can't do this—I can't fucking do this—I can't!" Wide-eyed and ravenous, he frantically paced the room, stomping back and forth until the shiny oval mirror drew him in.

Wrath in his eyes, he ambled towards it, a final act in mind. The mirror was no longer a vanity but a tool; a tool to ultimately build his fortune upon. He ripped it from the wall by the leather strap from which it hung. He whipped it violently at the ground. The boisterous shatter was orgasmic to his ears. At his feet, dozens of sparkly bits glittered the floor. One larger jagged shard stood out above the rest, just begging him to pick it up and worship it like his god—a new god that would deliver him from all that was evil and unholy, to all that is pure and just.

He held the idol in his hand, ready to submit every part of himself to it like the sacrificial lamb in exchange for the prize he wanted, needed, waiting for him on the other side. He tilted his head, staring straight into the burning light strip above. "I'm coming home, sweetie." He put the broken glass to his throat and squeezed every facial muscle he had until they nearly imploded.

The same knuckle he bared his teeth on when breaking his ankle rested firmly against his neck, overtop the rapidly pulsating artery he planned to gouge. With nothing left to stop him, Julian drew one final breath and whispered, "Peace." As he reared back to make the cut, the door burst open, startling him into dropping the glass and opening his eyes.

There, Pana stood, his mighty eyes bulging. He yelled, "What the hell are you doing, boy?!" in a mix of disgust and concern.

"I …" Julian had no answer. He had nothing but two knees to collapse upon as his tears rained once again.

Pana joined him, also falling to his knees and embracing the young vampire in his kind, understanding arms. "It is okay, boy," he whispered gently, patting Julian's back. "It is going to be okay."

Chapter Ten

It wasn't just getting caught, though he felt the terrible impression he'd made on Pana was something he could never make up for, even if he did imagine himself an excusable pity party in the elder's eyes. Julian was ashamed of himself. He knew Violet would not approve of such irrational behavior either. Surely his flower would object to following her heinous murder with an equally Shakespearean suicide—a romantic gesture disguised as a twisted union of ironic comedy and tragedy at the end of a happy dagger.

That was only part of his indignity. Julian survived his first attempt, ultimately leading to the love of his life and an ironclad understanding that suicide was not how he was meant to die. Yet there he was, attempting to defy an alleged God's predestined fate by imposing his own will for the second time. In her final words, Violet told him they would transcend all time and space together. *What if I had ruined it? What if suicide really could change things?*

After consoling the grieving widower until his ducts ran dry, Pana took him back to his living quarters on the other end of the bunker. Its front room was the same size as Julian's entire guest room. A strange smell filled the air: something he thought was sage, but with hints of citrus and honeysuckle.

Opposite the door, a black wood-burning stove sat centered against the wall—a fire glowing inside it. A hollow, cylindrical stack rose from the back and disappeared into the concrete ceiling. On the plain gray floor, next to the stove, lay a bundle of small branches and twigs. Facing the stove, sat two old rocking chairs.

Next to the front door, a chrome mini fridge sat in the front left corner next to a sink and two overhead cabinets. In the rear left corner, a hallway disappeared farther into the apartment. Along the wall on the right side of the room, a brown sofa rested below a large, centered painting.

Julian fixed on the old work. Two indigenous men stood beneath a midnight blue sky full of stars and illuminated by a cloud-covered moon. A dark ocean of rising waves and white ripples rose to tide behind them. He recognized the man on the left as Pana. He and the shorter man—with the same dark, mullet-esque hair as his, but thicker eyebrows and a longer chin—wore bulky, black, fur coats, each washed over in moonlight. "Who's that other man?" Julian asked.

"His name is Aput, my great, great, great uncle and maker. Aput taught me almost everything I know. He was more of a father than an uncle."

"What happened to him?"

"It was strange, really. Like Lusa and myself, Aput could not fly, though he was quite an adventurer. Once, while south, we believe he must've lost track of the stars, telling him when the sun's long hibernation was ending."

"That's awful!"

"His passing—yes," Pana nodded. "However, there are much worse ways for our kind to perish."

"Worse than burning alive?"

"We do not burn when touched by the sun. We merely dissolve into dust and cease to exist. Some even believe the transition is painless." Pana joined Julian at the painting. "We eventually found his clothing and supplies, but no real evidence of stray or anguish. I'd like to imagine he moved on peacefully."

Interesting.

"Don't get any ideas, boy."

Julian laughed. "What's the point?"

"The point of what?"

"Life, death, everything in between: what's the point?"

"I believe it is to learn and evolve. I believe our spirits are eternal. Our Mother Earth is billions of years old. The universe is even older. Outside this universe, beyond the realms of possibility as we know it, there was no beginning, thus there can be no end—only cycles and layers. What lies beyond that; who knows?"

"What do you personally think is waiting for us?"

Pana chuckled. Pointing at the rocking chairs, he said, "Have a seat." Along Julian's way to the chair on the left, the elder added, "How about a drink?"

"A drink? A drink of what?" Full of intrigue, Julian watched him go to the refrigerator. He removed a clear plastic milk jug, half full of a red substance. "Oh," Julian muttered, feeling a sense of embarrassment, assuming it could've been anything but blood or water. Pana retrieved a dull-green kettle from the overhead cabinet and poured half of the liquid into it.

He put the jug back in the refrigerator. Then he brought the kettle to the hot stove and placed it on top. "Just a minute," he said. "Not much heat is needed." Julian's gaze followed him back to the cabinet, watching him take two white coffee mugs. After returning to the stove, he filled one and handed it to Julian before pouring the rest into the other and taking a seat in the empty chair.

Julian put the mug to his nose and sniffed hints of metal and fish. It was nothing like the synthetic blood he'd already grown to loathe. "What is this?"

"Whale blood," Pana said before taking a drink.

"Whale blood?! Why do you have whale blood?"

"Whale meat is a delicacy to humans, this far north. There are butchers here in Utqiaġvik who sell it, and sometimes we can get the blood."

Julian sniffed it again, finding the scent more off-putting. Blushing, he said, "Please, don't take offense, but this kind of smells like period blood."

"Period blood?" Pana asked, tipping his head.

"Menstrual blood." Julian pointed towards his crotch. "You know, when a woman bleeds down there, and—"

"—yes, I know what menstrual means," Pana chortled. "I just never heard it referred to as 'period blood' before." Julian briefly joined the laughter. "Try it," Pana persisted. "You may enjoy it."

Julian looked inside the cup again, staring into the red and debating. *Fuck it,* he thought. *What's whale blood compared to any other?* He slowly put the cup to his lips and sipped. The rich flavor was not that of menses or fish, but more like sucking on a dirty penny with a sweet hint of fresh coconut. Before he could even swallow, all his nerve endings arose at once like microfibers throughout his body, tingling themselves into a form of relaxation he never knew possible. He took another drink, and his body became weightless and impalpable. His perceptive consciousness was all that remained. Any physical matter binding him to a three-dimensional universe melted away. There was no more pain, fear, or hatred—only pure, unconditional love, *her* love.

"Very nice, eh?" Pana asked, his deep, wise old voice reaching Julian's ears from what he perceived as a million miles away, gripping him tightly, and pulling him back from the everlasting void.

"Why do I feel this way?"

"Blood is the essence of life. Whether it be human or animal, each type has its own effect on us."

Curious, Julian took another drink, finding the taste more tolerant than the last. "I feel calm, like I'm high or something, but I'm not. It's as if every urge I had to pick up that piece of glass is gone now." He laughed, adding, "Now I feel like such an idiot!"

Pana smiled in approval of Julian's new mood. "So, you want me to tell you what I think happens to us when we die?"

"Go for it," Julian said, having another drink.

"First, what do you think happens?"

Julian smirked, allowing himself a moment to ponder and dig through his magical euphoria in search of an answer. "At this point, I would like to believe there is a heaven: one we create through our memories and experiences here on Earth. But I am man enough to admit I could be wrong about all that."

"That's the power of enlightenment, boy." Pana took a drink from his mug. "Faith is such a wonderful thing to have. It gives us purpose."

Julian had another sip and shut his eyes, taking himself back in time. "Not long before I met Violet, Xavier, and the others, I went to an *Ayahuasca* retreat. I sat for two nights in ceremony with a pink-haired shaman named Michele. She would say, 'You are the medicine, brother, and you manifest your reality.'"

"I believe that is true," Pana said. "Look around you. Everything you will ever lay eyes on that did not come from the earth or sky is a manifestation of man, brought from the fifth—or higher dimension—to the third—or physical: one universe to another, simply through thought and initiative."

"I understand, but how does this affect the way the rest of the world around me works?" Pana stared blankly. "What I mean is, I didn't want Violet or Xavier to die. I didn't want Daryl to become a vampire. All the horrible things that happened to my mother and me when I was a child—I never wanted any of that. I would have done anything in my power to have stopped it all, but I couldn't. So, in what way is that manifesting reality in my favor?"

"Say that last part again," Pana instructed.

"How am I manifesting reality in my favor?"

"Say the last three words again."

"In my favor," he repeated, throwing his free hand up and shrugging his shoulder.

"In 'your' favor," Pana stressed. "Everything is working 'in your favor.' You may not be getting what you want, but you are getting what you need. Call it God, the universe, Mother Earth, reality, what have you, but if you trust this—" Pana put his twisted right palm over Julian's heart. "And learn to properly use this—" His hand moved to the top of Julian's head. "Then you will understand."

Once the conversation grew scarce, Julian took another drink, then said, "I had another dream about Violet. She kept calling my name. I followed her voice outside. She was floating in the aurora borealis. I kept begging her to come down to me, but it was like she couldn't see or hear me."

"She was inside the Aurora?"

"Yes, the light was behind her, making her stand out to me. Why do you ask?"

"In many Inuit beliefs, the Aurora is where our souls go when we move on."

"Could she be up there, lost and trying to find me?"

"Perhaps, but personally, I wouldn't think so. Violet never followed our customs. As far as I know, she was a traditional Christian."

"But how would believing one religion or belief system over another change the entire outcome of where our souls go when we die? How could believing in one god over another send your soul to that god instead of whatever does await us?"

"What if it is all self-perception? As you said, what if our own idea of an afterlife is the afterlife we receive?"

"But what about all these people who claim they died and went to Hell? Who wants to go to Hell?"

Pana laughed, repeating, "'People who claim.' People lie and misinterpret damn near everything. It does not mean they are wrong, but it does mean that our place is not to base what we believe upon what someone else says. It is up to us to discover our own truth." As

Julian took his final drink, Pana asked, "Do you know who taught me that?"

He swallowed and said, "Xavier?"

"No, boy." He looked over his shoulder, pointing at his uncle on the wall. "Xavier did paint that portrait, though."

"How did you and Xavier meet, anyway?"

"Oh my, that was so long ago." Pana took his final drink. "Near the end of the thirteenth century—around my two-hundred-fiftieth year, Xavier and Caanis traveled here during the long winter months. In those days, our town was only a small village. Though others like us lived in the north, Aput and I were the only two of our kind here. The human Inupiaq of our village knew about us, but they also knew we would never harm them. Given our supernatural gifts, we could support them in ways they could not."

Pana took his and Julian's empty mugs to the sink, continuing, "Every winter, Aput and I traveled south, where caribou migrated. I never knew what the caribou sensed in us or why it frightened them to turn back, but we drove them all the way up here to be slaughtered for food and resources. We used the pelts for warmth and clothing, and along with massive whale bones and driftwood from the ocean, we'd use it for shelter too."

"That is so wild," Julian said. "I can't even imagine what the world looks like to you now compared to then, when survival in such a harsh climate was so difficult."

"It is still difficult," Pana said on his way back to the rocking chair. "However, thanks to modern advancements—like this bunker, for example—survival is easier than it was. But even today, the Arctic is not for everyone. Aside from the natives and people coming here to work, we only see tourists who are full of curiosity and wonder—until they find out how cold and harsh the climate is or how expensive all the imported food and supplies are. Then they leave and never come back.

"You could say Xavier and Caanis were also tourists. They loved exploring new places, and thanks to our sixty-five days of darkness, they both fell in love with the Arctic. As I said, I was nearly two-hundred-and-fifty years old when we first met. One trip down south, Aput and I had a run-in with another tribe, trying to steal our herd of caribou. Though we were much stronger, we were also outnumbered by at least a dozen others."

His attentive eyes glowing like polished sapphire, Julian asked, "What happened?"

"The other tribesmen began disappearing one by one into the sky, just to fall back to the earth. By then, those who remained were no longer interested in the caribou or us. They ran, but none made it far. Every one of them were killed. Xavier and Caanis happened to be flying over when they spotted us. Neither Aput nor I knew what to think. They were the first white men we met, and they saved our lives.

"Once we thanked and told them what we were doing with the herd, they helped us drive it all the way home. After that, Xavier and Caanis visited often, even teaching us and the other villagers their European ways of hunting, fishing, and construction. Soon enough, more visitors started coming with them—some even settling here permanently. That is how our coven began to grow from only two of us to what we have today."

"About that—the coven, I mean—with so many of you here, why isn't this a kingdom?" Julian asked. "I once heard someone say Raz Ahrim doesn't have very many vampires, but they are a kingdom. So, why is this just a coven?"

"The short answer is politics, boy. It is true, we have the numbers. Most covens are no bigger than what yours was. Even those are so scant, I wouldn't be surprised if there were none left. The thing is, Raz Ahrim, L'abisme, and Taltosia work together as an alliance. An alliance of what, I have no clue. There was a time when aligning with others added safety, but that was millennia before I was born.

"Now—or until just recently, I imagine—the kingdoms have all been at peace. They've had no enemy to merge and rise against. But let's say it were to happen; it would be the duties of the kingdoms to come together and eradicate the threat. I begrudge Caanis, and unless it involved my people directly, I would never spill blood for him. Neither would my people. If we were a kingdom, we would directly be held accountable whenever we were called. Even before Aput moved on, we both decided we wanted no part of that headache. Thus, we'd rather just use a less extravagant word and avoid the 'who has the biggest usuk' contest altogether."

"What happened between you two—you and Caanis?" Julian asked.

"The king changed; that's what happened. I'm just glad it was all after Aput moved on. Xavier and I shared a bond. My uncle shared one with Caanis."

"If you don't mind me asking, how did you and Aput become vampires?"

"My uncle went on many hunting and fishing expeditions as a human. Sometimes, he would be away for months. Once, he disappeared for nine years. His brother, my great, great, great grandfather, along with the rest of his family, believed he was dead until the night he returned—many years before I was born. When he came back to Utqiagvik, he brought the gift with him.

"Both my parents froze to death when I was young. Aput raised me as his own. Until my teenage years I had no idea what he was. I knew he was not like the others in the village, but I could never have guessed he possessed the powers of a demon. Once I was old enough to understand, he told me what happened to him."

On the edge of his seat, proudly invested in something other than himself, Julian asked, "What happened?"

"He said he traveled east and then far south—beyond the Arctic Circle and into the green forest. At this point, he was alone. He carried knives and a spear, but Aput was blindsided by a cougar. He managed to kill it, but not before taking it over the side of a cliff. The cougar expired on impact. Aput landed on top of it, breaking his fall but his back too.

"He was stuck at the bottom of that cliff for days, with no food or water. Though the climate was naturally warmer, the weather was still too frigid to survive like that for long. He told me he felt his life fading away. He said his prayers and made his peace. Then a woman found him."

"A woman?"

Pana nodded. "Aput said she was beautiful—green-eyed, with a seductive voice. He was stuck there so long, he became dehydrated. He saw visions. When she first came to him she appeared as a dreamy shadow. Unsure if she was real, he thought she was a wendigo or a succubus coming to devour his soul. But he was wrong. She was gentle. She took him somewhere far away, somewhere foreign, where she fed him from her own blood and nursed him back to health. He claimed that for a time she took him as her lover. Then a day came that he escaped her. He spent several years making his way back to us."

"Who was she—the woman?"

"He never told me her name."

"Why not?"

"Because sometimes, the less you know the better off you are. But from the way he spoke about her, the people, and the region, I believe it was somewhere much farther south than I have ever traveled … or ever care to, if I can help it."

"How did you become a vampire?"

"I was fishing a little too close to thin ice one day. It was early spring, and the ice was not as strong as during the winter. I was full of myself that day. I heard the crack but before I could move away, it broke, and I fell in. It hurt; it hurt bad. The water was so cold, it was like getting stuck with razors. Even amidst the pain and horror, all I thought of was my parents and how they both froze to death. I knew I would die the same way. I blacked out. When I awoke, I was no longer Pana the hunter and fisherman, but Pana the vampire."

"Jesus!"

"I was forty-nine years old when—"

Knock! Knock! came from Pana's door. Julian watched him promptly head in that direction and open it. In the hallway stood the long, rusty-red bearded man from the meeting. Before, a black hood had covered his head, but now it was down, revealing a shiny, bald, pink scalp.

Pana asked, "What is it, Roland?"

"We've got two visitors upstairs. They asked for you."

"Who are they?"

"Two of Caanis's guards from L'abisme."

What remained of Julian's euphoria slipped away upon the king's name hitting his ears, leaving only reality behind. "Ah, fuck!" he grunted under his breath, fearing they'd come for him, Anna, and Bernard.

Pana looked over his shoulder, saying, "Relax. I am going to go see what this is about. Go back to your room and wait."

Julian obeyed, following Pana and Roland down the hallway until reaching another. He turned right and the others turned left. Once he was out of their view, he picked up the pace towards his room, silently screaming, *Anna! If you can hear me, they've found us!*

Chapter Eleven

ang! Bang! Bang! "Hey!" Julian shouted, pounding on the metal door. *Bang! Bang! Bang!* "You guys—wake up! I think they know we're here!" *Bang! Bang! Bang!* "Hey! Someone said two people are here from Paris. I was with Pana, and that bearded guy from earlier came, I—"

"—fuck off!" Bernard groaned from behind the door. "We're trying to sleep."

Julian knocked harder. "I'm not kidding! There're people here from—"

The door flew open, and Bernard emerged. Droopy-eyed and lethargic, he shoved his index finger in Julian's face, growling, "What the fuck's the matter with you?! Don't you—"

"Shut up," Julian interrupted. "Two people are here from L'abisme."

"What?!" Anna yelped from behind the door. "Who?!"

"I don't know who it is. I was in Pana's room when that bearded man—Roland, I think—came and told him two of Caanis's guards were here. He told me to go back to my room, but I wanted to tell you guys first."

"Thanks," Bernard grunted, slamming the door in Julian's face.

"You're welcome, dick." Just like Pana instructed, he went back to his room, thinking, *He never told me not to tell them.* He waited, pacing, listening to Bernard go berserk on the other side of the wall.

"... I don't fucking care, Anna! They are here! Why else would they be here?!"

"Would you calm down, love? Maybe they are here over what happened, but it doesn't mean they know we are here. Even if they do, who cares? It would be strange going home after all these years and having to explain our sides of the story, but now you're the one making a much bigger deal out of this than you need to. You're scaring Julian. Him freaking out at the door was because he probably thinks they want to kill us or something."

"How do you know? Did you read his mind?"

"No, I didn't. I've not been able to since all this started."

What?! Really? Julian remembered Pana telling him, the others at the meeting couldn't read his mind either. But he still thought Anna could.

"Interesting," Bernard said. "Aside from myself, I've only known a handful of others who are able to keep vampires out of our thoughts."

"I don't need to hear his thoughts to see how traumatized he is," Anna professed. "Look at all he's endured."

"And I don't care!"

"You should! You've been terrible to him. He's a good man and he needs compassion, not you leaving him wondering from one minute to the next if we're going to stab him in the back, like you were talking about before. What if he had heard you say that?"

"Why don't you go be his friend? It would make sense. You can't have his maker now, and since his piece is dead too, why not both of you go for the next best thing?"

Fuming with rage, longing to charge next door and savagely beat the heartless Austrian within inches of his life for such a remark, Julian was only brought back to the present by the distinct sound of smacking flesh, echoing from behind the concrete. Following the one slap, Anna shouted, "I swear to fucking God, Bernard! If you throw that shit in my face one more goddamn time, I am going to—"

"You'll what?"

Before she could tell him, 'what,' a knock came at their door then Julian's. He and Bernard each opened theirs at the same time, finding Roland waiting. "Two men are here from L'abisme," he said.

Anna joined Bernard, asking, "What do they want?"

While Julian watched a pink hand imprint disappear from Bernard's cheek, Roland said, "Your sister, Princess Winter-Fae, seems to be missing."

"Missing?!" She gasped. "Where are they now—the men?"

"They are with Pana. He wanted me to come for all three of you." Roland shifted his gaze among them.

"Okay," Anna told them. "Come on."

Julian followed everyone back down the hall to the spacious room where Pana, a few others of his coven, and two men—wearing basic black suits and ties with white shirts—waited. As Anna grew closer to them, her expression changed. She knew them. "Paul?! … Teddy?"

"Princess Annabel," the shorter of the two men greeted, bowing his head. He was pale, slim, and sported a brown flattop.

"Where is Fae?! What happened to her?" she asked.

"We've not a clue," he said. His voice was deep, and he spoke with a thick Eastern European accent. "Since hearing the news of your brother, no one has been able to locate her."

"And you came all the way here?" Anna smirked. "Teddy, you know she wouldn't come this far alone." Her eyes moving to Pana, she said, "I don't think she's ever been here before, has she?" Appearing like a deer in the headlights, he was quick to shake his head.

"You've not been home in seventy-five years, Princess. You've no clue what any of us do," said the taller man, also thin and just as pale but with a thick, full head of dirty blond hair. His accent carried a more British aural. "Right now, we've no idea where she is."

"So, you didn't come all the way up here looking for us?"

"We did not," said the blond. "However, Caanis does want to see you." He looked at Bernard, adding "Both of you."

Bernard gulped, "Why?"

"You already know why," he said. "Teddy and I were ordered to search the north for Princess Winter-Fae, but we were also instructed to bring you back if we found you."

"Is that so?" Anna asked. Teddy and Paul both nodded. She sighed and her narrow shoulders sank. "And nobody knows where Fae could've gone?"

"No," said Paul.

Bernard asked, "Is the king mad at us?"

"He's angry at neither of you, but with the situation, yes. He is furious." Looking at Julian for the first time, Paul asked. "Who are you?"

"My name is Julian Frost."

"And you're with them?"

"Julian is Xavier's," Anna said.

"Really?" Paul asked, widening his eyes, staring at Julian. To Anna, he said "We heard Eric was killed, but where is Violet?"

"She is also dead," Anna moaned. Paul's eyes grew even wider, and Teddy's cheeks tensed. The two men shared an unpleasant glance. "It was her death—at her and Julian's wedding— where everything started."

Though Julian was beyond tired of reliving the events again, he and Anna told the men the same story they had told all the others. Once they finished, Teddy insisted, "Julian must also come," assuring them all, "No one will be harmed."

"Very well," Anna said. "We don't want conflict, especially brought upon our host." She smiled sincerely at Pana, and nodded in thanks for his hospitality. He returned the gesture. She resumed the conversation, saying. "We will go with you. If Fae really is missing, we must find her."

Pana stepped between the men in suits. He said, "It is currently daylight hours in Paris. Please, stay until nightfall, as my guests." The men bowed their heads in agreement. "Very nice," Pana replied. "Allow me to show you to your rooms." He led the men away to a hallway in the opposite direction of Julian's and the others' guest rooms.

Along the way back to their own rooms, Julian asked, "What's going to happen to us?"

"My father probably just wants me home, so he'll know I'm safe," Anna said.

"What about your sister?"

"I don't believe for a second she wandered off on her own, especially to come all the way here."

"Can't she fly?"

"She can, but that is not the point. You would have to meet her to understand. She's very shy, awkward, and because of her appearance she easily draws attention to herself. She's the cutest and sweetest little sprite you'll ever meet, but she rarely left the catacombs unless it was to come visit us in New York, but she always had someone escorting her. If she did go somewhere. It was either against her will or for a good reason."

Once reaching their rooms, Anna and Bernard went into theirs, and Julian, his. Simmering in a mixture of excitement, anxiety, and even a dash of optimism, he looked over the mess of broken glass on the floor, focusing on the end table next to the bed—specifically, what lay atop it. *Should I? Am I ready for another round of that yet?*

While trying to make up his mind, he took care of the broken glass, nicking the tip of his thumb on one of the shards. He watched the dark red substance pool over the wound. A microdot of light reflected from the growing red blob. He stared at the white dot as the surrounding puddle grew thicker. Finally, he pressed the tiny gash against his tongue, licking up the mess as if it were runny ice cream. The flavor was sweet. There was no euphoria like the whale blood had offered, but a chill overcame him. There was power in his blood. The sensation lasted only seconds, though it temporarily eased his anxiety.

He finished picking up the glass before looking at the diary again, knowing it might be a while before he had another chance to read it. *Fuck it. There's no time like the present.* He took it from the table, stretched out on the bed, and opened it to the next entry.

11/23/44
Dear Diary

    It has now been a month since I died. Xavier tells me I am not actually dead, but I will never be human again. Since my last entry, I have cried myself awake and back to sleep more times than I can count. Most of the time, now, I wish I was dead. I am trying to move past it, though. If Xavier wanted to kill me, he would have. Instead, he continues to show me kindness.

    I have been up, moving around more, and physically I feel better—perhaps a little too better. Last weekend, Xavier and Eric took me outside for the first time since it happened. It turns out I am still on Bleecker Street, but now I'm in the East Village. We walked all the way to Central Park. Everything looks different now. Everything is covered in snow, but that's not what I mean.

    This world is the same world I knew before, but the reality is different. Despite the freezing temperature, I couldn't feel the cold. My eyesight and hearing have improved tremendously. I can hear everyone's conversation in this building if I focus hard enough. I can even hear the preacher downstairs, on Wednesday nights and Sundays. I am so sick of hearing him repeat, "You've got to give yourself over to the Lord."

    When I was outside, I'd also hear occasional whispers from people as I passed them. The strangest thing was their mouths never moved. Xavier said I can read minds, but how crazy does that sound? He said it is one of my new gifts. I don't know anything about vampires other than a couple of movies. I tried reading "Dracula" once, but it gave me nightmares before I could finish it. I don't want to live like that! I don't want to have to survive on blood and only ever come out at night, crawling down the walls like a fucking lizard! Why would anybody want that?

Today was Thanksgiving. Xavier and I sat with the Grants while they enjoyed the most delicious smelling meal I have ever known. Xavier cooked and prepared everything. My stomach growled the entire time and I eventually had to excuse myself to keep from crying and ruining their dinner. It's not their fault. They have all been so good to me.

Ms. Grant has not had one bad thing to say about me being here. William—Eric's little brother—loves to play checkers, and we play daily. He is so smart for being only seven years old. He knows the Bible better than I do. And Eric's been the best friend I could ever ask for during all this. He holds me when I cry. He offers the most amazing ear and shoulder.

Last night, I helped Eric put up the Christmas tree while Xavier, Ms. Grant, and William were downstairs, at the chapel on the first floor. We wanted to surprise them when they came back. So, we put on a Bing Crosby record and spent the next hour throwing tinsel at each other until we finally got the ornaments on. Eric topped the tree with the prettiest angel.

We had so much fun. Sometimes he makes me forget all about this nightmare. He's not a vampire, like Xavier and I, but I wonder what it would be like if he was. Xavier says I will live forever. Forever is a long time, and I wouldn't want to get lonely—lonelier than I suppose I already am. Who knows what will happen? For now, I just need to learn how to accept my new life, I guess.

Violet

12/24/44

Dear Diary

It's the holidays, and I feel good. I am still living with Eric and his family. For now, I guess it will stay that way. Xavier pays the bills and makes sure we are all taken care of. In exchange, the Grants give him shelter—and now, me too. Xavier and I are the only ones here with this "gift," as he calls it. When he first brought me here, I thought I was hallucinating, but he can fly! He says I can too—I just haven't come fully into the ability yet. As a Christian, I still don't feel right about any of this. According to the Bible, I am an abomination. But I must admit, sometimes it feels good.

Today is Christmas Eve. Xavier told me he has a surprise for me tomorrow. Though he won't tell me what it is, Eric told me anyway. He made me promise I wouldn't tell. You'll keep my secret though, right, Diary? When it gets dark tomorrow, Xavier is going to take me home to Savannah to see my parents. I am excited, but I am so scared of facing them like this. Xavier says I should see them, and maybe get some closure for things from my past. I don't particularly want to bring up old wounds, but he says it will be good for me. I know he is right. I am nervous, but staying positive and optimistic. Wish me luck, Diary. I will probably need it!

Violet

1/22/45

Dear Diary

My life cannot get any worse. In some sort of twisted, fucked up freak accident, I killed both of my parents. I don't know what happened. My dad got so mad at me because he thought I was romantically involved with Xavier. Even though he is 800 years old, he looks like a teenage boy. My dad had the nerve to accuse me of fucking a kid!

In the middle of it, he called me "sweet pea." He only ever called me that once. I have been avoiding that night for so long. I almost ripped those first two pages out when I found you last year. The truth is my father raped me that night. He shoved me down on my stomach and put all his weight on me. He stunk of whiskey. I kept screaming and begging him to stop, but he only did it harder.

At one point he covered my mouth with his hand, and whispered, 'You will wake your mother, sweet pea.' When he was finished taking what he wanted, he staggered out. He didn't even remember doing it. I remembered. It hurt so bad. I felt him inside me for days after. I bled. I thought I was dying. I even thought I was pregnant.

I wanted to tell Mom, but I was scared. I never told anyone. So, I went on hating and blaming myself for years. I didn't date while growing up—in or out of school. Excluding my father, I am still a virgin. I even hated looking at myself in the mirror. That is mostly why I took such a fancy to acting. I got to be someone else for a while. I didn't have to be the 'dumb tomboy' victim who, beforehand, loved stealing her older brothers' baseballs and outrunning them when they came after me. I was whoever the scene required me to be.

At least my brothers weren't there. I miss them but I imagine there's no need to bother them anymore, especially now. After the incident, I shut down and we practically "unmet" each other, if that makes sense. They haven't spoken to me in years, anyway. They're going to get old and die. I might as well just move on now. I won't even write their names. In time, maybe I will forget them.

The night I met Xavier at the café, what my father did to me was what he confronted me with. I think it was also why he took me home—to confront him, but neither of us expected this. I am a murderer. Diary! There's a part of me that always felt like he deserved to die for what he did, but not my mom. She loved me, and she died because of me. In a wild fit of rage, everything around me caught on fire—even my dad. I can't explain it. It just appeared. My mom tried to get away, but part of the ceiling collapsed on her. It killed her instantly. The entire house burned down.

I was so excited to go home. I was scared, but I was still excited. Ever since my transformation, all I wanted was to see my mother's face again. I wanted her to know I was okay. It wasn't even a minute after walking in the door, my father started bitching at me. Even Xavier tried talking sense into him, but he wanted no part of his daughter's "boytoy."

I am in Alaska right now. I had to get away. Xavier brought me here to stay with his friends: Pana, Lusa, and several others. They've been good to me, and with the Northern Lights, it is so beautiful here. Since it is so far north, I think it stays dark for an entire month during the winter. It may be even longer than that.

Being here is helping, but I still feel so much guilt for what happened to my mom. I wish Eric was here. I am the happiest whenever I am around him. It is a little strange, me being a vampire and him being human, but should that matter? I miss him so much. I think I might even love him. I don't know. I have never felt this way before.

Reading the paragraph, Julian's nerves turned cold, but his curious, incandescent heart lingered.

During the first week of February, Xavier is going to come get me. I have discovered that I can fly now, but New York is a long way from Northern Alaska, and I would never try to fly that far myself. Depending on how I feel, I may try to talk Roland, Uki, or one of the others here who can fly into taking me home early. Then I could surprise Eric. I bet he would like that. I know I would. I will let you know what happens, Diary.

Violet

Fearing he was approaching dangerous territory, Julian closed his eyes and focused on his breathing, taking deep inhales through his nose and releasing them from his mouth. "She loved you, Julian. She married you," he said aloud, trying to shed as much ego and self-doubt as possible. He took one more breath before opening his eyes and turning the page. Then he saw the date.

2/14/45
Dear Diary

I thought today would be special. I thought we were meant to be. I was wrong. As I write this, Eric is dying in his bed, and it is all my fault. Last night, Xavier brought me home. Eric and I were so happy to see each other. Before he could even tell me, "Hello," I was in his arms, kissing him. I told him I loved him, and he told me the same. After his mother and William went to bed, and Xavier went out somewhere, we had the place to ourselves. I wanted him, so I came on to him. He did not resist.

The next thing I knew, we were in his bed, both naked, and I was on top of him. I know I went wild, but I didn't even know I was hurting him until he started screaming. I got off him and found the entire bottom half of his body covered in blood. His penis was barely hanging on by a thin piece of skin. His mother ran into the room, screaming. By then, Eric had stopped. He was losing blood so fast, he'd passed out. I didn't know what to do.

Xavier came back only a few minutes later and stopped Autumn from calling anyone. He told us both that Eric had lost so much blood, he would not survive. He had no choice but to feed Eric his own blood. Now, he is becoming one of us. Autumn took William and left. I don't know where they went. Now, I am so scared Eric will die. Xavier told me he's made others before me, but I was the only one who ever survived. He has stayed by Eric's side this whole time. I don't know why, but the only relief I have had during all this has come from writing about it. He'll make it through, right, Diary? He must! I pray to any God that is listening: please, save him, even if you must take me.

Violet

Even after reading something as difficult as the love of his life's account of falling for and being intimate with someone else, Julian was so shocked, he let the book slip out of his hands. It all made sense. He once asked her why Eric became a vampire, and she told him she didn't know. *No wonder she didn't want to tell me. I can't be angry with her for that.*

He never got to know Eric like he had all the others, but he cried anyway. He cried for Eric and Violet. *She loved him, so he must not have been a bad guy.* He could relate to what it did to her amidst all the other horrors she had faced since her transition— facing his own. Unable to read any more for the time being, he put the diary inside his backpack before turning off the light. He lay back in bed, covering himself with the fishy fur blanket and shutting his eyes. "I love you, Violet," he whispered. "Goodnight, my flower."

Chapter Twelve

When a knock came to the door, Julian awoke. His initial response was, "Who is it?!" but he couldn't help wondering, *Is this a dream? Is there even a difference? Who knows? Who cares anymore?*

"It's Anna! Time to go, love."

Julian crawled out of bed, wiped his eyes, and yawned. He opened the door, finding the Gaunts both waiting. "One second," he said, going back to get his black leather jacket from the floor. He slipped it on and then strapped his green backpack overtop. He straightened the fur blanket on the bed before putting on his sneakers and joining the others in the hall. "All right, let's go." He walked alongside them, heading back towards the meeting room. When they arrived, most of the vampires from the night before were gathered, conversing amongst themselves.

Julian scanned the crowd, finding Pana staring back at him. The Inupiaq smiled as he approached. "I am glad we met, Julian Frost."

"Me too," Julian replied.

"You are wise beyond your years, boy." He wrapped his arm around Julian's shoulder. Together they walked towards the two men from L'abisme. "If you ever need it, you always have a home here. Never forget that."

"Thank you, Pana; for the conversations, your wisdom, and your hospitality."

Lusa: the plump, white-haired old woman from the night before, emerged from the crowd. A wide, motherly grin stretched across her wrinkled bronze face—beneath it, a mouthful of discolored teeth. In her hand, she carried a thin brown band. Centered on the hide fabric, a polished oval stone reflected light and other translucent shades of dark green. To Julian, it looked just like the Aurora. The smile still on her face, Lusa held the band close to Julian's left wrist, mumbling, "May I?"

"You may," he said, extending his arm and watching her tie it.

"That is Labradorite," Pana said. "Legends say a mighty warrior once drove his spear into the stone, releasing the aurora borealis into the sky. The stone is used for protection and insight. It thins the veil between this world and the next. When we come into certain powers as strongly and quickly as you have, they can often weaken as they balance, and you adapt. Sometimes they can grow even stronger, but it is rare. With this talisman, you will find communicating with Xavier and Violet more sufficient than without it."

When Lusa finished firmly tying the ends, Julian said, "Thank you."

Like their first meeting, she cupped her frail hands over his cheeks. She softly kissed his forehead, and then moved her cracked lips to his ear. "With this, you will find your way ... where you need to be," she whispered. Pulling away, she smiled again. "Your flower will bloom in time." Julian smiled back, his gesture every bit as honest as hers.

"Remember, anything you need, we are here," Pana reassured.

"Actually, there is something."

"What is it, boy?"

Julian leaned closer and whispered, "My friend, Daryl. I am worried about him. He won't know where to get blood. He and his family live in Gunnar, Virginia. Do you think anyone here who can fly would be able to—"

"You have nothing to worry over. It is taken care of."

"What do you mean?"

"I mean, you, your friend, and his family have nothing to worry about. Just like you, Daryl is family too, now."

Offering no forethought, Julian reached out and hugged the elder. The once solemn expression on Pana's face quickly turned to surprise. Julian could easily sense he wasn't used to the affection. Regardless, he felt like he could cry if he had the tears to spare. "Thank you so much, Pana." He looked around the room, noting all the faces of those who were kind to him while he was there. He and Uki shared a nod. Looking back, he added, "For everything."

He joined Anna, Bernard, and the men in suits—Paul and Teddy—at the door. Making their way out, a man from the crowd shouted, "Hey, Princess!" First, Anna turned around, then Bernard and Julian. Roland stood out among the others. His bright, passionate eyes deadlocked with sheer intent; he used both hands to pull back his hood, his pink scalp shining in the fluorescent light. "Tell 'King Daddy,' brother Roland of Reinhardt says hello." Ignoring him, Anna and the others turned back towards the door. "… and remind him … he has no place at Odin's table. Remind the old wolf every dog has its day."

Paul swiveled around, demanding, "What did you say?"

Julian looked back, watching Roland turn his gaze upon the royal guard. Flashing a malevolent grin, he slowly slid the tip of his blood-red tongue across his teeth before barking, "Woof! Woof!" at them all like a famished hound.

The rest of the room awkwardly frozen in silence, Anna beckoned her husband and Julian, "Come on."

While following the others up the stairs and through the decoy house, Julian wondered, *What the hell was that all about?* Outside, in the pouring white static, he looked up, taking in the gracious beauty of the Aurora one last time. "If you really are up there—I love you."

Anna tugged his arm, drawing him away from the polarity. "You can ride on Paul or Teddy's back." She looked at the guards, waiting for one to respond.

Paul, the taller blond, said, "He can ride with me, Princess."

"Please stop calling me that," she said. "I am just 'Anna.'"

The vampires all made their way outside the town, far from unseen eyes. Just like when Julian, Anna, and Bernard had first landed, they all struggled through the snow before Teddy finally shouted, "All right! Enough of this shit! Let's go!"

After exchanging mutual nods of agreement, everyone prepared for the flight. Julian paired up with Paul, asking, "How long will this take?"

"Over an hour," he said.

Fucking hell! Julian groaned in silence. He focused on the unseen benefit—the silver lining Violet once presented—telling him flying wouldn't be so bad after becoming a vampire. He shrugged his shoulders and took a deep breath. "Fuck it," he grumbled. "Let's go." Seconds later, they were all airborne; bound for Paris and whatever fate a vengeful God chose to throw their way next.

***

Although he faced the speed in his cheeks, the wind ruffling his hair, and the resistance pulling his backpack, Julian managed to make the best of it. Unlike Bernard, Paul was gentler and more mindful of his passenger. With nothing else to do aside from not falling asleep, Julian could only wonder, *What's going to happen now?*

I've never met a king before. How will I even address him? Assuming he doesn't kill me, where do I go from here? When can I go home? I hope Daryl is okay. I wonder if my text message ever sent. I will check later. Why was Roland acting like that? Is any of this real? Am I even awake? Am I real? Many other questions followed.

It seemed like they had all been flying twice as long as the time it had taken to reach Alaska, but there was no sign of slowing down. He imagined they were several miles above Earth—maybe even crossing the Atlantic. As a human, he'd hated opening his eyes while in flight, but curiosity got the better of him and he indulged.

The heavenly stratosphere bled midnight blue. No clouds in sight, the eyes he never had as an impaired human expanded like satellites. He probed in awe over the gargantuan moon and endless array of stars, salting the astral field he grazed. It was a truly magical moment, the kind he thought only existed in fairy tales, the kind he wished Violet was there to see. He was moving too fast to say it aloud, but in his mind and heart he said it for them both: *To all time and space, my flower. It is so beautiful, and yet nothing compares to you.*

As a warm, loving sensation cuddled Julian's timid heart, he and Paul began slowing down. Ahead, light tiptoed from the dark, inching closer by the second. He caught sight of the Eiffel Tower—not the replica from Las Vegas, but the real one—standing twice as high and showering its surrounding city in a golden hue.

Against the wind, Paul shouted, "We are about to land! There should not be anyone close enough to see, but we are going to land fast. Once we do, stay alert and follow me!"

"Okay!" Julian yelled back, nearly gagging on the airspeed.

Seconds later, they touched down in a small courtyard with trees and bushes. Enclosing the area, dark old buildings and a sour, unpleasant odor loomed. Paul whispered, "Come on." Julian followed him alongside an old building with broken and boarded windows. They turned a corner and reached a short alleyway. Teddy, along with Anna and Bernard, caught up to them.

Together, they crossed the alley, reaching a populous city
street at the other end. Julian looked on, taking in the surroundings.
The crowded sidewalk and cobblestone road were both slightly
polluted with random trash and debris. Across the street, the
aesthetics were easier on the eyes. White lace curtains draped the
storefront windows of an old brown building. Bright, decorative red
lighting from an overhead sign lit the structure to the top. Julian's
ears wandered when, from somewhere nearby, upbeat trumpets and
drums belted a high-energy jazz tune. "So, this is Paris?" he asked, a
little underwhelmed.

Anna said, "Yeah. It's dirtier than I remember."

The men in suits stepped forward, motioning the others on.
They walked three blocks before entering a small diner. Wondering
why they were there, Julian scanned the various patrons sitting at
tables: some drinking coffee, some reading newspapers and
magazines while they did. He even saw a man in glasses, typing on a
laptop. He smiled, remembering where he was the year before. He
was that guy, typing on his own laptop, drinking coffee in a Las
Vegas diner, and witnessing true beauty, if there ever was such a
thing.

With Paul and Teddy leading the way, he watched them each
nod to the dark, young waitress behind the counter. After she
nodded back, they headed down a short hallway towards a closed
black door at the end. Paul opened it. On the other side, a wooden
staircase led nearly ten feet down.

A damp, unlit basement waited at the bottom. From there,
Paul squeaked open another door. Teddy pulled a small flashlight
from his pocket and clicked it on. He stepped through the door first,
instantly disappearing. Roughly ten seconds later, his remotely
distant voice echoed, "Clear!"

Bernard walked through next, also vanishing. Anna told
Julian, "There's no stairs, and it's a long drop. I'll take you down.
When we get there, stay with us. Under no circumstances should

126

you wander off. It is dark and dangerous, even for us. In some areas there's water. In others, we'll have to squeeze through small cracks. If you don't watch your step in certain places, you could fall and get hurt. Understand, love?"

"I do," Julian said. His morbid curiosity piqued, knowing where he was heading: through the home of six million skeletons, enroute to a subterranean kingdom of vampires. Following Anna to the door, he watched Paul take a small flashlight from his pocket and move aside. At the edge of the door frame, Julian wrapped his arms around Anna's shoulders. Just before descending, he laughed. "After you!"

Chapter Thirteen

From sixty feet beneath the City of Love, the fusty, earthly stench of dirt and decay set the mood. Upon landing in the mass grave, Julian's first impression was nothing short of macabre and flattering. To stand amongst the dead in such numbers, he couldn't help blushing with envy. What he wouldn't give to join them, gladly trading places and enduring the six million tragedies that claimed each of their souls. For one more kiss of his precious flower's lips, he would welcome it like family.

Once Paul joined the others at the bottom, he and Teddy beamed their flashlights along the narrow, dilapidated limestone walls, offering Julian a better view of his surroundings. Assuming he would find stacks and rows of bones and skulls, neatly arranged and staring back, like he'd seen in several pictures and films, he saw nothing of the sort. Disappointed, he asked, "Where's all the skeletons?"

"This is the restricted area," Paul said. "There are no skeletons over here, unless we happen upon someone who got lost and died, that is."

"Why is it restricted?"

"Because it is too dangerous for humans. They keep the bones in a charnel house and run it as a business and tourist attraction. It is the only area people are allowed to visit, down here."

"What?!" Julian shouted, his voice echoing in every direction. "They charge money to come down here?"

"Yeah, thirteen euros," Paul said.

"That's fucked up!"

"Quiet!" Teddy snapped.

"Why?" Anna asked.

"Because the police often patrol this part. Sometimes I think their ears are as good as ours. They only go so far, though. Once we get a little farther, we can make as much noise as we want. But for now, mind yourselves."

"You got to be fucking kidding me," Anna groaned.

"We told you—a lot's changed since you were here, Princess."

Walking along the heavily graffitied corridors, passing openings to various rooms and chambers, Julian listened closely for any sounds. Hearing nothing but the occasional drip, he asked, "How far do we have to go?"

"It is a decent way," Paul said. "The possibility of encountering others, not just the police, is high. So, we mustn't do anything to draw extra attention."

"Other people?" Bernard asked.

"Yeah, 'cataphiles,' they call themselves."

"What the hell do they do?"

Paul chuckled into his hand. "You'd be surprised. If we pass anyone, don't talk to them. If you see anything strange, ignore it."

"You will encounter many oddities down here," Teddy added.

Bernard shrugged, mumbling, "I guess."

For over a mile, everyone walked in silence. Along the way, Julian admired the higher quality pieces of graffiti decorating the subterranean walls. Everything from three-dimensional lettering to dragons and flowers popped in beautiful vibrant colors. He would have never recognized such intricate detailing, had he viewed them through his former sight. At one point, they stopped to rest, everyone sharing a laugh. After reaching the end of a flooded shaft, their tired, wet feet and shins all needed a break. They entered a small, mined-out chamber, another hallway beginning parallel.

Portrayed in several shades of pink, red, peach, and white; a crude, squirting vagina covered a sizable portion of the creamy-gray wall—the bordered entryway to the cathedral's vestibule. Centered above it, a shiny silver hoop pierced the temple's hood for good measure. Though vulgar, the intricate display would have taken the most skilled artist hours to complete.

Her cheeks glowing cherry-bomb red, Anna cupped a hand over her imploding lips, trying not to laugh. Amidst her bashful exhibit, she said, "That is just fucking minging!"

Everyone laughed at her response. Paul said, "Somebody did that a year ago."

After pushing forward another mile—crossing several more shallow pools, squeezing through a fissure, and even climbing over a short wall—the group met a synchronized beat like that of a heart, fading in from somewhere ahead. Bernard asked, "What is that?"

"It's music," Teddy said.

"Down here?"

"There's always a rave somewhere."

"Seriously?" Bernard snorted. "Why?!"

"Cataphiles—it's just what they do. We all have our pleasures," Paul said. "Remember, if you see anyone, do not speak to them, even if they speak to you. Don't make eye contact either."

Drawing nearer, the volume burgeoned. Finally, they encountered their first people since entering the cavern. Lightning-white lights blistered from a door-shaped opening on the left—the digital bath in sync with the beat. Human silhouettes smoldered in the strobe, conversing and crowding the hall. As Julian passed, he looked inside the ample chamber, observing the shapes of wild dancers in motion, roaring trance music coming from big black speakers stacked against the back wall.

Overtop the music, a boy in the hall shouted, "Any of you want to buy some molly?"

Everyone ignored him. Anna shrugged her nose and scowled at the entire scene while passing. Julian imagined himself enjoying it: under better circumstances and with the right company. Like Violet, he also liked to dance. *Maybe someday, my flower*. After trudging another mile through silent darkness, he asked, "How much farther?"

"We are close," Teddy said. "There's a hidden staircase that will take us down. After that, we are there."

Turning a corner, Julian faced new light, radiating softly from the far end of the hall, a somber tune weeping at a moderate volume. His jaw tensed, hearing such a dire lament. It was one he'd heard before. Leaving the corridor, a spacious cavity opened, exposing the source of the faction at its nerve.

Several feet to Julian's right, a projector screen—more than five times the size of his already massive TV back home—hung from a high wall. At least two dozen spectators sat in various chairs and some lounged on blankets, all seated with their backs to the passersby.

Don't look. You'll only hurt yourself if you do. Progress be damned, he looked, just long enough to catch a full view: the hideous, black-clad vampire, "Nosferatu," clenching his chest and vanishing in the sunlight, the tandem symphony of horror strumming Julian's heartstrings all the while. By then, he was frozen in place, his slimy black sneakers at one with the limestone as if it were Medusa who'd obliged. For the first time since Alaska, he wept.

"—the fuck are you doing?!" Anna hissed like a whispering viper. She hooked his arm and yanked him away, dropping a cow on the overstated vaudeville. By the time he'd shaken the cobwebs and returned to reality, he and the others had long since passed the makeshift theater. Anna griped, "I can't believe Father just lets people do that kind of shite here."

"What choice do you think he has?" Teddy asked.

When nobody answered, Paul said, "There's over two-hundred kilometers of tunnels, shafts, and other secrets hiding beneath Paris. Even the Nazis still have bunkers down here."

I bet I know who'd like those.

"Who?" Paul asked, leading the way, his back to everyone but Teddy. A lash of ice bullwhipped Julian's spine. He held his breath, praying the man would just let it go. "Who?"

"What?" Teddy asked.

"Julian said he knows who'd like the *Lycée Nontaigne*."

Teddy looked over his shoulder, asking, "Who?"

"Fucking hell," Anna groaned, her dragging timbre filling in the blanks.

Bernard glared, his carnivorous eyes locked in a rusty prison cell with Julian's like they were raw veal. "Who?" he asked, his expanding cheeks daring him to say something audacious.

Julian stuttered for words. "N—nobody—just somebody I used to know."

Smirking, Bernard said, "That's right." He winked, letting his amused, '*Do you honestly want to fuck with me?*' expression fall flat. Julian swallowed a lump, his heavy pulse and bad choices kicking him in the teeth.

"… back to what I was saying," Paul chortled. "We've been down here for almost a quarter millennium now. No one even notices. To think, all those people do in the name of commemorating darkness without knowing who we are. They eat, drink, fuck, dance, and sin here—none ever guessing just how close they are to—"

"Oh, thank God!" a shrill man's voice cried in the dark. As instructed, Julian ignored it, his eyes glued forward. "Hey! You've got to help me! I've been lost down here for days!" The sheer panic in his tone implied he wasn't lying. Julian shivered, recognizing an American accent. "Some asshole brought me down here! He knocked me out and took my shit! … Hey!"

Everyone continued as if he wasn't there. The man's pace thickened from behind, splashing through puddles, his shoes squeaking and clacking over the dry stone. Until then, Julian ignored his own feet. His shoes and socks were so muddy they were ruined—his jeans from the knees down as well.

"Hey! I need help!"

Julian empathized with the vagrant, but even he understood the unfortunate discipline. The hopeless man rushed by, his filthy stench of sweat, soured urine, and fecal waste trailing in the momentum. He darted before them all, throwing himself directly into the guards' light. In torn muddy blue jeans and a black, long-sleeved shirt, his greasy, dark hair hung ear-length—his wet mop and dripping diamonds of sweat glistening in the bright yellow flashlight rays. He was smaller framed than average and most of his tanned face was caked in dirt and grime.

Paul and Teddy, still leading the way, never stopped. "You sons of bitches!" As if putting all his weight into it, the little man shoved Teddy with both hands, screaming, "Fuck you, pieces of—"

Teddy worked so fast, even Julian's new eyes could not keep up. The man was already dead before his skull crunched the floor; his throat ripped back, gouged open, and collecting a red pool beneath. Startled, Julian jerked away like he'd grabbed a live wire, exclaiming, "Jesus! Teddy scooped up the remains and sunk his teeth into the gaping wound.

"Do share," Paul insisted meekly. His lips and cleft chin dripping red, Teddy complied, handing the cold one off to his friend like it was a juice box on the playground.

"Oh, come on!" Anna whined. "You've got to do that here? What if someone sees?"

Looking at her, Julian wondered, *Are you okay with this?* Bernard stared sadistically, grinning at the scene like a sexual fantasy. Maintaining his air of barbarity, his eyes twinkled in the light when shifting toward Julian's again. *'Watch what I can do,'* the grimace said without saying. *'You'll see.'* No other muscle moved between the two. No one else was watching. Time seemed to freeze until the next second, when the Austrian's orbs returned to the murder.

Also turning back, Julian knew the act should have sickened him. He'd never seen vampires feed like that before. Instead, the longer he stared—trying to forget Bernard—the dripping excess drew him in like the void, seducing him. Time stood still once more. "Julian," came a whisper to his ear, accompanied by another shiver up his backbone.

The silky voice resonated low. He could not distinguish a gender, but he knew it wasn't *her*. *Hello?* His stomach growled and a hunger emerged. It was a ravenous hunger, one he'd felt before. The craving had occurred on New Years' Eve, when watching the sweet red nectar flow from Kevin Cauldwell's open gashes, hurling like a half-clogged downspout while struggling to free himself. Julian mused for so long, he entranced himself into a desire to partake.

"… Guys!" Anna impatiently shouted. "Can we please get a move on? I'm tired and just want to get this over with."

Finally, the guards had consumed their fill. Teddy told Paul, "Take them on. I'll go dump this somewhere." Paul nodded and Teddy threw the carcass over his shoulder and disappeared down another corridor.

"Come on," Paul said, motioning for the others to follow him.

By the time he reached the end of another flooded hall, treading heel deep through the septic cata-juice, Julian took notice of how scarce the graffiti had become. *We must be a good way in by now.* Not much farther, the weary travelers reached a chamber unlike the others. The walls and floor of the limestone shrine had all been smoothed and shaped to resemble any rectangular room, but it was the writing on the walls that colored Julian's curiosity. The one flashlight gently brushing the cavity with just enough light, he observed intricate carvings in the stone, all depicting ancient still-lifes and concepts.

The dominant parable was that of early Rome. One wall boasted two ferocious warriors, bruting and engaged in battle—violently swinging their swords for glory: bread and circus. On the adjacent, extravagant pillars and architecture spread the twenty-odd-foot length of the room. Domed palaces, basilicas, church steeples and towers; the legendary coliseum, worn like God's crown atop the center of such a perfect, painstaking epilogue.

The other two walls featured angels, demons, cherubs, giants, and other humanoids: all posed in various positions. Some laughed, some cried, some danced naked. All were joined in union. Julian saw it as duality. Taking a moment to appreciate the work, Anna joined in. He watched her scan the walls, observing them like she never had before. She turned to her husband and smiled. "I remember this room. I always loved it here."

Bernard joined her side. Both facing the clashing titans, he said, "I like it too, my love." There wasn't much emotion in his response, but Anna smiled again like she admired the effort. She took his hand. He looked at her in a special way, offering a half-smile: something he appeared reluctant, yet relieved, to express. For a moment, they stared, losing themselves to each other.

"How did this get here?" Julian asked.

Paul said, "Long ago, before us and even the bones arrived, this was all a limestone and gypsum mine. Back then, Rome controlled France. *Lutetian* limestone—here in Paris and the surrounding region—is unlike any in the world. Miners spent years in here. These, and most others, took entire careers to finish."

"They moved the bodies down here because Paris was flooding, right?"

"Yes, and because the plague was killing people too fast to find space for them. The humor is the catacombs are already flooded and hollow for the most part. I imagine Paris will rot and collapse beneath its own weight someday. Then someone will just bury them." Appearing to grow impatient, Paul said, "Come on. We're almost there." Having stood together like they were finally enjoying themselves, Anna and Bernard moved on.

Leaving the hidden museum behind, everyone entered another corridor. This one had black-barred doors clinging to rusty hinges on either side. Paul stopped at the third door on the right. It squealed when he opened it.

Inside a small, empty enclosure, he rubbed his hand against a dusty brick wall, pushing in a specific slab. The entire barrier revolved sideways from the middle, creating a large enough opening for them all to pass through at once. *Wow*, Julian thought, amazed by such a thing he'd only ever seen in movies. From the other side, Paul pushed the wall back in place. He shined his flashlight down on the pitch-black floor, exposing the only other thing there: a big round hole, limestone steps spiraling back to the shadows.

Anna told Julian, "Beneath the surface, there's a rail. Hang on to it, love. It's a long way down."

After several minutes of going in circles, he thought, *Damn! Is this ever going to end?* He was exhausted by the time they all reached the bottom. There, another lengthy hallway stood before them. Over a hundred feet away, at the other end, he spotted orange light glowing through an expansive archway. "Is this it?" he asked.

"It is," Anna said. She released a long, deep exhale, hinting relief, but new anxiety rising in its place. Heading towards the light, she told Bernard, "Here we are, love. I always said I'd bring you one day." To him and Julian, she said, "Welcome to L'abisme."

Chapter Fourteen

L'abisme: the kingdom in the abyss, had mourned losing a princess for three quarters of a century. Though they now also mourned their fallen prince, the nocturnal creatures could relent some of their tears and rejoice in the glorious return of Princess Annabel, eldest daughter of King Caanis. From the arched entrance, she stood barefoot, having carried her expensive leather dress flats—her entire lower-half baptized in the smut and juices she'd picked up along the way.

The princess gawked pleasantly, as if everything was how she'd left it. Despite such a reunion, an overshadowing weight of concern pulled her down. To Julian's empathy, the obvious implied something more consequential was festering—one missing detail—a provocative question that must have tormented the hellfire-redhead to brimstone and back since leaving Alaska. It was her motivation for coming home. Even Julian wanted to know, '*Where is Winter-Fae?*'

Nobody was prepared for their arrival, but as the trio's footsteps cackled and echoed, any living soul within earshot came to see for themselves. Her only apparent interest being the welfare of her sister, Anna ignored all the wide-eyed stares aimed at her and the men who followed. Julian's intrigue was another story—scoping anything his vampiric eyes allowed.

The enormous chamber's sufficient light casting spells from a broad assembly of torches and firepits; he scanned the glowing faces of over forty men and women, scattered along the floor and gathering like flies on a pearly gray balcony in the distance. Like the Alaskan coven, the Parisian kingdom showcased a melting pot of shapes, colors, and fashions.

From the dead sea of awkward silence, a young baritone delivered a psalm to the unseen—his royal decree suffocating the great hall with promises of hopes and dreams, mightier than the Bells of Heaven themselves. "It's Princess Annabel! All come and see!"

Her head hung and jarring in disfavor, Anna grumbled, "For fuck's sake. It's not like I'm the goddamn queen of Brit—"

"—Annie!" came a high, feminine squeal from afar. In a blur, the voice practically flew into her arms; a little white specter nearly knocking the redhead down. "Annie!" the same voice cried again. A pair of thin white legs, with tiny, shoeless, dusty white feet firmly cuddled Anna's hips. Two colorless twigs clutched her upper half like vines. Mostly covered by a white crocheted robe, the tiny figure had barely any color at all.

A thick, virgin fleece rested like curtains along her narrow collar and nape. Tightly cropped bangs draped her baby-smooth forehead. The silky 'do was like that of a bedroom window on a warm, brilliant morning—the fat old sun shining in her optimistic eyes as she opened them.

"Oh my God—Fae!" Anna cheered, her gleeful change radiating more blissfully than Julian had seen thus far. After the long embrace, the kitten's paws fell to the ground, and she released her grip. Standing straight, the immaculate anomaly carried the elvish height of an adolescent, but she illustrated a petite bone structure and the toned pear shape of a fully blossomed woman.

"I missed you so much, Annie." Winter-Fae was soft spoken. Her shy, mousy speech rose just beyond a whisper, her accent English to Julian's ears.

"And I missed you." Though bright, Anna's sunny-day forecast quickly turned cloudy. "—but I thought something happened. That's what Paul and Teddy said—that no one could find you." Anna looked over her shoulder, she and Julian finding Paul had disappeared since returning.

"What? No. I've been here the whole time." The little sprite giggled, swaying nonchalantly, hands joined and twiddling her tiny fingers behind her back, her demeanor suggesting she had secrets.

Anna rolled her eyes like there was no need to argue. She grunted, but then her smile returned. "I figured as much."

Fae moved on. "Hi, Bernie!"

"Winter-Fae," he greeted, bowing his head just enough to show respect.

The porcelain doll looked up at Julian next, her forehead meeting his sternum. Though her tender features shone flawlessly, the frail, weeping cheeks of a gamine child offered clues that she had found suffering long before it found her. At the center of her face, a well-defined nose extenuated her deep, ocean-blue eyes and pouty pink lips—the only colors Julian saw. Fae looked back at her sister and smiled. "Regarding wanderlust, who's the glowstick," she asked, bobbing her head in Julian's direction.

"This is Julian Frost," Anna said. "He was Xavier's."

Fae's eyes twinkled, hearing the news. She offered Julian a crooked smile containing warmth and benefit of the doubt. but above all, caution and bewilderment. Looking back at her sister, she asked, "When?"

"Actually, it was just this past Christmas," Julian said.

"You have only been a vampire for a week?" The faery's eyes shifted between the two, both nodding. "Fascinating. It was like he knew, yeah?"

"Knew what?" Julian asked.

"He knew he was going to die."

"That's what he told me—that night. In a dream, he said it was prophesied, sacrificing himself to save the rest of us."

To Anna, Fae said, "I felt it when it happened. So did Daddy."

"Is Dad mad at me?"

"Not you, but the circumstances. He is desperate for answers." The reunited sisters began walking through the cavern, Julian and Bernard following. "Last year, we all heard about what happened at the club, with that soldier man. As you know, Daddy was already miffed over the place existing to begin with, but then once events turned so dramatic, he was beside himself. Now, it's just hitting him. Our father lost his heir and only son."

"We're not happy either," Bernard blurted, offering no condolence. "After the club got raided, we hid out in the city for a while, hoping Xavier would come back—well, Anna did. When he didn't, we took off, never staying anywhere longer than we had to."

"He's right," Anna said. "After the Christopher Cauldwell incident and Eric and William's murders, things got intense. Hell Belle took Julian to Virginia, and Xavier completely disappeared."

Fae said, "He came to Paris last summer. Daddy was so angry over all the attention from the nightclub—and it had been so long since they'd spoken, he refused to see him. I overheard him say Xavier was here, so I got Avice to go with me to the surface to meet him. He told me about Eric, and he told me you, Bernie, and Hell Belle were all hiding." Still walking, she flashed an eye at Julian, adding, "He never told me about you."

"He told me before, there are things I don't need to know. He was just trying to keep me safe. Violet, too," he said.

Fae giggled. "That's our brother: the man, the myth, the enigma." She twisted all the way around, staring past Julian and Bernard. "Speaking of Hell Belle: where is my little punk rocker?" she asked, unknowingly shooting Julian's heart out of the sky, sending it spiraling down in a fiery tailspin of remembrance to kiss its fate on the nose. "She always wanted to see the kingdom, but I never had the chance to show her."

Anna took her sister's tiny hand, drawing her attention back. "Violet died too," she said.

Fae moaned, "My sweet Hell Belle is dead?"

"It was her death, at her and Julian's wedding, that caused all this."

Fae's little doll head fell forward. From behind, Julian imagined her taking a moment to remember someone who could never be forgotten. Picking herself back up, she sighed and said, "Come on. Daddy must know."

Moving along, Julian further examined the cavern. Those who were not rubbernecking from every angle, followed at a distance. Ahead, two sculpted staircases curled their way up the whipped-cream walls from either side of the floor. The semi-spirals landed in the middle of a chiseled balcony. From there, a hallway disappeared in each direction, another centered.

On the ground floor, seven shallow steps lay ahead, leading farther into the unknown. All along, Julian admired the innovative craftsmanship. On his way in, he'd wondered why Caanis would choose such an inconvenient location to call home, even if privacy was the top priority. After seeing everything for himself, he understood why.

At the bottom of the shallow steps, a hallway led in each direction, like it had upstairs. Julian and Bernard followed the royals down the central hall, blazing mounted torches leading the way. At the end stood a glimmering gold door, its polished knob the size of a grapefruit.

"Don't speak, Julian, not unless my father asks you to," Anna said. "He is old-fashioned and demands the same regard you would expect from any king."

"He's lightened up some since you left, but he does take himself much too seriously" Fae said. Her eyes probing Julian, she added, "Respect goes a long way with him." With both hands, she reached for the knob, but Anna stopped her. "What is it?"

"Hold on," Anna turned to face her husband. She wrapped both arms around his neck and pecked his lips with hers. Her eyes chased his down. "Don't worry, love. I know you don't want to be here. Neither do I." She kissed him again. "You've come so far, and I love you."

"I know," Bernard uttered, awkwardly glancing at the others.

Julian turned away, focusing on the opposite end of the hall—where he'd just come from. On either side of the stairs, two other sets led even farther down. Winter-Fae snuck up by his side, placing her hand over his lower back. "That goes down to the stream," she said.

"There's a creek down here?"

"There is. We use it for bathing, but sometimes it's fun for a dip."

Hoping Anna and Bernard were done with their sentimental moment, Julian turned back, Fae's hand innocently sliding off his rear. The Gaunts were engaged in a kiss like it had been years since either felt such passion for the other. *Oh, come on, guys. I know you've been having problems, but get a room.*

Fae reached with both hands again, turning the big doorknob, the lovers breaking away as she did. "You ready?"

"Yeah," Anna said, taking Bernard's hand and facing the door. "Let's go."

Winter-Fae entered first. Anna and Bernard followed, Julian tailing everyone. "Please, close the door behind you," Fae instructed. He obeyed, pushing the heavy mass until it clicked. Before them, another open space of cavern waited. Just like the other, torches and fire pits flickered, bathing the walls in numerous shades of orange.

The modest hall stretched over fifty feet. At the other end, an empty chair set centered atop a carved, elevated area, three short steps leading to it from the floor. The cathedra was identical to the throne Julian first saw in Xavier's New York apartment: brass with red velvet cushions. He'd originally found it cliché, but upon seeing its twin featured in what he took as an underworld throne room, he wondered, *Where's the king?*

"I am over here!" a deep, Nordic voice bellowed from nowhere. The sudden high-energy declaration startled Julian, slightly knocking him off balance. To his right, a massive, broad-shouldered man with a round belly and the war-torn face of a dormant berserker stood, dwarfing everyone in his presence.

His caramel hair and beard hung wild, thick, and long. Between his lifeless eyes, a thin pink scar disappeared up his forehead. At his side, a sheathed dagger hung from a belt. He donned black slacks, shin-high black leather boots, and an untucked white shirt—buttoned halfway. From beneath the exposed crevice, a thick brown mass of hair emerged.

"Well, well, well," the king chuckled, strutting towards everyone, his royal smirk leading the way. "My lovely daughter finally comes home, gracing us with her presence. And it only took seventy-five years, a slain brother, and a missing sister to do it."

Flashing a smirk of her own, Anna said, "Imagine that."

"Excuse me?" Caanis cracked a wise grin. He looked at Bernard and said, "All these years, and she is still a bitch." Bernard offered nothing in response.

Each step Caanis took was powerful, echoing throughout the hall. Julian found the king's mighty presence unnerving. His heart pounded a strange beat like a drum and his breaths had grown heavy. He was already exhausted, having traveled so far, and not entirely healed from his transition or all the abuse his body endured since.

Caanis reached Bernard first. His eyes locked intently, he extended a hand. "Hello, Bernard—or should I say, 'son?'" He chuckled. Bernard nervously stroked his dark goatee, forcing a short-lived smile. "The last time I saw you, you were in that little cage." First glancing at Anna, he added. "But lucky for you, my daughter carries empathy, as any worthy queen should."

Bernard seemed hesitant, but he shook the king's hand, mumbling, "Lucky me." He cleared his throat, speaking up, and putting a little more life in his voice. "And how are you, your highness?"

"As good as the Gods, I suppose," Caanis said. Moving on, he took one look at Anna and continued, passing her without a word. He laid a large palm over Winter-Fae's head, petting her like a dog. "Thank you for bringing them to me." She looked up at her father and smiled. "But I am still disappointed in you." Her smile faded. "You don't do such things, my sweet *Vanir*."

"I told you, I needed to be alone," Fae pouted.

"Then you should have told somebody—at least your sister."

"I can take care of myself!"

The king's cheeks turned red, and his body tensed. In the middle of lifting a finger, presumably to put the faery in her place, his body and hand suddenly collapsed to a calmer state. "You know, it's not like you to vanish, and after what just happened; the way humans have always treated you; I worry for you."

Fae lifted an innocent finger to her father's chest, his sinking shoulders bending to her will. "I'm home now. So, please fret no more. I just needed a couple of nights for myself." She looked up high, deep into the king's milder eyes. "You did not remain in his life like I did—or Annie. You don't know how this past century and a half changed him. I know you love your son, just like you love your daughters, but we all shed tears in our own way."

Leaving it at that, Caanis arrived at Julian. With no introduction, he demanded, "What the hell were you and my son doing on the television?!" His eyes widened, turning sour again, and staring a hole. He loomed so closely, Julian could smell his foul breath. He imagined the mammoth could snap him in half if he so desired.

"I—I—"

"You … you … out with it!"

Julian looked at Anna, unsure what to say and too scared to say it, even if he knew. She said, "It wasn't their fault."

"I asked him!"

Julian swallowed a lump, never feeling so on-the-spot in his life. "We—we never meant for it to happen. The men who did it took us against our will."

"Was it the same men who attacked Xavier's establishment?"

"Yes, it was. They shot us with tranquilizer darts. We couldn't defend ourselves. Everything happened so fast. Bishop showed up and the next thing I knew we were in the helicopter. If Bishop hadn't been there, I don't know what would've happened, but Xavier and I wanted vengeance."

"Vengeance?" Caanis snorted. "So, you attacked them maliciously?"

Julian grew nauseous, fearing he chose the wrong words. "Your highness, we—we were not looking for a fight. Honestly, I'm surprised Bishop was there or even tried to help us after what he did to Eric and the others."

Caanis's expression changed from that of anger to confusion. "What do you mean?"

"After he killed Eric and all those other people, I nev—"

"What?!" the king barked.

"Wait," Fae interjected. "Bishop—Tony Bishop?"

"Yes," Julian said.

"Tattoos … drummer … that Tony Bishop?" Fae continued. Julian nodded. "He killed Eric and who?"

"He killed Eric, Eric's brother, and he also killed Christopher Cauldwell's daughter, which is apparently what started all of this," Julian said. "He also killed a few others around the city."

"Who told you this?" Caanis asked.

"Xavier did. Last year, when everyone went their separate ways for a while, he went to Queen Dajhri in Taltosia. She gave him a letter Bishop left for him, saying he did it. He said his mind was being controlled by the ..." Julian looked at Anna, asking, "What's his name—the guy who runs Raz Ahrim?"

"The Raja Kahiji?" Caanis impatiently answered first.

"Yeah—that's him."

"Let me make sure I heard you correctly," the king began. "The Raja Kahiji manipulated Tony Bishop's mind to control him and force him to kill Eric? Tony went to Dajhri and left her a note, telling Xavier what he did. Then Bishop later showed up to save you?"

"Yes."

"He's right," Anna said. "Xavier told me and Bern the same thing."

Caanis took a step back, completely caught off-guard by the revelations. He shut his eyes as if he were lost somewhere deep in thought. Opening them he said, "It is time we have a meeting."

"What kind of meeting?" Anna asked.

"If Raz Ahrim is attempting to rile me, I want to know. If Dajhri knows anything I do not ... I want to know. My son is dead. His son is dead."

And his daughter too.

"Violet too? You loved her, did you not?"

"'Loved?' No, your highness. I still love her. I will always love her. I gave her my mortal coil on a silver platter. The very last thought I have will be of her."

"Xavier made you, yes?" Caanis asked. "It was recently?"

"Yes."

"And you're all that's left of him?"

"Apparently I am."

Caanis rested his heavy hand on Julian's shoulder. He said, "I am truly sorry." He pulled away and turned his back to everyone, walking in the direction of the side hall from where he had first appeared. Along the way, he said, "I shall send word to the other two kingdoms, requesting the king and queen's presence." He stopped and looked back at everyone, adding, "Until then, none of you are to leave." Then he disappeared.

Julian stood at a loss. The king had been every bit as frightening as he imagined. Fae tugged on his hand. She said, "Come, everyone. I will show you to your quarters." She opened the gold door, motioning for them to follow. They did, none with a single word to say.

Chapter Fifteen

Winter-Fae led everyone back towards the main chamber, and then, to the top of the curved stairs. Already knowing their way, Anna took Bernard's hand, both giggling like a pair of hormonal teenagers. They disappeared down the hall on the left, leaving Julian alone with the porcelain princess. On their way down the central hall, Fae said, "Daddy's living area is downstairs, but the rest of us live up here." The hallway glowing in torchlight, Julian counted several carved-out doorways with hinges and black metal doors lining the walls as far as he could see. Each door featured a white hand-painted number on it.

31 ... 32 ... 33. Julian silently read as he passed. "So, how many vampires live here?" he asked.

"I believe we have one hundred thirteen with us—well, one hundred sixteen, now—but I could be wrong. You only saw some of us earlier. The rest are either in their rooms, down at the stream, or somewhere above."

34 ... 35 ... "This meeting Caanis was talking about ... what's going to happen?"

"That, I have no clue. Daddy's never called a meeting like this in all my years. I have only met the queen once, but I've never met anyone from Raz Ahrim. I do know if what you and Annie say is true, the outcome will be dire."

"That's what I'm afraid of." *37 ... 38 ...*

Fae stopped in place. She softly sighed. "There is something in your story that doesn't sit right with me."

"What do you mean?"

"You said Tony killed Eric and William and then he left a note, confessing?" Julian nodded. "He was here last year for Halloween. Upstairs, there's always a lot of fun raves and motion pictures being shown, but even more than usual on Halloween. Tony had been coming to the catacombs for years. When he was here, he showed no signs of distress. I could read his mind. He had no thoughts about killing Eric, William, or anyone you mentioned."

"What?" Julian gasped. "How is that possible?"

"I don't know, but when my other sister, Avice, and I met with Xavier last summer, he told us he saw Dajhri. He said nothing about Tony or the note."

"Maybe it was to protect you."

"Perhaps, but unless someone wiped Tony's memory— which I've never heard of before—either he didn't do it or he buried it so far in his mind, he never thought about it while we were together. I am thinking if he did it against his will or not, and he felt so compelled to leave Xavier a note, then he would have at least one thought about it, considering our close connection."

"When we saw him in Times Square, he told Xavier he made a mistake and he wanted to fix it."

"Hmm …" Fae touched an index finger to her puckered lips, rolling her oceanic globes back in her head. "Would you care if I searched some of your thoughts?"

Julian stalled at first, but then he said, "I guess."

Fae reached up and put a tiny hand over his forehead. She closed her eyes. "I see you lying in your bed, listening to Xavier reading Tony's note." She moved her hand to one side of his head and placed her other hand over the opposite. "Xavier told Violet it was Tony's handwriting."

Julian found relief in Fae's gentle touch, her pygmy fingers moving slowly about his temples. The sensation invoked chills and goosebumps. It reminded him of all the times Violet used to run her fingertips through his hair and along his scalp as he'd fall asleep with his head in her lap. For a moment, he shut his eyes, enjoying the delicacy while it lasted. Relaxed, he couldn't help thinking, *That feels so good.*

"I see you lying face up. People are standing over you, looking at you like you are dead. Tony takes your hand and says, 'Julian, I am here to help you.' Then he pulls you up and helps Xavier. I can hear him saying, 'I know I fucked up and disobeyed you. I don't deserve your forgiveness, but I am here to make things right. So let me make things right.'" Fae opened her eyes and removed hands. "Thank you."

"What does that tell you?"

"I don't know. Perhaps I just missed it before." She stared for a second. "I saw something interesting in your thoughts just now. You've experienced that memory twice—Tony helping you up. Am I correct?"

Julian blushed, feeling like she might think he was crazy. "I have, but it's hard to explain. I once had a psychedelic vision. I first saw it there. The faces hovering over me were all certain people from my past—my parents, grandparents, and others. In the vision, I took it as God lifting me up, offering me serenity, so to speak. Then when it really happened, I felt like the fall I took from the helicopter had killed me. I even saw Violet as an angel, holding me the same way another angel held me in part of my vision."

Her face glowing with astonishment, Fae said, "You're a seer. You had the vision before receiving the gift?" He nodded. She then bobbed her head, repeating, "You are a seer—perhaps in alternate contexts, but you can see things before they happen."

"It's funny you say that. I was born with a degenerative eye condition—Retinitis Pigmentosa. Until I became a vampire, I was almost completely blind. Throughout my life, people told me when you lose one sense, it enhances others. I used to believe it was nothing more than patronizing attempts to make me feel better."

"In my years, I have learned whatever strengths or abilities we already possess as humans become even more powerful once we receive this gift of ours. For me, I was intuitive, even before I became a vampire. I was not born with that strength. I had to learn it the hard way."

"How so?"

Before Fae could respond, a shirtless, dark-skinned man passed, politely saying, "Excuse me."

They moved aside, letting him pass. Fae then took Julian's hand and said, "Come on. Let me finish showing you to your room."

Moving on, he went back to counting the numbers on the doors. *41 ... 42 ...*

Fae pulled a lit torch from a mounted holder, approaching the upcoming door on the left. "Here we are—number forty-three." She opened the door and entered the dark room first, heading towards a small, round firepit in the corner. There was already unburnt wood inside it and another pile stacked nearby on the floor.

When she kissed the tinder with the torch, the small room instantly came alive, the limestone walls melting like orange creamsicles. Aside from the wood and pit, a twin bed on the opposite side of the room was all he had. Julian removed his backpack and jacket, laying them both on the floor, beside the bed. Then he removed his muddy shoes and socks.

Ignoring the soiled lower half of his jeans for the moment, he flopped down on the side of the bed and yawned, his legs dangling off the edge. "Thank you for showing me to my room," he said.

Fae stuck the lit end of the torch in the firepit, leaving the handle leaning away from the flames. She sat beside him, saying, "You're welcome, little Glowstick."

He laughed, finding her lingo quirky. "You've called me that twice now. Why?"

"I get it now. I see why my little Hell Belle loved you."

"Why's that?"

"Your eyes—they shine. They tell such a sad story. But at the end of that story, I see triumph. You are a warrior and a survivor."

"What's that have to do with glow sticks?"

"How do you make a glow stick work? It must be broken first. Only then it can shine."

"I like that," he said, truly meaning it.

"All of us have been broken at one time or another. For my sister, Avice, and I, it was the deaths of our parents," she said, her soft voice cracking along with the fire.

"When did it happen?"

"I lost mine late sixteen-sixty-five and Avice lost hers early sixteen-sixty-six. The Great Plague took them and everyone else we cared about."

"Did you and her already know each other before it happened?"

"No. We never met until we were orphans living in the streets of London. The first months were the hardest for me. I was alone and had to fend for myself. So many people were terrified of me. Some thought I was a demon. Others thought I was a witch."

"That's awful."

She snickered. "I was even lured into a church by a priest once. He promised me food and a bed, but he had other plans. He tried to burn me alive."

"Why?" A little reluctant, he asked, "Was it because you're an albino?"

"Please don't call me that. I prefer 'faery-princess.' Even my mother thought I was. She said I was born during a horrendous snowstorm, very prematurely, and I came out tiny and just as white as the snow. The fact I survived was a miracle from God. My mother said I looked just like a little faery, smiling up at her. So, that is who I became. People who believed in folklore were more scared of faeries than Jesus, but not my mother. She thought they were precious, like all of God's creatures." Fae took a moment, grinning and gleaming in the light, appearing to savor the past.

"But … yeah," she continued. "This looney old priest took me in out of the cold, one night. My gut told me not to trust him, but it was also empty. I hadn't eaten in days. He promised me food. Once he got me inside his empty church, he tried to have his way with me. When I told him no, he started calling me a demon and said he was going to 'burn me to Hell.'"

"What did you do?"

"He already had logs blazing in the biggest firebox I'd ever seen. When I refused to fellate him, he grabbed me by my hair and dragged me to the oven. Then he tried to pick me up to throw me in. Trying to wiggle free, I kicked him in the plums. Foolish for him but lucky for me, he had a wrought iron poker within reach. While he was hunched over, writhing in pain, I hit him across the head, busting him open, and dropping him to a knee.

"I went on, hitting him over and over with that poker. His blood went everywhere. I spent every ounce of energy I had left, beating him until he stopped moving and looked like raspberry jelly. Then, as he lay rotting, I ate the meal he had promised. It was potatoes and rabbit stew—the best potatoes and rabbit stew I ever tasted. I even took a hot bath to wash away all his filth and my own. That night, I slept in a soft, warm bed. It was the best night's sleep I had since my parents died." Fae's proud grin stretched in palatable triumph. To most, her story would have been appalling—enough reason to scamper in fear of the living doll; but not Julian.

When her smile faded and the light in her eyes balanced, she continued. "The next morning, I even helped myself to a scrumptious breakfast before filling my pockets with anything small and valuable I could carry and then running away. No one ever knew who or why—only that he would never take advantage of another fourteen-year-old girl again."

"You were only fourteen?"

"I was," she said. "Then a week later, someone else—someone more successful than the 'man of God,' had their turn. He wasn't a priest, but a much bigger and older boy. He was another orphan. Unlike the priest, he was strong, and I couldn't fight him off. It happened behind an old cemetery I'd sometimes sleep in. I screamed with all I had. He took what he came for, but that was not enough. After stealing my virtue, he beat me. I thought he was going to kill me."

"The only virtue he stole was his own," Julian blurted.

"Then, she came—Avice: a girl I had never seen in my life: my sister, my Christ. She had a knife. Before the boy even knew she was there, his throat was sliced wide open, and my face was baptized in his warm blood. Even as a human, it tasted good. It tasted every bit as good as it did watching it pour from his gash. That satisfaction lasted until the following nightmares stole that from me too."

Trying to sympathize, Julian said, "I can't even begin to imagine what all that must have been like for you at such a young age. Even after everything I have been through at my own age, including watching my wife get decapitated, I wouldn't wish what you had to go through on anyone."

"You're sweet," Fae said. "Please do not take this the wrong way, but you were not meant for this life. I told you I see why my little Hell Belle loved you, but she and my brother should not have involved you in this."

"Why would you say that?"

"Times were different back then. Maybe it's because I am much older than you and you are still so young at this, but I see an innocence in you that I don't see in others—not even what I still try to see in myself."

"I am not innocent. I killed two men. One of them was self-defense, but the other was rage. I even took enjoyment in watching

Violet kill one of my cousins and two of his friends. They were trying to rob and kill me, but their behavior was no reflection on mine. It is not normal to enjoy something like that, even if the karma was just. I kissed her lips for the first time that night, and I tasted their blood—not as a vampire, but a human. I liked it. Is that innocence to you?"

After only staring for several seconds, Fae said, "Why don't I let you get some sleep?"

"That sounds great, actually."

She stood from the bed and took the torch from the fire pit. "Feel free to put more wood on the fire whenever you need. If it goes out, just find a torch somewhere to relight it."

"Okay, thanks," Julian said, watching her at the door.

She took his muddy shoes. "I will have these washed and returned to you shortly. I don't know what is going on between them, but it might be a while before we see Annie and Bernie again. So, if you get hungry, let me know." She opened the door and began her way out before turning back, adding, "If you need anything else, my room is right across the hallway—number forty-four."

Chapter Sixteen

Julian awoke hours later, better rested, but now he was weak with hunger. He pulled away the red wool blanket he'd buried himself under before falling asleep. The fire was getting low, so he put a small log in the pit and watched the room glow. He opened his backpack and removed a clean pair of jeans, his dirty pair lying balled up on the floor next to it. His stomach growling, he wondered, *Is Winter-Fae awake?* He opened his door, facing the closed black door across the hall—*44.*

He approached, listening for movement. It wasn't much, but there was something. Cautiously, he knocked. "Winter-Fae, it's Julian. Are you awake?"

From the other side, a voice said, "Come in." Unsure who it belonged to, and thinking nothing of it, he opened the door. A fire crackling in a pit just like the one in his room, the natural light revealed a small wooden table against the opposite wall. Atop it, a chessboard sat with its pieces in their proper places for a new game. On either side of the table sat a matching chair. The one on the left was empty. The other was occupied.

With all the white pieces arranged before him, the man, the myth, the enigma sat slouched, facing the board, wearing the same black suit, tie, and eyepatch as before. Seeing his creator was all Julian needed to know what this was. Xavier looked up from the board and grinned, his miserable, broken teeth stealing the show. "You know, I became comfortable with my life in New York. I even enjoyed my brief time in Virginia. Germany was divine. But I must admit, there is no place like home."

"I met your sister," Julian said, taking a few steps closer.

"Which one?"

"Winter-Fae."

"Ah! She's a unique little imp, yes?"

"She is. She told me quite an interesting story, too." Xavier tipped his head. "She said you saw her last summer, but you never told her what Dajhri told you about Bishop. Why not?"

"For the same reason I cannot tell you certain things now. Many vampires can read each other's thoughts. If you knew something and a more powerful vampire wanted to know, you would be powerless to stop them. Your only defense is ignorance. I left sweet Fae in the dark about Bishop because I not only wanted to protect her, but I wanted to find out more information first."

"And did you ever find that information?"

"Take a seat." Xavier pointed at the empty chair. Julian approached the table, sitting where instructed and expecting to be asked for a rematch. "To answer your question: on New Year's Eve, I did find that information."

"And?"

"When Bishop acknowledged his guilt, it was not over what happened to Eric or William. His guilt was that of running away when I specifically asked him and everyone else to stay there the night after Cauldwell had threatened to come back. Instead of respecting my wishes, he fled."

"Fae said he was here last Halloween, but he showed her no signs of guilt or anything that would incriminate him. So, what does this mean?"

Xavier slid one of his center pawns two spaces forward. Then he stared with his one eye, waiting for Julian to reciprocate. Humoring his elder, he moved one of his own pawns forward. Continuing, Xavier said, "I caught a short glimpse of Bishop writing the letter, but he hadn't a clue what he was writing,"

"Are you saying he was being manipulated—even then?"

"Perhaps." Xavier moved his left knight. "With all else afoot, I only had time to see so much. I could not say if he was the one who killed Eric and William or not, but if he did, I do not believe he had any present memories of doing it."

Julian moved one of his knights. "Is it possible for a vampire to erase another's memory?"

"To my knowledge, no. Through mind control, a vampire can isolate another's memories and prevent them from thinking about it, but the memory remains lost and unseen."

"Hopefully it will be straightened out shortly. Caanis said he is calling a meeting with the Raja Kahiji and Dajhri."

Xavier smirked. "So, how is my dear old dad?"

"He is scary, and I don't like him much."

"Not many people do. The man's ego is inflated, and he takes himself far too seriously."

"I noticed. I also noticed he's not very popular in Alaska either, particularly with Roland."

Xavier snickered, asking, "What brothers get along?"

"Funny you should mention that. Pana told me the story of how Caanis became the king. He told me Caanis's maker made his own son a vampire and that son was the heir."

"Aellin was. He could have had everything, but then his father was betrayed."

Julian asked, "Why?"

"Aellin wanted to expand while Arvil did not. The night it happened, Caanis found Arvil in his bed, his heart impaled with the same blade he once gave his son."

"Anna said you and she were also there."

"We were close by—in another part of the palace, but not near enough to see it for ourselves. Caanis said he heard something coming from the king's quarters. He later came out with Arvil in his arms."

"Did anyone else see what happened?"

"They did not."

"You realize how sketchy that sounds, right?"

"I understand." Xavier used his queen to take one of Julian's bishops. "There were those who believed Caanis and those who believed Aellin. It was that division which led to the war and inevitably settling here."

Julian moved a rook. The game had gone back and forth several turns before he spoke up again. "Fae thinks I am too innocent to be a vampire."

"She's right. I never wanted you to be one of us—Violet either. After Dajhri's prophecy about Violet making a vampire, I was certain it would be you, but I never wanted her to turn anyone."

"Why not?"

"Because I have made many in my life, but all except for her, Eric, and you have died just after. That was another reason I was reluctant to make you—not just because of all your blind rage. Among other things, I feared you would not survive the transition. After Eric, along with Violet's love for you, the last thing I wanted was to put your life in jeopardy, when your transition was never forced by a matter of life and death like theirs was."

"I read a little about that in Violet's diary. You and her both feared Eric was going to die when making him. Why did all the others die?"

"Since your rebirth, I've held a certain suspicion, but I never knew for certain. I have seen numerous vampires made throughout my life and their transitions all went as smoothly as yours. When I made Violet, it was my first attempt in almost four-hundred years. I only went to that diner because Dajhri persuaded me, telling me it was crucial that I turned her. Even then, I did not want to do it. There had to be another way. I wanted to prove her wrong as a prophet. But then when I found Violet dying on the sidewalk, I knew turning her was the only way to save her. I was not about to let something so precious slip away when I knew I might have had a chance to save her too. That is when I realized the prophecy was indeed destiny." When he stopped for a breath, Xavier nearly wept.

The men continued their game. *Something just seems off,* Julian thought, forgetting Xavier could hear him. He waited, expecting his maker to respond with eye contact or banter, but he showed no signs of either. *Can you hear me?* Julian waited, but still, nothing. Unsure if Xavier was truly unable to hear him or playing possum, he thought to himself, *You know you're dead, right? When that building fell on you, it killed you. This is only a dream, and you don't know you're dead.* Still, he offered nothing.

Julian was ashamed of such drastic thoughts but all things considered, even attempting to take his own life again, he was running out of anything worth caring for—whether it be internal, external, dreams, or reality. The way he saw it, death itself was his kingdom come. Finally, he asked, "What could potentially happen at this meeting?"

"Hopefully, the truth will out. There has not been a meeting between the kingdoms since just before Arvil Reinhardt's assassination. Something is certainly amiss, but I have faith Caanis will reach the bottom of it."

"You sure have a lot of faith in a man who cut your dick off and excommunicated you for something as petty as sex."

"Technically, he never excommunicated me. He castrated me, yes. He kicked me out of L'abisme, yes. It was my choice to never return. He wanted me to go out on my own and mature. I cannot explain it, but once I left home, everything changed for the better. With what money I had, I began investing and flipping. As you saw with my club and in Las Vegas, I eventually became financially successful."

Making his boldest move yet, Julian took Xavier's queen with his own. The blond smirked and bowed his head in approval. "By the time I started making real money, I had reconciled with my sisters—well, Fae and Anna. Avice is a whole other story. After the incident that got me in trouble, I had spent over a hundred-and-fifty years with no contact from anyone."

Julian made another move, asking, "What changed that?"

"Anna came and found me. She told me she met another vampire for whom she had sympathy."

"Bernard?"

"Yes. She told me his maker: Eustice Golding, a vile beast who had survived the war but remained loyal to Reinhardt, had been keeping Bernard as a servant and sex slave for just as long as I had been away. When Anna came to me, she wanted my help to free him. With Caanis an enemy of Eustice, she never dared to ask him for help."

"What did you do?"

"I went to Austria with her. First, I tried reasoning with Eustice, bargaining for Bernard's freedom. Due to his hatred for our father, he spat in our faces. I took it personally. Other than having Bernard in his company, Eustice was alone. With barely any effort I snapped his neck. I didn't want to. It haunted me. But I had to, not just for Bernard, but Annie too. After that, it took time for Bernard to adjust, but he and my sister returned to New York with me. Eventually, they married."

"Was that before or after you met Violet and Eric?"

"It was after. I had met Eric, William, and their mother, Autumn, some years earlier. William was still a baby. There was a church at the bottom of their apartment building. One year, I happened by on Christmas Eve. From the streets, I heard everyone inside, singing 'When the Saints Go Marching In.' I enjoy that hymn, so I went inside, singing along with the congregation, welcomed like one of their own.

"When the service concluded, I approached a beautiful but sad woman, alone on one of the pews. She was cradling a newborn baby in a blanket. I saw right through her. I saw her struggles and needs. Being Christmas, I offered her money and even prepared a hearty banquet for her and her teenaged son, Eric. I eventually told them who I was, assuring them I would never harm them. Autumn then invited me to stay permanently."

Julian examined the chessboard, having paid far less attention to the game than Xavier's story. He moved a pawn a space, not caring so much about the outcome. Once the move was completed, he asked, "What happened after Anna and Bernard came to New York?"

"I bought the building where we all lived. They moved into one of the vacant apartments. I even had a special room set aside for Fae when she'd visit. She loved to travel, but on account of her size and appearance, she was always scared to go anywhere far or alone. The apartment building started becoming a hotspot for vampires to visit. Though their secrets remained safe, the church downstairs eventually disbanded."

Still listening to the story, Julian watched his maker closing in on his king. "Eric and William had a lot of problems back then. After several of William's outbursts, the priest who oversaw the congregation, and who also lived in one of the apartments, could sense something 'unholy in the air,' as he put it."

Julian laughed at the remark a little harder than he thought he would. He made his final moves before the game was lost. "Oh, well … I've never been good at chess."

"To be fair, I have centuries of experience on you. You did take my queen. Be proud of that."

Julian smiled, closing his eyes, and reminiscing over the past autumn and winter months leading up to Xavier's and Violet's deaths. "I miss you both so much," he said. When he opened his eyes, he found himself back in his room—beneath the red wool blanket, the orange embers in the firepit showing little signs of life. It took him a moment to catch his breath, but once he did, like Xavier, Julian wept too.

Chapter Seventeen

His empty belly nagging for attention, Julian climbed out of bed, wearing only his boxers and black shirt. He put on a clean pair of jeans. Then he took his keys and phone from the pockets of his dirty pair, putting the keys inside his jacket. He checked his phone. The time read: *7:06 p.m. CET*, and the date: *Jan 4, 2020.*

Though he didn't have a signal, he looked at the text message he'd sent Daryl in Alaska—overcome by a spark of relief when reading, *"Delivered"* beneath it. He turned his phone off to save battery power before also putting it in one of his pockets. He slipped the jacket on and faced the door. His black sneakers sat just inside it; clean, but still wet. *Fuck it*, he thought while examining them. *I'll just go barefoot.*

Now dressed, and every bit as weakened with hunger as in his dream, he headed towards the door. Hearing voices in the hallway, he opened it just in time to find Anna and Bernard heading his way. They were both smiling, appearing well-rested and wearing clean clothes. Anna wore a simple yellow sundress. Bernard wore black slacks, a belt with a shiny fat buckle, and a tucked blue shirt, its two top buttons undone. Like Julian, neither wore shoes. "Talk about good timing," he said, laughing at the odds. "Are you two as hungry as I am?"

"Famished," Bernard chuckled.

"So, since we're not allowed to leave, where are we supposed to get blood?"

"I don't know, love. That's why we came over here, to find Fae," Anna said. "Is she still in forty-four?"

"Yeah." Julian watched her approach Fae's door, lifting a hand to knock. Before she could, it squeaked open and out popped a smiling, little white face through the gap.

She cheerfully greeted them, squeaking, "Good evening, little moonshines!"

Julian patted his gut. "We're hungry."

"I heard," she said, joining everyone in the hall. "Follow me." She led them back towards the main chamber. Reaching the balcony, overlooking the grand cavern's entirety, Julian took in the view. Many vampires stood on the floor below, engaged in random conversations. Roughly two hundred feet separated the balcony from the kingdom's entrance—the tall, wide opening leading back towards the spiral staircase.

Julian and the others followed Fae into the hallway on their left. The first door on the right was open. Inside the torchlit room—three times the size of Julian's—a large, round hole engulfed the far-left corner. Over the trench, a crank was rigged. Metal poles rising from the limestone floor held a thick chrome bar with a handle on the end. Tied to the bar, a brown hemp rope disappeared into the void.

Bernard scratched his scalp, asking, "What is this?"

"It's the closest thing to refrigeration we have," Fae said. "Not everyone here likes to hunt. For those of us who don't, we have this." She trotted to the crank and twisted it with the rapid speed only a vampire could possess. The spool of rope thickened until an oversized, dripping wet fisherman's net emerged, packed full of shiny red IV bags.

Julian asked, "Are those safe to consume?"

"Indeed, they are. This well is deep. The bottom is full of ice and cold water. We go through bags so quickly, they don't have time to spoil." She took one from the top of the net and handed it to him. "Go on. Try it."

"Is this real blood or synthetic?" he asked.

"It is real blood."

"I—I've never had real human blood before—not like this."

"Then you're in for a treat."

"Where did you get it?" Anna asked, reaching into the net. She took one for Bernard and another for herself.

"Hospitals and donors from around the world. As many of us here who travel and explore; every day someone is bringing some back, giving us all we need."

Julian examined the cold bag. He watched Anna take a drink from hers, then Bernard. *Well, here goes nothing.* He put the tube between his lips, already tasting the metallic fumes before the substance reached his tongue. Once it did, the zapping sensation that followed was like licking a nine-volt battery. All his nerve endings simultaneously came alive, each mindful of its place.

A concentrated dose of love and understanding cradled his every thought and being in a snug, velvety blanket, the pint bag nursing the voracious infant like it was a loving mother's breast. Such warmth bathed what remained of his withering soul in bubbles—popping, fizzling, and tickling his perception. Then he swallowed. His entire body became weightless. He could no longer feel his clothing or the rocky surface beneath his feet. If it wasn't for his sight, Julian would swear on the fate of the universe he was floating. *Is this what it feels like?*

Watching and grinning all along, Fae asked, "What?"

"Flying: is this what it feels like?"

"Sort of," she said. "After drinking it so long, it tends to not have the same effect."

From behind, a deep feminine voice said, "I don't know how anyone can stand drinking that cold shit!" Everyone turned to face her. Like Winter-Fae, the tall, stocky brunette spoke in the same English accent. Her pointed chin and nose in the air, she first approached Anna. "I guess now that your meal ticket's pushing up rubble, you think you can just come crawling back to Daddy—with your husband—" she smirked at Bernard. "—and whoever the fuck this is supposed to be," she added, her enquiring eyes moving on.

"My name is Julian."

The woman sauntered his way, stopping so close she could have kissed him. Obnoxiously shaking her head, she whispered, "I don't care."

Anna grunted. "So, who fucked you up the arse and forgot to pay, sis?"

"Really, Annabel? Whore jokes … from you?"

"Excuse me?" Anna squawked. "It's your fault Xavier got kicked out of here, Avice—and you're calling me a whore?"

"It was his fault, not mine. I'm not the one who tricked us into smoking that shit!"

"That's not what I mean," Anna said.

"Jesus-fucking-Christ," Bernard groaned. "I don't want to hear this shit." Before anyone could stop him, he took his IV bag and stormed out the doorway, heading in the direction of his room.

Anna turned back to her sister, her eyes burning just as red as her hair. "Good going, you fucking bitch! I've had a hell of a time with him lately! We literally just started making up. You just had to come in here, famously flashing that big cunt of yours, and drive another wedge between us, didn't you?!"

"So?" Avice grinned. "If your husband's really that jealous of a dead man, then perhaps Bernard should change his name to Bernadette because you ain't got a husband; you got a wife."

Her cheeks pumping, Anna shoved a finger in Avice's face, shouting, "What the fuck's your problem?!"

Julian watching from a million miles away, unsure what was happening, Fae broke into a sudden fit of laughter. He and the clashing sisters gave her their attention. Once she caught her breath and contained herself, the faery asked, "Is it wrong of me to admit I have missed this a little too much?"

In a calmer tone, Anna said, "To answer your question, Avice, I came home because Paul and Teddy found us when looking for Fae. Father wanted me here—all of us. We didn't want any trouble for Pana or his people, so we came back."

"He's not very happy," Avice said. "I heard he barely had anything to say to you."

"Who told you that?"

"He did. He told me what happened to our dear brother, how it happened … his daughter, too." Avice looked at Julian and said, "He told me it all started at yours and her wedding."

"That's right," he awkwardly mumbled.

With no hint of empathy in her deep voice, she said, "Tough break."

"What else did 'Daddy' tell you?" Anna asked.

"He said he sent word to Raz Ahrim and Taltosia, seeking an audience with Dajhri and the Raja Kahiji. He said they will arrive in a few days. It should be interesting. I have heard Dajhri's a delight, but I don't believe anyone here aside from Daddy has ever met the self-proclaimed 'King Death' before or any of those other tongueless monsters."

"That's what his name means: 'King Death?'" Julian asked.

Avice nodded. "Edgy, is it not?"

"And he doesn't have a tongue?"

"As far as I know, nobody from Raz Ahrim does."

"How do they communicate?"

"They don't," Fae said. "Apparently, they think they are too good to need to communicate with anyone else."

Julian sipped from his pouch, his head still buzzing. He watched Anna, listening to what she and her sisters were saying. He witnessed a new pain burrowing deep in her wounded eyes. Her physical presence offered nothing, but he observed the helpless dread the gut-wrenching fear of another fight with her husband, forcing her into a dark corner again, just as it was him.

"Oh, God—please don't let Bern be mad at me," Anna said, but Julian never saw her lips move. "Last night was so good. I ain't been fucked like that in centuries, not since Xavvy. God, that was so good! I always want it to be that good. Please, God, don't let things go back to the way they were before all this, again. I just want to be happy."

Julian continued watching her speak without speaking. He wondered, *Am I hearing her thoughts?* He looked at his half-empty IV bag. *Could this be why?*

"So, what are your plans after this meeting?" Avice asked. "Are you, Bernard, and 'Julian' going to stick around, or are you going to take off again?"

"I honestly haven't thought about it," Anna said.

Julian took another drink. He could almost see the shape of Anna's face change: her eyes drooping out of their sockets, an exaggerated, umbrella-sized frown overtaking the bottom half of her freckled face. It was like a hallucination, the heartsick countenance of a sad clown overlapping hers. "This is weird," he said.

"What is?" Fae asked.

Acting purely on impulse, Julian took Anna's hand. "Go to him," he said. "Tell Bernard you love him, and this conversation was neither of your faults." The obscure false face he'd watched forming over Anna's began to fade like his words controlled the weather. Then, real tears began to fall.

The way she stared at him; he knew she knew. She said, "Thank you," without saying it.

Out loud, Julian said, "You're welcome." He watched her tears persist as she turned to leave the room, heading in the same direction Bernard had.

Avice shrugged her shoulders. "What the fuck was that all about?"

Fae smiled and said, "That was beautiful, Glowstick."

Julian blushing, Avice grunted, "'Glowstick?' Where the bloody shit d'you get that from?"

"It's a nickname."

"You just met him, and you've already given him a nickname?" Avice glared at Julian. Looking back at her sister, she said, "Remember; the nice ones will hurt you the most."

"What are you saying?" Julian asked.

Avice ignored him, adding, "Don't be a rebound."

Julian said, "Listen here, I don't know what you think, but I have no intentions of doing anything inappropriate with anyone. I love my wife and—"

"And that's sweet," Avice interrupted, her tone still lacking emotion. "I am happy for you, but your wife is not here anymore. My delicate sister is. I don't know if she told you this, but I killed a boy who raped her. I slit his throat and never regretted it once. I had never met her before then, but I knew I had to save her. She was only fourteen. From then on, I have been with her. As humans, we survived the streets, the plague, and the Great Fire—together. As vampires, we have survived nearly four-hundred years—together. I wouldn't lose sleep over killing anyone else for her, including you. Never forget that, 'Glowstick.'"

Fae said, "It's okay. Julian's not going to hurt me."

"If he does, I will—"

"If I do, please kill me. Chop me up into little bacon bits and feed me to rats, dogs, or the homeless, for all I fucking care! I don't give a shit anymore. But whatever you do, make sure it kills me. You'd be doing us both a favor. Then go on with your life and forget I was ever in it, okay?!" Julian didn't give Avice the chance to retaliate. He'd heard enough. Looking at Fae, he held up the IV bag, forced a smile, and bowed his head, toasting her kindness. He walked back to his room, leaving the sisters to their affairs.

Chapter Eighteen

Julian sat in bed, finishing his breakfast. Staring into the new fire burning in the pit, he'd worried over what could happen when the other king and queen arrived in L'abisme. *If Bishop really did kill Eric, what does this mean? What if Bishop had nothing to do with it? Christopher Cauldwell murdered my Violet, an innocent woman. Did he also murder an innocent man? Did Bishop die for nothing? Was Eric's death the sign Dajhri prophesied to be the start of a war? Was it Violet's? Times Square? Has it even happened yet?*

Julian took his final drink, now thinking of Anna. He wondered if the human blood had allowed him to read her mind and see her emotions so vividly. *What is happening to me?* He questioned life, death, and everything in between—dreams and reality—desperately searching for the difference. One was just as troublesome and painful as the other. His torment had become an infinite loop of self-inflicted mental abuse: a personal Hell he was never meant to escape.

Infinity. He laughed. *Goddamn you, enlightenment. If only the certainty of peace after suicide was truly certain. I could go home now and call it a day. Then we could begin our eternal anew, my flower—unravel an endless understanding of transcending all time and space together. That's the only 'infinity' that appeals to me.*

Finding the notion of taking his own life so beautiful and poetic; Julian cried. Vampire or not, he was unwell to crave such desires once again. He knew he needed help; even a temporary release would do. He looked at his backpack, his mind levitating towards Violet's diary. He removed it from his bag and flipped to the next unread page. He took a deep breath and then he dove, headfirst, back into his lost love's past once more.

2/19/45

Dear Diary

   Eric survived the transition! Thank you, God! I was so scared he was going to die. Even Xavier thought he might. He said no matter how many times he tried to make a vampire before, back when he lived in Germany, they always died. He never understood why.

   I am so glad Eric made it through, but I hate myself for what I did to him. With his penis only hanging on by a little bit of skin, Xavier had to cut it completely off. He told me we can heal ourselves much faster than humans, but if we lose vital parts like that, they don't grow back. I don't know how this is all supposed to work. All I know is I have now destroyed three lives—not to mention what this might do to his mother or little William.

   I was shocked to find out Xavier had once lost his parts, too. He told me the story of why he left Paris. He was once a very reckless man. Not long after moving back from Germany, he gave his sisters opium, and they all went wild. That is why he is here now. It angered and frightened his maker, King Caanis. He was so angry he castrated Xavier and sent him away.

   So, what now, Diary? Where do I go from here? Where does Eric go from here? Where do "we" go from here? Even if we can't make love, will he still want me? Am I a bad person to wonder if I would still want him? An eternity is forever, after all. I never thought I would want to be intimate with a man before I met him. I guess only time will tell.

                                                                  Violet

   Digesting Violet's guilt was hard enough, but Julian spent the next few minutes thinking, *That's what happened—he gave them opium? I didn't know vampires could smoke anything. No wonder Caanis reacted so harshly.* Just when he found his way back to the present, turning the page to read the next, a thunderous, vibrating knock struck his door.

"Who is it?" he asked. Hearing nothing, he repeated, "Who is it?!" louder than before. Still, no one answered. Grumbling, "For fuck's sake," on his way to the door, the diary in hand, he tugged it open, thinking, *Is it really that fucking hard to say your goddamn name?* It was only then he saw who it was. His jaw dropped, all his color fading at once.

"'For fuck's sake' … is it really that hard to open your door before you address a king that way?"

"I … I …"

"You … you … what?"

"My apologies, you—your highness. I—I've been having a really difficult time lately and I—"

Caanis belted a jolly laugh. He planted a heavy hand on Julian's shoulder, jarring him when he did. "I understand. It is a stressful time, but you must mind yourself."

"If I may speak frankly, your highness, I kind of got that hint earlier."

"How do you mean?"

"I met Avice, and—"

"Ah, yes! She told me. She believes a mutual attraction exists between you and my youngest daughter." Though the king had carried a smug demeanor thus far, his expression changed. The nearly seven-foot ogre looked down on Julian, firmly staring into his baby-blue eyes. Unsure if it was the blood still amplifying his sentiment or if he truly was that mortified, he swallowed a lump. Caanis moved his hand to Julian's face, patting his cheek. "I can see that is not so," he said. "You've a rare heart. I advise you to cherish it, lest you wish to spend the rest of your days in regret."

"Thank you, your highness."

"Ah, please! You can call me Caanis. Bernard only called me that because he knows what is at stake." Julian tipped his head. Caanis stepped to the side of the doorway. Motioning towards the main chamber, he said, "Walk with me." Having no intentions of denying such a request, Julian stuffed Violet's diary into a large hidden pocket inside his jacket lining before leaving the room and shutting the door behind him. "So, how are you liking L'abisme?"

Following the king, Julian said, "It is nice down here. I couldn't really tell you why, but I always felt a strange attraction to the Paris catacombs … long before I knew our kind existed."

"The catacombs have quite the history. It is no wonder such a place would inspire and tempt those who choose to dabble and embrace their own inner darkness."

"Is that what drew you here?"

"It is … and is not. I am sure by now you know the story of Reinhardt's demise. Since discovering I could fly, centuries before the king's murder, I enjoyed traveling. Having the ability to quickly go anywhere I so desired in the world was a joy unlike any other." For a moment, Caanis shut his eyes and smiled. "In all my travels, Paris became my favorite place to visit. Not only in Paris did I meet my son, your maker, but I fell in love."

"With who?"

"Her name was Rosalyn." He smiled, whispering, "My *Valkyrie*," under his breath. Moving on at a normal volume, he said, "She was a vampire who knew nothing of her maker and little of our kind."

"How did you meet her?"

"She first came to me in a dream. It was her eyes that stood out the most. They were the heartiest shade of green. Only one other time have I seen eyes like hers." Reaching the end of the hall, Caanis stopped at the balcony. "It was but mere days before finding Xavier floating in the Seine River—so close to death—mine and

Rosalyn's eyes met for the first time outside our slumber. For so long, I questioned whether that was a dream too, but she was with me when I saved my former heir."

"Did you take Rosalyn back to Germany with you and Xavier?"

"I did not. She said Paris was her home, and she refused to leave this cavern. I spent six-hundred years courting her, longing to convince her to marry me. She always refused. She offered me her body and pieces of her heart, but never the entirety."

Caanis headed towards the stairs. Julian followed, asking, "What happened?"

"I wanted Paris to become my new permanent residency. Even my daughters enjoyed the city. Unfortunately, neither they, nor Xavier—who was unconscious throughout the entirety of his transitioning—ever met Rosalyn. I begged and pleaded to King Arvil for his blessing to break away from Reinhardt and start my own coven. Like so many others before me, he too refused my request."

At the bottom of the stairs, Caanis froze. "I still visited Rosalyn for years after, but she always insisted I came alone. It was not until the king's death and my victory over his murderer that I chose this location for a new kingdom. It was to be our kingdom. Rosalyn was to be my queen."

"I can't imagine how that must have felt to finally have the woman you gave six-hundred years of yourself to."

Caanis said, "I never knew. When the war was won, I came home to propose marriage and start anew. Thanks to the French Revolution, any authority figure was too busy hiding or dying to notice our arrival. That was the easy part. The dismay came after finding Rosalyn was not here waiting for me like she promised. She left nary a note or even a sign that she was ever here or existed at all."

"What do you mean?"

Caanis snorted. "Aren't you paying attention? All that time she was here. Then she no longer was. I tried telling Xavier and the others. They humored my ambition but had no choice believing she was only ever a dream—perhaps it was Loki's trickery. Only the Gods could fool me in such a way."

"That is so sad."

"Indeed—and it was all for nothing."

"What was?"

"My brother, Aellin, murdered his father because he thought we deserved freedom. It was loyalty to my king that drove me to seek vengeance." From the black sheath on his belt, Caanis gripped the decorative gold hilt of a dagger. He pulled it free, the whip of sharp metal on leather releasing a chill into the air. "This is the blade he used. It is the blade I pulled from my maker's heart; the same blade with which I sought my vengeance, driving it into Aellin's." As if entranced by the long blade's sheen, Caanis stared with deep intent in his tired old eyes. "I kept it all this time, to covet as a reminder of what love and loyalty to anyone but yourself will only accomplish."

Julian also gazed upon the weapon. The final chills of what Arvil Reinhardt and his son must have felt, as the icy hands of death added them to its collection, wiggled its way up his spine. Following such a shiver, he took a deep breath, exhaling something much colder than the air he took in. Uncomfortable with the feeling, he cleared his throat and said, "Forgive me, Caanis, but why are you telling me all this?"

The giant patted him on the shoulder before moving onward, down the stairs leading towards his throne room. At the bottom, he said, "I see greatness in you. At our previous encounter, I knew then why Xavier chose you. At thirty-eight years old, you are much wiser, intuitive, and humble than he was at that age. For him, the gift was a game, a way to indulge in matters more of the flesh than the mind or heart."

"Is that really why you castrated and banished him … because of what he did to your daughters?"

Snickering, Caanis said, "You're bold—another good quality. I admit but do not regret emasculating him, though I did not banish or strip him of his title. He did that on his own. Opium was newer to Paris, and quite popular at the time. My son shared it with his sisters before tearing up the city in a drug-fueled fuck-frenzy. From the accounts of all four, it was never his intention to violate them in such a way. But no matter how obscene the act might have been, that was not as much my qualm."

Entering the throne room, Julian continued following Caanis towards the brass chair ahead. "Once the war began in Germany, a vicious, equally bloodthirsty band of hunters hit us hard. Amidst the fight between vampires, we also had to deal with the hunters. It took some time, but we finally escaped them and made our way here, where I thought I would find my beloved Rosalyn waiting for me.

"Though I was left to build this kingdom on my own, it quickly became all I could ever hope for. The night Xavier, Avice, Winter-Fae, and Annabel sowed their wild royal oats, it was a public spectacle all throughout the city. They were seen by humans— fornicating in midair, on rooftops, up and down the streets, even. I imagine if the Iron Lady was standing back then, their stink would probably still be rusted on it."

Julian tried to resist, but unable to see anything other than the mental image of all the king told him, he put his palm over his mouth to keep from laughing. Caanis took notice. "I see how most would find the humor in it. Going from such devastation in Germany, less than a decade before, to hunting down and killing dozens of humans to keep our new home a secret, I felt I had no choice but to teach my irresponsible son a lesson."

Caanis lifted the dagger to eye-level. He smirked at the blade before putting it back in its sheath, walking up the three steps, and then squatting on his throne. He laughed, saying, "I hate this chair. It is fucking uncomfortable. But as the saying goes: 'appearances are everything.'"

"But having that kind of power must be nice."

"Power, yes. Power is what makes the world spin. This power was meant for Xavier, whether he wanted it or not. I might have held anger and even some resentment towards him for what he did, but I'd heard stories of how he'd matured over the centuries. I know this popular new-age notion of feeding without killing or hurting humans was his idea. For these more modern times, it was a cunning initiative. He did well, and he will be missed."

"I miss him already … him and Violet."

"I never met Violet, but Winter-Fae told me about her. She looked up to Violet. She gives everyone names. She named her 'Hell Belle.'" Julian grinned, his day suddenly growing brighter. He'd known how she received the name, but not who christened it. "So!" Caanis blurted, slapping his hands together once and changing the subject. "Now that Xavier is gone, I am without an heir. I have yet to make it official, and I am trusting this will stay between us."

"Of course."

"The most obvious choice is my eldest daughter."

"If you want my honest opinion, I'm not sure how she would respond. She seems adamant on telling everyone to not call her 'princess,' but, personally, I think she would be an excellent choice."

"Yes, she would be a fine queen indeed. Unlike my other daughters, she is married. What queen could expect to properly rule the largest vampire kingdom in the world without a king to make all the big decisions for her?"

Julian snickered, imagining lowering his moral fiber and standards. Remembering what Pana said about training himself to keep other vampires from reading his thoughts, he said, "I also think Bernard would make a great king." The truth: *Bernard can go fuck himself.*

"I am glad you agree. His maker and I were never friends, even before we became enemies. I only met Bernard once before, but it was while he was still in Eustice Golding's 'company,' if you will. We never shared a word that day. If my daughter loves him enough to have saved and married him, he must be fit enough to rule my kingdom when I am gone. I plan to make the announcement when everyone is gathered in two days' time for the meeting. I only hope the rest of it goes as well."

"About that," Julian began, nervously rubbing the back of his head. "What will happen if Raz Ahrim was responsible for all these deaths and all that happened in New York?"

"You need not worry about that right now. You are here, and you are safe. Please, enjoy yourself. Life is too short to worry. All I ask is that you stay here until the matter is resolved."

Julian said, "I will, your highness." Caanis laughed, jokingly pointing at him while winking. Once the guffawing concluded, he asked, "Is there anything else I can do for you, Caanis?"

"No, that is all. Go, enjoy yourself."

"You too, sir." Julian turned to walk away, his eyes focused on the stairs ahead, centered between the two flights of stairs leading down to the stream. Until he knew he was far enough away from Caanis, he put all his thoughts into grabbing some clothes and taking a bath—anything to keep his mind from screaming what he couldn't help but really think: *Pompous son of a bitch!*

Chapter Nineteen

Julian had not bathed since his wedding night. Though he knew he needed one, he wasn't thrilled about the idea of washing himself in front of others. With no alternative but for his stink to linger, he gathered some clean clothes and an old red bottle of bodywash he'd packed when leaving Las Vegas, but never unpacked in Virginia. Then he headed down to the stream.

He descended the first set of stairs, glaring at the closed, polished gold door on his way down the second. At the bottom, he turned to face the third. The shallow decline led a dozen feet to the embankment. He stopped there, slowly panning his surroundings. The deep, narrow creek bed appeared from the far end: a steady stream of clear cave water, spewing from one black abyss and then swallowed by another.

The overhead ceiling arched high, and though they appeared harmless, a small group of bats hung throughout the humid chamber. Near the center of the fifty-foot waterway, the oval opening to a small grotto led away from the current. Every ten feet, a mounted burning torch lined the walls, creating sufficient lighting for the entire area.

Julian found a spot on the river's edge to set his clothes. He scanned the water again, counting three males. One of them was in the grotto which was also lit, but not as brightly as the rest of the cavern. Despite his naked antics in New York, Julian was bashful when removing his rags; stripping down to only his labradorite bracelet, gold wedding band, and the silver ankh pendant Violet gave him on a chain for his last birthday.

With the bodywash in hand, he inched into the flow. Sensing the cold, his own temperature never changed. He advanced farther until the water reached his waist. Then he lowered to his knees and dunked his head. When he came back up, he brushed his long, wet hair aside, catching a small, feminine silhouette approaching from the stairs. For a moment, he imagined his precious flower, there to join him for a bath. When passing the first torch, the dark figure turned white, dashing Julian's hopes.

After all the unwarranted uproar, he tried to ignore her. He squirted a handful of dark blue bodywash to use as shampoo, lathering his hair and dunking his head again to rinse. He emerged and rubbed any remaining soap from his eyes just in time to see what he was trying to avoid. Facing away, on the nearby bank, Winter-Fae let her white crocheted robe fall to the limestone floor. Julian knew he should've looked away, but her flawless milky-white skin and perfect backside were intoxicating to his eyes.

She stepped away from the pile of fabric, kicking off a white pair of sandals. She turned towards the water, Julian still watching, curious and shamefully aroused. On her way to the stream, she never looked directly in his direction, but the smirk on her face implied she knew he was watching. To Julian, her careless strut—taking her time to jump from a three-foot boulder—suggested she didn't care if he was. Just before diving in, he caught a full-frontal view.

Once her head pierced the surface of the water, she looked directly at him and said, "Hey. Come to the grotto with me. You'll like it there."

Unsure what she wanted or where the moment was leading, Julian reluctantly followed. Approaching the entrance, he discovered the man, previously there, was now gone. He waded through the passage, sensing an instant rise in his body temperature. Inside the limestone rotunda, he faced at least fifteen feet of lagoon. A single torch provided just enough light to follow the ginger walls high above his head. There, they domed like a martini glass at the center of a stalactite-heavy roof.

Settled in the back, Fae lounged like a mermaid. Stretched along a boulder near the wall, her curved hips sank just beneath the waterline, leaving her entire upper half exposed. Though fit, the faery was lean—so lean, in that position, her rawboned ribcage appeared more voluptuous than her modest bust. At the center of each breast, a perfectly proportioned areola offered the same hue as her soft pink lips.

Walking hunched, also waist deep in the water, and carrying his red bottle of bodywash, Julian made his way towards the back wall. "It's nice in here," he said.

"I like it," Fae said, her low chirps echoing, her eyes never straying.

He chuckled anxiously, his heart beating in his ears, his intuition screaming, *Violet is the one you want*, from somewhere in the backdrop. Having come to the creek with the intention of bathing, he looked at his bodywash, then, at Fae again, blushing. He was becoming erect beneath the water and not sure why. *This is weird.*

"I am so sorry about all that earlier with Avice," Fae said. "She is very protective of me. Many men have tried taking advantage of me in the past. Now, she likes to jump to conclusions."

"I noticed."

"She has a heart, I swear. Avice has saved my life more than once, and I owe her everything."

"What does she have against Anna?"

"Annie was Daddy's first, and Avice was always jealous of that. Over these last seventy-five years, it has only been the two of us. The bond we first created as orphans became even stronger after Annie left for America. Now that she is back home, Avice feels threatened, like she might not be Daddy's favorite anymore."

"Really? How could anyone choose her over you as their favorite anything?"

Fae smiled, but then it faded. "I am an oddity," she said, her soft, self-conscious tone nearly bringing Julian to tears.

He said, "No, you are not."

"Avice had to practically force Daddy to turn me."

"Why?"

"By the time I met her, she'd already had tuberculosis. It is still so hard to believe … all the time we spent together as humans, and I somehow never caught it. We met Daddy one night while begging for food. He took one look at her and knew death was close. In those days, finding food or money to buy it was difficult for orphans like us. So we could eat, Avice occasionally did things she still doesn't like to talk about. Caanis saw these things in her. It broke his barbarian heart. Rather than letting her die, he gave her something better."

"What about you?"

"The night Avice disappeared, I thought she might've been trying to make us some money, but the next day she never came back. I was so scared he'd killed her. For the next two weeks, I avoided everyone. I occasionally stole bread and fruit from random stalls when I knew I could get away with it.

"Then one night she found me. She wasn't the same Avice. She was healthy. Her skin had color again, and there was a light in her eyes I never saw before. At first, she was scared to tell me what happened, but eventually she confessed. She told me exactly how he did it and that she would live forever, cured of her disease."

"How did you feel about it?"

"Any ordinary person would have called her mad, but I knew she was telling me the truth. She said she could not be outside in daylight anymore and she had to go away. I begged for her to take me. She said she'd already asked, but he said no. She also said the others like her would kill me for my blood."

Fae rubbed her eyes. Julian moved closer, resting his back against the wall. "I loved her," she continued. "She was my sister before any of this. I cried and cried all night, saying anything I could to keep her from leaving me, but before the sun came up, she told me goodbye. And then, she left." Fae melted down the rock, easing further into the water until dunking her slender shoulders. "I spent the next day wandering, so certain I would never see her again. But that night, she came back. She said she told Daddy she would not live without me, and if he refused to offer me the same gift, she would stay by my side until the sun rose and took her from us both."

"And that is how it happened?"

"Yes, that is how it happened," she said, bobbing her head. "Not long before sunrise, Daddy came and took us to a nearby cellar he was using while in London. That very next night, I gave myself over to darkness, and in that darkness, my sister and I have dwelled ever since."

Surprised, Julian said, "I was starting to think I was the only one who willingly gave themselves over without sickness or impending death forcing it."

"There's more like us than you'd think."

"Do you regret it?"

"Sometimes, but overall, no. I learned long ago how to cope with who I am. I accepted my life, and though I mostly stay confined to the cave, I make the best of it."

"That's a good attitude," Julian said. "Honestly, I wish I was dead more often than I don't—at least now."

"We've all felt like that at one time or another. The way I see it, we are not doing anything we are not supposed to do. If it is God's will we roam this Earth forever, is that not the way it is supposed to be?" Once the conversation grew quiet, Fae pointed at the bottle in Julian's hand. "Aren't you going to take a bath?"

"I …" He blushed again. "I'm not used to bathing in front of other people. No offense, but it's a little strange."

Fae giggled. "I understand. How about I leave you to it?" Before Julian could answer, she stood. With the water swaying just above her abdomen, she splashed through the grotto towards the exit. Before leaving, she turned back and asked, "What are you doing later tonight?"

"What am I doing?"

"Yeah, what are you doing?"

"I don't know … reading, maybe? I don't know. Why?"

"There'll be a rave upstairs. Want to go with me?"

"To a rave? I—I didn't think Caanis wanted us to leave the cavern."

"It's not far, I promise. He probably won't even know we're gone. You'll be with me, so even if he did, I don't see why he would mind."

"But my shoes are still wet, and I don't want to walk through more water."

"Unless people from the surface bring an extra pair with them, nobody will have dry shoes. I promise we won't have to walk through any puddles or water of any kind. I know exactly where it's going to be."

"Well …" *Fuck it. Just go with her, you idiot! You deserve to have some fun.* "… all right, I'll go."

"Yay!" Fae squeaked with excitement, bouncing from the water, and giving Julian another full view. "It'll be closer to midnight, but I'll knock on your door when it's time to go."

"Okay." He watched her turn and leave. Then he spent the next several minutes frozen in place, thinking, *What the fuck is wrong with you, Julian? Widower or not, you're a married man. You never even consummated it. In dreams or the hereafter, you'll have your wedding night soon enough. You love Violet. You gave her your soul. Don't sell it to someone else.*

Taken so far from the present, the red bottle slipped from Julian's hand. When the water splashed him in the face, he snapped out of it, his arousal fading. Then, he finished his bath and left the creek, having little else to debate or think about than the obvious, and apparent night to come.

Chapter Twenty

Julian sat quietly in his dark room, watching what remained of the glowing embers in the pit. He wore blue jeans, a red shirt, and clean socks. The time on his phone read, *11:55 p.m. CET.* When he heard the door across the hall squeak open, he slipped on his damp sneakers. Three soft knocks tapped against his door as he did.

"Hey, Glowstick, it's me!"

"Coming." When Julian opened the door, he lost his breath. There, stood Winter-Fae: decked out, head to toe, in all purple. A pair of dancing shoes hugged her toothpick ankles. A silky, shimmering miniskirt hung halfway down her milky-white thighs. Fishnet stockings emerged from beneath. A narrow, purple sequin tube top covered her breasts but left her remaining torso exposed. Attached to her back, a pair of transparent faery wings, like one would find on a child's Halloween costume, spread out over half a foot—each dappled in tiny white lights. Her happy little face was neatly painted in purple lipstick, eyeshadow, and blush.

Atop Fae's head, a purple band held two short wire antennas, each crowned with a purple star. Her arms, shoulders, and the visible areas of her chest and stomach all sparkled with vanilla scented body glitter. On her wrists, hung glow-bracelets, and around her neck, glow-necklaces. In her left hand, she held a long white faery wand with a star on the end: the entirety flashing in bright multi-colored light. Aside from what glowed, everything was purple, even her short fingernails.

Julian's eyes bugged out as he tried to find the words. He had nothing. "Tonight is for our Hell Belle," Fae said.

"Wow!" he finally managed. Julian was utterly blown away—not just by the all-out appearance, but her touching tribute to his fallen angel, most of all. "You are a beautiful treasure," he said.

Fae chuckled. "I'm just me." She took a step back, tipping her head towards the main chamber. "Shall we?" Julian joined her. At the balcony, she said, "Before we leave, are you hungry?"

"Not necessarily, but I guess I could—"

She held up a finger. "Wait right here." He watched her skip away towards the room housing the well of blood, her wings flapping behind her.

While he waited, Julian peered over the balcony at several vampires on the floor below. He spotted Anna and Bernard talking. Though he could not distinguish theirs over all the other conversations, he noted their pleasant smiles and shared enthusiasm. *Good for her.* Still not Bernard's biggest fan, he even thought, *Good for them both.*

Further scanning the sea of people, he spotted a silhouette matching Violet's. Her hair appeared every inch as long. Her shape and size also matched: slim and short, but still nearly a foot taller than Winter-Fae. His eyes stayed locked on the figure until she moved closer into the light, revealing jet black hair and a golden olive face. She was pretty, but she was not Violet.

His hopes dashed again, Julian shut his eyes and sighed. *I miss you, my flower. I wish you would come back to me. How I long to touch you, to kiss you, to make love to you.* Then it was like a soft, warm hand took hold of his heart, safely nestling the muscle in a tender embrace. A series of light squeezes followed. The speed fluctuated, each set of pulsations coming in threes: *squeeze-squeeze-squeeze ... squeeze---squeeze---squeeze ... squeeze--squeeze--squeeze.*

Julian released a cool breath, muttering, "Violet? Is that you?" He put his palm over his heart, tapping his chest three times, once with each spoken word: "I love you." As if Violet was saying it back, her affectionate claps returned. *Squeeze-squeeze-squeeze ... squeeze---squeeze---squeeze ... squeeze--squeeze--squeeze.*

The moment became surreal. He grew weak in the knees, losing his balance. Before he could fall, he threw his arm out and took hold of the carved parapet separating him from the floor below. Carrying an IV bag, Fae returned just in time to see it happen. "Are you all right?"

Julian sucked in a deep breath and cleared his throat. "I can't explain it, but yeah. I'm okay."

"Here, have some." She handed him the bag with a drink already taken from it. "This will make you feel right." First, he sipped. The flavor was similar, but he could tell it was not the same blood he'd tasted last. He took a bigger drink. The sudden frailty that overwhelmed him resolved itself. He was refreshed, energized, and euphoric again. *"Thy drugs are quick."* Fae looked on with concerned eyes, asking again, "Are you okay, Glowstick?"

He handed her the bag and said, "Yeah, let's go dance."

At the bottom of the stairs, he looked over his shoulder, towards the steps leading down to the throne room. Since his last encounter with Caanis, he'd felt uneasy. It wasn't just his thoughts about the king of L'abisme, but what might happen when the king of Raz Ahrim and the queen of Taltosia met to discuss the possible betrayal of a truce intended to keep peace amongst the gods.

"Come on, little Glowstick," Fae said, tugging Julian's arm and pulling him on. "You're safe with me." Once they reached the other end of the chamber, she offered him the bag again. "There's one little gulp left. You want it?"

"Sure, why not?" He took the last drink, and they were off. Heading away from the light, he said, "I know you're glowing, but don't we need something brighter, like a torch or a flashlight?"

Fae held up her wand and smiled. She twisted a small dial on the handle. The star glowed, surrounding them in a bubble of bright white, offering more than enough luminosity to lead their way down the long hall to the equally long spiral staircase. Halfway up, Julian laughed, remembering all the times he'd climbed up and down the old wooden stairs of Leviticus. Leading the way, Fae asked, "What is so funny?"

"Déjà vu. Stairs and clubbing, just like last year."

"You mean, at Xavier's club in New York?"

"Yeah. Violet talked me into flying there with her from Las Vegas. That was before she even told me what she was. The first time I saw her fly, I thought she'd killed herself. She jumped off the side of a hotel without first telling me the punchline to her fucked-up joke." Now laughing, he added, "She scared the shit out of me quite a few times that day."

"Hell Belle was certainly spontaneous. Aside from her big heart, that wild spark was always my favorite thing about her."

Julian sighed. "I sure do miss her. Our time together ended before it really began. I never even got to make love to her."

With another fifteen feet of stairway left, Fae stopped and faced him. "That really meant something to you—making love to her?"

"I was only ever with one person I loved. I had a couple other intimate experiences, but they were all unfulfilling. It wasn't until after my time with the shaman and *Ayahuasca*, I began to heal and let that part of my life go. That is when Violet entered. I didn't question it. I followed my heart and fell in love with her; but being so sexually 'repressed,' for a lack of a better word, I craved intimacy with her.

"Am I selfish or shallow to feel so angry and cheated by a God who could do that to me … to let me feel like I could finally make love to a woman I am both physically and emotionally attracted to, but denied such things because 'He' decided I wasn't good enough for that by 'His' standards instead of my own?"

From two steps ahead, Fae gently caressed Julian's cheek with the back of her bent fingers. She said, "Some are far more and less reserved than others, but we all have needs. We all have desires. Such a sad, misled world will try to shame you for it, but to have these fantasies does not make you a monster. It means you are alive and breathing." She pulled away and turned back around, continuing, "… as for what God imposes, I believe we are all on a predestined path. You were only given what the universe felt you needed. It can be truly melancholic, but what we need is not always what we want."

"That is exactly what Pana told me in Alaska."

At the top of the stairs, Julian watched Fae push in the third brick from the right, on the eighth row, on the wall leading to the rest of the catacombs. When it unlocked, she spun the secret door wide enough for them to pass through. She put it back in place and opened the metal gate. From the other side, she closed it, and they turned right. "It's not far from here."

Julian followed her down a long corridor lined with bricks on each side. From a distance, a steady, rhythmic beat swirled into his ears. The closer they drew, the louder it grew. After turning a left corner, red and white lights bounced and reflected off the pale walls. Just ahead, the vampires reached their destination. From outside the entrance to a chamber full of people, lights, and speakers blaring deep trance music, Julian said, "I've never been to a rave before."

"You'll be fine. Just stay near me. If I grab your hand and tell you to run, follow me until we get out of sight. Sometimes the coppers will run up, but they won't catch us."

On their way inside, Julian was approached by a young male. "Hey! You want to buy some ecstasy?"

"No, thanks."

"Fuck you, then, you wank!"

He didn't see the boy say it, but Julian glared at him as if he did. He wore a backwards white baseball cap and a studded nose ring. The acne on his face said he was no older than his late teens. Ignoring everything he was told, Julian shouted, "What did you call me?!"

"What?!" the boy yelled back, wide-eyed and his color fading fast.

"Come on!" Fae took Julian's hand and led him inside the sizable chamber, packed with more people dancing than he could count. Most of them were lit up with glow sticks and flashy costumes as colorful as Winter-Fae's, but from what Julian saw, her attire was by far the best. At the front of the chamber, a large DJ-manned booth stood, its border of red and white strobe lights blasting with the beat. Behind it, Julian counted two generators.

Fae released his hand and started dancing. He watched, bobbing his head along. She took one look at him and laughed. "Come on, Glowstick! Do what I do!" Still holding her wand, again flashing multiple colors, she raised both of her hands as high as she could, swiveling her hips, and bending her knees with the rapid beat. Julian tried to copy her but only laughed at how silly he imagined himself looking in comparison.

He eventually started getting into it, feeling the music, and twisting his body more accordingly. Fae smiled, yelling, "That's it, Glowstick! You got it!" Seeing her happy filled him with joy. He was also happy for himself. It was good to feel something positive, for a change. Over the next several minutes, they danced facing one another. Julian watched Fae move like a professional, bold and unafraid of anyone's judgement. He wondered how long it took her to become so good at running circles around everyone who was running circles around him but couldn't hold a candle to her.

Those closest also took notice of how well she moved. As the music progressed, they began crowding them both, moving in unison to the throbbing pulse that was the bass coming from all the massive speakers around the room. When the beat dropped, so did they. At one point, Julian heard someone behind him shout, "That faery girl is fucking awesome!"

She sure is. Fae looked Julian's way and smiled. He smiled back. She came closer, so close that the soft starry ends of her antennae occasionally poked and prodded his neck and chin. He didn't mind. She slid her hands over his hips, letting him lead.

"… hey! What's that guy doing over there with that young girl!" Julian heard it. Fae must've also heard it, letting go and taking a step back. To avoid conflict, they spent the next hour dancing at a more reasonable distance. Julian assumed he would be exhausted, but he felt like he could dance forever, especially with the great company of the little faery princess.

Eventually, Fae's advanced moves caught everyone's attention again. This time, a tall, slender boy in a blue hoodie—appearing no older than the one at the door—danced his way directly between the girl and Julian. He couldn't even see her. Still dancing and trying to at least get close enough to know where she was, he moved to the boy's left. As if purposely trying to cut him off, the young man blocked him again. *You little shit!*

Julian heard, "Damn, girl, the things I'd do to you," coming from his direction. He was the only other one close enough to hear whose mouth Julian couldn't see. Trying to be civil and not cause a scene, he ignored it, knowing Fae would not fall for something like that. A moment later, he heard the boy again. "I want to take you in one of these empty rooms and fuck you raw. I'll show you my faery wand and wreck you with it in every little hole you got."

Mother fucker! Julian tapped the boy's shoulder, but he ignored him. He tapped harder. The boy glanced but kept dancing. "Hey! You need—" The boy turned his back towards Fae. The next time, Julian didn't tap. "I said, 'hey!'" He slapped his hand down hard on the boy's shoulder. He spun around fast, shoving his finger in Julian's face.

"What the fuck is your problem?!" the kid yelled, furiously spitting every syllable. As if any inhibition to remain on his best behavior was suddenly lost, Julian said nothing. Instead, he wrapped his hand around the boy's finger and without even trying, snapped it all the way back, ripping it from the socket.

The teenager howled like there was no tomorrow. That was when all the others close by saw the blood gushing. Some screamed for their lives. Fae pushed the boy aside on her way to Julian, shouting, "What the shit?! Why'd you do that?!"

"I heard what that thirsty little fuck said to you."

"Thought it! He didn't say it!"

The boy continued wailing in agony, his blood already covering most of his hand. Those who were the closest had started backing away. The music was still blaring as if news of the incident hadn't reached the DJ or all the others too busy dancing, tripping, or otherwise oblivious to the chaos they hadn't heard over their own good time. Before any further attention could be drawn to them, Fae grabbed Julian's hand, pulling him towards the exit. "We've got to get out of here!"

Making haste out the door, an older male voice yelled, "Hey! Stop!"

After turning the first corner and leaving any prying eyes behind, Fae held up her wand. Glowing solid white again, she said, "Put your arms around my shoulders and hold on!" Julian complied, and they were gone, blazing through the ancient mine. It took only seconds to return to the hidden doorway. Fae pushed the brick and opened the wall. On the other side, she put it back, and they both rushed down the spiral staircase, across the long hall, and back home safely.

Julian followed Fae towards the stairs on the other end of the main chamber. Those they passed along the way stared. Trying not to say anything anyone could hear, Julian only muttered, "I am sorry."

"Not here," Fae whispered back, in a cautious, not-so-sweet tone. Julian said nothing else. He followed her up the stairs and down the hallway towards their rooms, only able to wonder what the can of worms he had just opened could potentially do to him, Fae, or his other friends.

Chapter Twenty-One

Having spent the rest of his night lying awake, Julian's stomach churned, battering himself with guilt. *My new friend must hate me now.* The way she had looked at him when he ripped the kid's finger off—so angered and mortified—he feared he ruined everything. *What if Caanis finds out?* He shivered at the idea.

Trying to relax, he shut his eyes, desperately hoping to sleep and start over when he awoke, but there, he saw *her*, his one true love: his night, day, and everything in between. Winter-Fae had even tried to pay tribute to her, not just because she adored her, but because she knew it would bring Julian one step closer to the happiness he left buried across the ocean. He knew that. *And this is how I repay her, permanently disfiguring some snotty pervert in front of her and so many others. Shame on me!*

With the fire long gone, the room lay dark and silent. Julian used his vampire ears, listening for anything from the room across the hall—number forty-four. He occasionally heard others passing, but nothing from the princess. He even imagined Violet bursting through the door, taking him away from such a place, and going home. Then he could have his so-called "perfect life," and maybe even fix things with Daryl. Anything was ideal over just lying there, worrying.

Finally, he got up and checked his phone. *8:22 a.m. CET. Jan 5, 2020*, it read. Having given up on trying to sleep, and still a full day before the meeting of the kingdoms, he thought, *What now?* Little time passed before receiving an answer.

First, the knock came to Fae's door. When it cracked open, a soft, not-so-chipper voice said, "What?"

"Daddy wants to see you."

"Okay."

"He wants to see him too. Is he in there with you?"

"What?! No! Why would …" Winter-Fae sighed.

Already nauseous, his head reeling and thinking the worst, Julian's heart dropped when the knock came to his door next. He took his time getting there. When he opened it, he first saw Avice. Fae stood behind her, wearing her usual white robe. Though most of it had been wiped away, faint traces of purple makeup remained on her cheeks and in the corners of her eyes. Grimacing, Avice said, "The king would like a word with you."

"What does he want?"

"He wants you to go have a word with him," she remarked. Julian looked past the stone-cold brunette. Fae's oceanics splashed the floor, unable to match his wave of intent. "Put your shoes on and come," Avice demanded.

"Goddamn it," Julian grumbled, sliding his feet into his dry shoes. He tied them and followed the sisters. The entire way, no one said a word. They walked down both flights of stairs, through the open gold doorway, and into the throne room.

At the other end, Caanis sat on his chair, his eyes locked directly on Julian's. From analyzing his mouth, cheeks, and posture, he could not discern the king's mood, but in his gut, he felt certain the king knew what he had done. During the entirety of the long walk, Caanis never blinked or looked away. Finally, when everyone stood just five feet from him, he held up his hand, stopping them at once.

To Avice, he said "Thank you, Princess. You may go now." She smiled at him and curtsied before turning and walking away. His eyes roamed beyond Julian and Fae, watching his loyal daughter leave the room, her echoing footsteps fading away. Once she was gone, Caanis looked back at Julian, then Fae. "I trust you had fun last night?"

"Daddy, I—"

Caanis raised his hand again, silencing her. "Paul, Teddy, Avice, and others were approached by policemen in the caves before daybreak. None of whom were the least concerned with their trespass, but a specific incident. Last night, a sixteen-year-old human boy was attacked at one of these 'rave-dance' socials you suddenly enjoy attending so much."

He distinctly glared at Julian, sending a sharp chill throughout his already frozen frame. Returning to Fae, he continued. "A 'little purple and white faery girl,' as they all claimed—" Caanis pointed at the little white faery girl's purple-speckled face. "—was with a 'grown man with long brown hair and wearing a red shirt.'" Caanis pointed at Julian's red shirt. "I even spoke to some here this morning who saw you both coming back in, appearing distressed."

The king panned between them both, adding, "Which of you want to begin telling me how and why this happened, and why you—" he pointed at Julian. "—were there when I commanded you to stay here!"

"I … I did it," Julian said. "We were dancing, and the boy kept butting in front of me. I—I couldn't see his face, but I kept hearing him say some crude and disrespectful things to her."

Fae said, "I told you he did not say those things. He only thought them."

"At the time I didn't know that. I—I have no clue how reading minds even works."

"Silence!" Caanis shouted. "What were you doing there?"

"I—I was just trying to enjoy myself, like you had suggested. Fae told me you—"

"What?" Caanis interrupted, his gaze shifting to his daughter. "Fae told you what?"

"Sh—she said you wouldn't mind, since it wasn't far from here and she would be with me."

Caanis asked Fae, "Is this true?"

"Yes, Daddy, it is true," she muttered, bowing her head in shame.

"It wasn't her fault!" The king turned his attention back to Julian. "Princess Winter-Fae knows how torn up I've been since my Violet died. She just wanted to cheer me up. That is why she was wearing all purple—not only because of Violet's name, but because purple was her favorite color. I swear she meant no harm."

Ignoring him, Caanis asked Fae, "What did you do when he attacked the boy?"

"We got out of there. I waited until we were away from anyone in the hallway, and then I flew us both to the wall." Julian nodded to confirm the claim. "Daddy, there were so many people in there. The music was so loud and dark, the only people who saw it were those closest to us."

"The number of people who saw what happened does not matter. Enough saw it to involve the police."

"Daddy, it's not like they don't find bodies up there all the time. Julian didn't kill him. He only ripped his finger off."

"That is not the point!" The king's cheeks swelled. He asked Julian, "What do you think will happen if anyone who is not supposed to know we are here, finds us?"

"I—I don't know."

"You don't know?" Shaking his head and sneering in disbelief, he threw his hands up when looking back at his daughter. "I really don't understand what has become of you lately. First, your brother passes, and you disappear … to only Odin knows where, and now, this?" He stared at her in silence for several seconds, likely contemplating his next words before finally settling on, "Thank you for your honesty. You may go now."

"But Daddy, please don't do any—"

"I said go!" he shouted. Fae jumped before turning to leave. "Oh, and do not do this man any more favors, my precious daughter." Once the tiny footsteps dissolved into silence, the mighty Viking stood from his throne, staring an even mightier hole through Julian. He took his time descending the stairs, every step echoing louder than the last.

Just like the first time they met, the king looked down on the helpless whelp. He took in a series of deep, angry breaths, the kind a raging bull would just before charging. Trembling with all he had not to strike, Caanis spoke calmly, instead. "If you were not needed tomorrow, and if Violet or Eric were still alive—leaving my son another heir to his coven—I would kill you for this. I would kill you just like I killed all the others Xavier once made."

Julian gasped. *It was you!*

"Yes, it was," he confirmed. "My son was irresponsible in his youth. He put his cock in anything that would allow it. He truly believed he could make other vampires and pass that legacy on to them. After all we suffered in Germany, and like it was nothing to him, my son nearly jeopardized everything for the gilded cunts of my daughters."

His body tense, Julian listened, a terror rising that even his darkest longing for death could not contest. "I told you yesterday, I had later become proud of my son and the coven he created, but while here and in Germany, I would not dare allow him to create another. So, as he'd slumber, weakened from offering his blood, I'd suffocate them while they too slept, healing from the change." Caanis smiled like he was proud of it.

"Not even a week has passed since the entire world saw what happened in New York. Again, my son was at the forefront of it. He opened that establishment to spite me. It was that which led to his own demise. What he did cannot be undone. And now, you add logs to my pyre. After I spoke so highly of you—commending your maturity and confiding in you, a stranger, who I plan to name as my new heir. This is how you honor the respect I have shown you?"

When he paused, Julian took it as a sign he was waiting for an answer. "Your—your highness, please. If I knew what was happening last night, I swear to you, I would have—" Caanis snapped like a whip of lightning. Before Julian knew it, he was violently hoisted high above the king's head, one massive professional-wrestler-sized hand crushing his throat. Julian gasped and grunted, unable to breathe. He kicked his legs by instinct, losing both shoes, trying to wiggle free.

"Listen here!" Caanis growled. "We all have sickening thoughts! We are all monsters! Humans … vampires … we are all cruel, aberrant vultures of filth and habit! It is only when we act on those atrocities, we become them! Do you understand?!"

"Ye—ye—yes!" Julian struggled. Even his vision blurred. "Pl—please … c-can't breathe!"

Caanis released his grip, and Julian fell to the rock floor, coughing, wheezing, and gasping for air. Above all the horror of trying to catch his breath while fearing the king wasn't finished, he thought he was going to die. For the first time since Violet's death, he was afraid to join her. Caanis shouted, "Get up!" He was slow putting his shoes back on, but he obeyed, standing and trying to take a full breath without coughing.

"Now, when I say stay here, I mean, stay here! Do you understand?" Unable to speak, Julian bobbed his head repeatedly in compliance. "After tomorrow, you can go run into the sun for all I care, but for right now, I still need you to tell your side of the story to the others. However, if you do anything else to defy me or bring any further attention to us, I will see to it that you suffer. Mark my words: I know how to make someone suffer. Do you understand me?" Again, Julian nodded. Caanis returned to his throne. "Now, get out of my sight."

Julian turned and walked away, focusing all his thoughts on the only thing that still mattered to him. He pictured *her* perfect face so intensely, he could even smell her vanilla. No thought of her was ever as graceful as the one he forced upon himself now to avoid anything inconspicuous. When he made it back upstairs to the balcony, he could finally breathe properly and groan, "I'm tired, Violet. I just want to come home."

Chapter Twenty-Two

Though exhausted, Julian was too scared to shut his burning eyes. He didn't want to believe Caanis would just barge in and murder him in his sleep, but the more he learned about the man, the more he began to despise him. *How could he claim to love his son and do something so horrible? If he would kill Xavier's others, what would stop him from killing me too?* Unsure if Winter-Fae could hear his thoughts from across the hall, he took a deep breath, trying to refocus. *Get up and go get some blood.* Minding his inner voice, he put on his shoes and headed to the room with the blood well.

Lucky for him, someone already had the net cranked to the surface. To his surprise, it was the woman he'd seen the night before, with jet-black hair and golden olive skin. When approaching the pit, the young woman's bright green eyes met his, and she smiled. "Hello," Julian said. She bobbed her head, and though her welcoming twinkle remained, she said nothing. Julian reached toward the fishing net, asking, "May I?" Again, the woman nodded. He took a bag and bowed his head. "Thank you," he said, stepping away from the well and watching her lower the net.

"Oi!" a familiar voice yelped from behind. Julian turned to find Anna wrapped in a beige bathrobe, her frizzy red hair a mess. Staring past Julian at the other woman, she said, "Hold on, Yara." Still smiling, the woman backed away. Anna took the crank and brought the net back up. "Thanks, love," she said. The woman nodded again. Then she took her own bag and left the room.

"That's Yara," Anna said. "She is kind, but I guess no one has ever taught her English. She speaks Arabic."

"Is she Middle Eastern?"

"Egyptian, but she's no Ahrim. She found us not long before I came to New York. My father welcomed her in."

"Speaking of Caanis, that man is a fucking psycho!"

"Says the bloke who tore a kid's finger off."

Watching Anna take two bags from the net, he said, "You heard about that?"

"Everybody heard."

"First of all, I didn't know he was only sixteen. He had his back to me, and he was blocking me from Fae."

"So? Was she not allowed to dance with other people?"

"It's not like that."

"You got a thing for her or something?"

"I love Violet. What is it with everyone assuming there's something going on between us? First, it was Avice, and now you. Why?"

"Because you've been spending an awful lotta time with her since you met. I saw you together last night."

"She was nice to me, and we were friends."

"'Were?'"

"After last night, and earlier, Caanis telling her not to do me any more favors, I doubt she'll ever talk to me again."

"Nah, she will. She knows Dad's pissed, and she probably just wants to wait for things to die down."

"He picked me up by the throat and choked me out. It hurt, and it scared the fuck out of me. I seriously thought he was going to kill me. I don't feel safe here."

"Dad has a lot on his mind right now, and although he shouldn't take it out on you like that, you shouldn't have attacked that kid either. There were cops up there looking for you. After New York, can you blame him for being so paranoid?"

"I guess not, but I still think he overreacted. I told him, the boy's back was to me, and I had no idea I was reading his mind. I thought he was telling Fae he wanted to fuck her raw. I was only trying to protect her."

Anna laughed. "Fae can protect herself against horny teenage cunts."

"I didn't know he was a teenager. He was tall, and like I said, I couldn't see his face. I only heard him going on about wanting to put his 'faery wand' in her. Believe me, I know she can protect herself, but I was still trying to be a gentleman. I really didn't mean to break off his finger like that. I got caught up in the moment and forgot my own strength."

While he took a drink from his IV bag, Anna said, "Do you remember last year, when we were talking at the bar? I was telling you about all the dirty things I'd hear men thinking about me, and how Bern would react if he knew—remember?"

"I remember."

"People think all kinds of dirty things. People just never know it because they are meant to be private. Aside from the person having the thought, we are the only ones who can hear them. Just because that boy had those thoughts, doesn't mean he would have done it."

"Thinking shit like that … if he had the chance to get with her, you're telling me he wouldn't do it?"

"No, I'm not saying that. I am saying we are all deviant creatures. We all have intense thoughts. Thoughts ain't actions. Actions are actions."

"I get what you're saying, but the way it came out sounded like he wanted to have his way with her."

"What if he did?" Anna held the ends of both bags in one hand, using the other to crank the net down into the well. "Can you honestly say you've never had any sexual thoughts about Violet?"

"Yeah, but not like that."

"How old are you, Julian?"

"Thirty-eight."

"A mature thirty-eight, I might add. And how old's that boy?"

"I get it." He sighed, almost snickering. Everything Anna said resonated. Knowing he needed to come clean and confide it in somebody, he said, "Maybe you and Avice are right; I don't know. Yesterday, while I was bathing, I saw Fae. All of Fae. She showed up not long after I did. When I saw her like that, I admit it: I was aroused. It's not that I have a 'thing' for her. It's that I—"

"You're grieving, Julian. You are lonely and confused. Believe me when I say I understand it more than you do. It's like Fae even said when we first arrived, we all grieve differently."

"I love Violet. All this has been for her. I don't want to feel these things for other women. Last year at the club, I had the chance to get with two attractive ladies who liked my song. I didn't want them. I wanted Violet. That was before I fell in love with her. And now—" he shrugged his shoulders.

"Fae is amazing, and I think she has a perfect body. It's no wonder that boy wanted her. Even though I thought he was saying those things, maybe my reaction was more of jealousy than protection. Either way, I feel like it's an insult to Violet, what we had, and what we can hopefully have again. I've even insulted myself, feeling that way for someone else, whether it be sexual, emotional, or both."

"So, you do feel something for my sister?"

"I don't know." He sighed again. "Like you said, I'm lonely. What kind of hypocrite does that make me? I don't know if I'm going crazy or what is happening to me, but every shadow I see is Violet. Everything I physically feel inside my body is Violet. I've had two lucid dreams of her since she died. In one, she tried to make love to me. In the other, she couldn't find me. It's like we are in limbo. I keep trying to convince myself, when I die, we will be together forever in a heaven created by a God I sometimes believe in, and other times wish I knew existed so I could spit in its face."

"It sounds like you've got a lot to think about, love."

"But I don't. Fae has been such a welcoming presence since losing Violet, but she's just that. I took a vow, a vow I intend to keep. Honestly, I don't even see mine and Fae's friendship recovering now, anyway. Besides, after the meeting tomorrow, I want to get out of here. What Caanis did to me was unacceptable. I don't want to be here any longer than I have to."

"Relax, love. Dad's not going to kill you."

Julian wondered if he should tell her what Caanis did to Xavier's children. Then, he remembered what his maker said that there are some things people don't need to know. With Caanis telling Julian he'd chosen Anna to be his heir, he thought it would be better to say nothing, assuming she would believe him if he had. "Regardless, I want to leave."

"Then what? You can't fly. Where would you get blood?"

"I don't know. Maybe I could go back to Alaska until I adapt."

"Only you know what's right." Anna turned towards the doorway. "I'm going back to mine and Bern's room now. I just wanted to come grab us some lunch."

"How are things between you two?"

"They're getting better. Aside from that shite with Avice the other day, it's like Bern's a whole other man since we got here. I don't understand it, but I ain't complaining. I've not felt this way in a long time."

"Not since Xavier?" ... *Oh, fuck me! Goddamn it!* He cringed, immediately regretting the slip-up.

"Xavier?" Her jaw fell open. "What do you mean?"

"Nothing. It's just ... I had this weird dream recently."

Her eyes growing concerned, she asked, "What dream?"

"The day after Violet and Xavier died, when I woke up and told you about the diary, I also dreamt of you." He glanced at the doorway to make sure Bernard wasn't there. "You told me you and Xavier were once lovers."

"Once," she said. "That one time. But that one time was a mistake."

"Not that. Before then, in Germany."

Anna gasped. "How did you ..." She turned towards the doorway. "It doesn't matter. It was just a dream."

"I'm sorry. I wasn't trying to impose. I just—"

"It's fine!" Standing just outside the door, her back to him, and starting to sadden, Anna quavered, "Just stay out of trouble. Let Fae come to you. After tomorrow, do what you want." As her footsteps receded, her wailing grew shrill but quickly silenced just as it began.

Like he didn't already have enough to feel terrible about, Julian also wanted to cry. Unlike the future queen, he had no tears. *Everything I touch burns to ashes*, he thought, leaving the room, headed back towards his own. While passing the balcony, he came face to face with Avice, walking in the direction of the blood well. They briefly made eye contact, but neither spoke. Julian respected the princess for her love and devotion to Winter-Fae, but like Caanis, he wanted as little to do with her as possible.

Back at his room, before opening the door, he looked at the one opposite his—eyeing the two white fours, hand painted over the black metal. Though he wasn't trying to listen, he thought he heard humming on the other side. It was Fae, and it sounded just like one of the first beats they danced to at the rave. Julian smiled, feeling a small flicker of hope—not for anything romantic or sexual—but friendship. He needed a friend, one just as every bit weird and free-spirited as him.

Chapter Twenty–Three

Having spent the afternoon and evening resting in his room, Julian was still unable to sleep. Throughout the day, he'd heard Winter-Fae occasionally leave her room, never staying away long. *What the hell does everyone do around here for centuries on end and never get tired of?* Though his eyes seared with restlessness, he gave himself an idea. He retrieved his leather jacket from the floor, removing Violet's diary from the hidden pocket where he'd put it the day before. Finding his place, he started reading to himself.

3/3/45

Dear Diary

Since my last entry, Eric's body has healed! The rest of him, not so much. He only talks to me when he has to. Otherwise, he says nothing to me or Xavier. Autumn came back last week for her and William's belongings. She said she can't live here anymore. For the love of her oldest son, and out of respect for all Xavier had done for them over the last seven years, she swore our secret was safe with her. I tried talking to her, but she refused. She wouldn't even look at me. She hates me. I don't blame her. I stole her baby from her. It is my fault Eric is like this now. I hate myself too.

Just like when they were all living here as a big happy family, Xavier is paying Autumn's bills at her new place. He feels as responsible about all this as I do. I have asked him so many times these last few weeks, why? Why any of this? Why do we learn to love something so deeply only for it to be taken from us so soon? Is this truly life as we know it, or is it Hell, run by a devil disguising itself as God?

When I first began this journey, I believed in God. Now, I don't know if I want to anymore. For the first time in my life, I fell in love, but I couldn't express that love physically. Even if Eric can ever forgive me, I will never forgive myself. It will never be the same, and neither will he nor I. What a world we live in, Diary. What a world, indeed.

Violet

"Wow," Julian breathed. "She was feeling so much—many of the same feelings then that I am now, I suppose. I wonder if that's why she wanted me to find her diary." He turned the page and continued.

4/13/45

Dear Diary

My birthday was two days ago, but it was uneventful. I haven't had anything to say lately. Perhaps it's because I wanted to wait until I had something positive to share. This book only has so many pages in it, and I don't want to waste them on nothing. Forever might take a while. Over these last five weeks, things between Eric and I have started to improve. He is coming into his powers. He can even fly faster than I can, but I seem to be better at reading people's minds than he is.

So, last night we finally talked about it. I'd been dreading it. He had been too. He told me he forgave me. It was relieving to hear. I know it just happened, and he has no idea how it will affect him in the long-term, but I also know he meant it. I still don't know if I will ever be able to forgive myself. Do I even deserve to? As a vampire, I have an eternity to try, I suppose. Though it is our fate to roam this Earth forever, along with our creator and "father figure," Xavier, I still don't know where Eric and I stand beyond that. I've got time. I'll just have to wait and see. This is progress, though. Wish us luck!

Violet

7/4/45
Dear Diary

    Today is Independence Day in more ways than one. A couple of nights ago, I met Xavier's sister, Annabel. She came because she needed Xavier's help. She said there is an Austrian vampire, named Bernard, being held captive by another vampire. She seems to have a big heart like her brother. She asked him to help her free Bernard.

    After dark, Xavier left with her to go to Europe, leaving me and Eric here alone together for the first time like this. Xavier has forbidden us from killing anyone for blood, so he left us enough in the freezer for a week. I don't know where he gets it, but he swears it came from donors.

    I worry for Xavier, his sister, and Bernard. I don't really know the situation, but I wish them a safe return. I am so nervous about being here alone with Eric, though. I love him and I believe he loves me, but I don't think he feels like a man anymore. I tried to kiss him last month, but he wasn't interested. I told him there are other things we could try, but he's not interested in anything at all. I understand why he feels that way, but I hope one day he changes his mind.

    Although my biological father stole my innocence, I gave my virginity to Eric. He's the only man I've ever wanted that way, and despite how it ended so horribly, at first it was great! I never knew it would feel so good. Now, I want more, but I can't have it … at least, not with him. I will never try anything like that with a human again.

    Xavier feels just as guilty about it as I do. He knew we had feelings for one another, but he had no clue I would try to fuck him out of nowhere like that. Honestly, neither did I until it happened. Xavier said he never thought to tell me to exercise caution. What I wouldn't give to go back in time, like something in a science fiction book. I could change everything. But then, if I could do that, knowing everything I knew now, would I have even come to New York at all?

Violet

She had married Julian in the end, but naturally he wasn't very comfortable reading his flower's confessions of wanting another man. But he also knew it was like Anna telling Bernard in Alaska that she'd lived many years before he was ever born. How could he or Julian expect their lovers to remain celibate for someone who didn't even exist yet? Beyond her feelings for Eric, Julian understood Violet's frustration, having just confided his own desires to Winter-Fae, the night before. He turned the page and read the next.

7/11/45

Dear Diary

Last night, Xavier and Annabel came home. They were not alone. In addition to Bernard, who seems so lost, I met one of Xavier's other sisters. Her name is Winter-Fae. She's the cutest little thing I've ever seen, and though she is almost three hundred years old, there is a youthful charm about her. Her skin and hair are solid white, and she is so short. I thought I was tiny, but she's nearly a foot shorter than me!

She said she was eighteen when she was turned, but she was born prematurely, and it must have stunted her growth. She seems so sweet and gentle. She took one look at me and said I was an auburn Aries—a real "Hell Belle." Eric and Annabel both got a kick out of it. Now they keep going out of their way to call me Hell Belle. As for Bernard, he's not said a word to me or Eric. I don't think he's even said anything to Xavier since they got here. I have an idea of what happened to him, but to what extent, I have no clue. Something seems off about him, though.

Right now, I don't know if any of them are planning on staying here with us, but I hope they do. Annabel and Winter-Fae are great. Although I don't see it, Bernard must be great too, or else someone as old and wise as Annabel would not have come to her brother for help, over 150 years after parting ways.

Xavier had told me all about what happened between him and his sisters, but I wonder if there is more to it. The way he and Annabel looked at each other when she first got here seemed more personal than a normal brother-and-sister relationship. I know they aren't really brother and sister, and after so long apart, I am sure they were just naturally happy to see one another.

Their interactions together now since returning with Bernard, compared to before leaving for Austria, seem so reserved. Even Eric noticed, so I know it's not just me. Xavier said their time together was an accident and it only happened once ... but a woman's intuition, combined with vampiric insight makes me wonder. Maybe I am overthinking it. Either way, I am just happy they are back home and safe!

Violet

Julian mumbled, "Even she thought something was going on between them ... and right from the start." He remembered Anna's confession in his dream and her reaction when foolishly confronted. Along with Violet's entry, he could no longer help believing there really was more than just a single engagement. Curious, and wanting to know more, he continued.

9/15/45
Dear Diary

I am sad, Diary. Last night, Anna took Fae back to Paris. Fae can fly, but she was too scared to go so far alone. I completely understand that. I never learned to swim, and I would not want to fly across the ocean by myself either. For a while, I thought she might stay here with us. I wish she would have. We got along so well. Xavier even rented apartment 33 for her, downstairs.

Four nights ago, Xavier took Fae and Anna to see a Broadway play called "A Boy Who Lived Twice." Apparently, people kept heckling Fae over her appearance. Someone even called her a witch! I felt so bad for her. She told me she hated going out in public because nobody understands her condition. She said living in a cave, where she only associates with people who already know her, is so much easier than pretending like she can fit in with a society of such dangerously misguided people. So, she went back home tonight.

Bernard stayed here, instead of going with Anna. Not only did Xavier get that studio for Fae, but he also got Anna and Bernard the empty apartment down the hall—number 41. I heard Anna tell Xavier, Bernard has really bad nightmares. She wanted to be near him. Since they moved down the hall, I haven't seen him.

Xavier and Eric have both tried to bond with him, but Bernard acts like he wants nothing to do with either of them. Xavier says it is like he became so desensitized through all the abuse from the vampire who kept him locked away for so many years, Bernard has no idea how to function without him. He said Bernard needs space and time to readjust. He will never be the same. I can't even imagine what that must feel like.

Speaking of Xavier, I finally grew brave and asked about his and Anna's past. He swears, beyond the orgy, there isn't one. He wouldn't say anything else. I want to believe him, but I don't. He has told me, in the past he loved many women, but after his castration, everything changed. Considering what I have seen from Eric, I believe him. Like Eric, I think losing his penis shattered Xavier as a man and made him feel inadequate. If only he had not smoked that opium with his sisters, nothing would have happened. Then again, would I be alive right now if he hadn't? I know opium and alcohol are different, but from my own experience, I know the damage intoxication can cause.

If there really was something more between Xavier and his sister, I can only hope it does not lead to any problems now. Anna is sweet and compassionate like her brother and little sister. I feel like she could be the big sister I never had. I don't want her to leave us the way Fae did. I still don't know enough about Bernard to develop a proper opinion about him yet, but after everything he has endured, he deserves a fair chance, along with peace and happiness, just like we all do.

Violet

Julian turned the page, prepared to read more, when a shout, "It's the Taltosians!" came charging through the room. "They are here! Queen Dajhri has arrived!" The shrill, upbeat male voice came from somewhere in the hallway. "Everyone, come see!"

His interest piqued, Julian put on his shoes and shot out the door, just as Winter-Fae did the same. Their eyes briefly met. Hers offered no signs of animosity, but she said nothing. Together, they rushed down the hallway. Julian stopped at the balcony, where others were quickly gathering. Fae continued down the stairs to the chamber floor. She joined Avice and their father, both standing at the center, facing the vacant entrance at the other end.

Julian mumbled, "Well, where are they?"

From his left, a tall pasty man said, "They're either coming down the stairs or the hall, mate. I reckon someone came ahead to prepare us."

Anna and Bernard caught Julian's eye, descending the stairs on his right, and then joining the other royals in the center. Many vampires crowded either side of the chamber floor, parting it like the Red Sea, creating a wide, central walkway. Julian said, "I didn't think the meeting was until tomorrow."

The same man said, "It ain't. Peru time is several hours behind us. Their sunset's only a few hours before our sunrise. It is a very long journey, so coming early just makes more sense, you know?"

"Yeah, I suppose so," Julian said, watching movement appear at the entrance.

Two figures took shape from the darkness, trudging side by side, each covered in a brown, hooded cloak. Two more emerged five feet behind them. As the cloaks marched onward, a lone figure came forward, dressed in a simple green gown. From two hundred feet away, Julian could not distinguish their facial features, but he recognized a dark-haired woman. She ambled several feet into the chamber before stepping aside, offering a clear view of the shadowy entry. The four cloaked figures ahead of her halted. The two rows turned to face their opposites. Each figure then took five steps backwards, leaving an open space for everyone to see what was to come.

The woman in green was small to Julian's eyes, even from a distance, but her high-impact delivery rocked the cavern like a quake. "Presenting: Queen Dajhri of Taltosia!" Julian thought everyone might cheer, but the only sound came from his heart, rattling with anticipation.

A petite figure came into the light. She wore a shimmering white gown, so long, its spotless hem nearly brushed the floor. From a distance, Julian fixed his gaze on a dark mass bundled atop her head. Though he could see everything as a vampire compared to nothing as a human, between such a distance and the low lighting, the finer features of the queen remained a mystery.

With poise, Dajhri sashayed by the woman who presented her. She followed her queen from there. When they both passed the hooded figures, they too followed; first, the row nearest, then the farthest. The six Taltosians made their way along the chamber's center. Everyone they passed looked on in astonishment—as if the historical moment Queen Dajhri graced the haunted halls of L'abisme with her legendary presence had never and would never happen again. By the time the queen and her entourage reached the king and his, Julian recognized the mahogany mass above her head as hair. Only a shade or two darker than Violet's auburn, her royal locks tightly constructed a beehive, so tall it would be obnoxious if not so elegant and decoratively tied in place by thin gold twine.

Still not close enough to see her face, Julian observed the queen's fair mocha skin. Although every woman he'd seen since her death resembled Violet in one way or another, Dajhri's shape and colors seemed almost identical. Caanis stepped forward, his daughters and Bernard close behind. "With the heart of a queen and the emerald eyes of a goddess: as I live and breathe. Queen Dajhri, you are as stunning as ever." He took the queen's hand in his and kissed the back of it. "Those eyes," he continued with such admiration. "Only once before have I seen such eyes as yours."

"Caanis," the queen softly moaned as she curtsied. Her silky, venomous voice was like a heavenly harp to Julian's ears. If he could float to such a heaven, the air would be her voice. It was pure entrancement: the most relaxing voice he'd ever heard.

Dajhri peered beyond the king first, at Avice. She gently bowed her head and Avice did the same. Next, was Winter-Fae. She approached the porcelain doll and took both of her tiny hands. "I've seen many of our kind since we first and last met, little one. In all the years, you are still the most breathtaking of them all, darling Winter-Fae." Again, Julian shrugged. There was something about her voice that he could not resist.

"Your highness …" Fae smiled as she curtsied.

Dajhri moved on to Anna, bowing to her. "Please accept my condolences, Annabel. Of your father and sisters, I know you were the closest to your brother." Anna returned the gesture but said nothing back. The queen looked in Bernard's direction but only addressed him with a smile and nod. In response, he did the same.

Caanis stepped forward, facing all the Taltosians. "You have traveled far, and you must be tired. Please, allow my daughters to show you to your rooms." To Dajhri, he said, "We can meet in the morning to discuss some matters before the Ahrims arrive."

Softly, the queen said, "Very well."

Caanis turned and walked away, disappearing beneath the balcony. The four cloaked figures removed their hoods. Beneath them were a group of swarthy men. All but one featured a headful of dark chocolate hair. The exception was bald, a narrow, tawny mustache running the distance of his broad upper lip. Fae and Avice led them up the stairway on Julian's left. Bernard lingering behind them, Anna led Dajhri and her maiden up the stairs on the right. By the time they all reached the top and met in the middle, the local vampires were already returning to their rooms or elsewhere.

Now only ten feet away, Julian caught a better view of the queen's teardrop-shaped face. Her full, naturally puckered lips rested comfortably beneath an aquiline nose. Symmetrical to both, a pair of high cheekbones and distinctly dramatic eyes completed the ensemble. Each iris—such a deep, vibrant forest of green—forever circled in a bold black ring.

Julian gasped, finding such depth in her eyes. Before him stood an exquisite specimen of woman, highly dignified in her own acclaim, who had endured biblical mounds of war-torn oppression to claw her way to the prestige she'd come to hold so dearly. When she and her handmaiden were led right by him, Dajhri looked directly into his eyes, reversing the microscope.

Though she never stopped walking, time became an abstract concept, leaving nothing to disturb them from sharing a glance that went on forever and never. As if the virulent gaze wasn't enough to shatter his universe in such a way he'd find acceptable, the same venomous voice he'd let in his heart like it was Jesus Christ, whispered a lullaby. "Are you the one?" Her lips never moved, and it was not like he heard the queen's thoughts, but her thoughts became his own.

Once she, her company, and the others disappeared down the central hallway and out of sight, Julian snapped back to reality. *What the hell just happened? Fuck, I really need some sleep.*

Chapter Twenty—Four

Ever since Violet's death, Julian begged for his own. Not until Caanis whispered it in his ear had he opened his eyes. Until then, he thought he'd be happy, drawing his final breath and falling into his lover's arms. But he wasn't ready. Not yet. To him, the sudden will to survive meant his journey was far from over. Still, it was rightful guilt and fear that had kept him awake the night before. Now, he lay restless—no fire in the pit or sounds within earshot—asking himself, *Why? What purpose could I still have here?*

He yawned and closed his eyes, hoping to finally sleep. His chaotic thoughts adrift, Julian retracted, centering on the dreams he'd come to love and hate. He was thankful for receiving Xavier and all he still had to offer, but he craved Violet the most. He only wished she would come to him in the same capacity as their maker, offering something more than a shadow or an interrupted rendezvous.

He hadn't slept since the night he arrived at L'abisme. He was so tired and weak, not from hunger but running on fumes all day. Though it was nothing compared to the carnage in Times Square, Julian loathed his actions at the rave. Among the pressures of an angry king attacking him and all but gloating over murdering Xavier's fledglings as they slept, how could he, another of Xavier's fledglings, sleep comfortably with that information?

Even his own self-indulgent desires were keeping him awake. First, it was his undying love for Violet, then his fizzled lust for Winter-Fae. Now at the forefront, two cosmic green eyes had gazed far beyond his own, piercing the veil with her sweet, venomous voice. '*Are you the one?*' *What does that even mean? Am I the one what?*

Damp with moisture he never knew accumulated, he pulled the blanket closer and rolled onto his side, facing away from the door, wishing with all he had for it to open behind him. It could be Caanis, there to end his misery and disprove his theory of a journey unfulfilled. *If it was him, I'd already know it.*

It could have been Violet: there to crawl in bed with him, to whisper sweet nothings in his ear and spoon him to sleep. Either way, he held his breath when the door creaked. Refusing to look, he clutched the blanket tighter in his sweaty palms. When her "cheap vanilla bean" scent overcame the musty cavernous air, Julian cooed.

The sounds and motions of her discreetly crawling in bed behind him invoked Julian's deepest chills yet. "You found me," he cheered heartily. She burrowed beneath the blanket, her cold, bare upper half gluing itself to his back. Through his shirt, two erect nipples moved about in search of a comfortable space. Then she wrapped her arm over his waist, her bare hand gently resting below his navel. Her hair tickling his cheek, Julian took her hand and said, "I love you, Violet."

"I love you, Julian," she barely muttered back. He trembled at her voice. It was the first time she'd whispered in his ear in some time. While he savored hearing it again as if it was the first time, she softly kissed his neck. That too made him quiver. Returning to his ear, she repeated, "I love you," whispering at an even lower volume than before. Her warm breath dusting his flesh was like magic fingers tenderizing his bittering nerves. Julian was lucid and knew it was only a dream, but at least it was a good dream, contradicting his previous mixed feelings for such a damning new ability.

"I love you too," he said. "I wish forever was now, and now was forever."

She kissed his neck again before laying her head on his shoulder. He wanted to turn around and look at her, but his intuition told him to stay where he was and enjoy the moment while it lasted.

Without another word from either, Julian fell asleep in his lover's arms, believing he was safe, sound, and divinely protected.

***

Sometime later, a series of knocks came to Julian's door and awoke him. He yawned and stretched, dragging his feet towards the door. The knock was mighty, like that of a king. Naturally, he was reluctant to open it, but assuming the bleak result of disobedience, he took a deep breath and turned the knob. Waiting on the other side was not Caanis but a man he did not expect to see again so soon. From his one eye to both toes, he wore black, as always. This time his pale blond locks hung free, bordering the sides of his face and hiding the more prominent features of his long, narrow jawline.

"Xavier?" Julian croaked. He was at a loss. *Was that not a dream? Am I dreaming now?*

"Put your shoes on and come with me," Xavier said.

"Where are we going?"

"Out."

"Out where?"

"Put your shoes on, and I will show you." After Julian complied, Xavier took his young creation's hand. "Come." He followed him to the balcony, down the steps, and to the floor below. Along the way, he heard nothing and saw no one. He looked over his shoulder towards the stairs leading down to the throne room, but Xavier beckoned him to keep up.

Since Julian started following him, Xavier hadn't said a word. Growing frustrated, he asked, "Is this a dream?" knowing what the question could do.

"It is," Xavier said as he and Julian crossed the main chamber together, heading towards the exit. "And I know I am dead."

"What?!" Julian stopped. "You know?" Xavier faced him and nodded. "Did you always know, even in Virginia and here before?"

"I knew."

Gasping in disbelief, he whipped out each extended hand as if he was Jesus on the cross, and yelled, "Why the fuck didn't you tell me?!"

"Because I felt it was not time for you to know."

"And now?!"

"And now I can no longer pretend to be something I am not without causing you even more confusion and pressure. I am telling you now because tomorrow my name will be slandered."

"What do you mean?" Xavier refused to divulge any further. Instead, he turned back around and took a lit torch from the wall, moving onward from there. Gritting his teeth and debating on giving his creator the finger, Julian thought, *Fuck it*. He followed Xavier out of the chamber, down the long hall, up the spiral staircase, and into the catacombs. "Now what?" he asked.

"Let's go to the surface."

"For what?"

"Because I want to show you something."

Xavier turned away, walking in the direction of the room with all the carvings on the limestone walls. His frustration turning sour, Julian gouged the elder's shoulder and spun him around. He growled, "No! You need to tell me right now or I'll do something to wake myself up. No more games and no more bullshit! Tell me what the fuck is going on!"

"All right," Xavier sighed. "You win. As you know, the Ahrims tried to set me up. Eric, William, and the others; their murders were all intended to look like I was the one responsible."

"But I know it wasn't you, and so does Dajhri."

"You and she may know, but all the others who knew are dead. That is why I had to see you. I told you I do not believe Bishop knew what he was doing when he left that note for me. If that is true, the Ahrims really were alone in this. Tomorrow, they will try to convince everyone that I killed those people."

"Since you can talk to those you shared your blood with, why don't you tell Caanis? He was your maker."

"I'm not so sure he would believe me, but I have nothing to say to him."

"Caanis is not a good man."

"No, he is not. I have known that for centuries. It was not until I was forced to leave this place. I felt I had nowhere else to go. Before then, I lacked the confidence in myself as a vampire to risk a life away from the kingdom. So, I turned blind eyes when needed, to fool the king into believing he had my support. Only after I was forced to be a brave sigma, I became one. It was later I became an alpha."

Julian groaned, "Cut the shit, Xavier. I know you're much more resourceful than that. I think you really stayed for your sisters, didn't you?" Xavier said nothing. "I know you loved them, and you wanted them to be safe. I've noticed how Caanis talks about them, and some of the words he uses." His maker turned away and started walking again.

"And I know things changed—especially after Bernard came into the picture, but you and Anna were in love once, weren't you?" Xavier froze in place, still maintaining his silence. "Caanis is naming her his heir tomorrow, but he's only choosing her because she is married," Julian continued. "He cares more about making Bernard, a man he doesn't even know, the future king of L'abisme, than he cares about making his own daughter the queen. He's a sexist, and he cares more about the sake of appearances than morality."

Xavier appeared to listen, but he offered nothing to address his child's concerns. "Come," he said. "I really do want to show you something."

Though angry and growing more apathetic by the second, Julian's curiosity got the better of him and he followed the phantom for what felt like miles. They passed crude graffiti, waded across a knee-high pool, and inched their way through two tight crevices. Finally reaching a chamber with a visible opening, high above their heads, Xavier dropped the torch and asked, "Can you fly yet?" Julian shook his head. "Then hold on to me."

He wrapped his arms around Xavier from behind. After one big leap, they stood in the doorway of a small, dark basement. Xavier flipped on a light switch near the door. Other than the foul stench of urine and a short stone stairway, the dirty old cellar was empty. Julian followed Xavier to the top of the stairs, entering a vacant corridor, where the smell lingered. Walking down the hall, he squinted at a distracting overhead lightbulb, buzzing, and flickering like there was a short in the wiring. Upon reaching a closed white door at the other end, Xavier opened it, giving way to the cool Parisian nightscape.

They walked down a dark alley. Like the basement and hallway, it also stank of piss. Julian asked, "Why does everything smell so bad?"

"This is Paris, not a botanical garden."

"Yeah, but I thought the City of Love would smell more like love and less like bodily fluids."

"No matter," Xavier chuckled. "We did not come to the surface for the smells."

At the end of the alley, they reached the edge of an empty cobblestone road. Julian noted the surrounding buildings and working street lights but no cars or people—not even a breeze in the

January air. It was like the only signs of life came from the creator and dreamer themselves. "So, what did you want to show me?"

"Hop on," Xavier said, patting himself on the back. "Don't fret. We are not going far." Julian held on as Xavier leapt into the air. Without fear of anyone noticing, he lingered in flight and Julian took in the sights. Other than spotting the Eiffel Tower again— glowing purple, of all colors—nothing impressed the man who'd seen practically everything.

Leaving the bright city lights behind, Xavier landed in a dark, wooded area, only seconds later. "Where are we?" Julian asked, staring at what he thought were headstones in the distance. Each unique silhouette topped off like icebergs, the moonlit sky exposing the tips, an ocean of shadows concealing the rest. "Who's buried here?"

"Dead people," Xavier giggled. "Come." He urged Julian onward, through an old cemetery, passing rows and rows of tombstones. "Last year, on Halloween, you shared an intimate piece of yourself with Violet and I when we took you to visit your uncle James' burial plot. Tonight, I wanted to share with you an intimate piece of my own."

They continued until halting before quite the monument: a dark marble headstone, standing roughly four feet high and eight feet wide. Julian stared at the slab until *Van Abarrow* appeared, each bold, beautiful, cursive letter etched high across the center. The stone was in no way as old as Xavier. It was modern, its corners inscribed with flowers and moons. The stone was far too big for just one person. Julian looked closer, finding other names chiseled below it. Starting on the left, he read the first name and timeline aloud.

"Ragno Van Abarrow—February 11, 1098 to April 7, 1159."

"That's my father," Xavier said. "He was a knight for King Louis the Seventh. He was killed in battle only two years before I jumped in the river."

Next, Julian read, "Creada Van Abarrow—July 6, 1128 to November 4, 1156."

"My beloved mother," Xavier continued. "She died young from pneumonia, although I believe a broken heart played the biggest part. After my baby sister died, my mother was lost."

Unsure how to respond, Julian read on, "Sibilla Van Abarrow—September 24 ..." Upon reading the date, he looked at Xavier and said, "September twenty-fourth is my birthday, too."

"Yes, I remember. It was much later that night, in the early hours of the twenty-fifth that I came to Virginia. I was here first, putting flowers on her grave—as I do for her and my parents every year on their birthdays. When I arrived at your house, Violet told me you two had been celebrating."

Julian started over, reading, "Sibilla Van Abarrow— September 24, 1149 to October 23, 1154." He paused for a moment before moaning, "Aww, poor little thing."

"My sweet Sibby was the world to me," Xavier said. "After losing her and both my parents so close together, it was just too much for me to bear. At seventeen, I was a man, but even men from an unforgiving era such as that could still feel pain. I felt it. The anguish cut so deep that I intended to take my own life when I threw myself off the cliff. I wanted the torture to end."

After reflecting, Xavier snickered. "To think, if Caanis—a vampire who was not even a resident of Paris at the time—had not sauntered past the river with his alleged mademoiselle at just the right moment, you and I would have never met."

"There is no such thing as coincidence, only synchronicity," Julian said. "It is all tragic, but it was meant to happen."

"True," Xavier sighed. "But if you could change certain events in your life, would you not?"

"I'd want Violet back."

"What about your past ... your younger years?"

"Maybe. I mean, I suppose, but if I did, I wouldn't be who I am."

"And who is that?"

"I don't know anymore," he said, bowing his head to sulk. From there, he caught one last name on the Van Abarrow family stone. Like the others, he read that one out loud as well. "Xavier Van Abarrow—October 27, 1144 to …"

"Imagine the look on people's faces if they were to see that full timeline," Xavier chortled. Julian also laughed, unable to deny the humor as anything but hilarious, even in such dark circumstances. "I loathe this now being the only way I can ever visit my family again, but I suppose beggars cannot be choosers."

"I hope I'm not about to put my foot in my mouth, since I seem to do that a lot lately, but why does your name sound so modern compared to theirs? I mean, your father's name reminds me of a Viking. Yours sounds like something from the Middle Ages."

Xavier laughed. "I take no offense. In fact, you are the first American who's noticed. Violet and Eric knew, but not until I told them. You are correct. 'Xavier' was not my birth name, and neither was 'Van Abarrow.'"

"But I clearly remember you telling me on Halloween, your sister used to mock you for calling her Sibby—calling you 'Xavvy.'"

"I also remember it clearly. She called me 'Xavvy' because that was my name. She mocked my voice and posture when I'd scold her for misbehaving, not my name."

"So why did you change it?"

"By the time I fully embraced my vampirism I could speak Early French, Middle English, and some Romance and Latin. In time, I learned many other languages, words, and names. I became a student regarding all the world had to offer. You could say 'Xavier' came from my pride. I chose it as a way of declaring myself a better

Xavvy—'Xavvy-er,' if you will. I cannot speak for when others began using the name."

"What about 'Van Abarrow?' Where did that come from?"

"When I was born, surnames were not so common. It wasn't until the 1500s Germany required them. Even then, we still had to fit in with society. King Arvil had chosen Reinhardt centuries earlier, when first establishing his kingdom. Caanis and many others refused to conform. I chose 'Abarrow' after reading it in a historical archive, on account of my Anglo-Saxon heritage. 'Van' was my own addition. I thought it would sound 'cool,' as you would say."

Though highly intrigued by the truth, Julian said nothing. After a moment of silence Xavier said, "Come. Let us lighten the mood, shall we?" He motioned his youngling to join him again before flying away. Returning to the city, they landed on the high viewing deck of the neon-purple Eiffel Tower, the night lights of Paris blazing beneath.

Julian had a look around at all the multicolored lights surrounding tall buildings and even a giant Ferris wheel off to his right. Had he never seen Las Vegas from an airplane or the top of the Stratosphere after dark, the view might have been more breathtaking. He had nothing against the ancient city, but like his earlier reaction, he wasn't as impressed as he thought he'd be. To humor Xavier and respect his efforts, he said, "It's nice up here. I always said I wanted to travel abroad at least once before I die."

"I have always thought the city was beautiful from above, even before the invention of electricity or this tower was erect." Julian giggled, imagining himself no different than the perverted boy he had disfigured, hearing Xavier express his love for the city from above and erecting towers. Then, his maker joined in the laughter, saying, "Yeah, yeah, funny, huh?"

So, you really can still read my thoughts? It felt good to laugh like a human again. The crude and childish innuendo reminded him of Daryl, back home—probably scared and mentally ripping himself to shreds. He asked, "Is Daryl going to be okay?"

"I cannot say. He presented himself as strong-willed, but I imagine his world is falling apart. He does not strike me as the kind of man who'd dare challenge his beliefs."

"Daryl's a proud man. He always has been. Pana told me he would look for him and offer him help. I know you told me not to tell anyone about Daryl, but I—"

"I trust Pana. Certain others, not so much."

"You mean, Caanis?"

Xavier nodded. "And others."

"What others?" Facing the city, Xavier held his tongue. Moving on, Julian asked, "Did Caanis kill Arvil Reinhardt?"

"Don't you think it would be easier not knowing such things, for now?"

"Would it really matter?"

"It would if Caanis knew you thought he was a murderer."

"But he already admitted to me that he is." *Oh, fuck!* Julian gasped, knowing he had said too much again. *What the fuck is wrong with me?*

His one eye leading the way, Xavier turned fully in Julian's direction. "Who did he say he killed?"

"Caanis, he …" Julian took a deep breath. He didn't want to be the one to tell him, but he knew he had to. He deserved to know the truth. Throwing caution to the wind, he forced it out, already squirming over the potential outcome. "Caanis is the reason all the other vampires, that you made before Violet died. He said he didn't think you were fit to create others, so he'd smother them as they slept."

Julian watched as what little color his creator had drained instantly. A single tear squirted out from beneath the loose-fitting eyepatch. The unholy dab took its time rolling down his long, melancholic face before dripping over the tower's edge and landing somewhere on the dirty ground below.

"I always wondered if it was him. I just never knew for certain. Thank you for telling me."

Watching Xavier tremble and do all he could to keep more tears at bay, Julian put his hand over his shoulder and said, "I am so sorry. He told me while he was angry. Honestly, I thought he was going to strangle me, too."

"How so?"

"In some weird, jealous rage, I attacked a teenager at a rave I went to with Winter-Fae. It brought unwanted attention to the catacombs, and Caanis found out. He choked me out good."

"That's Caanis: the world-renowned hothead," Xavier grumbled.

"Why is he like that?"

"He has demons. He's carried guilt that's haunted him for centuries now."

"Why?"

"Caanis has many regrets. He knows he made terrible choices in his life. He is so wounded, he takes those regrets out on others."

"Regrets about what?"

"As you know by now from my own faults, love and lust can do much damage in the proper context." Looking back on the city, Xavier asked, "Did he tell you about 'Rosalyn?'"

"He did. He told me they were in love, but because she would not leave Paris, they only ever saw each other when he came here."

"No one else ever saw her. Supposedly, she was with him when he pulled me from the river. I do not remember any of it. He told everyone he had spent six hundred years devoting his heart to her, but he never even spoke of her until just before our king, Arvil

Reinhardt, was assassinated. Even then, he said she mostly stayed hidden in the shadows—that, and her green eyes, were all he ever told me about her. Caanis was a very private man before he took the crown. Apparently, even I didn't know him as well as I thought."

"Caanis told me she lived in the catacombs, and that is why he chose that location for L'abisme." Xavier nodded. "Do you think it was an excuse to kill the king—to get away and start his own kingdom?"

"If Rosalyn truly existed, perhaps."

Again, Julian asked, "Do you think he really did it?" Xavier said nothing. To him, it said everything. While the silence lingered, he scanned the Parisian landscape below, noting all the empty streets. "Since this is my dream, does that mean you and I are the only ones here?"

"It does."

"So, I guess we could do anything and not get caught."

"Indeed. In fact, that is why I brought you up here."

"What do you mean?"

"Any vampiric ability you have in the waking world, you have here. Any ability you learn here, you can take back to the waking world."

"And?"

"Now that you are somewhere safe from potential injury, I think it is time you have your first official flying lesson." Julian tipped his head. "I saw what you did in New York. Your instincts took over when you thought you were about to be shot by Kevin Cauldwell. It proves you can fly. You just need to fully awaken it."

"What should I do?"

"I want you to throw yourself from this deck."

"Why?!"

"Because one of two things will happen. Either you will fly back up to me, or you will wake up in your bed." Hesitant, Julian took a step back. "I assure you, it will not hurt if you hit the ground."

"I know," he groaned, minding his pooling nausea and growing heartbeat. "It doesn't mean the fear of doing it in the waking world isn't every bit as real here as this conversation, though."

Xavier shrugged his shoulders. "Meaning what, exactly?"

"Meaning I'm scared!"

"Everything you have endured in this past week, and you fear waking up? How many times have you fallen now?"

Julian cried, "It's not like that!"

"I understand," Xavier said, warmly patting him on the cheek like a proud father. "Just allow me to say this first. Even though I am dead and gone, there are many still living I continue to care about. Tomorrow at the meeting, I want everyone to know the truth. I want those I care about to be safe, like you."

"And Anna?"

Xavier almost smirked, but then a certain look of guilt washed over his visible face, a look that told Julian, "I am so sorry for what I've done to you, and to *her*," without actually saying it. As if something he'd been trying to avoid had found him lying helpless on a silver platter, his cheeks, shoulders, and demeanor all wilted downward in self-disgust. Julian wondered why, but before he could ask, Xavier suddenly picked himself back up like he'd forgotten why himself. Moving on, he said, "I love you, Julian. Please, forgive me."

"For what?"

"For this." Before getting hurled over the railing could properly register, Julian plummeted from the tower. His field of vision quickly twirled between purple and dark—purple and dark—occasional white flashes creating tracers. He had no time to think or react. Though he fell fast, the lung-punching descent lasted far longer than he expected. Finally, it all went black. Julian leapt from his bed, landing on the hard floor beside it, basted in sweat, and breathing so fast that he nearly hyperventilated. It took him over a minute to catch his breath, but once he did, all the petrified vampire could manage was, "Holy-fucking-shit!"

Chapter Twenty-Five

For the first time since Julian's transformation, he was cold. It was not a temperate cold but an icy-hands-of-death cold. His body shivered and his teeth chattered in ways reminiscent of the morning after his second, and most horrifying, *Ayahuasca* ceremony—spending hours questioning whether he was dead or alive before vowing to never touch the sacred plant medicine again.

He knew he was alive, but despite all the times he'd fallen over the last week, in dreams and reality, that specific plunge from the neon-purple tower awoke such a fright. Even wrapping himself in his blanket was not enough to comfort him. He let the cover fall to the floor when he got off the bed. He put on his leather jacket and shoes before heading out to the hallway, thinking, *Maybe some blood will make me feel better.*

When he reached the balcony, a small gathering of vampires caught his attention down on the floor. He had no idea what time it was, but he assumed he slept all night. After making it to the blood well, he started turning the crank to raise the net. Everyone else he'd seen turning it did it with a super speed he did not possess. It took some time, but finally, the net reached the surface, and he took a bag.

Just as he started to lower it, Winter-Fae trotted in. He stopped and said, "Hi."

"Good afternoon," she replied, approaching the well with a vague hint of hope in her eyes.

Julian stepped back, watching her take a bag. Wanting to say something, but not sure what, he asked, "What time are the Ahrims supposed to be here tonight?"

Facing away, she rapidly turned the crank, lowering the net back into the icy water below. "I've no clue. Daddy met Dajhri earlier. I imagine he'll want to talk to you too,"

"Why?"

"Because you're a witness." When Fae finished, she turned back towards the doorway, her eyes focused on the hall beyond.

As she passed, Julian gently brushed her forearm with the back of his fingers. "Hey, listen," he began, stopping her, each meeting the other's gaze. "I wanted to apologize for my behavior at the rave. I was immature and stupid."

"You're right. You were."

"I don't know what I was thinking. If you want me to be honest, I was having a lot of fun with you. It felt so good to have a friend I could talk to so openly about my feelings. I guess I got wrapped up in that and took some things the wrong way. Then when I heard that boy, not only was I angry, thinking he was talking to you that way, I …" He paused and awkwardly scratched the back of his neck.

"You what?" Fae asked. She put the IV hose to her lips, sucking in the red drink without breaking eye contact.

"I got jealous."

Her sparkling eyes bugged out before she burst into laughter, nearly choking, spitting out the hose and some of the blood she'd started to drink. Regaining her composure, the little sprite croaked, "Jealous?! You—a man with such words—such heart and soul— jealous of a dirty little bloke whose idea of romance was taking me off and 'wrecking my every hole?'" More of her precious laughter followed.

"I never said I was perfect. I only wanted to say I am sorry for everything."

Fae broke eye contact, bobbing her head, then going to the door. On her way out, she turned back and said, "Apology accepted, my friend." She skipped off towards the balcony, radiating far more positivity than when she entered. *'My friend.'* Julian smiled, hoping their friendship could go back to the way it was. That was when he noticed his shivers and chattering, which had carried over from the dream, had vanished.

As he walked along the balcony, headed towards his room, a loud, manly voice bellowed, "Julian!" from the floor below. He looked in the direction it came from, finding Caanis staring back, his hand extended upwards, and a big smile stretching his bearded face. The king was not alone. Bernard was at his side.

Oh, God. Here we go, With what Fae said, and the king's expression, he knew Caanis was calling him to come and join them. Having no choice, he took a drink and began down the steps, silently telling himself, *Positive thoughts, Julian. Only think positive thoughts. Don't think about him being a prick. Just stroke his ego, smile, and be who you need to be to get through this. It will all be over soon, and you can go back to Alaska. Positive thoughts, Julian—positive—* "Well, good afternoon, your highness," Julian greeted, offering a huge plastic grin.

"Good afternoon," Caanis replied. "I trust you had a pleasant night's rest?"

"I did."

"Very good! I was just telling Bernard, the Ahrims should arrive no later than midnight. As for the meeting, we will gather at my throne once they've arrived. I do not want them here any longer than they must be. The sooner we can settle this, the better. As I told you before, you will be asked to give your account of the events. I may have further questions, as may Dajhri."

Julian asked, "What about the Ahrims? Without tongues, how are they supposed to answer anything or give their side of the story?"

"That, I know not. I have spent very little time in the Raja Kahiji's presence. That was long ago. To my knowledge, Dajhri and

I are the only two living vampires outside of Raz Ahrim who've ever laid eyes on him. He had nothing but blank stares for me then, before I was king. Tonight, if the ancient one knows what is good for him, he will answer mine and the queen's questions one way or another."

"Exactly," Bernard added.

Julian asked, "Is there anything else you need from me before then?"

"There is not."

He motioned back towards the stairs and held up his bag of blood. "Then may I …"

"Yes, of course. Go enjoy the rest of your day. Just try not to enjoy it too much." Caanis chuckled, shooting him a glare. Julian watched Bernard also laugh, further kissing the king's ass.

He, too, played along, forcing a smile before saying, "I will." After he walked away, Julian went back up the stairs, Bernard following not far behind. Once he reached the top, he hurried to the middle hallway, avoiding any potential conversation.

He was happy that Anna was happy, and he was excited she was about to be named the heiress apparent, but some of the things Bernard had to say about him and Violet in Alaska and Virginia remained tattooed beneath his skin. He couldn't help wondering what lengths a man who knows torture better than anyone would go to, or who he would sell out if his life were on the line.

Julian knew he was probably overthinking, but all he could see when he envisioned the man who resembled his ex-lover's brother, was the image of him calling his wife a whore in his dream before attempting to hit her. He shook it off and went back to his room, drinking his blood, and spending the rest of his day deep in thought, wondering, *What now?*

Before he knew it, several hours had passed. A knock at his door snapped him out of a meditative trance he'd sat in since returning to his room and finishing his brunch. When he opened the door, Winter-Fae was there, wearing an adorable, white, hand-crocheted dress. "Hey."

"Hey, it's almost midnight. The Ahrims should be here any time."

Julian nodded, put his shoes on, and joined her in the hall. On their way towards the main chamber, he asked, "Is everyone going to be in the throne room?"

"The Taltosians, the Ahrims, my sisters and I, you, Bernie, and Daddy will be. No one else is permitted."

By the time they reached the stairs, all the others were gathered in the same areas as the night before, greeting Dajhri and her entourage. Vampires crowded each side of the chamber, leaving the center wide open. Avice, Anna, and Bernard stood side by side, just below the balcony. Caanis and Dajhri both stood a few feet further ahead. The queen's guards and handmaiden flanked her right. As Julian caught a profile view of Caanis from the stairs, he had to swallow his lips to keep from laughing at his haughty attire.

He wore black slacks, leather boots, and a belt, the sheathed dagger at his side. He also donned a white poet's blouse with full bishop sleeves, its cuffs and central chest all decoratively frosted in thick, eccentric frills like those that might border a wedding cake. Cloaking the pirate shirt was a majestic red velvet cape, its high, broad shoulder pads and white fur trimming each royally peppered in black speckles. Despite the king's impressive height, much of the robe lay in a crumpled pile behind his feet. Atop his head, over his unkempt caramel locks, rested a gold crown with shiny red jewels circling the base and larger purple jewels centered on each of the crown's five points. Julian rolled his eyes, maintaining a straight face while gazing upon the massive ego and cliché.

Assuming he was not meant to stand with the others, he stopped at the bottom of the stairs, but Fae took his hand, leading him towards her family. Though his view of the entrance was clear,

Julian also had a perfect rear view of the queen. She wore the same simple white gown she had arrived in, her thick, twine-wrapped mahogany hair still neatly styled in a daunting beehive.

From the crowd, someone yelled, "They are coming!"

At a distance, Julian observed movement stirring in the darkness. Closer in the light, he still could not see the gangly figure's face, but he recognized a man: bald and wrapped in a shimmering gold tunic that reached his knees. His walk as odd as his turtling posture, the barefooted figure moved slowly. Once several feet separated him from the entryway, a massive, man-shaped animate object squeezed its way through the natural, high-pointed cathedral opening.

Julian fixated on the rock-solid behemoth with brown, brick-colored skin, standing roughly nine feet tall and at least five feet wide. A thick head of dark, dreaded hair rested comfortably on its colossal shoulders. An equally thick, dark beard seemed to only lack an inch or two from brushing the beast's exquisitely sculpted pecs. Its only clothing was a brown fur loincloth and thin leather-like straps, wrapping its clean bulbous feet and spiraling two-thirds the way up its fibrous calves.

Along with others in the crowd, Julian gasped at the sight, mumbling, "What the fuck is that supposed to be?!"

Appearing astonished, Fae whispered, "Buldgera!" in such awe. "I've heard of him before. I just never knew he was real."

Following the strange man ahead of him, the monster strutted with the grace and confidence of a Greek god, cursed with the bottled rage of a rabid gorilla. Julian looked at the others, asking, "How in the hell could something like that even get down here with nobody noticing?"

Avice said, "I don't know. Why don't you go ask him?"

Julian looked back at the entrance, expecting to see others, but no one else came. By the time the strange front man reached Caanis and Dajhri, his face was clear. His smooth, shiny skin boasted the discolored shade of a bruised peach. Not only was his egghead shorn, but his entire face was hairless. Not even eyebrows or visible lashes were present.

There was something Julian found unnerving about the intensity in the cryptic man's sunken, pale gray eyes. They seemed to follow everywhere at once. Along with his thin, dark lips, stretched upwards in a sinister grin so creepy it could haunt a house, Julian recognized him, along with the mammoth in his backdrop, as vile creatures not of this age.

"Where is the Raja Kahiji?" Caanis demanded.

"Such matters lie beneath the One True King." The strange man's voice was deep. "I am Rasul, the translator and messenger of Raz Ahrim and the Raja Kahiji: the one and only true king of all our kind."

Dajhri, who'd stood dormant thus far, said, "You can talk?"

"I would not be a worthy translator or messenger if I hadn't the ability to translate or deliver messages, would I?"

Caanis growled, "I requested the presence of the Raja Kahiji! He is your king, and it is his actions in question, not yours or that 'thing' behind you!" The beast whom Fae referred to as 'Buldgera' roared like a mighty lion at the king's outcry, instantly raising Julian's heartbeat.

"Then perhaps you should have come to request his presence yourself. No matter our distaste for any others who parade and peddle our stolen gift as their own, a spine still goes a long way with the One True King."

Dajhri said, "You do realize how guilty your king's refusal to answer another king of the truce's call makes him look, yes?"

"We have no concern," said Rasul. "We came as a courtesy to the truce. We received news of the exposure in America on the eve of their new year, and you dare accuse the One True King of instigating such blasphemy?"

"That is why we are here—to gain answers," Dajhri said. She pointed over her shoulder towards the throne room, her left green eye aiming directly into Julian's. To everyone involved, she said, "Come, friends. Let us settle this in peace and with a pleasant conversation."

Chapter Twenty–Six

Everyone whose presence was required gathered in the throne room. Caanis sat on his brass chair, presiding over the event. His daughters were all by his side: Avice and Winter-Fae on his left, Anna on his right. At the bottom of the three short steps separating them from the floor, everyone else stood side by side. From the king's view, left to right, were Rasul, Dajhri, Bernard, and Julian. Behind them, Buldgera hammered up the left corner while Dajhri's handmaiden and hooded guards stood bunched on the right, alert, but keeping a safe distance from the colossus.

"Now then," Caanis began. "We all know why we are here. However, before tensions have the almost certain displeasure of growing, I've an announcement to make." To Julian's right, a pleasantly soft exhale came from Bernard. "As most of you know, Xavier Van Abarrow was my heir."

Rasul took one step forward, interrupting the king. "Pardon, but was Xavier not excommunicated from your 'kingdom?'"

"By his own admittance, yes, but not mine. It is true, I once sent him away. He was nearly a six-hundred-fifty-year-old boy, refusing to mature until I punished him for his deviancies." Again, Julian heard Bernard, grunting, not as pleasantly as before. "After years of growth and self-reflection, my son knew he was welcome to return. It was his decision to refrain."

Rasul took a step back to where he started, and Caanis resumed. "As I said, I am now without an heir. So, before we get to the point of why I have summoned you all here, I wanted to announce my choice to replace him." He looked at Anna and smiled. Then he addressed everyone.

"My eldest daughter will make a wonderful queen. Before she returned home, I'd never properly met her husband, Bernard. It is true, his maker was my enemy and a traitor to the crown. However, as I have taken time to get to know him over these past days, I am proud to call him my son." Julian watched the smile burrow its way up Bernard's cheeks, his dark mustache stretching with it. "My daughter will make a fine queen, indeed. And since every fine queen needs a great king to rule, I hereby declare the heir of my throne and the Kingdom of L'abisme to be: Bernard Gaunt."

All three of the king's daughters simultaneously gasped. Even Julian had the wind briefly knocked out of him. Avice appeared the least happy of them all, shrieking, "Excuse me?!" She stomped out of alignment with Fae, throwing her hands up in frustration.

Caanis returned the putrid glare. "Quiet!" he barked. "I have made my decision."

Avice put one hand against her waist, shoving her free index finger forward, growling, "No! You made the wrong decision!"

"I beg your pardon?" Caanis spoke as calmly as he could, but if he were a dragon, his nostrils would spit smoke. "You dare speak to me: your father and king that way?"

Ignoring his attempt to silence her, Avice snarled, "Oh, I more than dare, Daddy. We are your daughters! Anna and I never saw eye to eye, but even she would be better to name than this acquiescent … molly-boy!" She threw a pointer at Bernard in such a hateful way that flicked everyone in its path with intangible droplets of anguish and disgust.

Caanis rose from his throne, aiming his own sausage finger back in his daughter's face, the Viking's smoldering orbs burning redder than *Hel* itself. "You bite your tongue, child!"

"Or what? Are you going to cut it out and send me off to live with the freaks?!" She pointed at both the Ahrims. Rasul emitted a cackle as odd as his appearance. From behind, Buldgera grunted in something resembling a chuckle but that was more of an unpleasant, guttural skid. "You think that crown, silly cape, and throne make you powerful? What I did for my sister and I, when we were just blackguard youth—the way I protected and supported her—that was true power, goddamn you!"

Winter-Fae, her precious little face melting with impending dread, tugged Avice's hand, begging, "Not here, Sissy."

"No!" Avice hissed, swatting her away. Caanis rolled his eyes, appearing to let his daughter have her fun while it lasted. Seeing this reaction, she only seethed harder, waving her finger in his face again. "… and how did you get your power? You sold out your maker, his heir, and our entire kingdom for—an imaginary cunt!" Without warning, Caanis violently backhanded Avice across the nose and cheek, striking her with such force that it sent her flying down the steps and smacking face first into the hard limestone.

"Avice!" Fae cried, rushing to her big sister's aid. She knelt to help her but was pushed away again.

Between her whimpers, Avice screamed, "Leave me!" Fae complied, jolting away as the resilient brunette stood on her own. She wiped a narrow red ribbon streaming from her nose and spat a tooth from between her quivering lips. All along, Julian's heart ripped. Each breath was shallow. Anxiety filled his gut with nausea. The scene took him back to his childhood and all the times he'd watched his father—and then later, his mother's boyfriend, Bill— strike her down.

Caanis retook his seat. Eyeing his daughter, he pointed at the exit. "Your presence is no longer needed. Leave."

Avice dusted off her silky blue dress, grunting, "Fine!" She looked at everyone else in the king's presence, even Julian, saying, "I don't give a fuck about any of this, anyway." Her eyes met Winter-Fae's, who'd reclaimed her place by her father's side. She tried to smile at her little sister but could not. Instead, she turned towards the others and stormed away. As she passed between Julian and Bernard, she shot the heir apparent a cold, stern gaze, muttering, "Fuck you," under her breath.

Bernard whispered back, "You would."

Julian watched the distraught princess, barreling away, doing all she could not to cry on her way out. She even ignored Buldgera, passing him without a glance. Once she left the room and began up the stairs, Julian turned back to the others, instantly drawn to the heartbroken looks on both remaining sisters' faces. He looked down the line at the others beside him. Rasul and Dajhri appeared indifferent, but Bernard's smirk had grown to a snide grin.

Caanis loudly cleared his throat and said, "Now, then. Bernard, why not come up here and join your queen's side?" He lifted a hand, curling his fingers inward while Bernard obeyed his master like a loyal lapdog, prancing up the stairs and joining his wife. Fae stared at the floor, her trembling bottom lip tucked over the top.

Again, Rasul came forward. "My apologies, 'King,' but now the sentiment has passed, may we resume?"

Caanis cleared his throat. Addressing everyone, he said, "We are here because a vampire by the name of Tony Bishop allegedly murdered another vampire: Eric Grant. Eric's brother, a human Christian priest, and dare I say ally, named William Grant, was also slain. Furthermore, others in New York City fell prey, including the daughter of a soldier and hunter named Christopher Cauldwell. That name is familiar. If memory serves me correctly, the Cauldwells— quite the revered family—were among those the Vatican used to wage their war against Reinhart in its final days."

Rasul said, "No, Caanis. You are the one who waged war on Reinhardt. The queen can attest."

"The civil war waged from within the castle walls," Dajhri said. "It was not until it became public, the Vatican intervened, and it escalated into 'their war.'"

Rasul cackled. "Be that as it may, it is queer you assume the One True King is to blame for these recent events."

Dajhri stepped forward. "Tony Bishop—not of my making but another in my kingdom—came to me with his confession. I know for our kind, reaping blood can be a very dark act, no matter the method. As a shamanic healer, I detest the cruel methods Raz Ahrim use when hunting or simply killing for sport."

"May I ask your point?"

"Eric Grant and the other humans were decapitated, their spines severed. Whether it be for food, self-defense, justice, or pleasure, no others in the history of our kind have used such disturbing, unnecessary methods but the Ahrims."

The messenger's sunken eyes burst in absolute offense. "Are you implying the One True King put Tony Bishop up to this?!"

Dajhri said, "I am only stating facts."

"And because a vampire and some puny humans were executed by means we have not practiced in centuries, it must be the One True King who is responsible?"

"I assume nothing, Rasul. I only state facts. Tony Bishop came to me on his own accord, knowing the consequences of such a confession. I was angered when he told me what he'd done, but I took my concerns to Mother Lilith in prayer. She implored I spare his life. I followed my Goddess's order, banishing him from Taltosia."

Caanis leaned forward on his throne. "Julian Frost tells me Tony Bishop wrote a note in your presence to be given to Xavier. Is this true?"

"It is," she said. "I knew Xavier would come. I saw it in a vision. Tony Bishop wanted to explain himself and apologize to him personally. For the safety of my people, I refused his request. Before I sent him away, he asked if he could leave the note. I agreed to his terms if he wrote it honestly. I would then later give it to Xavier when he arrived, for guidance and to mourn the loss of his son."

"What did the letter say?"

"Allow me a moment." Dajhri closed her eyes and took in a deep, concentrated breath. "It said, 'Dear Xavier, what can I say that could make up for the damage I caused, the innocent lives I took, or the unwanted attention I brought upon the coven? Nothing. What I can say is it was never my intention for any of this to happen.

"'I was manipulated and forced to act against my will. The truth is, I killed everyone: Eric, Father Grant, and all the others. I started a chain reaction, on the command of the Raja Kahiji, to lead a trail back to you. The Ahrims' king ensnared my mind. He told me what to do, how to do it, and I had no control over my own thoughts or actions. I know the horrible mistake I made, and though I do not deserve it, I beg for your forgiveness.

"'I returned home to Taltosia, but upon arrival, I was banished by Dajhri for my crimes against you and for disturbing the truce. She said you would come to her, and as I am a child of Taltosia, she spared my life and allowed me to leave you this letter as a confession in hopes that if our paths ever cross again, you will show me the same mercy Caanis once showed you. Until that day comes, please accept my apology. Forever or never, Bishop.'"

Rasul hurled himself forward again, snarling, "Lies! That is a damnable lie!"

The king's view shifting between them, he said, "Queen Dajhri, do you swear to this?"

"I do."

"It is true," Julian said. Every eye in the room turned on him.

"Word for word?" Caanis asked.

"I cannot say if it was word for word, but that was the point he made. I heard Violet read the letter out loud, the night Xavier returned to us. I swear that was at least roughly what it said."

"So, you've no proof either?" asked Rasul.

"I can find out," Fae said, drawing everyone's attention to her. "If Julian heard it, I can find it and read it back exactly as he heard it."

"Go on," Caanis said.

Julian stepped forward, meeting her at the bottom step. She was still shorter than him, but the difference made it easier to place her small hands on each side of his head. She closed her eyes, her little face squinching in concentration. She then repeated the entire letter back to everyone, word for word, in comparison to Dajhri's recount. She opened her eyes, asking, "Xavier comes to you in your dreams?"

"Yes."

With her hands still on Julian's head, Fae closed her eyes again. Seconds later, she opened them, gently releasing him. She told her father, "Xavier saw Tony the night they died. In a more recent dream, he told Julian he searched Tony's thoughts, and he saw him writing the letter while Queen Dajhri watched on."

"That is correct," Julian confirmed.

Addressing everyone, Fae said, "Tony was here last Halloween. I was unable to pick up on anything in his thoughts regarding any of this. It was as if he had no knowledge of it. So, I believe them."

Rasul cackled again. "Your opinion matters not, ghostly baboon!"

Caanis launched from the chair, his planted feet and arching knees aimed at Rasul, sneering, and pointing. "Don't you dare speak to my daughter that way!"

From the back of the room, Buldgera came alive. He growled along the walk to his fellow Ahrim's side. Even Dajhri appeared alarmed, taking a big step to her left. From behind, her four guards steadily approached, bare hands and balled fists exposed, ready to fight if needed. Rasul held a hand up to the beast, putting him at ease. He told Winter-Fae, "My apologies, 'Princess.'"

Tensions calming, Caanis retook his seat while Fae, Dajhri, and Julian reclaimed their original places. Moving on, Rasul said, "Regarding Xavier and the alleged murderer's deaths, they occurred on the same night as the other deaths; the deaths everyone watched on their televisions?"

Caanis said, "They did."

Rasul's unnerving grin returned. "Was it not Xavier who originally brought all of this unwarranted attention upon himself when opening his establishment for humans?"

Anna said, "No. The nightclub had nothing to do with it."

"Oh?" Rasul stroked his narrow chin.

"It is no secret, we played with fire when Leviticus opened, but we never had any problems until people started getting killed around the city. Just like Eric and William, they all had their spines cut up and were beheaded. One night, Christopher Cauldwell came into the club, accusing Xavier of killing his daughter.

"Xavier kicked him out, but he came back the next night with his brother and another man. They started shooting, and that's when it all began. We split up after that. Bernard and I hid in another apartment Xavier had in case we ever needed a safehouse. Julian and Violet went to Virginia, and Eric went to his brother's."

Rasul asked, "Were this 'Eric' and his brother killed together?"

"No, they were killed a month apart," Anna said.

"Where was Eric killed?"

"At the club, the night after Christopher Cauldwell and his men came in."

"Who found the body?"

"Xavier."

"Well then," Rasul chuckled. "That is convenient."

Caanis asked, "How so?"

"A murder victim's father accuses Xavier of such an act. Then the accused finds the body in his establishment, killed the same way as all the others."

"Xavier would never kill his son!" He could not explain where it came from, but the powerful urge to blurt such a claim in his maker's defense overtook Julian's inhibition to keep quiet. Everyone looked at him.

Rasul said, "How can you be so sure? Were you there?"

"I was."

Stroking his chin again, the ancient said, "Do tell."

"The night Eric died, Violet and I started in Las Vegas, but then we flew to New York. We landed on the roof and first went to Violet's apartment, above the club. Then we went downstairs. At that time, I was still human. I wore eyeglasses, but I lost them the night before, when all the shooting started. While Violet and I were in the lobby looking for them, we heard Xavier screaming from the other room. That is where we found Eric."

"So, Xavier found him first?"

"Yes."

The Ahrim laughed. "Forgive me, but finding the accused with the dead body is the furthest from proof of his innocence."

Dajhri came forward again. "When Tony Bishop came to me, I saw Eric's face as if it were through Tony's eyes. I assure you it was Tony who committed these murders, not Xavier."

"Dajhri, I respect your position." Quickly glaring over at Caanis, he added, "—more than his, I should say," before his attention returned. "… but being a queen does not mean you are immune to deception."

"What are you saying, Rasul?"

"For all I know this has been an attempt to slander the One True King's name! I am saying, other than hearsay and accusations, you have no proof of anything! And though we may not have proof to exonerate the One True King, we have proof and accusations of our own!"

"And what are those?" Caanis asked.

"We learned of the incident leading to the helicopter crash, when your men came to summon us for this meeting. We know it all started at the wedding of this thing over there—" Rasul pointed at Julian. "—who somehow believes he has the right to be one of us. We know the instigator in all this was the hunter. However, assuming the killer was not Xavier, is there anyone in this company who can say if it was not for his dance club—prompting the culprit to act out in such a way—all those people would still be alive?"

"No!" Julian shouted. "It happened because somebody knew who Christopher Cauldwell was from the start! I believe his daughter, Catherine Cauldwell—just like Eric and William—were specific targets."

Caanis said, "I appreciate your willingness and passion, Julian, but please stop interrupting us."

Rasul argued, "No, I want to hear what he has to say."

Caanis nodded and Julian continued. "Someone was trying to set Xavier up. Maybe it was because of the club. Xavier, even Anna and Bernard suspected it was someone who was angry with him for opening an opportunity to expose vampires."

"Who wouldn't?!" Bernard let slip. Julian looked his way just in time to see Anna smacking his hand with the back of hers, not enough to hurt, but enough to say, "Shut up." Her deep, grounding eyes also on him, Bernard's tense shoulders relaxed, and the meeting continued.

"… You are rightful in your theory," said Rasul. "Tell me, was Xavier your creator?" Julian nodded. "And are you his only living spawn?" He nodded again. "That would make you the heir to his coven." Turning to Caanis, he asked, "If Xavier had survived, would you deem the actions he and his coven took, exposing our kind to the world, punishable?"

"While the cause of the incident was not his fault, choosing to retaliate in the presence of humans was," Caanis said.

"I will take that as a yes." Rasul's grin expanding, he asked Dajhri, "Would you consider his actions punishable?"

"I do agree with Caanis. Retaliating was his fault. However, under the circumstances, it—"

"—three yesses!" Rasul wailed, his otherwise gruff tone cracking a high-pitch victory squeal. He took a few steps forward, slowly pacing the floor. His heartbeat ringing in his ears, Julian started fearing the worst. "There was a time when our three kingdoms would have never agreed to a gathering such as this. Any accusations would lead to a direct war without question. We are an ancient kingdom, the only true kingdom, but even as the oldest and most rightful, we too believe in evolution.

"We share more differences than we have laws in common. However, one law we have always embraced amongst our kind is when a coven commits an atrocity, such as exposing our existence to humanity at large, we punish the head of that coven. In this case, the coven's former head was killed. Now, the coven has a new head, who also took part in the events that currently has everyone across the globe speaking of 'biblical miracles.'"

Caanis asked, "What are you getting at, Rasul?"

"This man ..." He pointed at Julian again. "He deserves to be punished for committing such a sin."

"How about 'no?!'" Fae shrieked.

Caanis looked at her, a serious air of concern on his haggard face. "Please, be quiet," he said. Fae rolled her eyes and angrily stomped her foot. Julian stood frozen. Each breath he took was harder than the last.

"It is the law by which we have always lived," Rasul explained. "Breaking such a law would result in breaking our truce. Is this really something you want?"

Dajhri approached, gently placing her hand over Rasul's oddly discolored, bone-thin arm. "None of us want this, but you are correct. However, there is another law amongst our kind you fail to mention. How many vampires does it take to form and hold a coven?"

Rasul said, "Two or more."

"'Two or more,'" she repeated. "Until this meeting, Xavier's coven consisted of Anna and Bernard Gaunt—Julian Frost, the head: correct?" Rasul bowed. "Bernard was just named the heir to the kingdom of L'abisme. He accepted. That would mean he is now officially tied to this kingdom, not the coven. His wife, the king's daughter, will become the queen. That means she, too, is officially tied to L'abisme once again. This leaves the coven with only one remaining member. From your own tongue, you just said a coven cannot be of only one."

"She is right," Caanis said. Fae and Anna both nodded repeatedly while Bernard remained silent and motionless.

"Then, this coven is hereby no more," Dajhri said. "To punish Julian Frost—a credible man I have heard much about from Xavier and Violet—would be an attack against the kingdom."

"What kingdom?" Rasul groaned. "He is not a member of any kingdom."

Caanis asked, "Would you like to join ours, Julian?"

"Or Taltosia?" Dajhri added.

Julian looked back and forth between the king and queen, knowing he needed to make a choice like his life depended on it. He asked, "Once I join, will I be a member forever?"

"Not necessarily," Caanis said.

He looked at Fae, gazing back, her eyes practically begging him to pick the kingdom he already knew. *If only the Alaskan coven were a kingdom, I'd just go there.* Without even taking the time to remember all that happened over the past few days—or what Caanis had once done to Xavier, his children, and just did to Avice—Julian didn't even consider Taltosia when making his choice. "I will stay here."

"There you have it," Caanis said. Fae squeaked in joy. Even Dajhri smiled. Outside the Ahrims, the only one who appeared unhappy about it was Bernard.

"This changes nothing!" Rasul snarled. "You summoned us here to make claims against us, and yet you have no proof of any wrongdoing by Raz Ahrim or the One True King! You have insulted the truce—something your betrayed predecessor showed far more respect for than you, and by playing this little game of yours, you have insulted our own vampiric laws! Today, Raz Ahrim spits on the names of L'abisme and even Taltosia!" Though nothing appeared to come out of his mouth, Rasul spat towards the ground.

Caanis again stood from his throne, fuming at the messenger's insult. Before he could respond, Rasul had turned sharply and headed towards the exit. "Buldgera! Let us leave this cesspool!" The monster roared as they met near the gold door. Before leaving, he turned back to face everyone. "On behalf of the One True King: the Raja Kahiji, and all Raz Ahrim, if you ever disrupt us again with such ridiculous accusations, we will slaughter every last one of you." He looked at Dajhri, adding, "All of you. And when we are done, we will bathe in your blood." The translator and messenger of Raz Ahrim turned back towards the door, barking, "Come, Buldgera!"

Julian watched the anomalies marching up the stairs, main chamber bound. Caanis hurried by, his outlandish red cape sweeping the floor in the Ahrims' direction. From behind, Anna told Bernard, "He's probably going to make sure they don't hurt anybody when they leave."

Everyone remaining in the throne room now able to sigh in relief, Julian found Dajhri staring at him, her soulful green eyes piercing him deeply. He smiled and bowed in respect. He said,

"Thank you." Dajhri returned the smile and bow before joining her guards and handmaiden. Bernard caught Julian's attention next, smiling as if the pressure everyone else felt had gone completely over his head.

To the heir's left, a scowling, droopy-eyed Anna looked miserable. Even though she had been away for seventy-five years and hated being called "princess," Julian knew her father's snub cut her deeply. Her wounded expression said it did. Regardless, he watched her do what any majestic queen would: pick her chin up, rub her eyes dry, and make herself smile, even when it hurt to do so.

Chapter Twenty-Seven

Julian, along with Anna, Winter-Fae, Bernard, and Caanis, all stood gathered on the main chamber floor. The Ahrims were long gone, and the Taltosians had just begun their journey back to Peru, but each of their powerful presences remained in the musty air through whispers. Those who'd come to see the evening's events unfold from outside the king's court had been spreading rumors of what they believed transpired as if it were the common cold.

Once the crowd finally started to thin, Caanis returned to his quarters, leaving the others behind. Julian turned to them, sarcastically exhaling. "Thank God that's over."

"The meeting is, but the Ahrims just broke the truce," Fae said.

"So, what does that mean?"

"It means they could attack us or Taltosia any time," said Bernard.

"What would happen if they did?"

"Alone, neither kingdom would stand a chance. Together, it would still be a hell of a battle, one we would probably still lose," he said.

Anna took her husband's hand. "Give it time, love. Hopefully, it'll all blow over soon."

"Anna …" Bernard groaned in frustration, releasing her hand. "You saw Rasul when he and Buldgera left, didn't you? For all we know, they could come back tomorrow."

Fae said, "He is only the messenger." Snickering and mocking Rasul, curling her fingers with air-quotes, she continued, "The 'One True King' has the final say in what they do."

"Yes, but I don't trust them, and if I ever hope to be a great king, I cannot ignore what my heart says, right? Besides, that beast looked like he came prepared for a fight."

"Speaking of that big-ass motherfucker … what is he?" Julian asked.

"Buldgera is a half-giant. He could be a Nephilim," Fae said. "He was born thousands upon thousands of years ago, when biblical creatures still roamed the earth. They say his father was either a giant or an angel, but his mother was one of the first humans."

Only able to picture the terror and carnage such a war machine could unleash when commanded, Julian asked, "What now?" wanting as far away from the spine-tingling image as possible.

"I'm hungry," Fae moaned, patting her flat belly. She turned towards the steps before looking over her shoulder at the others. "Let's have a snack to help us sleep. We can worry about 'what now' tomorrow."

Anna said, "I could eat." Bernard nodded and accompanied his wife towards the steps. Fae and Julian followed. At the blood well, Anna turned the crank and brought the net to the surface. Everyone took a bag.

All having stood quietly around the room, feeding, Fae broke the silence, asking Bernard, "How's it feel to be next in line?"

He smiled, his pressed lips damming a mouthful of drink. Before he could swallow and answer, "… I am sure it feels great, since that's what he wanted all along," came blistering from the doorway. There, Avice lurked, her messy bangs in her face, her eyes widening, the rest of her sneering in a mix of rage and heartache.

Bernard swallowed and asked, "What did you just say to me?"

"You heard me."

Anna glared at her disgruntled sister, imploring, "Not now."

"Really?" Avice laughed. "You're just going to stand there and pretend like you are okay with the very poor choice our father just made?"

"What do you want me to say or do about it, Avice? It's his decision."

Bernard said, "You could be happy for me."

"I am happy for you, love. I swear, I am. You're a good man and you'll make a good king."

"But?" Bernard grumbled.

"… but you're a nobody!" Avice interjected. "You spent two centuries as a slave to one of Father's enemies—which in my opinion, should make you an enemy too. Then you come in here with our sister after she's been away for seventy-five years, and you're suddenly named the heir—just because you're a man?! Fae and I have been far more loyal to Father than either of you, but he completely disregarded us both!"

Bernard laughed. "Was it not made clear to you earlier how irrelevant a whore's opinion is to a king?"

Avice darted at Bernard, growling, "You son of a—" but Fae grabbed her waist, wrapping her skinny white twigs over her sister's raging frame. "Let me go!" Avice roared.

"No! You need to calm down," Fae squeaked. Still holding her sister back, she shot an evil glare at Bernard. He smirked at them both.

While watching the scene unfold. Anna's face kept Julian's attention the longest. The mystical effects of the human blood showed him the future queen's emotions painted over her false expressions once again. Fat, cartoonish tears fell from overlapping swollen eyes in bright turquoise. Her thoughts came flowing without effort. "Oh no! What if she's right? What have I done?" she silently cried as if struck by an epiphany she only wished was a dream.

Once Avice was calm, Fae released her. She looked at her little sister and said, "Don't ever do that again."

"But I am tired of all this anger!" Fae snapped, blaring more emotion in her soft little voice than Julian had seen thus far. "There's nothing any of us can do now. I don't think it's fair either, but fighting won't change it!" Sparkling moisture gathered in the faery's puppy-dog eyes.

"Fae, I love you more than life itself, but our father has sold out his kingdom once again." Avice then looked at Bernard. "You were only named because of me."

The smirking heir raised an eyebrow, asking, "How do you figure?"

"I am the one who came on to Xavier that night. Everyone else was far too canned to remember—at least for a while, but I remembered. I remembered everything." Pointing at her sisters, she added, "So did they. But I wanted him. I wanted to know what all the fuss was about, so I got him. If it wasn't for me, he would have never lost that beautiful cock of his and Anna would've never—"

"—Avice, don't!" Anna yelped, her eyes burning hellfire red in Julian's perspective.

"No!" Bernard insisted, holding up his hand to silence her. "… Anna would have never what?"

"You are a stupid, stupid fool," Avice giggled, clearly enjoying her personal therapy. "You really think Anna saved you from Eustice Golding only because she felt sorry for you?"

Now blubbering, Anna begged, "Please. Don't do this, Avice!" Her alert, accusatory eyes briefly met Julian's. No words accompanied the exchange, but his gut turned rancid, fearing what her unpleasantly surprised expression meant, knowing the look was intended for him.

Disregarding his queen's sorrow, Bernard said, "What the hell are you talking about?"

"She and Xavier were in love long before Fae and I were born. They just never wanted anybody to know about it. They often met in secret, sometimes going at it hard for hours, assuming nobody knew." She simpered at her crumbling sister, adding, "But I knew. I always knew about you two."

Bernard's rounded shoulders deflated instantly. His face turned a sickly green. The entitled smirk he famously wore like a training crown faded to nothing. Of all the angry outbursts and assertions Julian had seen from him, it was like he had never believed any of them himself, not until now. He sighed and asked, "Is this true?"

Against her thickening tears and despair, Anna nodded. "Before Paris and before you and I met: yes. It was true. But I swear, Bern, when we rescued you, it all changed. I fell in love with you. Now, you are the only one I love. I swear!"

"Oh, please, Anna!" Avice barked. "The only reason it ended was because Xavier couldn't please you anymore. If it wasn't for me, he would have never left and the two of you would probably still be together." In the chaos, Julian thought vividly about Violet and Eric's relationship meeting a similar fate. The triggered afterthought was quickly interrupted when Avice, facing him, said, "Yeah, kind of like how she would still be fucking him if they were alive, and he hadn't lost his stick too."

"Hey!" Julian squealed. "What is your problem with me, huh? What the fuck did I do to you?"

Avice ignored him. Turning back to Bernard, she said, "You and Julian are only here because you were both second choices."

"That's not true!" Anna sobbed. Her eyes shifting between Avice and Julian, she said, "I don't know what the fuck you two are playing at, but—"

"I didn't do anything!" Julian yelped, his soft voice breaking. "I can't help what I dream!"

"What dream?!" Bernard asked, one eye on Anna, the other on Julian.

"Just a dream," Julian said. Seething, Bernard's eyes centered on his wife, his pale saggy cheeks pumping with each hard breath.

Avice finished, saying, "After all those years apart, Anna cried day and night for her long-lost love—her real motive for rescuing you. My sister probably cared about you, but your daring rescue was only an excuse to see him again. Otherwise, you'd likely still be a chamber maiden."

Fae stepped in, rabidly shouting, "That's enough, Avice! You need to stop!" The brunette laughed, but she complied to her sister's demands, turning, and leaving the room, the damage done.

Anna's wails persisting, Bernard carelessly stared. With little hope in his voice, he asked again, "Is all this true, 'my love?'" Anna tried to speak, but her anguish was so intense, she could not. "Answer me!" he viciously growled.

Julian took a step forward. Calmly, he said, "Bernard, right now is not—"

"You shut the fuck up!" he screamed in Julian's face. Again, the heir asked his wife, "Is it true?" All the broken redhead managed was a single bob of her dispirited head.

Fae said, "Bernie, it's not like that. She didn't even know—"

"You shut up too!" Bernard hissed, scaring her back a step. He squinted at his future consort in sheer disgust. "And just like that: your perfidy. I was always right. You weren't just mourning a brother, but your lover. And alas, I knew. I always knew. I just wanted to hear you say it yourself."

"Bern, please!" Anna finally managed. "I love you!" she screamed in such a disheartening way. "I should've told you. That's on me! I swear to you though, nothing else ever happened after that night he was with all of us. You're the only man I've been with in over two hundred years!"

As if not one word of it registered, Bernard snarled, "You fucking whore!" When he raised a fist, Julian raised his, struck like a flash of lightning: taking him back to Caanis striking Avice; his father striking his mother; but most of all, his dream: the heir attempting the same. By the time reality checked back, he'd tackled Bernard to the floor, savagely throwing fists in his face as quickly as his arms allowed, fulfilling his own prophecy. His right fist came up just long enough to hammer his left one back down. Blood spattered out from Bernard's nose, but it didn't matter to Julian. Beating him senseless was euphoric; not bloodsucking euphoric, but enjoying a cigarette after great sex euphoric.

Fist after fist, Julian's therapy continued. From behind, Fae shouted, "Stop," but he paid no mind to her until a monstrous hand ripped him away, slamming him into the nearby wall.

"You dare attack my successor!" Dazed, Julian rubbed his eyes, finding Caanis towering over him. "I just saved your life, and this is how you repay me?! Get up!" Julian stood, watching Bernard taking longer to do the same, then wiping the blood from his face onto his buttoned blue shirt. A red smudge remained, just like in the dream.

Julian caught his breath and tried to speak. "Caanis, I—"

"You are done here! Consider your place in this kingdom void as of now. I will not kill you, but you are hereby banished from L'abisme."

Staring at her husband in disbelief, her chafed eyes bugging out and her narrow jaw gaping, Anna turned her back on him, sighting Julian next. She repeated, "What have I done?" without saying it. Though she did not have to say or think it, her dying eyes whispered, "How fucking dare you, Julian Frost." The queen-to-be looked at her father next. She wanted to say something, but when her tears began pouring like rain, she ran from the room without another word.

Before anyone else could speak, Fae said, "Daddy, it wasn't Julian's—"

"And you! Your loyalty is to me, not him!" Fae stepped back, her little face starting to quiver. To Julian, Caanis said, "Out of respect for the memory of my son, and for the information you supplied earlier, I will give you the rest of tonight and tomorrow's daylight hours to find yourself a way back across the ocean. After that, you must leave and never return. And if you think I will let you live upstairs in the catacombs, you are wrong. Up there, you would be a greater threat to me. If that happened, I would kill you before you could make another mistake. Do you understand me?" Panicked, Julian had no choice but to nod.

Caanis went to Bernard's aid, asking, "Are you okay?"

"I'll live," he moaned, spitting a wad of his own blood, glaring at his attacker.

Caanis then began towards the door. On his way, he told Julian, "I suggest you start looking for a way out now. You have just over twelve hours."

The king exited, leaving Julian, Bernard, and Winter-Fae behind. Fae picked up Julian's unfinished bag of blood from the limestone floor and gave it to him. "Come on. It's late and we both need sleep," she said.

"But I need to look for somebody to—"

"I'll take you. I can do more than people think." Julian nodded and followed her. On their way out, Fae shot Bernard another hateful stare, adding, "There is no love here anymore."

Once outside the room, headed towards his own, Julian swore he heard Bernard say, "Sweet dreams."

Chapter Twenty–Eight

L ike every night since Violet's death, Julian lay awake, picking his scabs, and sousing in the mental anguish that followed. He couldn't sleep. He hadn't even taken his jacket off. He only rested his eyes and body while his endurance ran on fumes. All that transpired during the meeting and its cataclysmic fallout had played on loop for hours.

There was still so much left to process, but with his time running thin, there were more pressing matters at hand. Fae said she would take him home, but Julian knew she was always scared to fly far on her own, and despite her determination, he worried how his size compared to hers could endanger them both. Having given up on sleep, he sighed, thinking, *If there is a will, there is a way, I suppose.*

From the silence, synced footsteps of at least two people came stomping down the hallway. The march endured until reaching Julian's door. A loud, powerful knock followed. *Great ... what now?* He yelled, "Who is it?" on his way to the door. Before he could open it, the metal barrier imploded—after Paul, alongside Teddy—kicked it in. Julian squawked, "What the hell?!"

"You're coming with us," Paul said.

"Why?! Caanis said I have until it gets dark!"

Teddy punched Julian between the eyes with a closed fist, sending him stumbling backwards. He tripped over the empty firepit and fell. "What the hell are you doing?!" The guards stood him up, each taking an arm and pulling him into the hallway, his bare feet sliding along the limestone. Panic setting in, he squealed "What is this?!"

About that time, Fae's door opened, and she pounced into the hall. Her tired eyes half shut, she yelled "Hey! What are you doing to him?!"

Paul said, "We're taking him to see the king. Go back to your room and we will get you when it's time."

"Time for what?" Fae gave chase, catching up to them. "I am coming too!" she insisted. "Father gave him until tonight to leave!" As Julian struggled, Teddy kneed him on the side of his abdomen, knocking the wind out of him. The vicious strike burnt more than it hurt. Fae screamed, "Stop it! He didn't do anything!" They ignored her, dragging Julian on towards the balcony. Still following, Fae shouted, "I want to see my father!"

Clenching Julian tight, Paul and Teddy stopped just short of the stairs. Paul said, "Your father is dead, Princess."

"What?!" Fae's jaw dropped and she looked back and forth between the two men before locking eyes with Julian.

"But I—I didn't do anything! I've been in my room the whole time!" he said.

Teddy growled, "Shut up!" and punched him in the gut. He fell forward, and the men nearly pushed him down the stairs before Fae reached out and grabbed him.

Like a frightened child, she screamed, "Where is he?! Where's my daddy?!"

At the bottom of the steps, Julian was led down the next set, towards the throne room. Beyond the open gold door, men and women crowded the area leading into Caanis' living quarters. "Get the bloody hell out of here!" Paul snarled at them. Everyone quickly but quietly scurried away towards the main chamber like roaches in the light.

Pointing at the entryway, Fae quavered, "Is he in there?"

Teddy said, "Yes, but stay here. It's not a sight for your eyes."

Fae disappeared into her father's quarters, anyway, ignoring the guard's wishes. While his tempest of a heartbeat drowned most other sounds, Julian clearly heard, "Get out of my way! ... I said get out of my way, Bernie!" Seconds later, the faery cried, "No! Daddy! No! Oh God, no!"

The broken doll's wails instantly depleted Julian of any hope for a peaceful resolution. He shut his eyes, praying it was only a dream—one of 'Loki's tricks,' as Caanis would say, but he knew there was no hope or prayer that any god would grant him—not now. He opened his eyes to face reality. He knew he was awake, and he knew it was all true. The king was dead, and he was the convenient scapegoat. With his own tears forming, he looked at the men in suits and asked, "What happened?"

Paul said, "You already know, murderer!"

"Who told you I did this?"

"King Bernard," said Paul. "He told us of the incident you caused earlier, and how you attacked him. He told us Caanis banished you, and if anyone had a motive to kill him, it was you."

"This is bullshit!" Julian snapped. "Winter-Fae was there too! Ask her!" He shouted, "Fae! I didn't do this! You know I didn't do this!"

"Shut up!" Teddy yelled, punching him in the face again, knocking him down.

Julian shook it off and asked, "Where is Anna? She also knows I wouldn't do this."

Bernard emerged from the king's quarters, wearing a clean, buttoned white shirt. Resting comfortably, atop his head flourished his shiny new crown. King Bernard: the judge, jury, and executioner took one look at the accused and smirked. Julian tried to stand, but the royal intervened, gaining a running start and punting him in the nose. He fell flat. A thin red stream flowing from each of Julian's nostrils, Bernard said, "It doesn't feel so good, does it?"

He wiped the blood away, groaning, "I only did it because you were going to hit your wife. I didn't do this, though, Bernard. Surely, you know that."

Bernard kicked him in the nose again. "That's 'King Bernard' to you! Piece of shit … what was it you called me, 'a neo-Nazi-looking Adolf Hitler worshiper?'" He kicked Julian in the mouth. Even his new tolerance for pain couldn't block it all. "You wiseass motherfucker! I despise Adolf Hitler—even more than Napoleon. I am ashamed that he came from Austria!"

Bernard raised his shirt tail, unfurling a plump oval belt buckle. He pushed the shiny hunk of silver aside. "… but since you insist that I am a Nazi …" He pulled the entire belt free from his black slacks, firmly wrapping the loose end over his closed fist. "… let me oblige."

Before Julian could brace himself, a sharp piece of the buckle caught him in the ear. Then he took one on the bone just above his left eye socket. Every other second, the buckle came crashing down on some part of his head. He shut his eyes and tried to shield himself with his hands, focusing hard on the only one who could possibly take his pain away, but by the seventh or eighth lashing, Julian was numb to all but the taste of blood and the love of Violet.

"Stop it!" Fae cried, running to Julian's side. She knelt to his level, looking him over with her somber, tear-stained eyes. Shoving her finger in Bernard's face, she growled, "What the fuck's the matter with you?! You know Julian wouldn't do that! Even if he had, not like that!"

"This does not concern you," Bernard said.

"Caanis was my father and maker! Now he's lying dead in his bed! It damn well does concern me!" Fae broke down in tears again, squealing, "Someone put that God-forsaken dagger through his heart!" After catching her breath, she whimpered to the guards, "Weren't you watching him?"

"We sleep too," Teddy said.

"Who else could have done it," Bernard asked. "Avice? Anna? I haven't seen either of them since earlier."

Fae's eyes burned a hole through the new king. "Do you really want me to say who I think did this? Do you really want me to say it out loud, 'your highness?'"

"Are you implying what I believe you are? Because if you are, I can take you down to the dungeon and lock you away with your new friend."

"You're going to put him in the dungeon?!" Bernard grinned. "You know I can read Julian's thoughts. I can see right now he stayed in his room after we parted in the hallway. As for you, nobody can read yours, can they?"

"If you have something to say to me, 'former' Princess Winter-Fae, then say it!"

"You can strip me of my title. I don't care. It doesn't matter anymore. But I won't let you threaten me!"

"I don't make threats, Winter-Fae. Try me and find out." Pointing at Julian, King Bernard faced the guards and said, "Take him away."

The servants obeyed their master, picking up Julian's bloody, battered carcass from the ground and dragging him towards a doorway opposite the king's living quarters. Fae moaned, "I will fix this! I know you are innocent!" The last thing he saw before he was pulled out of view was Fae getting in Bernard's face again, repeating, "What is wrong with you? This is not the Bernie I remember!"

Once Julian was dragged into the darkness, someone shoved him down a set of steep, narrow stairs, carved into the stone. He flipped, flew, and bounced at least ten feet down before hitting the bottom. By then, he'd found his wrist had popped out of place, and he was sure his nose was broken from Bernard's assault. He winced. His pain—dull and sharp—attacked from multiple locations at once.

The men approached, Paul carrying a lit torch. He used it to ignite a fire pit at the bottom of the steps and another torch mounted on the wall at the opposite end. Julian stood at the center, nearly gagging on the small room's damp, rotting odor. Along his left, thick black bars, resembling those of a jail cell, stretched from one end of the room to the other, a closed door in the center. On the right, the setup was identical.

From the wall beside the fire pit, Teddy snatched a large keyring with two rusty keys. He used it to open the door on the right. Paul dragged Julian to the doorway and shoved him inside. "What's going to happen now?" he asked. Neither man replied. They shut the door and turned away, heading back up the stairs, leaving Julian alone with nothing but the clothes on his back and the holes in his heart.

Chapter Twenty–Nine

S everal hours had passed since Julian was locked in the dungeon. Voices occasionally stirred from upstairs, but he could not make out who they belonged to or what they said. His broken nose, along with all the other cuts and fractures he'd acquired in the fray, had healed. Though it hurt like a "Motherfucker," he'd even popped his wrist back into place. Physically, he was better, but he was still exhausted and otherwise scared and uncertain of what to expect from the new king.

His sore, baggy eyes occasionally collapsed only long enough to fly open again, jolting him back to life. *You just had to be a vampire, didn't you? You had to be 'trendy,' 'cool,' and ruin your fucking life—all because somebody worth having was finally good to you. Now, she's dead and you're alone again, thrown in a cell to rot. The joke's on you, asshole! But hey, at least you're a vampire. Everybody wants to be a vampire because it would be so edgy and glamorous to live on blood forever like a parasite.* Julian snickered aloud. *You are goddamn pathetic! No wonder Faith got away with all her bullshit for so long. Why wouldn't she use some stupid cunt like you? Even your own mother chose dick and drugs over you. Who wouldn't?*

"That's not a very positive attitude, Jul," a familiar, sweet southern songbird chirped. It was the voice which guided him in Alaska: *her* voice. Julian jumped to his feet, lunging in the direction it came from. There she stood: his flower, confined to the cell opposite his. Her perfect face squeezed between two of the narrow black cylinders, her hands tightly gripping the bar on each side of it. The blizzard of chills Julian invoked when looking into her brown almonds—he gazed into the eyes of God.

This was the first time he'd examined her face with such clarity since she was killed just inches over his body. After taking a moment to question her authenticity, Julian asked, "Is this a dream?"

"No, Jul. This is reality—your new reality. So, adapt."

As quickly as Violet's thick, succulent lips stopped moving, her image evaporated in a magical spark of smoke and insanity. Julian rubbed his achy, self-loathing eyes, squeaking, "What the hell?!" Frustrated, he paced the cell for several minutes. Unsure how long he would be there, he removed his jacket, figuring he might as well try to get comfortable. Without a bed or even a mat to lie on, he returned to the floor in the corner, wiggling and trying to find an ideal position before resting his head against the wall. He sighed, then repeated Violet's final words, "So, adapt." *Adapt to what?*

Everything in his life had changed in a day and he had such little time to think about it. Before the meeting with Dajhri and the Ahrims, he had remained hopeful about returning to Alaska afterwards—or at least home. He had no idea the Ahrims would hold him responsible for what Christopher Cauldwell did or how he and Xavier retaliated. To him, they were only doing what was right. Cauldwell unjustly took his wife and Xavier's daughter. *Who wouldn't want revenge?*

It was just his luck Caanis was murdered only hours after naming his new heir, and a jealous sister exposed the new queen to her husband and king. Julian already suspected Xavier and Anna were once in love, but he saw how the queen truly loved Bernard and how devastated she was when Avice lashed out. *But what about Bernard?* Julian hated the man, but he heard everything he said. *He said he always knew. But how?* The last of Anna's thoughts he heard was, "What have I done?" *What indeed, Anna? What do you know?*

***

Hey! Hey, wake up!" Julian's eyelids opened slowly, his restless gels burning. Paul stood outside the cell, waving a full IV bag. "Here," he said, dropping it through the bars. The pint bag landed between Julian's bare feet. "Eat up! We can't have you dying on us yet."

"What does that mean?" Julian groaned. "Where are Winter-Fae and Anna?" Offering no response, Paul turned to leave. "How can you just go from supporting Caanis to someone he named his heir right before he died? Doesn't that matter to you? Doesn't the new queen or either of the princesses still matter?"

Heading up the steps, Paul said, "Winter-Fae and Avice were stripped of their titles. There are no more princesses here, only the king and his queen."

"Then let me see the queen. I demand justice!"

Paul disappeared without another word, leaving Julian grunting in anger. He took a few sips of blood, hoping it would calm his nerves and help him go back to sleep. Luckily, it did.

***

He had no idea how long he'd slept, but Julian was rested and alert. He finished the blood, wondering, *Now what am I supposed to do?* He wasn't sure if it was the drink amplifying his brain activity, but suddenly, he remembered Violet's word, '*adapt*.' Though he took it as a hallucination from a lack of sleep, he wondered if her appearance wasn't of her doing rather than his. It was the only time he'd seen her outside of a dark silhouette since she was taken from him. So deeply rooted in his thoughts of her, it was at random, he remembered, *The diary!*

He checked the hidden pocket on his jacket, thanking God he started keeping it there instead of the backpack in his room. *At least this can keep me occupied until … what?! Where is it?* His newfound optimism was crushed, discovering the book wasn't there. Then it hit him. He'd left it on his bed the last time he read it, the night Dajhri arrived. At the top of his lungs—high-pitch and all—he roared, "God-fucking-damnit!"

Though he did not have the diary, he did still have his phone. It was zipped in one of the pockets. He turned it on, reading the time and date: *11:44 p.m. CET. Jan 7, 2020.* He knew he wouldn't have a signal, but he did a double take when he saw the battery power also read *44%.* To him, the number appearing twice was a pleasant omen. He knew it meant he was exactly where he needed to be, but he was certainly not happy about it.

Remember what Fae, Pana, and even Violet and Xavier have all told you: the universe doesn't always give you what you want, but it will always give you what you need. He turned his phone off to preserve the battery, laughing at the idea like it was a cliché.

***

What felt like another day came and went, followed by another, and more after that. Roughly the same amount of time passed between Paul's visits to bring blood. He still refused to answer any questions about the king, queen, or Winter-Fae, but at least he kept the fire going, though Julian felt it was more for Paul's own benefit rather than his.

Upon each visit, he used a small, jagged rock he'd found to scratch lines in the creamy gray wall. He did it to keep track of how many days he'd been there. After making four lines, he etched a fifth, horizontally crossing the others. By the seventh day, still no visits from the queen or her little sister, Julian began to consider himself a dead man walking; or in his case, waiting.

On the eighth day, when Paul brought Julian's meal, he begged him, "Please, just kill me and get it over with! I am losing my mind down here. If you're not even going to let me plead my case or talk to someone who can give me answers, just kill me!"

Paul laughed. "I am not going to kill you. The king has still not decided what he is going to do with you."

"Why are you doing this to me? Do you only follow his orders because he is the king, or do you truly believe I killed Caanis?" Having served his purpose, Paul turned away and left him alone again. Julian drank from the pouch and then scratched his third line in his second bunch. Two days later, he finished it. It was not until he had crossed off two more bunches, there finally came a change.

On his twenty-first day in captivity, Julian heard small footsteps—too light to be Paul's—come pattering down the stairs. At first, he thought the faery princess was another hallucination, like the one he had of Violet, but then she came close enough to reach inside the cell and touch his hand. "Julian?" she kindly whispered. He heard, saw, and felt her, but it was almost as if he was in a near catatonic trance.

"I am so sorry I didn't come sooner. My sisters were missing, and I tried to find them. Avice was hiding up in the caves, but we still can't find Annie."

Julian took a few breaths and blinked until his eyes were clear. Slowly coming to life, he cleared his throat. "What do you mean you can't find her?" he slowly asked, his voice scratchy and hoarse.

"Since she ran away that night, nobody knows where she is."

"Oh, God," he mumbled. "That son of a bitch didn't do something to her too, did he?"

"I don't believe he did, but we still don't know where she could be."

"What about Avice?"

"She came back. She was mad at Daddy, not Annie or you. After she calmed down, she felt horrible for the things she said."

"So, why are you here now, Fae? After all this time, why now?"

"I told you I was looking for my sisters. I don't mean to sound cold, but they come first to me. Besides that, the only way in here is from the throne room. Bernard is usually there, and he'd already stopped me from trying to come down here a couple of times before."

"How did you make it past him this time?"

"He left earlier, but I don't know where he went. After what happened, Avice wants to take me and leave, but we wouldn't know where to go, and I told her you have nobody. I didn't want to leave you behind."

"What is Bernard going to do to me?"

"I don't know, but he was right about the Ahrims. They have already sent us multiple threats."

"So, they are threatening the kingdom, and the king ran away?" Despite his slow, lifeless speech, Julian snickered at such a cowardly act.

Fae looked at his filthy bare feet, saying, "I wish I could have brought your shoes or some of your clean clothing, but if anyone saw them, they'd know I was here. I did take your belongings before anyone else could, though." She looked at the black leather jacket, balled up in the corner behind him. He'd been using it for a pillow. "I am glad you have your coat. You can use it to hide this."

She held up an old blue book: Violet's diary. Julian's eyes twinkled like stars, his other groggy senses blasting off like rockets to catch up. For a moment, he thought he might cry, but nothing perspired. Fae reached the thick hardback through the bars. His hand trembled when taking it. "Thank you," he said, observing the pitiful expression on her little white face while she sulked over his condition.

"I wish there was something more I could do, Glowstick."

He looked at the key ring on the wall. "You could let me out."

"If I did, they would never stop looking for either of us. They would know I did it, and it would end far worse than if I try to get you out of here the right way."

"What is the right way?"

"I don't know yet. I'm still trying to figure that out."

"What about Pana? Do you think Avice would take you to Alaska to find Pana?"

"I don't know, but what could he do?"

Julian sighed. "I don't know. I don't know how any of this shit works or what I can do to clear my name. I didn't do anything, and I feel like if Bernard is guilty, he's using me to get away with it. From what I've heard, it sounds like the Caanis and Aellin Reinhardt situation all over again."

"What do you mean?"

"The more I learn about him, the more I wonder if Caanis framed Aellin. He's your father and I know you love him, but if he did, what happened to him was poetic justice."

"You are right. I do love him. In hindsight, he was kinder to me than he was to my siblings. Xavier and Annie always believed he did it, but Avice and I weren't even there the night it happened. I never wanted to believe it, but to completely disregard the idea would be foolish."

Julian looked her in the eyes and said, "I don't want to die, Fae. When Violet was first taken from me, I did, but now I want justice or dare I say, vengeance. The more time passes, I can't help but think this is all leading to my execution for a crime I didn't even commit."

Fae reached through the bars and took Julian's hand. "Give me time, and I will try to figure something out." He smiled for the first time since he'd thanked Dajhri for saving his life.

"It's funny," he chortled. "Dajhri offered me a place in her kingdom, but I chose to stay here. If only I knew then what I know now."

Fae retracted her hand from the cell. "I need to go back upstairs before anyone starts looking for me. I will come back as soon as I can. I promise." She offered a heartfelt smile of her own before adding, "Stay strong, and remember, you are a glowstick." She headed to the steps, looking over her shoulder to get one more glimpse before ascending and leaving Julian alone again—now with something to read.

Chapter Thirty

8/1/46

Dear Diary

It has been almost a year since my last entry. Since then, mine and Eric's friendship has grown stronger. We mutually decided that is all it will ever be: just friendship. He has no hard feelings towards me, and we get along great together, but the romance is gone. I will never stop blaming myself for ruining his life. His mother won't even talk to him. She won't let him see little William either. Autumn still takes Xavier's money for her rent, groceries, and bills, but otherwise, she wants nothing to do with us.

We still find ways to have fun, though. Eric and I love listening to music and talking about cars. He's even taught me a little morse code his father once taught him from his time in the Navy. Back in February, he and Xavier took me to see "Adventure." It was Clark Gable's first movie since the war ended, and my first time back in a theatre since "Arsenic and Old Lace." The movie was good, and we all enjoyed ourselves, but Clark Gable will never be able to top his performance as Rhett Butler in "Gone with the Wind."

Bernard is becoming a little livelier and more talkative towards Anna and Xavier too. He still hasn't said very much to me. Anna said he sometimes cries himself to sleep. It breaks her heart, but it also gives her hope. When he first got here, he was numb and showed barely any emotion at all. Now, he can feel enough to cry. It is so sad, but they say we cannot heal until we feel.

Now, onto the reason I chose today for this entry. Last night, I was visited in a dream by Xavier. It was so real, like I was awake and in complete control of my actions and thoughts. In the dream, he told me vampires can communicate that way when we share our blood. In the dream, we were standing on a cliff. Of course, I thought it was only a regular dream, but when I woke up this morning, I told him about it, and he confirmed he really was there. I have been a vampire nearly two years now, and I still manage to be surprised by new discoveries and abilities. Eric and I have not shared our blood, but I wonder what would happen if we did. To avoid anything else going wrong, perhaps I should ask Xavier first this time.

Violet

12/25/46

Dear Diary

Today is Christmas! Last week, Xavier finalized the deal to buy our building! He owns the entire thing now, even the church downstairs. He, Eric, and I were just down there for midnight mass. The congregation didn't seem as lively as I had expected, nor as cheerful as Xavier told me they were the first time he attended, but I still enjoyed it.

Winter-Fae showed up and surprised us all last night. She went down to church too. She had a blast! When the pianist played Xavier's favorite hymn, "When the Saints Go Marching In," he and Fae got up and started dancing together. They got a lot of funny looks from the congregation, but they were having too much fun to care.

Fae was brought here by someone from Paris named Paul. I don't like Paul. He seems way too phony and uptight. Luckily, he didn't stay. I am so glad Fae came back. She even made me a Christmas gift. It is a white crocheted shawl, and it is every bit as adorable as she is! I missed her so much and I am glad she is here. I don't know how long she will stay this time, but the mood has been far more pleasant and light-hearted since she arrived.

Even Bernard seems happy. I see how he and Anna have been looking at one another nowadays. I could be wrong, but I think she may be falling for him. When she first came here, I could have sworn she and Xavier had something going on, but the more time passes, the less they act like they were ever lovers. Now they act more like siblings or just great friends.

I haven't talked to Anna about Bernard yet. I don't want to be nosey, but I do wonder about them. Anna is by no means damaged like Bernard, but she is very mysterious. Perhaps my New Year's resolution for 1947 should be to start getting to know her better. I'll check back soon and let you know how it goes, Diary!

Violet

Still most of the book left and no idea how long he would be there, Julian tried limiting his reading to just one entry per day, hoping the effort would give him something to look forward to. He spent his next several days scratching lines on the wall, drinking a blood bag when he received one, and keeping the diary hidden when needed.

12/31/47
Dear Diary

1947 wasn't really that special. I did accomplish what I set out to do, though. Last spring, I talked Anna into going on a night walk through Central Park with me. We had so much fun, it became a regular activity for us. She has been making a great deal of progress with Bernard, but I think our walks are therapeutic for her.

She has told me a lot about her past before her transition. I was shocked to discover her father was an advisor to Malcolm III, the Scottish king who succeeded the son of Macbeth. I made a bit of an ass of myself, trying to show off by telling her I read Shakespeare's "Macbeth" in high school. She told me about all the inaccuracies, but she seemed to admire my interest in hearing the truth.

She said just before King Malcolm's death, she was set to marry one of his nobles, an older knight named Gunther. Anna knew Gunther long before their marriage was arranged, and he was always kind to her. Gunther was a fierce warrior but a gentleman at heart. While courting her, he would recite poetry and often bring her Scottish bluebells, her favorite flower. She said he was beautiful. Like Xavier, he had long, pale blond hair. He was tall, muscular, and she even said he had a cute butt. Though the marriage was arranged by her father, she loved him, and he loved her.

In 1093, just weeks before Anna's sixteenth birthday and the date she and Gunther were to be married, he and Anna's father were marching home from England. Malcolm and his army had just invaded Northumbria. Robert de Mowbray, the Earl of Northumbria retaliated, ambushing them, and killing not just the king, but her father and Gunther too.

It broke her and her mother's hearts, but Anna said their grief failed in comparison to what it did to Malcolm's widow: Queen Margaret. After living a deeply religious life of constant, aggressive fasting, the queen was already ill. Only days after Malcolm died, she joined him. Anna said Queen Margaret was the most graceful and elegant woman she ever knew. She said Margaret was even canonized a saint in 1250 by Pope Innocent IV!

Anna's story started out so romantic, but then it turned tragic. I cried when she told me. I'm even getting teary-eyed now, just writing about it. After her father's death, Anna's mother wanted a fresh start as far away from that life as possible. She took Anna and her brothers to Arbroath, Scotland. After that, everything changed. ...

As the sound of Paul's footsteps approached, Julian hid the diary beneath his jacket. Like any other time, Bernard's new servant added logs to the fire and tossed the bag into the cell. Julian assumed he wouldn't answer, but he asked, "When is Bernard going to make up his mind about me?"

He surprised Julian when saying, "You'll know soon enough."

"What does that mean?" Paul left the dungeon, offering nothing else. Julian raised his middle finger towards the stairway, mouthing, "Fuck you." After drinking some of the blood, he pulled the diary back out from under his jacket and found his place again.

... Being the widow of one of the king's most trusted advisors, Anna's mother had wealth. She used it to buy an inn with a downstairs bar. Anna said, with Arbroath such a popular port city at the time, her mother did very well for herself and her children. The only downside was the bar attracted bad people, like pirates! Anna was often confused for a prostitute, and men were always chasing after her.

It took a little time for her to tell me, but just a few days ago, she told me the story of how she met King Caanis. By the time she was twenty-five years old, she ran the bar while her mother handled the more technical aspects of the business. She said she was tough and more than capable of breaking up bar fights, even getting caught up in one or two herself. I could see that. She might not be the biggest woman, but she has muscles and a tough "Rosie the Riveter" quality about her.

One night, an Irishman was in the bar, drinking heavily. Anna said she had a bad feeling about him, but she ignored it, thinking he was harmless. At one point, he tried to pick a fight with someone and was antagonizing others. Finally, Anna had enough, and she kicked him out. When the man refused to leave, she led him out into the street by his ear, and when she turned to go back inside, he stabbed her near the kidneys with a knife. Quite a few people saw it happen, but nobody stepped in to help until Caanis did.

According to Anna and Xavier, Caanis is a very big man. Anna said she blacked out quickly from blood loss, but before she did, he lifted her up and carried her away. She awoke as a vampire days later in Germany. She said she and Caanis eventually found the Irishman, wandering drunk near her mother's bar.

She wouldn't go into detail about what she did to him, but she did say the cruelty of her revenge gave her nightmares for a while. I asked her if she ever went back and saw her mother, but she wouldn't answer that either. Between us, I don't think she did. I imagine that choice still haunts her to this day. I am also willing to bet that is why it took her so long to tell me how it happened.

On a more positive note, just the other day, in only sixteen hours, it snowed twenty-six inches! To beat it all, it happened on the twenty-sixth! Weird, huh? I have never seen anything like that before. I just had to go outside and play in it. It is too bad Winter-Fae isn't here. She loves playing in the snow too.

She did come visit over the summer, but she only stayed a few weeks before she started getting homesick. I hope she comes back soon. I miss her so much. I think everyone does. Here's hoping 1948 will bring not just her back, but many other wonderful experiences. Happy New Year, Diary!

Violet

2/15/50
Dear Diary

Not much has happened since my last entry, not worth writing about until tonight. I am so happy for Anna and Bernard. I knew something was starting to bloom between them, and I was right. Tonight, they went on their first date! Bernard had never been in a theatre before, so Anna took him to see "Cinderella."

Yesterday was Valentine's Day. Though it has been five years since the fateful Valentine's night I almost killed Eric, I thought about it the entire day. Eric and I have moved past it, and now we act more like siblings than anything else. It is better that way. Hopefully, one day, I will find my true Valentine. I know he is out there somewhere, waiting for me just like I am waiting for him.

Eric has been trying to reconnect with Autumn and William, who is thirteen years old now! He is getting so tall. He and Autumn attend a Catholic church now near midtown. William loves it there. He says he wants to be a priest when he gets older. I really hope he sticks with it, but now that he is getting old enough to understand something is different about his big brother, I worry about how that is going to affect their relationship in the future. According to Xavier, our kind was originally spawned from demons and by the devil. I am not sure how a priest would feel about that, especially being his brother. I guess only time will tell.

Winter-Fae has not been here in almost three years now. I don't know what happened, but we haven't heard anything from her or anyone in Paris. I miss the little cutie so much and I hope she is okay. Even though she's not from Paris, I did get to meet another vampire last year: a queen, actually. Her name is Dajhri, and she lives in Peru.

Her kingdom is called Taltosia. It is an old, indigenous temple inside an extinct volcano! I had never seen anything like it before. Oddly, Dajhri looks a lot like me. We are both the same height, the same size, and her hair is as long as mine. Our only big differences are her hair and skin color. They are both just a little darker than mine. Her eyes are the most beautiful shade of green I have ever seen, while mine are just brown and boring.

She seems friendly and in touch with Earth. Xavier said she is a shaman, and she has taught him so much. That was his reason for taking us there. He thought Bernard might benefit from spending some time under her guidance. Xavier took us all down, but Bernard stayed two months before he came back, He does seem happier now.

With the forties gone and the fifties here, I hope this new decade brings many new changes and I meet even more wonderful vampires. It is so fascinating to hear their stories from points in history I've only ever read about in books. Even those mostly give false information. I hope this decade brings Anna and Bernard good fortune too.

Bernard and I have spoken some, but he is incredibly timid and so easily upset if I or anyone else don't approach him the right way. I still can't imagine what that poor man must have endured. Maybe one day he will open up to me. I see him as just as much a part of my family as Xavier, Eric, Anna, and even Winter-Fae. At the end of the day, us 'demons' are all we have, right?

Violet

6/23/50

Dear Diary

Though our friendship didn't last long, and for a while I admittedly resented her for shutting Eric out, it still breaks my heart to say Autumn passed away a few days ago. Eric is absolutely devastated, and my heart is in pieces for him. Apparently, she had lung cancer. I knew she was a smoker—like a freight train— especially after what happened to Eric, but she never told him or any of us she was sick. I am not even sure if Xavier knew. If he did, he never told us. He paid for her funeral and burial.

Little William has been all to hell as well. Eric has no clue where their father is. He left Autumn while she was still pregnant with that poor little boy. Trying to stay positive; something good did come out of it. William moved back in. Apartment forty-two, across the hall, had been vacant for a while, so Xavier let Eric have it for him and William.

It is only fitting they have their own place, especially since Xavier moved into forty-four last year, leaving me alone in forty-three. I would have taken forty-two, since this is still technically the brothers' home, but they both said it reminds them too much of Autumn, and they'd rather move forward.

Now they are living together again, I hope they can rekindle the close relationship they once had. William has always known Xavier and I were vampires, but when he was younger, it never registered with him the way it does now. I can tell he is not comfortable with it, but he is still kind and, like the rest of us, just trying to make the best of the situation. Say a prayer for them, Diary. They could sure use one.

Violet

4/11/51

Dear Diary

Today is my thirty-fourth birthday, but I could not care less. This entire year has been pure hell. Not only has Eric been taking Autumn's death hard, but William is also acting out. He and Bernard do not like each other at all. I have lost count of all the times William has screamed at other tenants in the building, calling Bernard the devil.

By now, everyone here knows he lost his mother, and like Eric, it is taking its toll on him, but two families from downstairs have already moved out. Even the pastor who preached down in the chapel moved out. He had lived in thirty-four since he was William's age, but he told Xavier he could no longer ignore the "evil presence" here.

Though Bernard has provoked William more than once, I do feel bad for him. He's come such a long way since Xavier and Anna rescued him, but he has a chip on his shoulder and an attitude if you push his buttons. His and Anna's relationship has come a long way too. It is obvious they are head over heels in love with each other. I think it is so sweet.

Although I completely understand why Bernard is the way he is, Anna recently told me something a little alarming, which might make William's outbursts not sound so crazy. Anna said she first met Bernard in 1944. She, King Caanis, and some of their men went to Austria to visit a vampire named Eustice Golding. Eustice became an enemy of Caanis after their previous kingdom split in half. They went to Eustice because a vampire from L'abisme was found dead inside the Paris catacombs. Out of fear that his old enemy was responsible, Caanis questioned him.

Anna said while they were there, she saw Bernard inside a small cage. When she asked Eustice to let him out, he cursed her, which in turn offended Caanis, and nearly caused a fight. Before things got so heated, Anna had a chance to talk to Bernard. She said he trembled uncontrollably, and though he physically responded in fear, he said he loved his father with all his heart, and he was only supposed to talk to him. Anna said she spent the next several days haunted by the image of him balled up inside that small cage, being treated worse than an animal.

She told me Eustice took Bernard from the streets in 1805, turned him in 1824, and kept him ever since. All that time, Eustice would go on and on about his hatred for Caanis. He was convinced the king murdered their previous king and framed the king's son. According to Bernard, all Eustice wanted was to avenge his king, but he knew he would never be able to. So, he remained bitter and took his anger out on Bernard until the day Anna and Xavier rescued him and killed Eustice.

What alarmed me is what Bernard has been telling Anna all this time. She said he would give anything to drive that same dagger into Caanis's heart, killing him the same way he killed his maker's maker and king. He said after all the years of punishment and abuse he endured, the man who made Eustice that way should die. Anna said over time, Bernard has eased up on saying such dark things, but he still occasionally goes on tirades where he blames all the abuse on Caanis and his kingdom. I am sure it's nothing though, right?

I told Anna it might be common for someone who endured all that torture to look for people to blame to cope, and that is likely what he is doing. I hope I am right, and it is just rambling. When Bernard is not upset by William or having a flashback, he is a nice man, and he makes Anna happy. In fact, I am just waiting for the day she comes running down the hall, glowing like a June bug, and telling all of us he asked her to marry him. It is just a gut feeling! I will let you know when and if it happens.

Violet

Chapter Thirty–One

O nce Julian received his bag of blood for the day, he etched his second line in his sixth bunch on the wall, marking his twenty-seventh day. With both dead, he knew Xavier and Violet could only come to him, but he did not understand why they had both stayed away for so long. He even wondered if his fragile mental state had something to do with it. His confinement to such a small space for nearly a month had pushed him to the brink of insanity. Reading the diary helped, but he couldn't see it bringing him any closer to freedom.

The last entry he'd read about Bernard was damning. Before that, he only suspected the man's guilt, but in retrospect, the new king's motives made sense. *If it really was him, he did exactly what he said he would: drive the same dagger that killed Arvil Reinhardt and his true heir through the heart of their murderer. Well played, you prick.*

Drinking his blood, Julian eyed the diary, unable to shake a feeling the king wasn't finished. *Not only could he have killed Caanis, but he may also want to see everyone else here die too.* He'd already stripped the princesses of their titles, and according to the diary, he did not just blame Caanis, but the entire kingdom. *What else could be hiding in there, waiting for me to discover?* He picked up the old blue book and started with the next entry.

3/13/52
Dear Diary

It took two years, but I was right. Bernard finally asked Anna to marry him. The church downstairs closed when the preacher moved out of the building, so we are going to decorate it and use it for the wedding. Xavier even hired someone to install lighting behind the stained-glass windows in the chapel and to fill in the outside with bricks to keep any sunlight from shining in.

I think he is more excited about the wedding than anyone. It makes me so happy to see him happy. He said he wants to invite everyone he knows from L'abisme, Taltosia, and Alaska. He even wants to marry them himself. The date has been set for April twentieth. Anna is excited, but just last week, while we were walking through the park, she said things got a little hairy.

Going into the marriage, Anna didn't want there to be any secrets, so first she told Bernard about Gunther, and then what happened between her, Xavier, and their sisters. Bernard was furious. Anna said he even changed his mind about the wedding until she spent all night pouring her heart out and trying to convince him he is the only man she loves. Given the circumstances, I could see how Bernard might be jealous, but living over the course of hundreds of years, I can also imagine we go through phases and feel so many things in different ways.

Anna told me something else. Until now I had only suspected it, but she said that night was not the only time she and Xavier were together. She was in love with him. According to her, they first became intimate near the end of the twelfth century, after the sexual tension became too much for either of them to ignore.

They met in secret, fearing what Caanis might think. She said the affair was passionate and risky, making her want him even more. She said the longer the affair lasted, the less frequently their rendezvous occurred. She said Xavier loved her, but he loved all the attention he got from other women more. He didn't want to commit to just her. So, between his fear of commitment and his carefree promiscuities, their relationship never went any further.

Even with my own suspicions confirmed, I was honestly shocked to hear such a thing. Anna said she didn't tell Bernard about it. She wanted to, but after the way he reacted over the opium incident, she was far too scared to tell him the rest. She broke down and cried when telling me. She feels extremely guilty about it, like she is a horrible person, and fears this will make her a bad wife.

She knows this is no way to start a marriage, but she just wants to be happy. She said she never planned on falling for Bernard. When she came to Xavier to ask for his help freeing him, her intentions were honest, but she'd also hoped it would rekindle their old flame. After telling me this, she said I am the only other one who knows about them. She made me swear I would never tell anyone. Aside from telling you, Diary, I will take this to my grave.

Despite Anna's secret, hopefully the wedding will show Bernard how much she truly loves him. We are all rooting for her. Even William seems excited. He keeps to himself most of the time, but now that he has scared off pretty much everyone in the building who isn't a vampire, he has calmed down a whole lot.

He only has a few more years of school left, and he still says he wants to join the priesthood. Xavier has already told him he would pay for him to go to college and study theology if that is what he truly decides to do. I never knew Eric and William's biological father, but Xavier has been a real dad to them both. He may not be human or perfect, but he is certainly a real man in every sense of the word, and also the closest thing to a father I've ever known.

Violet

4/21/52
Dear Diary

Well, Diary, the wedding happened not long before midnight, and boy was it something! There were vampires here from all over the place. From Alaska; Pana, Roland, Lusa, and Uki came. From Taltosia; Dajhri, her servant Serene, and four of the queen's guards came. From L'abisme, Paul and a vampire named Teddy brought Winter-Fae. Xavier even invited his other sister, Avice, but Fae said she didn't want to come.

The ceremony itself was really nice. Anna's dress and veil were both gorgeous, and Bernard looked quite handsome in his blue suit. As the maid of honor, I wore a purple dress. Eric was Bernard's best man, and because he wanted to match, Eric also wore blue. As always, Xavier wore black.

The newly Mr. and Mrs. Gaunt wrote their own vows. Anna's was sweet. Bernard got choked up and couldn't finish his without crying. It was the most vulnerable display I have seen of him yet. After the wedding, they had a lovely reception. Since we could not eat cake or drink champagne, we toasted with crystal glasses full of whale blood that Pana brought from Alaska. It tasted weird, and it made me feel a little bubbly, like it felt back when I first started drinking human blood as a vampire. I felt a little drunk. I don't particularly like to feel drunk, but I was in good, safe company, so it was an okay, interesting change.

I was mostly nervous about having William around the others since he is a human child, but surprisingly, they all treated him with the same respect as they treated each other. I didn't expect him to come downstairs at all, let alone stick around for the reception, but he did! He lasted longer than I thought he would, too. It wasn't until we all started toasting, he went back upstairs. Speaking of toasts, my favorite came from Winter-Fae. She made a joke, calling our building and gathering a modern Leviticus, a home for the forsaken.

It was so nice to see the Alaskans again, especially Pana and Lusa. I never knew it before, but apparently Lusa is a prophet. Though she keeps her visions to herself, she told me to trust and follow my dreams. She said they will show me the way and lead to Earth's salvation. I don't dream very often, but Lusa said I would eventually. I don't know what that means, but I am intrigued.

I wish her and the other Alaskans would have stayed longer, but they went back home immediately after the reception without even saying goodbye. I hope everything is okay. Just like Lusa, I discovered Dajhri is a prophet as well. It was she who told Xavier to come into my café the night I got hit by that car and would have surely died if he hadn't found me. So, I guess I owe her my life just as much as I do Xavier.

Dajhri, Serene, and the others from Taltosia are staying in an empty apartment downstairs until next nightfall. Paul and Teddy went back to Paris, but Fae stayed behind. She said she wanted to spend some time with us. As for the happy couple, they are next door. Anna wanted to go on a honeymoon, but Bernard did not. These walls are paper thin, and not that I am a pervert who is trying to listen, but I am surprised I can't hear them over there, consummating the marriage. Anna told me the other day, they hadn't even done anything yet, and she had looked forward to him giving her a "good pump."

Now that William is a little older and not so scared of Fae's appearance anymore, they've become friends. They are across the hall, playing chess with Xavier and Eric right now. Then there is me—here alone. I am glad everyone else is having fun, but I am feeling a little depressed and just wanted some time to myself. As I sit curled up on my leather chair, writing about everyone else, it makes me realize how lonely I feel on the inside. I even miss acting. At least that gave me purpose and something to look forward to.

I hope one day I can have my own wedding and wear a white dress and veil as lovely as what Anna wore tonight. Oh, Diary, is my one true love out there? If so, where is he? If I could have just one wish granted in my life, it would be to know what this fabled romantic happiness truly is. Is that too much to ask?

Violet

Up until then, Julian had used the diary to entertain himself and bide his time. Having faced a rainbow of emotions from sorrow to anger after reading the words once written by his love, he'd yet to encounter the specific shade of heartache her most recent entry bestowed upon him now. Violet wished for him long before he or even his own mother was born. Only lacking one more scratch on the wall from completing six full bunches, he cried for the first time since his imprisonment, taking in the pain and loneliness Violet once had. Still, he endured, making his daily scratch, and moving on.

***

The next time Julian slept, beforehand, he did something rather unorthodox for himself as of late: he prayed. "Dear God, spirit guides, guardian angels, and universe, have you forsaken me? Is this dirty dungeon cell meant to lead to my redemption, my own Leviticus, or am I meant to die here? Please, give me strength, guidance: anything. Deliver me to your gates or the devil's if you must, but if that is my fate, deliver it now. If it is not, free me and lead me where I need to go."

Julian had lain on his side with his eyes shut thus far, but he sat up straight, opening his lids and clearing his throat. Looking straight up at the creamy gray ceiling, he continued. "I miss *her*. I miss my one true love, and I beg you to bring her to me. In dreams or in death, bring me the paradise I deserve. I ask these things in the name of God, my spirit guides, guardian angels, and the universe. Amen."

***

Julian awoke, finding himself in a dark cave, but not like the dungeon where he'd fallen asleep. This cave was free of confinement. A light breeze blew through his hair, carrying a faint vanilla scent. He smiled and sat up on the rocky surface. His surroundings were too obscure to emit shadows, but he knew she was there.

Then came her touch, taking his hand and lifting him to his feet. It was the same feminine hand that had done it before. Three of his five senses had been stimulated, and though he could not see her leading him through the cave, he tasted her desire. It was the same desire she had for her husband the first night he dreamt of her coming to him like this. "Violet," he whispered. "I prayed for you, and you came."

She continued leading him but said nothing on their way out of the cave and into the snowy forest, the haunting green glow of the aurora borealis dominating the sky above, giving shape to the feminine silhouette. Just like before, she guided him through the equally black woods, full of tall, snowy trees, until arriving at the spring. In the more open, viridescent light, Violet's white dress illuminated.

Standing with her back to him, Julian watched his slain bride reach behind her bodice and unzip it. The dress fell to the ground surrounding her feet. The tips of her hair—appearing much darker in the weak light—appeared to lay just where her back ended and her bare bottom began. She stepped away from the clump of dress and into the water. Once the glowing green liquid reached her shoulders, she turned, slowly beckoning with her index finger for Julian to join her.

Like before, he removed the white tuxedo and shoes he never noticed he was wearing until then. Naked of all but his wedding band, ankh pendant, and labradorite bracelet, he entered the warm water and slowly approached his bride. Now only inches apart, Julian said, "I love you, Violet." He waited for a response, but it never came.

Though she was physically present, her eyes, along with the rest of her face, remained hidden behind a thick veil of dark hair. It was just like the last time they were there. "You don't have to be scared, my flower." Unsure why or how she could behave this way in one dream and another in others, he cautiously placed one wet palm against each of her unseen cheeks, unsure what to expect.

Violet's head slowly starting to rise, Julian trembled, the rumbling in his gut and static in his head begging him not to question or ruin this perfect moment, but to embrace it. He gave in, closing his eyes and puckering his lips. Moving in to kiss her mouth, his hopefulness was now flourishing. Just as his impatiently quivering lips grazed hers, something struck his arm.

"Hey, Julian! Wake up!" He opened his eyes, finding himself back in the dungeon, lying so close to the bars that Winter-Fae's little hand and arm could easily reach him.

Disoriented and frustrated, he whined, "Son of a bitch!"

"What?"

"I was dreaming of Violet."

"Well, sorry, but I have news."

"What is it?"

"It's about Bernard. In this past month, Raz Ahrim all but declared war. The Raja Kahiji felt personally offended by Rasul's treatment. I found out Bernard has not just been away, looking for Annie. He's trying to reach a deal with the Ahrims that will reinstate the truce and prevent any danger of a war against him."

"What kind of deal?"

Fae sighed and her eyes began to sag. "In exchange for peace, Bernard has agreed to give them you."

"Why?"

"Because they hold you responsible for publicly exposing us in New York City. To them, Bernard handing you over would be a peace offering and show them the new king is not their enemy."

"Are they going to kill me?"

"Either kill you or enslave you. From some of the horror stories I have heard, death would be better."

"What the hell am I supposed to do?"

"I don't know, Glowstick." Fae put her tiny hands over her eyes and cried, whimpering, "I am so sorry."

Julian took a deep breath and nodded, accepting his fate. "I asked for this."

"No! This was not your fault."

"I mean, I prayed for this to just end already. Perhaps there is a God, after all."

"I just wish I knew what I could do, but nobody will listen to me. I've even tried convincing Paul and Teddy that you are innocent, but they ignore me now. Their loyalty is to the kingdom, not me. They were both a part of Reinhardt, and they served King Arvil with the same loyalty as my father and, now, Bernard."

"I read something incriminating in Violet's diary the other day," Julian said. "Back before Bernard and Anna were married, he told her he wanted to stab Caanis in the heart." Winter-Fae gasped. "The way Violet described it, she thought he was only saying it because he was traumatized and wasn't actually going to do it."

"I can't believe this," she grunted. "I didn't want to believe it, but it really was him. That bloody shit killed my father." She released a series of short gasps in disbelief.

"Have you been able to find Anna yet?"

"No, I still haven't, but since Bernard has also been looking, I don't think he did anything to her."

"Unless that is what he wants everyone to think. After the meeting, when Avice started everything at the well, I heard Anna thinking 'What have I done?' and it had me wondering what she meant. After reading Violet's diary entry, I wonder if she realized what bringing him here has done. From the moment Caanis named him, Anna just had a look on her face—like something terrible had happened. What if this was always his plan, but she, nor anyone else thought he would actually do it?"

Fae asked, "Can you show me the diary entry?" He removed the book from his hidden jacket pocket. Turning to the correct page and handing it over. After reading it, she said, "I am not going to take the whole book from you, but may I take this page? I need to show it to someone."

"Yes, you may," he said before watching her gently rip the old piece of paper from the book. "So, when are the Ahrims coming for me?"

"I don't know, but I imagine it will be soon."

"What are you going to do about Bernard?"

Again, the porcelain doll cried, repeating, "I don't know." Desperate, mousy little squeaks followed, symbolically driving a dagger through Julian's heart. In his youth, he'd once heard a mother cat cry. It had come home after a night of prowling to discover all her kittens had been eaten by coyotes the night before. That same helpless requiem is what Julian heard now—until footsteps descended the stairs, abruptly silencing the orchestra.

Their eyes both froze on the steps when Paul appeared with Julian's IV bag for the day. He took one look at Fae and shouted, "What the hell are you doing down here?!"

She scrambled for words as Julian watched her hide the piece of paper in her white robe. "I—I—I just …"

Paul growled, "Get out of here!"

After leaping in fright, she hurried towards the steps. Before leaving, Fae turned back towards Julian and said, "Keep glowing."

Paul snarled, "Get out!" Fae ran up the stairs, leaving him alone with Julian. "What the hell did she say to you?"

"She just wanted to check on me, Paul. She knows I am innocent, and she is worried about me. Please, don't be mad at her. You know how sweet she is."

"I know," he said, tossing the bag inside the cage. He turned to walk away, adding, "I just don't care." He walked back up the stairs, leaving Julian alone again, with his meal and an idea of where his journey might soon end.

Chapter Thirty–Two

More days passed, each bringing new blood and another scratch on the wall. The only solace with which Julian could distance himself from the impending doomsday clock was dwelling in Violet's past. Bernard's motives were clear, but he felt there was still much more to absorb from his holiest of bibles, even if it meant taking all he learned to the grave too.

6/1/61

Dear Diary

It has been a while, I know. After Anna and Bernard's wedding, I fell into a deep depression for a few years. I had little desire to interact with others, and nothing good or bad was worth writing about. So, I tossed you in my closet like I did when I was a little girl. I recently found you after searching for a photo album I also put away a long time ago. Xavier and I want to make a collage for little William. Well, I suppose I shouldn't call him so little anymore. He is a man now. With their dark hair and thick eyebrows, he and Eric almost look identical.

As a child, William had a dream. Now, his dream has been realized. He has since graduated from college with a master's degree in theology. He even spent a year studying at the Vatican in Rome. Tomorrow, he takes his vows and officially joins the Catholic priesthood!

Xavier and I are so proud of him. Eric is too, but the brothers' relationship has not been the same since William moved out and started college. While he was still in high school, they had a big argument after Eric caught him smoking. It upset him because of what happened to Autumn. Unlike with Eric, William gets along so well with me, Xavier, Anna, and even Fae, but maybe that's because we are not his blood relatives.

Anna and I still have our walks through Central Park together. For a while, I wasn't sure she and Bernard were going to make it. She told me he was mean to her. She said behind closed doors, he was constantly throwing her past in her face. She said he's called her a "whore" more times than she can count. She never even told him the rest about she and Xavier either. After all this, she said she never will.

I couldn't believe what I had heard. Anna is often a sister and sometimes like a mother. She's not perfect, but she is a sweetheart, and she never deserved that. Since then, Bernard has gotten more help and Anna seems to have forgiven him. Xavier took him back to Taltosia for a couple of months. I don't know what shamans do, but after he came back, he returned with a more positive mood than he did the last time. He's even more outgoing now. According to Anna, his jealous outbursts occasionally still occur, but not like before.

Fae still visits sometimes. She never stays long because she either gets home sick and misses her sister or somebody will heckle her in one way or another out in public and it scares her. It breaks my heart just how cruel people can be. She told me all about how she and Avice met. They were orphans during the Great Plague, and Fire of London. She said Avice killed for her more than once, and she would even sometimes prostitute herself so they could eat when they were on the streets. Avice always put her little sister first.

I wish Avice would come with her someday. She sounds like a hell of a person, and I would love to meet her. The way Fae talks about her leads me to believe she is a lot like Anna: a strong woman with a tough exterior but also the type who probably cries in the shower. Fae said after they became vampires, they made a pact. If something ever happened to one, the other would immediately follow. That is love.

Xavier is doing well. Not long before my transition, he invested in a local hotel. The hotel has since become a chain, and the five thousand dollars he invested has already turned into almost a million! Now, he has his eyes set on Las Vegas. It is a desert town out in Nevada. He's considering investing big because many people are predicting Las Vegas will become a major tourist attraction. It's already a hotspot for celebrities like Frank Sinatra, Jerry Lewis, and Dean Martin! If he invests now, he believes he will eventually never need to worry about money again. I told him to go for it. Only time will tell if it is a smart move. Until then, wish us all luck, Diary, especially 'Father' William!

Violet

12/31/63
Dear Diary

I haven't had much to write lately. Everyone is doing well. William seems to be happy in the life he has chosen, but he occasionally reminds Xavier and Eric that we are sinners. William has a great heart, but I think his time in the priesthood has already started convincing him we are abominations. Xavier handles it well, and he told me no matter what William may say to him, he will continue to love him like a son. William loves him, too, but our family has always been unconventional. "One day at a time," they say.

Xavier decided to go through with investing out West. It is a hotel casino called the Las Vegas Parliament. Though fifty years is still a long way off, he predicts his stock will be worth ten million dollars by then! That is a lot of money. I am keeping my fingers crossed. We all are!

Violet

12/31/65

Dear Diary

Life is so fucking boring! I hate never having anything to do. I've wanted to get back into acting so bad, but Xavier forbids it. I hate it, but I understand why. What the hell am I supposed to do for all eternity if this is all it's going to be? Fucking hell!

Violet

9/27/67

Dear Diary

"Are You Experienced?" My God, I certainly am now! Jimi Hendrix is the greatest guitarist ever! A new record store opened down the street. It's called Bleecker Benny's New and Used Records. I had been meaning to go in there for a while. It's going to start getting wintery soon, and the new store gave me an excuse to beef up my record collection and have plenty of new music to listen to over the Holidays. One of those records was the debut of the Jimi Hendrix Experience.

His talent is so raw! The old man working at the record store was telling somebody about seeing him perform at this big music festival in Monterey, California, back in June. He said Hendrix was amazing, and he even lit his guitar on fire! The guy said he wasn't the only talented artist there. That's when he told me about another newcomer named Janis Joplin and her band, Big Brother and the Holding Company. He said her voice was nothing like he'd ever heard. He called her a white Tina Turner.

Unfortunately, he said the best song she sang wasn't on their debut, also called "Big Brother and the Holding Company." I bought it anyway, and I am very happy! First, I put on "Are You Experienced?" Would you know it, the first song is called "Purple Haze!" The whole album is great. I've never heard anyone play a guitar like that before.

Next, "Big Brother and the Holding Company" was every bit
as amazing as the guy said it was! Janis Joplin is still so young, and
with such a big voice like that, I can't wait to see what she can do!
The guy said there were so many great bands at that festival. Man, I
wish we had something like that here, a little closer to home.

I've spent so much time during these past years moping over
the life I used to have while ignoring the life I currently have, or the
times I could still have. The Village is starting to come to life with
music, art, and culture. New York is a great city! I've spent so long
locked away, and aside from my walks with Anna or occasionally
going on a solo flight, I'm always here. I'm bored of that. This new
music I bought hasn't only given me something to listen to, but I
think it is also inspiring me to find something new to fill my time
with. I shall see!

Violet

5/22/68

Dear Diary

Phew! I thought I lost you, but you were just hiding under my
bed. I have the coolest story to tell you, Diary. One night, not long
ago, while Anna and I were out walking, we happened by Max's
Kansas City, a popular nightclub. There was a huge crowd of people
outside, so we got curious and went in. The Velvet Underground was
playing on stage, and I shit you not, but Andy Warhol was there! He
and his entourage were sitting at a booth, people-watching. His art
was on display everywhere too.

Anna and I both had a blast! I'd heard one or two of Velvet
Underground's songs before, but wow! They played one called
"Venus in Furs" that was so dark and hypnotic. I loved it! At first, I
think they freaked Anna out just a little bit, but eventually she
started getting into it just like I was. I never knew she could dance,

but she has got some moves! Now it looks like I will have to go back to the record store!

Violet

8/14/68
Dear Diary

Well, I found the album with "Venus in Furs," but I found something else too. As soon as I walked in the record store, Benny, the old man who owns it and was working the last time I went in there, played me some of the new Janis! The album is called "Cheap Thrills," and my God almighty! Benny had said before, there was a song she sang at the Monterey Pop Festival, but it wasn't on the last album. It's on this one, all right! It's a cover of Mama Thornton's "Ball and Chain." It's the greatest song I have ever heard in my life! This whole album is gold, and I am in love with Janis Joplin!

Violet

8/17/69
Dear Diary

Holy shit! I think tonight was the greatest night of my life! I just got back home from the Woodstock Music and Art Fair in Bethel. There must be over a hundred thousand people there! I have never seen anything like that in my life. Thank God I can fly. Traffic was backed up for miles and miles and even more miles. They were flying all the musical performers in and out by helicopter. Bethel is a small farming town about a hundred miles northwest of NYC. It was certainly not meant to host that many people.

I got there close to ten, while Mountain was playing. I wish I had left home a little earlier and could have heard the end of Canned Heat's set. Somebody in the crowd said they were fantastic. After Mountain, the Grateful Dead performed. It was probably because it was raining, but they had some technical difficulties with their equipment throughout their set. They made the best of it and still put on a great show!

I was a little disappointed—not with the Dead, though. I'd heard Janis was supposed to be there, but her performance was going to be much earlier in the day before I could come outside. After Creedence Clearwater Revival finished their amazing headlining set, I started to leave, but just before I did, the crowd near the stage started coming alive again, chanting, "We want Janis!"

Just as I turned around and looked at the stage, the guy came over the speakers: "Miss Janis Joplin!" This big, extravagant band starts up with horns, trumpets, and saxophones! Then here she comes, screaming the lyrics to "Raise Your Hand." What energy! I couldn't believe it was her! For the longest time, I was frozen to the ground, unable to move or do anything but gawk, listen, and tingle all over. She started at 2:30 and performed until almost 3:30. She even closed with "Ball and Chain!" I danced my ass off! Apparently, due to all the chaos, her time slot was moved several hours back. Because of that, I finally got to see her! Thank God! She was every bit as powerful and magical as I knew she would be. Even on stage, she showed how precious her heart truly is.

Between songs, she asked the crowd if everyone was staying hydrated, had a place to sleep, and she even asked if everyone was stoned. I'd say! There was enough grass in the air to stone a dinosaur! At first, some of the people responded with boos to her questions. That's when she got concerned, asking what their negative response meant. She said everyone needs to take care of themselves first and not put themselves in a situation where they are going without anything. It reminded me of something Anna would probably say.

After she finished, I tried sneaking backstage, hoping I could meet her. Between security and all the people crowding everything, I didn't even try. I wish I could have stayed longer. On my way out, Sly and the Family Stone were playing, but after them, the guy who introduced Janis announced The Who and Jefferson Airplane were coming later. Regardless, I am so excited, I can't sleep! While I was there, I heard Jimi Hendrix is supposed to be there later tonight! If I see him too, I think I can die a happy woman. Hearing so many thoughts at once was a little overwhelming at times, but to see Hendrix, too, it will be well worth it to go again. I'll let you know how it goes, Diary.

Violet

8/18/69

Dear Diary

    I just got back home from Bethel again, and Hendrix wasn't there. It has been raining all weekend. Along with the traffic issues and performances getting delayed and rearranged, I guess he was canceled. The Band was playing when I got there. Blood, Sweat, and Tears and Johnny Winter played after them. I wish Fae was here. I know she despises the word, but being a fellow albino, I think she would have loved Johnny Winter and perhaps even be inspired. She's so scared to go out in public, but he embraces who he is and never lets diversity stop him from doing what he loves. Neither should she.

    The highlight of the night was Crosby, Stills, and Nash. I think they said it was only their first or second live gig ever, but they were amazing! I came back home as soon as they finished their set at around 4:30. I guess after leaving so early before, I got a little cocky this time and waited, hoping for another surprise. Hendrix is my favorite guitarist ever, and it's a bummer he didn't show up, but at least I got to see Janis! I am staying positive. He is so young; I am sure I will have many more chances to see Jimi Hendrix, and Janis Joplin too.

Violet

10/4/70

Dear Diary

What the fuck is happening? In less than a month, Jimi Hendrix and Janis Joplin have died! My heart mourns. I was so devastated when I found out about Hendrix, I locked myself in my apartment, blasting his records and crying. He died on September 18th. Janis died today. I have no words other than, "Thank you both. I love you." I will never forget the greatest night of my life, watching Janis perform in front of so many people.

What a horrible way to start the seventies! I was already upset as is. In August, Lou Reed quit the Velvet Underground. I went back and saw them a few more times after Anna and I first went. Every show was great. I don't understand why all of this had to happen. I was happy, goddamn it!

Right around that same time, I actually thought I could have met Janis. She finished her final tour over the summer. There was a rumor that she was staying over in the West Village, not far from my old apartment. The guy who owns Max's Kansas City also owns a steakhouse in the basement of the building where Janis was supposedly staying. Sometimes she would randomly show up and sing a song or two, and apparently Jimi Hendrix did the same.

I wasn't even sure if the rumor was true, but I got excited. I took my vinyl copy of "Cheap Thrills," hoping she would autograph it if we met. I went four times in two weeks, but she never showed up. I wanted to go more. I even wanted to roam the halls for her, but I didn't want to be a stalker or draw the wrong attention. I let it go after that. Now she is gone. She died on October 4th: 10-4—over and out, I guess. Fuck the seventies!

Violet

Turning the page, Julian softly whispered, "I'm so sorry, baby."

1/1/73

Dear Diary

 It took two years, but I think I am finally starting to feel better. Last night I attended a show at the Mercer Art Center: a multipurpose performance venue in the old Grand Central Hotel. It is huge! Conveniently, the venue is just a little way around the corner from my building. The building is old, but the venue itself has only been open a year.

 Last night, I saw Ruby and the Rednecks, Wayne County, New York Dolls, and Suicide. It was a hell of a New Year's show! I enjoyed myself. I've been a few times before, but last night I explored. It is so damn big in there! The entire place is a labyrinth of theatres and performance halls. I bet those cinemas could each hold two hundred people. They all fill up almost every night too. Every hallway had something fun to discover. Everywhere leads into a central lobby. Everything in the lobby is white and has a really trippy vibe. I've heard some people call it the "Clockwork Orange" room.

 The music itself is heavier and far more wild than I am used to, but is different, bold, and I like it! Maybe the 70's won't be so bad after all. Even Lou Reed put out two solo albums this year. I just recently bought his last one, "Transformer." "Perfect Day" is such a beautiful song, but my favorite is "Walk on the Wild Side." I love it!

 Anna and Bernard still seem to be doing okay, as does everyone else. Winter-Fae was here until last week. Xavier took her home. I think he misses Paris. I can tell he is lonely, maybe even a little depressed. I wonder how those who have lived as long as he and Anna find new ways to enjoy life. I can't imagine living forever being as fun as it might sound. I'm only fifty-five though, and I have a long wait before I can answer that myself. Until then, I'll enjoy it the best way I can. Tonight was a great new start!

                 Violet

Other Music for Uplifting Gormandizers. According to Xavier the know-it-all, a gormandizer is a glutton.

The place had an interesting vibe. It used to be a dive bar for country music, but I guess they rethought their marketing strategy because the bands I saw earlier were the furthest possible from country. The opening act was fun! They call themselves the Ramones, and this was their first live gig ever.

They all wore leather jackets, and their music was so energetic! There was barely anyone there while they played, but I cheered my ass off for them. The headliner was called Angel and the Snake. Their singer is this pretty blonde girl. I am keeping my fingers crossed for this one, Diary. Third time's a charm? This place reminds me of Mercer. I guess we'll just see how it goes, but I do have a good feeling this time!

Violet

8/16/75
Dear Diary

I have been going to CBGB for a year, and I fucking love that place! I love this new style all these great local bands are creating. I've seen the Ramones several times, and lately I've been stuck on a newer band here: Talking Heads. Since their first show two months ago, I've seen them seven or eight times.

Even Lou Reed was in there, watching them. He was right there. I wanted to ask him for an autograph, but I chickened out. Don't ask why. He seemed to like them as much as I do, though. Their bass player is great! She can jam! The first time they played, their singer seemed a little nervous. Now, he owns the stage. They have a song called "Psycho Killer" that I absolutely adore. That bassline is so killer!

Even the Ramones have gotten better. I love those guys! I bought a leather jacket because of them. It looks just like the ones they wear. I was happy to see Patti Smith and Lenny Kaye have

8/4/73

Dear Diary

Either God has it out for me, or something really fucked up is happening! Yesterday, part of the Grand Central Hotel collapsed without warning, taking all of the Mercer Art Center with it. I think four people died. I knew the building was old, but my God! The art center had only been open a year and a half, but the building itself was 123 years old, and I believe the hotel had been closed for some time.

Something good did come out of it, though. After a nearby apartment building suffered some damage, everyone in it lost their power. William, who has been working at a cathedral down the street, persuaded the bishop to open his doors to those affected. Now they have a place to sleep, shower, and eat until their power is back on.

I wish it were under better circumstances, but I am so proud of William. Eric and Xavier are proud of him as well. If Autumn were here, I know she would be too. He's come such a long way from that little boy who loved playing checkers and reading his Baby Bible. I am so happy he turned out this way. As for me, I feel like I am back to nothing again. After acting, I found music. Everyone I love dies or something completely unexpected happens. That's life, I guess.

Violet

8/17/74

Dear Diary

Against my better judgment, I am going to try this one more time. Earlier this year, I found a new place on the corner of Bleecker and Bowery, not far from here. It's called CBGB and OMFUG. That is an acronym for Country, Bluegrass, Blues, and

formed their own band, the Patti Smith Group. I remember them
both from Mercer. Patti was usually an opening act. She read her
poetry. A lot of people booed or laughed, but she ignored it. Patti
Smith is a badass!

Last night I saw Talking Heads, Heartbreaker, and
Blondie—which is what Angel and the Snake call themselves now. I
like Blondie, and I think the name is catchier. Debbie Harry, their
singer, is so pretty. She's a great vocalist too. Among her, Patti
Smith, and Tina Weymouth—the bassist for Talking Heads—women
kick just as much ass there as the men do! Please, God. Don't take
this place from me too. Outside of home, these are my people.

Violet

4/9/77

Dear Diary

We call it punk rock. The crowds of CBGB have gotten so
fucking wild! For the first time ever, a British punk rock band
played in America. They are called the Damned. The crowd was
intense and violent, but that's just how punk is. Some call it slam-
dancing. Some call it moshing. I just call it beating the shit out of
each other. It is common, and I enjoy it. Consider it "hands-on
stress relief," Diary. I've come home before with some bumps and
bruises that hadn't yet healed. Neither Xavier nor Anna liked that,
but tonight, I think I finally went too far.

After the show was over, I walked home. As I was getting
ready to go into my apartment, Anna screamed bloody murder from
down the hall. Before I even looked at her, I thought something had
happened and she had died right there. When I looked, I saw her
staring at me—completely mortified, the look on her face was like
something out of "House on Haunted Hill." I asked, "What? Does
my hair look that bad?" She appeared so freaked out, I thought she
was exaggerating.

So, then she screams, "There's a fucking blade in your back!" Sure enough, a switchblade was sticking out from between my shoulder blades. I walked all the way home like that and didn't even know. I can only imagine why it scared Anna the way it did, considering what happened to her. I feel terrible about scaring her. There's a serial killer loose in the city right now, anyway. She pulled it out with no problem, but she and Xavier are both pissed off at me for being so careless. They said I'm not allowed to go back to CBGB. I understand why it would scare them, but I don't want to shut myself away again. I will figure it out. I am more pissed off that some asshole ruined my jacket than that he stabbed me. Sure, I can patch it, but it's still got a hole in it now. Fuck you, random stabber person!

Violet

7/14/77

Dear Diary

After the craziest lightning storm that I have ever seen, we just went twenty-five hours without power! That was a first. There was so much rioting and looting all over the city last night, it was insane! Xavier forbade me from going out anywhere. He and Eric are gone right now, to get us more blood, since what we had in the freezer was ruined. They left just after dark and should be back before daybreak. Xavier knows people across the world who work at hospitals and can get him all he needs.

I don't know if it was the power outage, the heat, or what, but for the first time in quite a while, Bernard threw a fit last night, after hearing Xavier say Eustice Golding's name. He was talking to Anna about the night Arvil Reinhardt was assassinated. The conversation had nothing to do with Bernard, but he took it the wrong way.

He and Xavier almost got into a fist fight over it. He stormed off, saying he was going out to look for the .44 Caliber Killer—some fucking psycho that's been shooting and killing people in Queens and the Bronx for the last year. There's a city-wide manhunt, and I think Bernard just needed to blow off some steam.

While he was gone, me and Anna had some girl time. She told me the night Arvil Reinhardt died, there was some kind of public dispute between Caanis and Eustice Golding. That's what she and Xavier were talking about. She said just hearing the name set Bernard off. Somehow, he also thought Xavier was mocking him.

I never realized just how much hell Bernard had actually been through. He is completely bald, but he has a thick mustache and goatee. I always thought that was an odd look for him, especially for his age and coming from Vienna in the early 1800s. Anna told me the story of how that happened. She said Bernard once told her, "Eustice liked his boys smooth and hairless, but he also enjoyed a little tickle."

Bernard was born in 1800. Just five years later, Napoleon Bonaparte seized Vienna. Though Napoleon was fair to the commoners, some of his soldiers were not. Anna said Bernard hid when they came. Soldiers were looting and raping their way through the city. Before Bernard's father could do anything, they shot him dead. Hiding under a pile of dirty clothes and rags, he watched Napoleon's men take turns on his pregnant mother until they all finished and shot her repeatedly for fun.

After they left, Bernard went straight to the constable. Eventually the soldiers were caught. Napoleon himself had them publicly beheaded by the guillotine. Their charge was treason. Bernard watched them die too. He was then taken in by the Vienna Foundlings and Orphans Home. Anna said as soon as he got there, he knew something wasn't right. Almost every child was dying from some kind of stomach disease. He said nobody cared about their living conditions, not even the nurses. The moment he got his first stomachache, he snuck off while everyone else was sleeping.

A few days later, Eustice Golding found him. Bernard was so sick by then. He might have died if he hadn't taken him in. For the longest time, Eustice was kind to him. He treated him like a son. Even at such an early age, Bernard knew what Eustice was. He'd bring in older boys almost every night, but they'd never leave. In exchange for food, warmth, and health, Bernard didn't care. But one day, he became an older boy himself.

At sixteen, Bernard had turned a hobby into a passion and became quite a skilled brew master for his age. He felt confident in his recipes and wanted to open a tavern. Then he could make his fortune and a life of his own. Up until then, their relationship was friendly and platonic. When Eustice told Bernard he wasn't allowed to leave, everything changed. Like he had as a child, Bernard tried to sneak away, but Eustice caught him. Anna said that was the first time he beat and forced himself on Bernard. After that, she said it happened almost every night over the next eight years.

He tried more than once to escape. That was when Eustice first put him in the cage. Eventually, he regained his captor's trust and was set free. Then as Eustice slept, Bernard slit his own throat. He wanted the nightmare to end. He only survived because Eustice awoke and found him. He turned Bernard, against his will. After he healed, Eustice rarely ever let him out of his cage again until Anna and Xavier freed him, 120 years later. I still can't believe Bernard went through all that and survived. I wonder how long it took him to tell Anna everything. That poor man. I honestly don't even know what to say.

Violet

11/1/77

Dear Diary

For the first time in a while, I had a great time last night! Back in August, the police finally caught the .44 Caliber Killer, or "Son of Sam," as he calls himself. What a relief! He shot and killed six people and wounded seven others. The city was tearing itself apart, but us New Yorkers can finally relax now that the boogeyman is gone.

Being Halloween, that is exactly what me and Eric did. We wanted to do something new and special. We'd heard about a horror musical called "The Rocky Horror Picture Show" making a huge impact. The movie is so popular, it gets shown all the time and people go dressed up like the characters, throw confetti, squirt water pistols, and have an absolute blast! Me being me, I had to take Eric to check it out!

I absolutely loved it! Eric liked it too. I think it might be the best musical I've ever seen. It's the most fun I've ever had at the movies. The songs were great, and I laughed so many times. It was so cool seeing so many people dressed up as their favorite characters! Not to sound like a stupid valley girl, but Dr. Frank-N-Furter is so dreamy!

Eric said if we go back and see it again, we should dress up. I don't know who I'd want to go as, though. He was joking, but he said we should go as the two main character's, Brad and Janet, in their underwear. Yeah, right! Honestly, I can't stop thinking about how perfect Xavier and Anna would be as Riff Raff and Magenta.

By the time we got back, Bleecker Benny's was already closed, but first thing tonight, I am going to go in there and see if they have the soundtrack. I think it's been out for a few years, so it should be there. It felt so good to go out again, and I know Eric had fun too. Isn't that what life is about—having fun? I think everything is going to be all right now, Diary.

Violet

On Julian's thirty-third day, he scratched his third mark on his seventh bunch of lines. Still waiting, wondering, and suffering every second of the dreaded countdown in his murky depths, he opened Violet's diary again, ready to dive headfirst into the only peace he knew. Lately, he'd read more than just one entry each day. He couldn't help it. His one true love's story had become so powerful and captivating thus far, and he refused to die before he could finish. Turning to the next entry, he gasped, reading a familiar date at the top.

9/24/81

Dear Diary

    Sorry I have been away for so long again, Diary. I've not really had anything to say. I am only writing this now because I experienced something interesting today. Earlier this morning, Eric gave me such a beautiful gift. An even more beautiful feeling came over me when he did. The gift was a silver ankh pendant on a chain. It was so random, especially since it is not my birthday. I love it!

    Eric told me the ankh is the second oldest symbol in the world, after the swastika. I already knew it is the symbol of Raz Ahrim, but I learned it is also the Egyptian symbol of life. I asked him why he would give it to me. He said he saw it in a shop window and felt called to buy it, unable to explain why.

    When he clasped it around my neck, I shivered. I have slept since then, and I had a dream. In the dream, I was searching for someone. I don't know who or where they were, just that I was supposed to find them. I remember seeing flashing blue and purple lights. I also seem to remember the desert. I want to say it was Las Vegas, but I don't know. I was there, walking around outside at night, feeling so lost but knowing there was someone I had to find. It was so real and lucid but hazy. I believe someone really was there, and I was so close to finding them, but I woke up before I could.

    It's funny. I have always believed in the idea of a fairy-tale romance and my very own Prince Charming. Once upon a time, I thought it was Eric, but now I feel like it is whoever was in my dream. As I slept while wearing my new necklace, that feeling I had when Eric first put it on me returned. In the dream, I was loved by somebody. I think I might know why. What if I found him? What if soulmates are real? What if this is what Lusa meant about trusting my dreams all those years ago? If so, what does the necklace have to do with it? This is so weird but fascinating! I'll keep you posted, Diary!

Violet

Julian smiled, finishing the page. A warm sensation engulfed him like a hug in a way that almost seemed real. He gently pulled the same ankh pendant from behind his shirt collar. Eric had given it to her on the day he was born. "She felt me enter the world." He rested his hand over his heart, tapping it three times, saying, "I love you," like he'd done the night of the rave. *Squeeze-squeeze-squeeze ... squeeze---squeeze---squeeze ... squeeze--squeeze--squeeze.* Julian gasped, breaking out in chills when the soft tugs came. It was just like before, her telling him she loved him in threes.

Little footsteps suddenly came rushing down the stairs, snapping him out of it. Before he saw her, Winter-Fae yelped, "Julian!" Then she appeared at the bottom, carrying his black sneakers. The wide-eyed expression on her little face was alarming. She tossed his shoes inside the cell and said, "Here! Put these and your jacket on. Quickly!"

Julian hopped to his feet. "What?! … Why?!"

Fae grabbed the keyring from the wall. "I'm getting you out of here, but we must go now."

"Why now?"

"I just heard. The Ahrims are coming for you tonight." Without hesitation, Julian slipped his dirt-riddled feet into the sneakers. After tucking Violet's diary away in the hidden pocket, he put on his jacket. Fae unlocked the door and let him out. "Okay, here's what's going to happen. When we get to the top of the stairs, you're going to put your arms around me and hold on for dear life."

His heart racing, Julian asked, "What about Bernard and the others?"

"They are distracted. That's why we must go now!"

"Distracted how?"

Fae took his hand, pulling him towards the stairs. At the top, she held a finger up for him to wait while she peeked around the corner. She whispered, "Okay. Hold on to me." He wrapped his arms around her miniature, robed shoulders. Instantly, the faery shot off, whipping through the main chamber like lightning, far too quick for any eye to notice.

They landed at the top of the spiral staircase only a second later. Fae pushed in the correct brick and moved the wall. They both passed through, and she put it back. Then, she withdrew a small black flashlight from a pocket in her robe and clicked it on. Freedom bound, she took Julian's hand and said, "Come on, Glowstick!" And off they went.

Chapter Thirty-Three

The runaways fled for over a mile before stopping to catch their breath. Graffitied above their heads, an enormous, olive-gray anaconda with black oval spots and almost twinkling beady green eyes instantly stole Julian's awareness. The daunting serpent's vast jaws pried open like a bear trap: over one hundred massive razor-sharp teeth glistened with eager anticipation. The ophidian was hungry for blood—his blood. "We need to wait here for someone," Fae said, bringing Julian back to the light.

"Who?"

"Me," came a whisper. A soft crunch followed. Winter-Fae raised her beam on Avice's pointy nose and chin. Walking forward, the rest of the sturdy brunette appeared.

"Was anyone suspicious?"

"Bernard at first, but I lured him into my room and took my dress off." The former princess cringed at her own words. "I told him a king deserves everything he wants. I said I could please him in ways he never dreamt of if only it meant I could be his new queen. I wanted to vomit—I still do—but I played it so well, my sweet baby Fae, up until he finally called me a whore. He reminded me I will never be as good as his true queen. Then he left my room.

"I was worried you wouldn't have enough time." Her eyes moving to Julian, she added, "Clearly, I was wrong. You're lucky my sister and brother care so much about you. I know you're innocent, but we are risking everything for you. Never forget that."

"I won't," Julian said, nodding in thanks. "So, where are we going? Alaska?"

"What could they do?" Avice asked. Lifting a flashlight of her own, casting light down a lengthy passage that eventually disappeared into more shadows. She motioned the others to follow her. While walking, she said, "First, we must get you out of Paris. The Ahrims are coming. After that, we will go to Taltosia. The Alaskans have numbers, but Dajhri is the only one who can help us now. She knew what kind of man our father really was, but she would not stand for this. Then, we can reach out to the Alaskans. With them and Taltosia on our side, we'll have a better chance of survival if a time comes when we all must fight."

"Do you have any idea where Anna could be?"

Avice sighed. "I do not. But it's all my fault. I was so angry with my father; I took it out on you both. I … I am sorry."

"I don't care about that now," he said. "I just want to get out of here."

Fae took her big sister's hand as they walked. "Don't worry, Avy. We'll find her. Wherever Annie is, I imagine she's devastated. After Bernard's naming, I think it all hit her at once—what he always planned on doing. Even before all this, there was no way she could have known he would go through with it. She really loved him, and she wanted to see the best in him. We all did. Sadly, I think that was his plan."

Patting Fae's shoulder, Avice said, "We will take our home back one day, even if it is by force. Nobody may believe Bernard is guilty, but everyone who is still there remains only because they don't know where else to go. They don't care who the king is as long as they're all safe and taken care of."

They continued for nearly another mile, passing through other caves, chambers, and flooded walkways. By then, Julian's shoes and his pant legs up to his knees were soaked. Approaching an intersection, Fae said, "I think we are almost—" but it was then a heavy ruckus came barreling from the left adjacent corridor, connecting to the others just ahead. All three froze in place.

Not a second later, the mammoth, bearded beast, Buldgera appeared in the glow. Sauntering close behind was Rasul. Both stopped to look. Rasul's sunken, gray eyes protruded at them all.

Visibly gritting his rotten teeth, the decrepit old being raised a long, pointed finger at the end of a jagged nail, snarling, "Him!"

"Run!" Fae screeched. Wedged between them, Avice grabbed her sister with one hand and Julian the other—not flying, but rapidly gliding upright through the cave at extraordinary speed. From close behind, the beast roared. Avice picked up pace, yelling, "Hold on!" Haphazardly maneuvered through the caves, Julian scraped and skidded along the walls at some of the narrow turns. When something sharp and fierce broiled his arm, he knew he'd been cut good.

After it seemed they had lost the behemoth, Avice came to a stop. Somewhere along the way, she had dropped her flashlight, but Fae still held hers. She aimed it at Julian, exposing a thick tear down his left jacket sleeve, from wrist to elbow. Beneath the gash, a long filet of missing flesh exposed a fat strip of moist, red tissue. The raging wildfire sensation had only intensified when he looked at it. Then the red turned pink, and finally, peach, as the damaged layers and any hint of pain healed to completion almost instantly.

Between frantic breaths, Fae whispered, "What are we going to do?!"

"Turn that light off," Avice whispered back, more calmly than her sister. Fae complied. Everyone listened closely. Aside from their breaths and the occasional dripping, there was nothing else to hear. Finally, Avice muttered, "Okay, I think we are—"

An earth-shattering, sonic boom of a roar nearly blasted Julian's eardrums out of his skull. It was the angry roar of a god—a vengeful god. The monster's call gave way to Fae's sharp howl in the dark. Amidst the chaos, her abandoned flashlight clicked on, exposing Buldgera gripping Avice in his overlording clutches. Fae charged, leaping onto his back and gouging the giant's eyes. He released Avice. Dazed, she fell to the ground. Unsure what to do, Julian stood motionless, only able to watch the ancient monstrosity struggle, desperately fighting to grab the little white speedball. Her pencil-thin fingers dug deep, skewering a slimy white golf ball from its socket. Buldgera squealed like a wounded pig. Scuffling wildly, he slammed hard into the wall, dazing the faery and gaining control.

Half consciously, Avice screamed, "Fae!"

Otherwise fastened in fear, Julian picked up a rock the size of his fist and chucked it at the mighty beast. It bounced off his face, doing nothing. Buldgera gripped each of Fae's bony ankles in his catcher's mitt sized hands. Face-first, he violently slammed her into the jagged limestone wall on his left. She yelped like a dying puppy. Then, he slammed her into the wall on his right.

"Fae!" Avice cried, trying to stand. Buldgera repeated the assault, slinging her back and forth until her red and white robe peeled away. Then, he started smashing her face and upper torso into the ground like he was shaking out a rug; bending his knees while taking her down before standing and forcefully whipping her at least another twelve feet back down. Julian, still too scared to move, Avice finally got to her feet. "Fae!" She charged, but the doll's limp body was used as a bat, viciously knocking her away again.

Cackling demonically, Buldgera held his achievement up high. Numerous red gashes and gouges covered her naked white body, each sparkling in the abandoned light's ray. Her perfect little face was completely destroyed. Emitting whistles, small green mucus bubbles popped from the torn pink outlet where her little nose had been attached. From her cherry-red mouth, she gasped, using her final effort to catch a breath she couldn't find.

Something then finally awoke in Julian. He shot forward with no plan in mind other than to save her. But like Avice, he, too, was knocked away with the makeshift weapon. While trying to get up, he watched what little life remained in Winter-Fae's oceanic eyes die while rolling back with the tide into her shattered skull.

From the ground, between her sobs, Avice shrieked, "Stop it! Just stop! She's dead! Please … just put her down and leave her alone!"

Still clutching her ankles, the devil creature made a wish, yanking each little leg with all he had until splitting her several inches down the middle. A grotesque, wet ripping of rubbery flesh filled the air until one leg and a thick flap of meat tore from the rest. Globs of the faery's precious blood and entrails landed at the killer's feet. Julian screamed, "No!" until losing his breath. Buldgera tossed the inanimate pieces aside, his only eye locked on its target. He marched forward until Avice jumped on his back.

While squirming with the beast, there was a split second her unforgiving eyes met Julian's. *'Never forget that.'* From between her quivering, bloody lips, she wailed, "Run, you fuck!" Julian did not want to leave her, but he didn't know what else to do. So, he ran into the darkness as fast as he could, his co-savior's selfless agony and death rattle serenading him until it became nothing at all.

By then, he'd turned many corners and slammed into several walls, completely losing track of where he was. Knowing he'd made more sound than progress, he stopped. Reaching out with both hands and fingers, he slowly tiptoed until finding the nearest wall. He gently pressed his back against it, minding his breath and pounding heart.

He spent several minutes in that position, listening and waiting for any hint of the evil lurking in the shadows. At one point he swore he heard footsteps from somewhere close. He held his breath for as long as he could, hoping it would be to his benefit. As more time passed, he remained firmly glued against the wall, not daring to move a muscle. Many more minutes of listening and waiting for the next time he would have to fight or fly passed, but as the silence lingered, he began to wonder if reality could be manifesting in his favor.

After standing in place for nearly another hour, his legs were trembling like tender veal. He'd been sitting for a month anyway, and even as a vampire he was discovering he was not impervious to fatigue. Then, he took his first full deep breath since it all began. With that breath, he nearly vomited, revisiting the grisly image of sweet Winter-Fae's delicate body, torn apart in such a wicked way. *I could have done so much more! Why didn't I?* The intense, crippling pain in his gut forced him to the ground. Goosebumps followed in the heightening fear that someone or something caught the clear squeak of leather on its way down the wall with him.

He searched his surroundings in the dark, running his shaky hand along the edge of a crevice at the bottom of the wall. It was tight, but it was just big enough for him to slide through. Trying to make as little noise as possible, he gently wiggled his way inside it. Not even five minutes later, light appeared in the tunnel.

Loud, heavy stomps and two muddy sets of feet went trampling past his eyes; one massive and wrapped in dirty cloth, the other bare and meager. Each left behind a shiny set of footprints less than a foot from his face. The Ahrims—none the wiser of how close they were to the man they sought—never stopped. They hurried onward; they and their light slowly fading back to nothing. Even after they were gone, Julian remained inside the crevice for at least half a day, exhausted, but knowing he'd be damned if he slept at a time like that. So, he waited, praying they wouldn't double back and find him.

Another full day must have passed with no sounds, sights, or movement from outside the crack before Julian grew brave enough to remove his phone from his pocket and turn it on. The time and date read: *2:22 a.m. CET, Feb 11, 2020.* He'd hoped his phone would have a signal, but it did not. He turned it off again to avoid making any sounds, debating whether he should make a run for it.

Not only was he tired, but he was also extremely weak and shaky from hunger. He knew if he stayed in place, he would soon die, so he made the only choice he could. He slid out from the crack, slowly climbed to his feet, and turned his phone back on. Using its flashlight to lead his way, praying it be a way to freedom, Julian walked softly, his eyes and ears on high alert.

Though he couldn't perceive it, the air was so cold that his unsteady exhales blew white. He took baby steps with caution, fearing any corner he turned would bring him face to face with the Ahrims. He hoped they had given up their search by then but refused to assume what any of them were capable of.

The only thing he knew for certain was amidst the cruelty behind Winter-Fae's tiny white body ripped to shreds, he did nothing but stare: too scared to be anything but a coward. *She and Avice gave their lives for you, and you just let it happen! How fucking dare you!* As if Julian's fragile emotions and blunt self-opinion could not sink any lower, he'd spent the last day and a half chastising and eating himself alive over what he did—or didn't do.

While trying to find his way through the black labyrinth, in the back of his mind he thought, *If the Ahrims are still here, maybe they should find me. Maybe I do deserve to die. Then I could be with you, my flower.* Julian had aimlessly wandered for hours, finding it harder and harder to keep his balance. A weight was pulling him down. The weight pulled like an anchor. He knew what it meant. Death was close, but he was lost and just wanted to find someone who could help him get out or at least tell him where to go. At one point, he saw his phone's battery power: *22%*. His time with the light was drawing to an end.

He'd come to a flooded corridor. Though he didn't know where it would lead, he advanced. All the other flooded areas he'd waded through had only reached his knees thus far, but after just four steps, he was almost thigh deep. When he took his fifth, the floor was not there to catch him. He fell forward, submerging his hands, wrists, and the lower part of his stomach in the putrid water.

The instant his phone touched liquid, his light and lifeline died. He furiously shouted, "Goddamn it!" loud enough to alert anything close by. "Fuck it! Come and get me, you ugly-ass motherfuckers! I'm tired! I am fucking tired! Here I am! Come kill me! Just fucking end this already!"

Crying out in agony, Julian splashed his way through the dark, crossing the hall until reaching the other side. By then, he was so exhausted, he just wanted to lie down and sleep forever. But instead, something inside him just kept glowing. Though it was of no use to him, he stuffed his wet phone in his pocket. He extended both hands as far as he could reach, taking slow steps and feeling for another wall. From the silent darkness, a genderless voice whispered, "Julian."

"What?! ... Who—who's there?"

Again, it whispered, "Julian." Using only his sense of touch to make his way through the dark, he ignored it and moved on, assuming it was only in his head. "You do not belong here." Despite the terrors already haunting him, the spirit's words and alarming way they were calmly hissed raised every hair he had.

"Help me, please!"

Raspier, and even more annoyed than the last, something fiendish groaned, "Leave us!"

Julian desperately cried, "I am trying! ... I am fucking trying!"

From only inches away, the aberrant specter declared, "Leave us or die!" Julian nearly jumped out of his shoes before the adrenaline kicked in. Fueled by a second wind, he broke into a full-blown sprint towards whatever the darkness was hiding in his path. When he thought he'd lost whatever it was that chased him, he started slowing down. It was then something like a tangible hand shoved him from behind. His balance faltered, he stumbled forward, trying to regain his footing until there was nothing left to tread upon. Headfirst, he toppled over himself for what seemed like an eternity, taking in every last cut, thump, and effort of pain until spiking headfirst into something hard like a lawn dart and blacking out cold.

***

Sometime later, Julian gained a conscious thought. He was disoriented and unsure where he was, but he knew he was awake. Seconds passed in the dark, then minutes, before he knew he was stuck and couldn't move. When his consciousness began fading once again, he knew it was for the last time. *Could it be?* From the darkness, a central white ball of light appeared in his dying view. It hurt like life to smile, but upon such a sight, he used the last of his earthly energy to grin wider than he ever had in his entire life. *Yes! Thank you, God. Sweet death, at last!*

The light expanded as it drew nearer, growing extravagantly until the winged silhouette of a vanilla-scented angel appeared at the forefront. Two gentle hands reached down and took Julian's broken body and empty soul from such an unforgiving world. Knowing, even in death, he was now safe, he closed his eyes and used his final breath to emit the only word that ever truly mattered: "Violet."

Chapter Thirty-Four

Julian's first conscious breath was not of vanilla or subterranean rot but alluring sage and dragon's blood, gently guiding his senses back into the light. Once there, his eyelids slowly began to crack, instantly drawing his baby blues to the orange flicker on a gray overhead ceiling. His hands at his sides, he rubbed his clean fingertips over the soft mat beneath him. *Wait a minute!*

His eyes opened fully, and he shot up straight, expecting the worst but finding himself in the middle of a small, foreign room. Lining three of the four walls were many tiers of at least one hundred white candles per wall with calm flames resting atop their blackened wicks. Otherwise, the room appeared empty. A doorway stood centered on the barren wall to his right. In place of a door hung a thick green blanket.

Unlike the creamy limestone of the catacombs, Julian instantly noted the darker walls and ceiling were not rough in texture but smooth and man-made. *Where the hell am I? Is this Raz Ahrim?* Only wearing his silver ankh, gold wedding band, and the labradorite bracelet Lusa gave him, he looked for his clothes or something to cover his naked body. All he could find was a white sheet on the mat. While wrapping himself, a pleasant, feminine hum began from somewhere beyond the doorway. Startled, he gasped.

The humming ended abruptly. A silky, venomous voice announced, "You're awake." The blanket ruffled when a mocha hand emerged and pulled it aside. Then she appeared. It wasn't her white dress, mighty beehive, or her starlet figure Julian saw first, but her eyes—her vibrant, emerald-green eyes—piercing his veil with no effort at all.

"Queen Dajhri?!"

"As I am," she said, smiling on her approach.

His heartbeat and breath rising with uncertainty, he asked, "Where am I?"

She rested a hand over his shoulder, her calm touch invoking instant relief. She said, "You are safe. This is Taltosia."

"In Peru?!" She bowed her head. "But how did I get here?"

"I found you at death's door. Had it been any longer, you would have expired."

"How did you know I was there?"

"I saw you in a vision. You were hiding from the Ahrims. You roamed those caves for so long." She moved her palm to his cheek and whispered, "You were so brave."

Presumably safe, and free to be vulnerable, Julian broke with pleasure. The tears gushed from his eyes like they were hydrants. He cried until he screamed. He screamed until he cried again. He fell to his knees near the bed-sized mat, shaking uncontrollably, purging something deep from within. Dajhri went down with him, wrapping her thin arms over his head, cradling him firmly against her gentle bosom. "Shh," she softly moaned in his ear. "You are safe now."

Julian snorted. "Am I, though?" he asked, looking up at her. "Bernard killed Caanis, and he framed me. He offered to trade me to the Ahrims in exchange for saving himself. Winter-Fae and Avice were …" *'Never forget that.'* "Winter-Fae and Avice were both killed trying to save me." Just saying their names was enough to bum-rush his conscience. His tears returned. "I just fucking stood there! I could've done so much more, but I didn't. I was such a coward!"

Dajhri pulled him close again. As he wailed, he caught a whiff of her rosewater scent. The aroma triggered a random memory from his past. Wanting so desperately to focus on something new and forget all the hell he'd endured, Julian wiped his eyes and cleared his throat. "You're a shaman, right?"

"I am."

He snickered through the anguish. "The smell of rosewater … it takes me back. At the end of 2018, I sat in ceremony with *Ayahuasca,* and the shaman—her name was Michele—she occasionally sprayed rosewater in my face to keep me cooled off. Now, every time I smell it, I think of that, and …" His vocal cords were strumming so fast, longing to outrun the memory of his most recent catastrophe, that he got choked up, started coughing, and gasping for air. For a split second he remembered Winter-Fae and how her final breaths were drawn.

Dajhri, who'd been watching and listening patiently, took him in her arms again when the tears returned. "It's okay," she whispered. "On the power and honor of Lilith, you are safe." The queen slowly waved her hand through Julian's hair, invoking chills down his back while rocking him like an abandoned baby.

He spent several minutes heaving and crying into her. Knowing his suffering was nothing in comparison to others, Bernard included, he was only as good as he could be. He also understood it was the life he'd chosen and there was nobody to blame for his choices or the trauma they created but himself. Still, he had every right to feel human, even if he no longer was one.

When his tears dried, he asked, "What now?"

"Without you to give the Ahrims, L'abisme is likely unsafe."

"Everyone I cared about is either dead or missing. After the way I was treated by Bernard and his men—just for being a convenient patsy—forgive me, but I don't give two shits about them."

"Who is missing?"

"Anna. She ran away after a fight with Avice. Bernard tried to hit her, and I attacked him. Sometime that night was when Caanis was assassinated. All that time, she just left me there. I don't guess I blame her, though. I think she got the impression we were all ganging up on her. It was a mess after you left."

"I see," said the queen.

"Where do you think she is?"

"I imagine she is somewhere safe, but I wouldn't know where. The new queen and I were never well acquainted, not like her brother and I." She smiled, mentioning Xavier. "He was a fine man; certainly one of the better of us." She took both of Julian's hands. "He likely never told you this, but I once saw his death in a dream. I did not know how or when it would occur. I only knew he would die for those he loved. When he last came here I swore on my life that I would counsel you and Violet when his time arrived."

Even the sweet sound of Violet's name nicked another delicate thread binding Julian's already unraveled soul. Everything hurt. More saltwater gathered at the ducts, but he held the drip back. "Xavier told me your prophecy. I didn't know you, but I should have gone with you when I had the chance. By then, I already knew Caanis wasn't good, but I stayed because I had made a friend."

"Caanis had demons, not just the obvious. He made very poor choices in the past. He put all his love and loyalty into an idea that tumbled. From the moment he first settled in the catacombs, knowing he'd been duped, he never took another breath without regret. He never learned from his mistakes. Thus, his misogyny became his demise. Some men never learn."

Almost snickering, Julian said, "The man also had a temper. Although, considering some of the shit I did, I suppose I have no room to talk."

Peering deep beyond his wilted blue eyes, she said, "You do have tremendous rage in you. I fear that rage may lead to your downfall. It could lead to your divine purpose, depending on how you choose to harness such power. You are a rarity, Julian Frost. All you've faced as a human and now as a vampire … and yet a soft, beating heart is nestled beneath that rage. How does such division not torment you to madness?"

"What is madness?" he asked. "What is rage, for that matter? I always tried to see the best in everything, but that is my problem. I want to believe goodness is burrowed deep inside of everything. I want to believe somewhere the birds still sing. I want the world to be the peaceful place society tries to trick itself into believing it is.

"This world is a parasite without consequence. It's like somebody could kill someone else and then go to their funeral, look at all the sad faces and wonder, 'Why is everyone crying?' That is when I ask myself, if I can see this, why is it so hard for others to understand such basic morality and refuse any accountability? Am I really so rare to be one of the few who still understands the basic idea of common sense—or am I just like everyone else?"

The queen's endless gaze never strayed from his honest outpour. "I know it is not my place to judge others, but lately, I cannot help but wish it was," he continued. "I wish I could be the one responsible for choosing who should stay and who should go. Sometimes, I wish I could be that consequence this world so rightfully deserves. And sometimes, I picture the world burning around me while I rejoice like Nero with his fiddle, wondering why everyone is running around, screaming and on fire.

"To answer your question, Dajhri, I was tormented to madness and became self-aware of my rage long before I knew our kind was real. Does that make me a monster? I know I shouldn't feel this way, but I just can't care anymore. They say we cannot help how we feel." Dajhri's deep green stare remained fixed as if she were at a loss for words but still every bit as enthralled.

He took a breath, snorted, and wiped his eyes again, nearly shaken by his domineering proclamation, and the unusual warmth and love he briefly inhaled before suddenly any notion of an orgasmic apocalypse was as dead and gone as everything else that mattered. "I—I'm sorry," he said. "It's just that … I think I'm losing my mind. At this point, I don't care what this world does. I just know I don't want to be a part of it anymore, especially knowing what awaits me on the other side."

"And what is that, Julian?"

"Violet."

Dajhri pumped a smile. She said, "I mean no disrespect, but how do you know this? How do you know your ever-after will be with her?"

"Faith, I suppose. I know that doesn't make it certain, but that is what I choose to believe. I refuse to believe in an eternity without her. Enlightened or not, there is nothing wrong with wanting something that exists beyond this life, is there?"

"There is not."

"Violet and I have a bond. The day I was born, she even wrote about me in her diary." *Her diary!* "Where is my jacket?!"

"It is in your room."

Julian looked around, asking, "Is this not my room?"

"This is my personal prayer room. I kept you here because this is where I often spend hours in meditation."

"But why am I in here?"

"You nearly expired. I even thought you had while I was bringing you here. For a week, I have spent many hours praying over you to Mother Lilith."

"I have been here a week?"

Dajhri bowed. Julian tried to imagine how badly his body must have been damaged when he first arrived, but his growling belly caught both his and the queen's attention first. Dajhri smiled. "It is doubtful that you would remember, but I fed you. In your state, I could only give you so much without overwhelming or choking you. Now that you are awake, I can show you to your room so you may dress. Then we can feed."

"How do you feed here?"

"We do not drink from bags. but I will not make you kill."

"Would it matter if I did?"

A warm, motherly smile and wide-eyed stare brightened the queen's already perfect complexion. "Dear one, you are so lost. I will find you."

"Like you found Bernard?"

The queen sighed. Her sunny expression withdrew but her universal enchantment remained. "Bernard's demons are beyond saving. I thought I could reach him. He fooled us all."

"Didn't he come down here a couple of times? According to Violet's diary—"

Dajhri took his hands again. "He did. And that is my burden. You need not worry about Bernard." Facing the door, she said, "Come with me. The night has arrived, and thus so has the hunt."

Chapter Thirty-Five

Before he was taken anywhere, Dajhri showed Julian to his room. It was small and bare like his last, containing a bed, covered in a black blanket set on one side, and a round, lit fire pit on the other. Julian's clean and neatly folded clothes lay on the bed. Beside them was his black leather jacket, the torn sleeve now patched and repaired. On the floor, at the foot of the bed, sat his black sneakers, also clean.

Julian checked the hidden pocket beneath the breast of his jacket. He sighed joyously when running his fingers over the hard rectangle beneath the fabric. In other pockets, he found his keys, wallet, cellphone, and its charger. He set the phone aside to continue drying out. Then, he removed the white sheet he'd wrapped himself in and started putting on his clothes.

After wearing the same red shirt and blue jeans for a month in the dungeon, he shuddered at the idea of sporting them again. Despite his newfound hatred for Bernard, while dressing, he couldn't help wondering how the new king survived over a century of living in captivity when only a month had pushed him to the edge of his own sanity.

Once dressed, he joined Dajhri, who waited in the hall. He followed her past other covered doorways and mounted torches until reaching an opening in the middle of a narrow stairway. Glowing in torchlight, the gray stairs fell fifty feet or more to the bottom, where the queen's living quarters and prayer room were located.

She beckoned Julian to ascend with her. After climbing the steep stone stairs for at least fifty feet, passing other hallways with their own blazing torches and covered doorways, they reached the top. A closed bronze door awaited. Dajhri used a rusty old key to open it, giving way to a small mausoleum-style room. On the other side, a closed gate door was all that separated them from the Peruvian nightscape. For a moment, the narrow bars of the squeaky old gate resembled those of the same one housing L'abisme's hidden passage where Fae and Avice once lived. '*Never forget that.*'

Outside, Julian found a clear view of the starry sky. Though his closer, earthbound environment hid all its nature beyond the black, the strong scent of moist vegetation and soil became that of a humid forest. Dajhri asked, "Would you believe my temple is at the summit of a volcano?"

"That's what I had heard," Julian said. "It is a very interesting spot, but I would be worried it might erupt."

"This volcano was extinct long before man was ever here. It would take a tremendous act to wake it once again. My husband and I chose this location to build our temple upon—after it was revealed to me in a vision."

"Your husband?"

"Yes. His name is Sami. He was my king and savior. It is ironic that he expired at nearly the same time as Christ. This temple is not just our home. It is a monument to the bravest warrior I will ever know." After a breath *in memoriam*, she said, "You cannot fly yet, can you?"

"I cannot."

"Then you may hold on to me. We are going somewhere far. It is never wise to feed close to home."

When Julian wrapped his arms around the queen's narrow shoulders, a powerful yet welcoming surge unlike in their previous exchange rocked his innards. Dajhri emitted such calming vibrations, washing away his timidity like a warm bath. He gasped at such exhilaration, a momentary stroke of bliss he'd never received from any immortal but her. Both now prepared for flight, she instructed, "Hold on tight."

She began slowly. Once they surpassed the massive summit, Julian caught a view of the entire volcano, basking in the brilliant moon's aura. Even at such an altitude, the mound drastically overshadowed the beautiful but miniature 3-D landscape of ridges and valleys beneath it. Such a sight took him back to the day he had flown over the Sierra Nevada Mountains on his way to San Francisco, just a month before meeting Violet. He was in an airplane then, observing such a natural elegance on his way to see a shaman. Now, the shaman was the airplane, flying him who-knew-where to see who-knew-what.

Dajhri made haste through the night, but for Julian, riding shotgun with her compared to others, Violet included, became something else entirely. She remained as smooth and steady as a flowing pipeline. He found breathing and looking around without the wind burning his eyes or taking his breath away easier. *Perhaps it is my power. Even though I can't fly, maybe I am adapting.*

"That is correct. You are evolving." Julian gasped and squirmed. Dajhri's voice did not enter his ears but his mind, like a thought.

He wondered, *Are you talking to me telepathically?*

"Yes."

That night we first saw each other in L'abisme, did you ask if I am the one?

"I did."

Julian was truly amazed by what the queen could do, but the most obvious question he could ask was, *Why?*

Decelerating, from her mouth, she said, "We are here." Julian stared in awe at the massive growing galaxy of little white specks amidst a great black universe beneath him. The queen steadily floated downward. Eventually, a big white blob came into view, also expanding and taking the shape of a cross. Julian slowly began to recognize the enormous, bathed-in-bright-light figure. It was a statue—a human-shaped statue, each extended hand reaching far outward. Even closer, the face of Jesus Christ appeared, looking down upon the big city of sinners below.

"Are we in Rio de Janeiro?"

"You know your geography," Dajhri chortled. Moments later, they landed in a vacant wooded area, at the base of the mountain below the giant statue, and only a few hundred feet from civilization. The queen said, "Follow me," and Julian obeyed, stumbling through the thick and unseen. The scent of spicy barbeque began filling the air and sounds of upbeat pop music grew louder while following the streetlights ahead. "Some of these *favelas* are dangerous. Crime and violence are very bad here, so stay close. Let me do any talking. Do nothing to draw attention."

"What are *favelas*?"

"Poor neighborhoods. Rio is home to over six million people. A quarter live in poverty. These underdeveloped areas are home to drug dealers, traffickers, murderers, and others who have no place in our world."

They passed down a walkway between two dingy white houses with chipped paint sidings and broken windows. Next to one of the houses, a rusty red tricycle lay tipped on its side. Julian was unable to imagine whomever it belonged to growing up to be anything more than a contributing stereotype. He shook the feeling as they reached the sidewalk, joining what appeared to be a block party in full swing.

From somewhere nearby, the loud music blared, and the smell of grilled meat hit Julian's nostrils more intensely than before. Men, women, and children all conversed in the street, along the sidewalks, and in front yards. Mixed with the sweet scent of human food, Julian occasionally caught whiffs of burning cannabis. At one point he saw a young, tan-skinned boy sucking on a blunt before passing it to a skinny, dark-haired little girl. She couldn't have been more than five years old. The child wore cut-off jean shorts, a skimpy, red, string-bikini top, and her young, round face was caked in enough colorful makeup to leave Julian wondering if she had parents or pimps.

After walking a little farther down the street, the pop music had been drowned out by funk *carioca*, playing much louder from a radio on someone's front porch. Next to the radio sat an older, obese man with honey-colored skin, a thin, dark mustache, and a receding hairline. Wearing jeans and a wife-beater, the man gripped a brown beer bottle in one hand and a nearly finished cigarette in the other. Dajhri was the first to spot him. With no one else close enough to notice, she shouted, *"Ei lindo!"* from the sidewalk.

The man smiled. *"Oi, boneca!"* he replied.

Having no clue what they were saying, Julian watched Dajhri take a few steps into the man's yard. *"Meu amigo e eu estamos procurando um terceiro."*

"Um terceiro?" said the man, stroking his chin and offering a curious gaze.

"Que tal se divertir de graça conosco?" Dajhri asked. The man giggled and blushed.

Julian wondered, *What the hell are you saying to him?*

Dajhri winked at him while the man on the porch said, *"Sei não. Como vou saber que não vai dar ruim pro meu lado?"*

She laughed. *"Ah, vamos, lindo. Eu quero muito! Você mora sozinho?"*

"Sim," said the man.

Dajhri took a few steps closer, seductively batting her eyes at him. *"Eu vou deixar você colocá-lo em qualquer lugar que você quiser."*

The man's fat red cheeks turned an even brighter shade of bashful as he practically leapt from his rusty metal chair, nearly tripping over himself as he did. He motioned them both forward, saying, *"Ta certo, pode entrar."*

Dajhri took Julian's hand. "Come on," she said, giggling under her breath with the joy in her eyes of a cat about to devour a canary. Though he had no idea what to expect, his obscene imagination ran wild with ideas. He followed her lead up two wooden steps to the porch and past the old screen door. The giddy round man eagerly slammed a larger white door behind them. From inside a small living room, an old box television displayed a *futebol* game at low volume and the smell of freshly cooked black beans and ham filled the air.

Roughly five feet in front of the television sat a brown recliner. Beside it, a two-tier wooden end table caught Julian's eye. A dirty paper plate sat atop, along with a green coffee mug next to it. On the bottom tier, the dark outline of what looked like a handgun lay next to a tied-off plastic baggy, half full of a white powdery substance.

His jolly face already glistening with sweat, the big man took his final drag from the cigarette before dropping the butt into the empty beer bottle. He tossed it through an open doorway leading to his kitchen. The bottle clanked when landing in the trash can. He looked at Dajhri with dirty intent in his narrow eyes. Pointing towards an open door beside the kitchen, he said, *"Vem aqui querida. Eu vou te der a foda de uma vida."*

Dajhri playfully cupped a hand over her mouth and snickered. She then took Julian's hand and led him towards the dark room where the man was already waiting. Along the way, Julian's heartbeat raised a click. Taking a full breath was becoming difficult. He knew what was coming. All he wanted was to escape it, but he couldn't, not unless he truly was prepared to die for it himself. Bernard had warned him a day would come when he would have no other choice but to kill. Dajhri said she would not make him do it, but he knew that fateful day was inevitable.

Once inside the room, Dajhri shut the door. Julian said, "I can't see anything."

"Turn the light on," she replied. By the time he found the switch and flipped it on, the big round man stood before them both completely naked. His hairy stomach hung low and the fleshy fanny pack beneath it draped over a small, flaccid penis, half buried in its surrounding girth.

Caught off guard, Julian jolted in surprise, squeaking, "What the fuck?!"

"Relax," Dajhri said.

Doing whatever necessary to avert his eyes from such an unwarranted sight, he scanned the man's dirty tanned carpet and unmade bed. The floor was littered in clothes, but not all of them were his. A little pink t-shirt with a big, glittery silver star—like a little girl would wear—lay spread out. Next to it, a small pair of white underwear with brown teddy bears lay, also spread out as if it were intentional.

His raised heartbeat and shortness of breath was guilt creeping in before, but now, it was his own eager anticipation. After what he just saw, he welcomed the change, the urge. The old Julian might have protested, but his ghost was lost in the ancient catacombs of Paris with all the others. The new Julian trembled with possibilities. He understood why the queen chose such a place to feed. As the fat man grunted and wiped the sweat from his forehead, ready to get his, he grinned at Dajhri, and in broken English, uttered, "Let's fuck."

She approached the man slowly and provocatively, placing a hand on each of his bloated cheeks. He closed his eyes and scrunched his lips. Julian's heart pounded faster and his body trembled while watching Dajhri lean forward, also closing her eyes and puckering her lips. Instead of kissing his mouth, she went for his throat. Her jaws chomped down on the side of his neck, blood instantly seeping from between her lips and the man's greasy flesh.

He screamed in agony, shouting incoherent Portuguese until Dajhri released her grip and spit a mouthful of blood, skin, and other gore into the man's horrified face. High-pitched wails continued as the blood poured from the mouth-sized hole in his neck. All the while, Dajhri laughed about it. Julian watched, still excited and nowhere near as appalled as he knew he should be. In his eyes, the man deserved every second of pain, and even that was an orgasm compared to what he likely deserved. Dajhri knew it too. She smiled with pride at the man waddling around the room, still squalling in his native tongue.

From the porch, the blaring music drowned any chance of escaping such a fate. Still, Dajhri slapped her palm over the man's mouth, likely just for her and Julian's own benefit. While catching the gushing blood in her mouth, the man struck her in the head with his fist, ruffling the queen's beehive. She grabbed the hand he had struck her with, unnaturally twisting it back and forth, around, and around, laughing harder at the torture.

She bit into the other side of his neck and spat out the raw meat. Practically glowing, her vibrant green eyes peered up at Julian. "Won't you come feed with me?"

The man struggled far less as he lost more blood, but Julian was hesitant. His stomach growled at the sparkling red fountain. "Fuck it," he said, approaching while Dajhri held their victim still. She sucked on one open wound, and Julian, the other. For the first time, fresh, warm human blood touched his lips. The taste was metallic like all the others, but this blood also contained the flavor of corn oil. His eyes popped open in such a way he'd never felt before, and though he was the furthest from sexually aroused, his bodily functions would show otherwise.

Attempting his last stand, the man wiggled an arm free and punched Julian in the ear. "Ah, fuck!" he groaned. Dajhri twisted around that hand like the other. The man gurgled, unable to energize a scream. After Julian rubbed the pain from his ear, he returned to the wound, just as happy to know of the fat man's suffering as Dajhri. Sensing the Brazilian's life slipping, he pulled his blood-soaked lips away and said, "Rot in Hell, pedophile."

Visibly tired of holding the man at bay, Dajhri twisted his head and Julian heard the snap. The blood continued pouring and they drank until each had their fill. Once they finished, they released the man and he collapsed. Just like the carpet, walls, and parts of the ceiling, the vampires were also painted red. With more energy and life pumping through his veins than he'd ever felt under any other circumstance, Julian burst into a mad fit of laughter. Once it ended, as if the pain, guilt, and other anguish had never lurked at all, he said, "Damn. Now I need a cigarette."

"We must go," Dajhri said. "There is a lake near the volcano. We can bathe there."

Julian followed her out the back door, into a dark yard. Ahead lay the mountain's base. At the top, Christ the Redeemer stared down, looking directly into Julian's eyes, saying, *Depart from me, wretched one, for I do not know you*, without speaking a word. Julian laughed at the inanimate object, the fresh blood providing his own ethereal bliss, free from Him or any other fabled storybook character. He didn't need Him anymore. In a crude, blasphemous mockery of the idol, he extended his middle finger upward at it, muttering, "Fuck you," before he and the queen departed from Him, the wretched ones they were.

Chapter Thirty—Six

Once returning to Peru, the blood-drenched demons landed on the dark, rocky edge of a small lake—no bigger than an acre or two—near the base of Dajhri's volcano. In what light shone from the late blue sky, Julian watched the queen begin removing her stained white dress. Her nude silhouette identical to Violet's, his memories took him back to the night she returned home, saving him at the last minute. She too had worn white, and by the time they shared their first kiss, she was painted in the same karmic red aftermath as the queen was now.

Though Julian found her familiar shape remarkable, he respectfully turned his attention away, stripping his own bloody rags before trotting into the cool, welcoming water. Back home, it may have been winter, but in the southern hemisphere, summer thrived. He waded through the water, listening to an array of exotic birds singing and chirping from the surrounding trees.

When the water reached his shoulders, he dunked his head and began wiping the dry blood from his face and other areas. Having not said a word to each other since leaving Brazil, Dajhri was the first to break the silence. Washing herself nearby, she said, "Normally I do not behave like that when I feed."

Turning to face her, Julian asked, "What do you mean?"

"I try to visit bad places when I hunt, hoping the person I choose has done something they deserve to die for. It is easier than thinking I took someone more innocent. Like you, I became angry when I saw the child's underclothing. I too wanted him to suffer."

"And what does that make us? Even if they are bad people, who are we to justify killing one human over another?"

"Because it is our nature," she said, moving closer. "We are human on the outside and even on the inside, but our physical form is just that: a physical form. When we become a vampire, we release those human bonds. In the wild, animals indiscriminately kill other animals for food. Do you think they ever stop to question the nature of morality before or after the hunt?"

"Probably not."

"And do you know why? Because the bias laws of man do not apply, but natural unadulterated instinct does. It is instinct to survive. Just like animals, we too have that primal instinct. It does not mean we have to enjoy killing—normally, I do not—but survival is a necessity."

Julian dunked his head again. When he emerged, Dajhri was so close, their hands and feet occasionally bumped while moving to stay afloat. He said, "I understand, but in hindsight, I feel like I should not have enjoyed slaughtering that man the way we did, no matter the drugs in his living room or clothes in his bedroom. Out of context, they could have meant anything."

"'We' did not slaughter him. 'I' did. You only drunk."

"The point is I enjoyed it. Just before you finished him, I called him a pedophile and told him to rot in Hell. I even laughed at him. That is not me."

"What are you—if not a man who's suffered dearly and held back for so long, he had no choice but to break?"

"I don't know how to answer that. I thought I experienced Hell before my transformation. I thought my childhood was Hell. I thought the deaths of my mother, grandmother, and Faith's infidelity—all driving me to attempt suicide—was Hell too. I was wrong. Hell is watching the woman you waited your entire life for getting her head cut off right in front of you. Hell was watching the otherworldly horror in her eyes, knowing there was nothing either of us could do to stop it. Hell is that image haunting me to the point I almost tried to take my life again.

"Hell is getting thrown into a dirty dungeon for over a month, unsure if my love was coming to me in dreams or hallucinations. Hell is knowing you got the only two people who tried to save you killed!" That is who I am: a man raised on true Hell: who sometimes wants to believe this world can be saved, and others—I just want to burn it all down and piss on the ashes."

Dajhri's hand rose from the water and she caressed Julian's cheek. "You are stuck and divided in two. Chaos and order are two sides of the same coin as up and down, light and dark. You cannot have one without the other. My beliefs and philosophy are based entirely on balance—as was my mother's, Lilith."

"Your mother?"

"Yes. My creator and goddess is Lilith: the first vampire. I was her final child, and while I am certainly not the oldest living vampire, I am only one of two second generation vampires who still roam the earth."

"Who is the other?"

"The Raja Kahiji. Lilith was not just his maker, but using Adam's seed, she birthed him. Everyone else who remains in Raz Ahrim was either later transformed by Lilith, her son, or those who have since expired."

"Anna once told me about Lilith and how she was banished from the Garden of Eden when she became defiant of Adam. She didn't tell me any of her children were still living though."

"She likely doesn't know. Lilith was such a wise and important woman. Thanks to the book of lies, most of her existence is shrouded. She taught me the universe does not know one side of the coin from the other. All things in life must be equal. If we take, we must give. If we give, we must take.

"When Mother Lilith and the children she bore with Adam were banished—not from a literal garden, but the human species— she embraced the night. Adam remained in the light and day. For his loyalty to the man-made God, he was given a new slave wife from his rib, who'd obey his every command. It was Lucifer that gave

Lilith her gift—not for honoring him or disobeying God, but for honoring herself."

"So, it really was the devil who created us?"

"Yes, but it is not as frightening as it sounds. Man's bible says Lucifer approached Eve as a serpent, tempting her to eat the 'forbidden fruit.' It was not fruit, but truth, empowerment, and free will: offered from the heart and soul of God's equally opposite. Another lie suggests it was Eve who first took from the tree. It was Lilith. That was the moment she declared herself Adam's equal. For her 'frailty,' God punished Lilith—cursing her and the children who followed her to forever roam the dark as cold-blooded parasites lest the sun be their demise. That is when Lucifer blessed her and her children with all the gifts our kind still share."

"Of course, the Bible was written by men, and men in those times would never allow a woman to appear so powerful. Why else would God be depicted as a man? Men do not give birth. If the Bible was meant to spread truth, it would include the books of Lilith, Enoch, Barnabas, Mary Magdalene. and even Judas. Alas, it does not. In place of truth, man wrote the worst lie of all. Eve consumed a pomegranate from the same tree God placed and forbade her to feed from. Then after Lucifer came to her as a serpent, offering free will and a choice to indulge, her decision to also defy God and tempt her husband—ignoring the original tempter—was used to justify a false claim: to think for yourself is to sin."

Taking a moment to wipe her face, Dajhri laughed. "Because a woman acted upon God's temptation we blame Lucifer for, we are damned to suffrage in Hell, lest we live outside the garden as tormented slaves like Adam and Eve rather than open our eyes and free our minds like Lucifer and Lilith. That is man's God: the real devil. To indulge in what He saw fit to create does not make us sinners. But God—the true deceiver who killed so many in the Old Testament for His own pleasure—creates to trap and punish those who think for themselves. Lucifer was only the first to taste God's wrath. To spite his creator, Lucifer created Lilith and she created me."

Having been washing himself while listening, Julian said, "That makes sense. I always wondered why Anna was so adamant about calling God a narcissist. After hearing that … now I get it."

"Man's God is not just a narcissist but an unforgiving slave holder, which is why he cast a rebellious Lucifer from paradise and an equally rebellious Lilith and her children from humanity. Neither were evil. They were enlightened and independent. That is what a 'loving God' considers sin." Changing the subject, she looked up at the sky. "The next nightfall will bring a new moon. Every new moon, I visit the nearby village of Pacha: my first home. I provide spiritual guidance and medicine to those who need it. I would like you to accompany me."

"Okay."

"You said you have taken *Ayahuasca*, correct?"

"I have."

"I do offer it to humans, but as I am sure you know, such an acidic substance would kill a vampire. However, there is something I would like for you to try—something to help with clearing your guilt, suffering, and to realign your third eye and other chakras." Dajhri dipped her head in the water. When she emerged, her beehive had collapsed. Her thick dark bundle covered her face until she brushed it away.

Turning towards the shore, she said, "It is time to leave. We can find you some clean clothes, and I will ask Serene to rewash the others." Julian followed her to the rocky bank where he put his boxers and shoes on. Once collecting their bloody clothes, Dajhri, dripping wet and completely naked, said, "Hold on to me and I will fly us up."

Julian blushed, feeling as bashful as the man Dajhri manipulated into letting inside his house. It wasn't arousal, like when he saw Winter-Fae, but something closer to unworthiness. Nonetheless, he obeyed the queen, wrapping his arms around her shadowy frame from behind. Pressing his own wet body against hers, he shivered.

After what seemed more like a giant leap than a flight, they stood at the gate inside the volcano. Dajhri used the same key as before to unlock the bronze door. From the other side, she called, "Serene!" Seconds later, a dark-haired woman in a green dress entered the stairway near the bottom. Julian recognized the queen's handmaiden from L'abisme.

In a strong Peruvian accent, but a soft tone, she said, "Yes, Dajhri?"

"My robe, please, and Julian needs clothes."

"Yes, right away." Serene bowed and then rushed to the bottom of the steps, disappearing to the left and then shortly reappearing with two white robes. On her way up, she said, "Julian can wear this until I see what else I can find for him."

Dajhri began down the stairs, motioning Julian to follow. They reached Serene near the middle. The handmaiden gave the queen her robe first, and then the other to Julian. "Thank you," he said. She smiled and bowed. He wrapped himself in the fluffy long robe, again saying, "Thank you."

Serene said, "You are welcome."

"That will be all," Dajhri said. She bowed her head once more before glancing back at Julian and smiling again. She turned away and disappeared into another hallway seven steps farther down.

In admiration, Julian said, "This is what it's like to be a queen, huh?"

"Yes, but I do not consider myself above anyone here. We are all equals." She winked, adding, "But as the queen, I do have the respect and final say in all matters. It is something more useful to have than not."

"About that final say, I imagine not only the Ahrims, but also L'abisme are looking for me." Dajhri nodded. "How long do you think it would be before it is safe for me to leave? I imagine I should probably go to Alaska, but I just want to go back home if I can."

"Neither kingdom will forget what happened—nor will they forgive—whether you were at fault or not. Let me ask you, Julian: what awaits you back home?"

"My frie—" Then, he remembered Xavier didn't want him telling anyone about Daryl. He thought fast, settling on, "—my friends and family."

Dajhri snickered, her alluring, deep forest of green neutralizing Julian's shallow orbs of baby blue. She said, "I enjoy you. You are very intelligent and intuitive for someone your age … at such a poor point in society, as well. It is no wonder Xavier and Violet loved you so. I only ask two things of you, here. Is that okay?"

"What are they?"

"Never lie to or defy me."

"I—I am sorry," he stuttered. "It's just that Xavier told me not to tell anyone what happened to my friend, Daryl."

"And what happened to your friend Daryl?"

Julian sighed, figuring by then she probably already knew everything. Having two kingdoms as enemies was enough, and the last thing he needed was to disobey such a powerful ally. "The night Christopher Cauldwell and his men killed Violet, they also shot Daryl. He was there because he was my best man. Violet's blood entered his wound, and it turned him."

Dajhri closed her eyes, bobbing slowly in thought. When she opened them, she said, "I am sorry about your friend. I knew Violet would make a vampire, but after the way she spoke of you when she was here, I imagined you would be the one. When I look at you, I see her power."

"You are right. Her power is in me. She was decapitated over top of me. I was paralyzed, and since I couldn't move, I swallowed her blood."

"Ah, I see. Now it makes sense."

"What does?"

"In one of my dreams, I saw someone rise from her blood with not just her abilities, but new powers that most of our kind have never known before. When we first met in Paris, I saw the same blue eyes staring back at me from the dream. The eyes are the gateway to the soul. Tell me, are you also a prophet?"

"It's funny you should ask. I had a vision with *Ayahuasca*. I saw Bishop taking my hand and picking me up from the ground in Times Square, a year before it happened. Before then, I thought little about it. I thought it was meant to be some sort of triumphant symbol of picking myself up from all the bullshit I took with me to the retreat, but after Xavier and I fell from Cauldwell's helicopter, Bishop proved me wrong. My vision was a premonition. I told Winter-Fae …" *'Never forget that.'* "I told her about it in Paris." His friend and savior's broken little face appeared in red and white flashes. "She told me I am a seer."

"You are, indeed." As if the queen bewitched herself deep into another thought, her eyes remained stuck on Julian's. He stared back, equally enchanted. The engagement endured until Dajhri blinked first. She cleared her throat and said, "You need rest. You slept for a week, but you pushed yourself tonight. Serene should come to your room soon with a new set of clothes. If you need me, I will be down where I was before."

"Okay, but you never answered my question."

"And that is?"

"When can I go home?"

"I don't know. It would not be safe right now. I would prefer you stay for the time being. Here, I can protect you, and if I may be so bold, you need guidance. You are traumatized. I can help you work through your turmoil, adapt to your new life, and I can also help you hone your abilities. Even if the other two kingdoms weren't looking for you, it would still be very challenging to survive on your own right now."

It was not what Julian wanted to hear, but following a sigh, he said, "I understand."

Standing shorter than him, Dajhri floated just high enough off the ground to lightly kiss Julian's forehead at his level. The innocent peck sent a relaxing vibration throughout his body. He almost smiled. Back on the ground, the queen whispered, "Sleep well," before turning to head down the steps.

"You too," Julian replied. "And, Dajhri …" She stopped and peered over her shoulder, one green eyes ripping straight through him and beyond. "… thank you for saving my life twice."

"It was an honor."

As she descended the stairs, Julian headed towards his room, occasionally hearing voices coming from behind other blanketed doorways. Most of them spoke Spanish. Others spoke a more primitive language he didn't recognize. Not long after he entered his room, Serene brought a clean pair of cotton pants and a matching white shirt. He put them on and climbed into bed, unsure how he felt overall, but certainly more optimistic than when he'd last awoken.

Chapter Thirty-Seven

Julian tossed and turned throughout the night, haunted by Avice's words, *'Never forget that;'* haunted by sweet Winter-Fae's broken little face and body. He was tucked beneath a blanket he never remembered covering himself with. His own words, *'Rot in hell, pedophile,'* rang over and over. *But what if he wasn't? What if those clothes were his daughter's or granddaughter's? What if they were just dirty and in his room? What if we killed an innocent man?* He sighed and mumbled, "It's too late. I am a wild animal now, and like Dajhri said, wild animals kill indiscriminately. The world never cared about shitting on me, so why care now if I shit back? Isn't karma supposed to be a bitch?"

Lying on his side and facing the wall only inches away, he yawned and rolled over. Even in complete darkness, he sensed the sudden change in the room and stale air. He saw and heard nothing, but he knew someone was there, standing over him and glaring down upon his negative monstrosity of a child and student. It was a man—the same man who neglected him for over a month. "What do you want, Xavier?" he tirelessly groaned, wishing it were someone else.

"Well now, try not to sound so excited," the teenaged elder chortled.

Following a short series of skidding, almost sarcastic grunts of disbelief, he repeated, "'Excited?'" A few more slipped, practically telling his creator to go fuck himself as they did. "Yes, Xavier. I am over the moon with joy. I must live out the rest of my waking life in darkness, falsely accused and pursued by your maker's assassin, his new kingdom, and the Ahrims. Meanwhile, I can't even face what I did to your sisters. Now, I am ashamed of myself for the enjoyment I took in killing someone tonight, just so I could feel guilty about that, too. I can't even sleep the regret away without either dreaming of you—since Violet won't come for whatever reason—just so I can wake up and lose you all over again. So, yes, I am so goddamn otherworldly excited right now that I might just start doing naked backflips."

"If my presence burdens you that deeply, I shall take my leave and torment you no further."

"That is not what I meant." Julian sighed. "It's just … I am tired. I am mentally exhausted, and I just want the pain to go away. Is that really so wrong of me?"

"I am so sorry this is happening to you, my son. I see how and why it hurts you. I am not going to patronize you, but I hope you understand it was never my intention for any of this to happen."

"Wasn't it? You are the one who went with Anna to free Bernard. I've never liked him. I know it's because he looks just like Faith's brother, Travis, but I sensed Bernard was a bad person from the first time I saw him. I wasn't an eight-hundred-year-old vampire when I met him like you were. I was a thirty-seven-year-old human who until then didn't even know vampires were real—until he told me."

"What do you want from me, Julian? In case you've failed to realize, I am not impervious to mistakes. When Anna came to me, she wanted my help. When she told me about Bernard and how troubled she was by what she had seen, I also pitied him. I did what I thought was right—not just for Bernard's sake, but Anna's. When we saved him, neither she nor I knew she would fall in love with him, but as I am sure you know, we cannot choose who we love."

"If only you wouldn't have rejected her from the start—everyone acting like it takes a dick to love someone," Julian grumbled. "She loved you, but a pretty little boy like you loved your options more, didn't you?"

Following an awkward grunt, and then almost a giggle, Xavier said, "I did not reject her. I brought shame to our kingdom. I just never realized it until I had to pay for my sins. I had it coming. When Caanis sent me away, I had no clue where I would go. I was not about to take Anna from her home to face such uncertainties with me. It had nothing to do with losing my appendage."

"I think your daughter's diary is more honest about it than you are with yourself, but that's just me. Regardless, I know none of this is your fault and I don't mean to be an asshole. I feel lost right now, though. I miss Violet, and I just want to die and join her. At the very least, I want to go home and make sure Daryl is okay. With everyone looking for me, Dajhri says I have to stay here. I told her I was worried about Daryl and—"

"You told her about Daryl?"

"Yes, but only because she knew I was thinking about him. I've been trying to hide my thoughts, but sometimes I still forget, and I can't prevent myself from thinking."

"I know."

"Why does it matter so much if anyone knows about him, anyway?"

"Not so much now, but before, I was afraid the Ahrims might try to also hold him responsible for Times Square."

"They blamed me for it, since you weren't here."

"I know. They blamed you because as my only living creation, you became my heir and the leader of my coven."

"Thank you, Captain Obvious, but there is no more coven. Dajhri said so."

"There is," Xavier amended. "Violet was my daughter. I created her and she created Daryl. That makes Daryl a part of the coven. It takes two or more vampires to create and keep a coven. You and Daryl make two. I didn't want certain people to know about him because his making was a mistake. He is innocent, and unlike you, he never chose to be a part of this.

"I know that might not sound fair, but since I felt the Ahrims might blame you, by keeping Daryl's name out of it, the coven was disbanded, and you escaped punishment. Had it not been for that, I am not so sure Caanis or even Dajhri would have protected you from the Ahrims, since doing so would break the truce and endanger their own people with no lawful reason."

"I might have escaped death at the meeting, but the Ahrims felt disrespected, and the truce was broken anyway. Bernard was going to give me to them to rebuild it. What now? He knows about Daryl. Since he tried to sell me out to the Ahrims, what if he tries to do the same to him?"

"Daryl is not the leader of the coven, so it would not matter if they knew now or not. Even if Bernard told them about him, the Ahrims would likely take it as a desperate lie to save himself, especially since nobody can read his mind to prove him right. Besides, Daryl is Violet's. You are mine. It is you the Ahrims want. No one else. For all they know, you died in the catacombs. I imagine not delivering you as promised will bring even more heat on the new king and L'abisme."

"Doesn't that bother you, though? L'abisme was your home once."

"Once. Aside from Anna, everyone there whom I once cared about is dead. All of my sisters—vampires and human—mean everything to me. At one time, so did Caanis, but when he killed our first king, everything changed. Now that I certainly know the truth of how all my other children passed, I feel nothing for those who remain in the catacombs."

"A lot happened surrounding Caanis' death. He named Bernard his heir, not Anna. That infuriated Avice. Out of jealousy, she confronted Anna and Bernard. She used yours and Anna's secret affair to insult Bernard. He was so angry, he almost hit Anna, but I attacked him. Caanis was going to banish me for it. Later that night, he was killed. Bernard blamed me, and I was thrown in the dungeon for a month. Anna had run away before Caanis died. I had previously said some foolish things to her, and I know it upset her, but after becoming the new queen, I had hoped she would return and set me free. She never came back."

"And she never will," Xavier said. "Monarchy was in her blood all along, even before Caanis gave her the dark gift. Sadly, she never wanted it. After she and Bernard wed, she pulled me aside and said he fantasized about killing Caanis. I should have taken her more seriously than I did. Wanting to see the best in him, I presumed it was a way for him to deal with his post-trauma. So did my sweet sister. When I died and he realized Caanis had lost his heir, he acted. I believe Anna brought him, believing he left those dark ideas behind long ago. Anna is highly intelligent, but she is grieving, and when she feels something she feels it hard. When she is overwhelmed, she runs. Avice is the same way."

"Fae too," Julian added. *'Never forget that.'*

"Her not so much."

"But she ran away too, that is how we ended up in Paris to begin with—Paul and Teddy came to Alaska looking for her. … And why there, of all places?"

"Winter-Fae does her own thing."

"'Did,'" he corrected. *'Never forget that.'* Both men sighed and lingered silently for several seconds before Julian asked, "Where do you think Anna could have gone?"

Xavier released another sigh, "I cannot say," riding the waves behind it.

"What should I do? As a shaman, Dajhri wants to help me with my grief. I like her. She makes me feel welcome."

"Then I suggest you stay here for now. If the Ahrims and L'abisme go to war, so be it."

"What will happen if they do?"

"L'abisme will be destroyed. Just like Reinhardt split when King Arvil was assassinated, I imagine something similar has happened or will happen in L'abisme. It would not surprise me if most of the vampires, especially those smart enough to know better, left while they could."

"Where would they go?"

A brief silence passed before Xavier said, "I could not say."

"… as in you don't know or you don't want me to know?"

Xavier never answered. Instead, Julian opened his eyes again, finding himself still in bed, but lying above the blanket as he had while falling asleep. The maker's presence was gone, and the only light came from the lit torches in the hall, their glow peeking through small openings between the blanket and the doorframe it covered.

Like the others, the dream was no less frustrating. If Julian had a choice, he would've rather it been his flower, but after a month of Xavier's absence, he wanted to be grateful for the time they shared. Then he focused on Violet, deeply fixating on the way she'd come to him in L'abisme: the big spoon, cuddling him to sleep, her naked body pressed firmly against his—holding him tight in her arms and protecting him from all the ungodly horrors of the world.

He'd hoped such a deep craving would bring her back like it did that fateful night, but after waiting so long, he knew she wasn't coming, at least not yet. He rolled back over in bed, curling up and getting comfortable enough to try to sleep. He thought of the more friendly vampires from L'abisme, like Yara, the Egyptian woman with jet black hair and golden olive skin, whose silhouette he'd mistook for Violet's. Remembering her pleasant smile at the blood well, he hoped she was one of the smart ones Xavier mentioned.

Before shutting his eyes and finally dozing off again, his final thoughts were for the safety of Yara, Anna, and the others like them, and for Bernard to receive all the karma he deserved. Then, there was Violet. Above all else, even when the universe ends and another begins, there would always be Violet. Her beautiful brown almonds, her thick lips when she smiled, her empathy: what passion, what fire. It is no wonder she inspired so many people like him, people like … *'Never forget that.'*

Chapter Thirty–Eight

By the next time Julian opened his eyes, he had a full night's rest behind him. He yawned out of habit, the obese old man's corn-oil flavor still lingering on his breath. Before his first balanced thought of the day could turn lurid, a soft, consistent drumbeat from somewhere inside the temple offered a welcoming wake-up call. Curious, Julian put on his shoes and went out to the hallway, heading towards the steps.

He walked all the way to the bottom, the drumming growing louder as he drew closer. Facing a hallway just like the previous one, Julian caught the pungent odor of something like tangy burnt coffee in the otherwise stale air. Intrigued, he followed his nose down the hall. The sound and smell both drifted out of the last doorway on the left. It was open, a mild orange glow flickering into the darker, surrounding corridor.

With no blanket in his way, Julian observed a room over twice as big as his. Near the center, a large black cauldron rested over a burning log fire. Behind it, Dajhri sat, legs crossed in the lotus position atop a white feathered mat. Facing the cauldron, a small brown drum with a tanned rawhide head sat firmly hugged between her thighs. Using both of her pale mocha hands, she slapped a specific rhythm at an upbeat pace. Wearing the same white robe as before, her mahogany strands were styled in a new beehive. Her smooth eyelids shut, the queen appeared lost in a meditative trance.

Unwilling to disturb her, Julian walked softly to the cauldron and peeked inside. Submerged just beneath boiling water, thin golden-brown strips of vine stewed with green leaves. Though he did not see or smell it prepared at the retreat in California, Julian knew what was cooking. He'd done extensive research before throwing himself headfirst into a psychedelic frenzy he still didn't quite understand.

Thanks to articles and videos on the internet, he knew the green leaves were of the *chacruna*, mingling with the vine to make sacred plant medicine: *Ayahuasca*. Having placed the smell with the substance, he shivered, recalling the foul acidic flavor when he drank, and the two horrific nights of unadulterated, abstract psychiatry that followed.

He turned to leave Dajhri to her ritual, but when he glimpsed the sight he'd missed behind him, he stumbled. To the right of the inner doorway stood a dusty old skeleton. The posed structure of human bones gripped a menacing spear at its side. The weapon's long wooden stalk featured a pointed copper head and thin green twine wrapped tightly over the connection. The apparent warrior was draped in a long green cape. Resting on its skull set a shiny, copper, bowl helmet with three decorative green feathers centered at the front.

Though Julian gasped when he first saw it, the display quickly fascinated him. He looked back over his shoulder, finding Dajhri's beady green eyes open, aiming directly into his. Her facial expression never changed. She said nothing and her drumming did not miss a beat. Julian pointed at the doorway, whispering, "I'll leave you be."

She slightly nodded before shutting her eyes and returning to her process. Julian returned to his floor. He took a lit torch from the hallway into his room, finding the fire pit already stocked with fresh wood. He set it ablaze and returned the torch, wondering, *What now?*

Back in his room, on the floor, beside the bed, his balled-up black leather jacket caught his attention. He knew several pages of Violet's diary had yet to be read. In Paris, he limited himself to bide his time. Now as a free man, an ardent desire to finish the book suddenly emerged. He took the diary from the hidden pocket in the jacket's inner lining and flipped to the page after the one Violet had filled the day he was born. Laying eyes on her handwriting again, he took a deep, refreshing breath and smiled. Then he began.

11/1/81

Dear Diary

Tonight was just too wild! First of all, don't freak out, but Eric and I might have been on national television. It is early Sunday morning now, but last night, we got in to "Saturday Night Live!" On Friday night, Eric was in Midtown. While walking past Rockefeller Plaza, he overheard somebody who worked there think or say John Belushi was going to make a surprise appearance on their Halloween show. Eric loves John Belushi. He's been obsessed with "Animal House" ever since it came out. He even bought a TV and VCR just for that movie.

He's wanted to attend an airing of "Saturday Night Live" ever since it started, so he got us tickets. He also heard them say Belushi only agreed to the appearance if they would let a punk rock band from Los Angeles called Fear perform as the musical guests. According to Eric, they said Belushi also wanted a bus full of "authentic punk rock fans" brought up from Washington D.C., to be in the crowd, since apparently the birthplace of punk and the city the show is filmed in isn't good enough to pool fans from. Basically, he wanted to ignore us and recreate the look of an "authentic punk show,' and boy-howdy, that is what they got!

Since we had to look the part, I gave Eric one of my Ramones shirts and he wore an old torn pair of blue jeans. His hair isn't very long, but it was perfect for spiking with some mousse. I also talked him into letting me apply some black eyeliner. That one took a little convincing, but I must admit, he looked sexy! I wore my patched leather jacket, an old Patti Smith shirt, a plaid skirt, and some old torn fishnets I found under my bed. The eyeliner looked so good on Eric that I wore some too. I also tried some matching lipstick and nail polish. I even painted my toenails. Not to brag, but I looked pretty damn good too! I especially love how the lipstick and nail polish turned out. I don't normally wear it, but this could be a new look for me.

When we got there, the bus from D.C. had already arrived. There were so many people outside, and not all of them were from the bus. They were from New York, and like us had probably also heard the news. Those people didn't have tickets, though, and they couldn't get in. Eric and I blended with the D.C. punks and were led into the studio, near the stage, while the more casual audience members were all seated behind us. Neither of us knew it would be like that. The crazy looks we all got from some of them was hilarious, but now we both wish we'd just gotten in line with them.

Donald Pleasence, who was hosting the show, introduced Fear early on—even first alluding to Belushi's surprise appearance. I can't believe it, but when the band started playing, they were actually letting people dive off the stage. It started getting rowdy fast. The looks on the people's faces off-camera were priceless! They all looked completely mortified. I got excited and wanted to go dive off the stage too, but Eric wouldn't let me. I understand why. I would have been on TV for sure. But, my God, it was tempting! In all the commotion, I wouldn't be surprised if our faces or heads weren't on TV anyway, but I still get it.

After the first song, the singer started saying random shit to the crowd. After a hurl of "fucks" from the punk crowd, Fear started playing a song called "New York's Alright If You Like Saxophones." By then, stagehands were trying to keep people from stage diving, but some were still doing it. At one point, somebody took the microphone from the singer—one of those "authentic" D.C. assholes, I'm sure—and they started screaming "Fuck New York," "New York sucks," or something to that effect.

The song ended abruptly. Not long after they started another, the stage manager or somebody came running out and stopped the whole thing. The band quit playing, and I assume they went off the air. Everyone went nuts. During the chaos, this freaking huge video camera got knocked over. They started running us off. Eric was scared somebody would call the police. That camera must've cost thousands! I think everyone in that crowd was from D.C. but us. We hauled ass out of there, and luckily, we made it back home with no trouble. That is punk rock, baby!

All I can say is thank God that Xavier, Anna, and Bernard don't watch television. Though it was incredibly fake, tonight was still kind of fun. The risk was exciting and new. Eric is bummed out that he didn't get to see John Belushi. I feel bad for him. He doesn't even really like punk rock. He only dressed up for me. Hell, even I don't dress up like that. I didn't get to see Jimi Hendrix at Woodstock or before he died, but at least I got to see my Janis. I hope Eric has a chance to see John Belushi perform in some capacity before something happens to him. As for me, I'm a little pissed off that the birthplace of punk got shit on like that, but us authentic punks are tough, and we can take it!

Violet

Though Julian sympathized with Violet's frustration, he giggled, reminiscing an early childhood memory. Both of his parents loved "Saturday Night Live," and all its comedians from that era—John Belushi included. Since they never really cared what Julian watched, at only five years old, "National Lampoon's Animal House" was one of his favorite comedies too. Unfortunately, just like Violet's idol, Janis Joplin, had died of a heroin overdose, so did Eric's; only four months after that infamous Halloween episode. Still, the fond memories of college pranks, dead horses and heart attacks, followed Julian on to the next page.

2/12/83
Dear Diary

There is two feet of snow outside! And guess what! Fae is here to play in it with me! We're having so much fun! We both feel like little girls again. We made snow angels, built a snowman, and even had a snowball fight! Fae told me, the first winter after she met Avice, London had a good snowfall. She said they played in it for hours, forgetting all their fears and uncertainties. For a while, they got to be innocent and vulnerable children again. Fae said I reminded her of what that felt like.

Since that dream I wrote about in 1981, I've had a couple more. They usually come at random, but there was one that stood out to me. I had it last year on September 24th, exactly one year after the first one. I didn't write about it or the others before because I am still trying to process them. I told Fae. She thinks they are interesting, but she also thinks I'm lonely and need to find a vampire guy to have some fun with. I got a good laugh out of it, but I told her I wanted so much more than just a good balling.

Just like the first dream, I had others after it, in which I was looking for someone, but I never knew who or where they were. In one dream, I was at a museum with trippy artwork on the walls. I wandered around until I woke up but found nothing. In another, I was driving through a jungle or rainforest. There were these oddly shaped, tall, narrow mountains along the road. I knew I was going to see someone, but like before, I didn't know who or where they were. Before I could reach my destination, I woke up.

Until I finally found him, I had one more dream like that. I was at a bar or something. The bartender handed me a brown mixed drink in a clear plastic cup with ice. Some random guy approached me and said, "Someone up there is looking for you." He pointed towards the ceiling, about twenty feet above my head. There was a *big window at the top of the wall, where someone could look down on the floor. As soon as I saw the window, I awoke.*

Last September, I finally saw him—well part of him. Do you remember the flashing blue and purple lights from my dream in '81? I saw them again. I was outside and it was dark, but I was in a desert. Like the first dream, everything was lucid but still hazy. From the dark came a man's shadow. He was taller and a little bigger than me. His shape was all I saw. He didn't say anything, but he extended his hand to me. Then I woke up.

Since then, I've taken his hand. We walk through the blue and purple desert together, but that is it. He still says nothing, and he is still hidden in the dark. The landscape reminds me a little of Las Vegas, but who knows? I feel like I am losing my mind. Xavier once said Caanis' lover, Rosalyn, was likely only ever in his head. What if my dream lover is only in my head too? What if this is just some kind of trick? Am I crazy? Wow! When I say it like that, I feel like I really am.

Violet

Turning the page, Julian whispered, "Why didn't you ever tell me about your dreams?"

7/4/86

Dear Diary

Tonight, Eric and I watched the fireworks from the roof of our building. They were beautiful. I finally told him about the dreams. Since my last entry, I have had more. Considering our past, I was a little nervous to tell him, but he was understanding and even fascinated. He told me I should follow my heart.

Something about that date: September 24th, 1981, still stands out to me. That was the day Eric gave me my ankh necklace and I had my first dream. I've now had one every year on that night since—and others too. They are also becoming more frequent and *vivid. Now, I can see part of him. He has brown hair, and he's as pasty as I am. Those details are clear now, and so is all his face, but not his eyes. Dark, round shadows are covering them, and I don't know why. He still hasn't said anything. I don't know why he won't talk to me. I talk to him. I tell him the kinds of things I tell you, Diary. He listens to everything, but he never speaks.*

Moving back to Eric, he's been a little upset this year. Although he and William had finally started to reconcile after yet another falling out, they are right back at odds again. Last year, William was appointed a clergyman at St. Patrick's Cathedral. He is normally busy or away doing outreach work, and he is hardly ever around anymore. With it being such a special day, and Eric knowing he would be there, he wanted to surprise him, showing up for midnight mass on Christmas.

His presence in the church made William nervous and when he tried to tell Eric to leave, they had an argument in front of other churchgoers. William is forty-nine years old now, and though he's always had so much love for me and Xavier, he still refuses to get along with his brother. I feel so bad for Eric because in spite of who he is now, he's still William's older brother, and he loves that sweet little boy with all his heart. It is breaking his heart that they cannot be as close as they were before their mother died or I came along. All I can do is hope and pray for the best, in dreams and reality.

Violet

7/23/88

Dear Diary

Finally, CBGB seems to be getting fun again. Until this summer, I'd only been to a small handful of shows. The best one I saw was Violent Femmes, back in '82, before they got famous. They opened for Richard Hell. I loved them! They reminded me so much of Velvet Underground's early days.

After the stabbing incident, I obeyed Xavier's wishes for the most part. I still went to a couple of hardcore punk shows. I saw Agnostic Front. I also saw Bad Brains. Back at the end of '81, not long after the "SNL" Halloween incident, Max's Kansas City closed its doors. Bad Brains played the final show. I didn't go because I wanted to remember the place as it was: The Velvet Underground on stage, while Andy Warhol watched with his and the Underground's muse, Candy Darling by his side.

Another reason I stayed away from CBGB for so long is because throughout most of the '80s, the bar has been a big hangout for skinheads and white supremacists. That's not my thing. Dead Kennedys have a song called, "Nazi Punks Fuck Off." Need I say more? Last month, I took a chance and went to see Sonic Youth. They were great! They played the next night and I saw that show too! Ladies and gentleman: Kim Gordon and Thurston Moore!

Last night, I had even more fun. I'd heard a couple of Black Flag's songs in the past, and I liked them, as well as their singer's stance against all these neo-Nazi assholes making a mockery out of punk. That man's name is Henry Rollins, and that is who I saw. I never knew what he looked like before, but he looks kind of like Eric, if only Eric has tattoos and were jacked!

The crowd was mostly drunk, which made it even better. CBGB drunks are funny. In Henry's second song, there was a part when his lyrics were spoken words without music. He said something about how he couldn't relax. Some guy in the crowd randomly yelled, "Why not?" A few people started laughing, but I absolutely lost my shit. Thank God the music started back up before I could make any more of an ass out of myself. I sounded like a monkey or something. People stared. How embarrassing!

When they played their next-to-last song, the drummer took his kit apart and put it back together. Henry said the guy wanted to see if he could do it in a certain timeframe. It did take a few minutes for him to do it. Finally, some drunk lady slurred out, "Play the fucking song!" Without any hesitation, they played it. Aside from that, the show ended on a high note, with a great response from the crowd.

On the walk home, I saw something interesting not too far from the bar. It is faster to take the alleyway home than the street. Unless I'm going to Bleecker Benny's first, I usually just take the shortcut. Tonight, I saw two people fucking over an old dumpster. I assume they were at the same show I was. The guy first had his face buried between this tall blonde girl's legs before practically hanging her over the side of the dumpster while holding her legs like a wheelbarrow. He was really giving it to her too.

It was so dirty, and I feel weird admitting it, even to you, but it turned me on. From a distance, I watched for a couple of minutes before walking away as quietly as I could. Is it strange to admit sometimes I wish I could get fucked like that? I once told Fae, I don't want it to be with just anyone, and I stand by that. I am not a whore, but does having such desires make me a bad person? How I long for my own ball and chain to get that hardcore with me. Is that wrong? Am I impure to want something so "sinful?"

Violet

4/26/92

Dear Diary

It has been four years since my last entry. I am sorry about that. Since it pertained to Henry Rollins, I figured I might as well follow up with another about him and the amazing band who opened for him! As soon as I heard Henry was coming back to the bar, I got excited. What I didn't expect was to see him out-performed by his opening act: Tool.

Tool can play! Their drummer is good—Neil Peart-from-Rush-level good. He's still young, too. I've said that before, but if he plays it smarter than other talented artists I've seen throw it all away, he will be remembered. And their singer—holy smokes! He was unlike any man I have ever heard before. He had this long, thick mohawk, but he wore it down. It makes me laugh to think about, but the easiest way to describe it is a "power mullet." The way he could stretch his higher, more aggressive notes, and hold them for several seconds at a time was mind-blowing!

I feel kind of guilty. I went there expecting to see a great Henry Rollins show. Don't get me wrong, Henry delivered and even outdid his previous performance. I just never expected to be blown away like that! I am glad it was a great show because I also realized something unfortunate. I have been going to CBGB for almost twenty years now and I haven't aged a day.

Somebody at the bar kept looking at me. I've seen him many times over the years, and I know he's seen me just as many. I am pretty sure he owns the place. If so, his name is Hilly Kristal. When he saw me he looked puzzled, like he was thinking about it, and the same realization hit him as it did me. He was on the other side of the bar, and I couldn't read his mind at such a distance, but he was probably questioning his sanity a little too much for comfort.

That is when you know it is time to call it a day and say goodbye. Goddamn it, Diary—goddamn it! Xavier once warned me about these things—how they'd come and go as time goes by—how I should never get too attached to anything or anyone. I guess I just never really thought about it until I had a reason to.

Throughout all this time, Bleecker Benny's has had so many employees and owners, I've blended in without anyone noticing. I love my music, but for the sake of the coven, I have to say farewell to that third charm I gave a chance to once upon a time ago. Besides, $12 is getting a little expensive for tickets anyway.

Everyone I first fell in love with there has all moved on to greener pastures. Talking Heads, who went on to become huge, finally called it quits last year. The Patti Smith Group and Blondie both disbanded years ago. They all got big before their days ended, too. The Ramones—those guys who invented punk—are still together, still touring, selling t-shirts, and reaching for that mainstream stardom they just haven't grasped yet. They have a cult following, but nothing like all the other CBGB alumni. That is irony in a nutshell.

Speaking of Bleecker Benny's, I stopped on my way home. I was so moved by their performance, I wanted whatever they had of Tool's. It turns out, they only have one album: a six-song LP called "Opiate." They played more than just six songs, so hopefully Tool will be putting out something else soon. Last year, I bought a new stereo system with a compact disc player, so I bought "Opiate" on CD and trotted home.

I can't explain it, but something about their singer's voice drives me wild! I don't do this often, and I am blushing thinking about it now, but after I put the CD on, I turned up the bass, lit some wild cherry incense, and took a long, hot bubble bath. What a way to end an era. I've still got my dreams, but now it looks like I need to find something new again. Oh, ball and chain, where are you already?

Violet

While finishing the entry, Julian chuckled. "I said it once, and I will say it again, 'you lucky little asshole.'" After taking a moment to savor one of many fond memories they shared in their final months together, he wiped a lone tear from his cheek and continued.

12/31/99
Dear Diary

I am starting to feel like you are more of a time capsule than a diary. I keep losing and finding you at the most random times. Not much has happened since the last time I wrote to you, aside from

William's hair. It is gray now. He and Dad often tease one another over who is really the oldest. A few years back, Anna pissed off Bernard bad, but that is nothing new. She was joking with William, telling him his gray hair was sexy. Bernard took her seriously and got jealous. For nearly a week, he wouldn't talk to any of us.

I know he and Anna still love each other, but you would never guess they are married now. Dad would make a more believable husband than Bernard. After all these years, I know she still loves Dad, and he loves her. I think Dad knows he fucked up by rejecting her, whether he will ever admit it or not. The way they look at each other, compared to the way she and Bernard do, there is no denying something is still there.

Speaking of Dad, he is filthy rich now! Throughout the '90s, he sold a lot of stock he owned in various hotels and other businesses he's held onto since before we ever met. He wants to use some of the money to open his own business but, as a vampire who is unable to do much during the day, he has no idea what would work. He is an innovator, so I am sure he will figure something out.

My dreams had eased off quite a bit for a while, but lately they have been intensifying again. His brown hair has grown long. I still can't see his eyes, but now sometimes when he visits me, he is crying. I don't know how, but I just know he is in pain. I even hear his voice sometimes now; It is so soft. I love it! He calls my name, but he doesn't call me Violet. He calls me his 'flower.' I wonder what his name is. Does he even exist, or am I just so lonely I've become whatever the hell this is? Almost twenty years later, I'm still asking myself that, still waiting for an answer that will probably never come. But, why not?

In just a few hours, the decade, century, and millennium are all ending. All of us, including a new friend from Taltosia, named Tony Bishop, are heading to Times Square to watch the ball drop at midnight. Bishop is a cool guy and I like all his tattoos, but I'm not

*attracted to him like that. Besides, I think he just wants to fuck
anything that moves. I guess he was repressed back home.*

*He's a big flirt. At first, I feel like he was trying to fuck me
too, but I'm thinking Dad or Eric might have told him to keep his
hands and other parts away from me because he suddenly backed off
in those regards. Now, he tries to act more like a big brother. Still, I
think he could be a good friend to the family. Dad likes him. I guess
we will see.*

*As I am getting ready to head downtown, I cannot help
thinking what I wouldn't give for the man of my dreams to be there
with me. I would kiss him at midnight and every other midnight
after. If only dreams were reality, what a reality it would be! Happy
New Year, Decade, Century, and Millennium, Diary!*

Violet

9/11/01

Dear Diary

*Today, our freedom was trodden upon. We all felt and heard
both towers fall. It is still daylight, but as far as I know, most of
Manhattan is covered in smoke and ash. I am scared—not just
because our city and country were just attacked, but because
William is in Midtown right now, doing his superhero priest work. If
there is a God out there, He'd better protect the best servant He
could ever ask for, or He will have Me to deal with when we meet.*

Violet

9/24/11

Dear Diary

*For thirty years, I've had memorable dreams of the same
man, and I still can't see his eyes. There have even been times I
knew I was dreaming and tried to make love to him, but I always
wake up before anything happens. Since the last time I wrote about*

it, we usually meet beneath the Northern Lights, somewhere up north. Every dream begins in a cave. I always lead him into a snowy forest and a small, rocky spring. I don't understand why the dream always ends the way it does. Could it be because I don't know what it would feel like to be with him like that?

Dad and Eric thought I was nuts for doing it, but a few years ago I searched all over Alaska and Canada for the cave. In some weird way I wondered if he would be there waiting for me. I never found him or the cave. Pana and all the Alaskans must also think I am insane by now, as much as I have bugged them over it.

After thirty years of these dreams, I still wonder if he is even real or if my mind just wants him to be. As a vampire, being able to fly and never age is great, but the loneliness is getting to me. I'm even scared to waste your pages now that you have so few left. You have become my closest friend, and you know more about me than anyone, but even that will have to end eventually. That is why I was away again for so long. Do you forgive me, Diary?

Considering Winter-Fae hasn't visited in a while, the most fun I have is mine and Anna's nightly walks, but even those aren't as often as they used to be. She and Bernard are having problems again. He's right back to throwing her past in her face. He just won't let it go. I think she feels guilty about marrying him, but after everything, and Bernard not having anywhere else to go, she just puts up with him. That is not healthy, and I fear it may eventually lead to bigger problems. I just hope if they split, nobody gets hurt. We've all had enough pain in our lives. That's all for now, I guess.

Violet

Why didn't you tell me all this? I love you so much, and I would have never thought you were crazy. In all their deep, late-night conversations, even at their happiest, Julian couldn't understand why Violet never told him about her dreams, or for how long she had waited for him. He'd read many other new trivial and significant facts about her that he didn't already know, but to withhold something so personal, he was at a loss for any practical reason why. Nevertheless, he moved his hand over his heart. Tapping three times, he said, "I love you." His declaration was met and returned with tender murmurs in threes he'd not received since the catacombs: *squeeze-squeeze-squeeze ... squeeze---squeeze---squeeze ... squeeze--squeeze--squeeze.* Now giddy, full of warmth, validation, and free of any doubt, Julian turned the page and continued.

5/3/15

Dear Diary

Well, Dad has been saying for years that he wanted to start his own business, and now he is, The coolest part is I inspired him! New York has changed so much in the seventy-one years I have been here. So much has come and gone. All four of the original Ramones are gone now. Lou Reed died a year and a half ago from liver disease. Back in 2006, CBGB finally closed its doors. Patti Smith came back and played that final show. I wanted to go so bad. I even heard Flea from Red Hot Chili Peppers was there. I didn't want to risk being recognized, so I stayed home.

And sadly, after all these years, Bleecker Benny's finally closed their doors two years ago. It is now a frozen yogurt shop. The Village I fell in love with, the one that started so many movements—not just for music, but freedom and equality—doesn't exist anymore. There isn't even anywhere left in this city for good music at all, hardly. Everything that's popular nowadays sounds like shit anyway. So, this all gave me an idea.

For decades, we have been humanely receiving our blood from donors, but it was always expensive. I helped Dad come up with a plan to have his business, make money, and get all the free blood we need. And the icing on the cake is we are going to have our own nightclub! The chapel downstairs has not been touched since Anna and Bernard's wedding. After Dad spent all that money to renovate it, he finally decided to use it by also building a bar, kitchen, stage, and having a state-of-the-art sound system installed.

Way back when Anna and Bernard got married, Winter-Fae made a joke during her toast. She called our gathering a modern Leviticus. That name always stuck with Dad and that is what he's decided to call the club: "Leviticus." Though it won't open for another month, we already have a house band lined up to play music. Bishop, from Taltosia, is a drummer. He moved into the building about ten years ago. Since then, he started a band with some talented human musicians who don't even know he is a vampire. His band plays heavy metal, and they are called the Black Casket Affair. They sound great!

Now, for the cherry on top! In addition to all the new renovations Dad is making, he is also turning the first-floor studio apartments into blood labs. The idea is anyone who would rather donate a pint of blood instead of paying the entry fee, can. Since that alone would look suspicious, Dad is going to keep enough for us and donate the rest. He is a little nervous the idea might not take off, but he is going to try!

The big question that has yet to be answered is what Caanis, Dajhri, and the Ahrims will think about Dad doing this. He believes he can pull it off, but he also knows it might rub some of the more elder vampires the wrong way. Dad's always been a rebel and the kind of man who would do anything in his power to prove someone wrong when they tell him he can't do it.

With all this excitement about the club, my dreams, which had been a little calmer as of late, started becoming vivid and constant again. Now, I dream of dancing with him. His hair and body have been clear to me, but his eyes are still hidden in the shadows. I don't understand what that means. Is he blind? Am I blind to something? I know I have been writing about him and wishing for him for decades now, and maybe I really am crazy, but I cannot help but feel as if Dad opening this club is what might bring us together. I guess I will just have to wait and see!

Violet

6/16/15
Dear Diary

Leviticus had its grand opening last night. Sadly, nobody came. Dad said that was expected. I'm a little bummed that nobody came, but he is right. I hate that I wasted one of your pages to say so little, but I just wanted to document June 15th, 2015 as the day we opened our doors. Keep your fingers crossed that my next entry has something more positive to report!

Violet

12/25/15
Dear Diary

Merry Christmas, Diary! Leviticus has been open for six months and it is on fire! My idea of accepting donated blood for entry took off fast. On top of that, Dad's made back all the money he spent on converting the chapel. I have never seen him so happy! He even bought Eric and I special Christmas gifts!

One thing my brother and I always had in common is a love for classic cars, so Dad bought one for each of us! He bought Eric a '69 black Mustang. For me, he bought a '69 purple Firebird with dual white racing stripes! 1969 was not just a great year for me, but a great year for both cars too. Eric is still out somewhere with his new toy. I took mine for a spin, but I didn't realize how hectic and scary NYC traffic had become. It is going to take me some getting used to before I feel comfortable enough driving in it.

I must admit, with the club doing so well, life is starting to look up a bit. The only real downside is the club has angered

Caanis. Fae came to visit right after it opened. She loved it! We even danced together. After she went home, the king heard about how popular the place had suddenly become after only two weeks. He didn't like that at all. He's worried we will get caught, but the thing is, nobody even knows what we are doing here, at least as far as humans know.

Aside from three of the four band members, the nurses in the blood labs, and a couple security guards, we run everything else ourselves. Anna tends the bar. Eric, Bern, and Dad rotate between the kitchen, office, and an extra bouncer. As for me, I just enjoy myself. I guess I am an ornament. Max's Kansas City had Candy Darling. Leviticus has Violet Trouton. The only thing that could possibly make me enjoy it any more was if my dream man was here. I know I am delusional, but it gives me hope, so I hold faith that he is close. Is he close, Diary, or am I wasting my life on nothing but a dream I keep questioning, even right now?

I have found something interesting as of late. When we opened the club, Dad bought a really nice computer. Eric taught us both how to use it. I still don't know how to do much with it, but he showed me a website on the internet called YouTube. We were both able to laugh when we found an old video from that Halloween '81 episode of "Saturday Night Live" we attended.

Throughout the entire thing, Eric and I managed to stay off camera. We couldn't even spot the backs of our heads. It's been years now, but what a relief! Furthermore, I found Hendrix's Woodstock performance. It was after daylight, but I had only missed him by a couple of hours. I also found that old Janis Joplin performance of "Ball and Chain" from the Monterey Pop Festival. All I can say is wow! Even Mama Cass from the Mamas and the Papas looked blown away! I can't believe what kind of technology exists nowadays. Here we go into the future, I suppose. It looks like I better hold on tight!

Violet

4/11/17

Dear Diary

    100 years ago today, I entered the world. Eric was the first to remind me I don't look a day over 27. Last night at midnight, I was thrown the best birthday party anyone could ever ask for! I already knew Dad had something in mind. He even told me I could choose the Black Casket's entire setlist. I got them to learn "Venus in Furs" by the Underground, but that wasn't even the best part!

    The club opens at 11, but the party didn't officially start until midnight. The big surprise came before any of us went downstairs. Around 10:30, a knock came at my door. I had no idea who it could have been, but when I opened the door, I damn near had the wind knocked out of me. There were Winter-Fae, Pana, Roland, and Uki: all waiting to surprise me. It had been a while since I last saw Fae, but I hadn't seen the Alaskans in years.

    I was so happy to see them, but Lusa didn't come. I asked Pana why. He said she doesn't like to travel, and after coming to Anna and Bernard's wedding she would never come to this place again. I remember them suddenly leaving afterwards, but I still don't know what could have happened. He wouldn't tell me, either.

    After the reunion, we all went downstairs. I think the crowd made the Alaskans nervous. Dad has a big, round corner booth, and it is reserved only for us. That's where Pana, Roland, and Uki stayed the whole time. Anna worked the bar all night, and I don't even think she got to talk to any of them. You should see how she handles that bar crowd all by herself, though. What a boss!

    At midnight, Dad took to the stage. For obvious reasons, he withheld my age, but he had everyone there sing "Happy Birthday." Before that, he helped Anna and Bernard pass out free plastic cups of Alizé Red Passion, to anyone over 21, so they could all toast me. The crowd loved that. I think Dad is their hero now. He's certainly mine! As they had their cups of Red Passion, we had our own.

Fae and I danced together again, but this time I got her to come out of her shell. At one point, while the band was playing a cover of Motörhead's "Ace of Spades," and Fae and I just happened to be on the side of the stage, where nobody else could see us, I grabbed her little hand and yanked her right out there with me, in front of everyone, and started going wild. It took me back to the good old days of CBGB. It scared her at first, and she froze, but when Fae saw everyone cheering her on, she got into it. We both went wild and had so much fun up there together! I wish I had a camera and could have taken a picture of the huge smile on her face. She was so happy!

At the end of the band's set came one of the biggest surprises of all. Just before they began to announce their final song, Fae gave me a birthday present: a new hand-crocheted shawl. The last one she made for me fell apart years ago. We were at Dad's booth, and I wasn't even paying attention to the band at that point, but suddenly, I heard Peter Harlow, Black Casket's singer and guitarist, say, "Would the birthday girl, Miss Violet Troúton, please report to the stage?"

I was so confused, but after Dad and everyone else at the table told me to go on, I did. When I got up there, Peter asked me if I knew the lyrics to "Ball and Chain." I immediately knew what was happening. I nearly fainted right there on stage in front of everyone. I embarrassed myself further, screaming, "Yes!" as soon as he asked. Some people laughed, but the band started playing it. I was so nervous and caught off guard, but I closed my eyes and went for it—my fucking God did I go for it! Wow!

I belted out every word just like Janis, but I sure as hell couldn't nor wanted to even try going off like she would have. All along I kept my eyes shut, picturing him: the man of my dreams. At the end, as I shivered from head to toe, everyone blew the roof off the place with cheers. I had chills! Finally, I knew what it meant to stand in front of a crowd and receive that standing ovation I always wanted. I did it, Diary! They cheered their asses off, and they were cheering for me!

Eric and Anna were whistling and cheering me on from the bar. Even Dad stood up on his table and clapped for me. I might not have gotten to be a big Hollywood starlet, but for almost ten minutes, I got to be a fucking rockstar! Not to mention, Peter absolutely shredded that guitar solo! The night I saw Janis, I said I could die a happy woman. It was the best night of my life. I love my sweet Janis to death, and I always will, but tonight is the first time I think I've ever been able to say that I am truly happy to be alive— right here, right now, in this moment.

It is daylight right now, but after dark, I think the Alaskans are returning home. I am so glad they came, but I still wish Lusa had come too. Fae said even Avice thought about coming but decided not to at the last minute. Fae said she's close to giving in, though. I think Avice is a little curious about the club. I really want to meet her. I wish Dad and Caanis would just grow up and bury the hatchet already. Maybe in another hundred years, everything will be different. I guess we'll find out when we get there.

Violet

12/11/18
Dear Diary

Remember the Las Vegas Parliament, where Dad once invested some money? Last year, he had no choice but to reveal himself to the Parliament's CEO, Charlie Castro, after he figured out Dad's young appearance and the age of his stockholder account did not match. Since then, I have felt a strong urge to go out West. Even my dreams are picking up again. His eyes are still hidden, but now he is walking beside me, in the desert again, while the flashing blue and purple neon lights illuminate our way.

Dad took Eric and I with him when he went out there. I didn't explore too much, but I loved all the palm trees and colorful lights. For being so beautiful, I learned Sin City has a very dark underbelly. Among other things, homelessness and child sex trafficking are really bad there. It is dangerous—more dangerous than anyone will admit to the public. And I know it sounds completely insane, but I really want to go back. Parts of New York got rough back in the '70s and '80s, but I made it through safe and sound, so why not try my luck in Vegas?

There was just something about the place, like it's where I need to be. If I went, I'd want to find something fun to do there. Thanks to Eric showing me how to improve my web-surfing skills, I checked out their local community college: the College of Southern Nevada. You wouldn't believe what I saw, Diary. They offer a Psychology of Dreams class, and it is at night! Is it crazy for me to believe with all my heart that is where I need to be? The synchronicity is too perfect!

It's ironic. I have wanted to make some new friends or find something new, which is difficult for a woman like me. I do feel a little conflicted about leaving now that I have just recently met someone. Her name is Chloe. She has long brown hair, but she is not him. Chloe came into the club alone one night. I saw her dancing and I joined her. She has a really nice dancer's body. After a few songs, we introduced ourselves. She is twenty-three and lives in Brooklyn.

Although I have never looked at women that way, I think she is gorgeous! She told me she is a lesbian, and the way she giggles at everything I say, I think she might have a crush on me. She is nice, but nobody else here likes her—not even Dad, and he likes everyone. I haven't told her I am a vampire. Now that I plan to go to Vegas soon, I don't really see a need to tell her. What should I do, Diary? Should I settle here or go through with my plans in Vegas? Help!

Violet

1/11/19
Dear Diary

 I am currently back in New York, but I decided to go forward with Vegas. Against everyone's wishes, I even drove my Firebird out there. What a trip! It only takes about thirty minutes to fly there but it took me five nights to drive it. It was such an amazing experience, though! I stayed in hotels during the day and drove through the night. I got to see a lot of the country. I never realized America was so beautiful!

 While crossing the Mississippi into St. Louis, I saw the Gateway Arch. It was so big! While passing through Colorado, I got to drive through the Rockies! They were covered in snow. There was something I found quite hauntingly surreal about burning rubber down I-70 at 2 a.m. with the windows down, icy wind blowing my hair everywhere, and Heart's "Barracuda" cranked at full blast and screaming the lyrics at the top of my lungs. If that is not the "American Dream," then what is? The next night, I finished my trip, after discovering how pretty Utah is.

 I have been back home for three days now, and I have seen Chloe twice. Regarding her: I am confused. Last night, she kissed me. It was just a small peck on the lips. I didn't resist, but I didn't return a kiss of my own. I think it upset her. I really don't know what to say. I want to tell her about me—I really do, but I am scared. They say everything that is meant to happen will happen regardless of any action, right?

 Maybe I should tell her. If she accepts me, I will know there can be something more. If not, maybe it is because my dream man really is waiting for me out West, and this could be my way of scaring Chloe off. I don't want to scare her, but I want my own happiness more. Self-love is not selfish, is it?

 It is settled! I am going to do this! My first psychology class is Friday the 13th, of all days. I am seeing Chloe tomorrow before she thinks I am headed to the airport. I am already nervous as hell, but I will tell her then. Whatever is meant to unfold from this will, right? Wish me luck, Diary! I think I'll need it.

Violet

Chapter Thirty–Nine

Having spent the last couple of hours reading and resting, Julian lay in bed, still wondering, *Why didn't Violet ever tell me about her dreams?* Before she died, he often asked, *Why me? Why choose me?* Now, it all made sense. She chose him because she patiently waited all but a year of his life for the universe to bring them together. *But why didn't she tell me?*

He'd become so wrapped up in reading and sharing the most intimate moment he still could with his love that Julian never noticed Dajhri's drumming had long since ended. He put his shoes back on and went downstairs, the *Ayahuasca's* pervasive aroma still festering at the bottom. In the room at the end of the hall, he found the queen with her back turned, stirring the cauldron with a long wooden ladle. From the doorway, he cleared his throat and asked, "How's it coming along?"

"It is nearly finished," Dajhri said, her focus never shifting.

Julian entered the room, saying, "I forgot how bad *Aya* smells."

"I grew used to it long ago. For me, the stench of vomit and feces from those who drink are far worse. Still, who am I to pay mind? The purge is key to the healing *Mama Aya* provides."

As she continued stirring the mixture, Julian turned and took another look at the green and copper-clad skeleton he'd stumbled upon earlier. Finding the posed warrior strangely mesmerizing, he asked, "Is that real—the skeleton?"

"He is. That is Sami, my husband."

Julian squeaked, "That's Sami?!" Though Dajhri's back was turned, he watched her head bob once. "I hope you don't take offense by my asking, but why would you keep him like that instead of burying him?"

"I do not take offense. I keep him here as a symbol and reminder of what true power, purpose, and motivation can accomplish. Do you see that spear in his hand?"

"Yes," he said, staring at the ancient weapon.

"It was with that spear he reclaimed our village and became my king when he was but eleven years old."

"Only eleven? How?"

Dajhri finished stirring the medicine, leaving the ladle leaning inside the cauldron. Turning to face Julian and the skeleton, she said, "There was a time my village of Pacha was nothing more than a few stone huts. Wild vegetation and livestock were bountiful for the small number of us inhabiting the land. Though we mostly lived in peace, our abundant supply sometimes made us a target for attacks from rival tribes.

"We had skilled *Inca* warriors to defend us against such threats, including the young Sami, but after one heavy attack, our village chieftain was killed. A vicious tyrant called Tupaca took his place, ordering his men to slaughter most of the village elders and force the rest of us into slavery. Some women collected crops for the tyrant to either keep for himself and his men or to send back to his home village as tribute to his previous chief. The women who could bear children were used in other ways.

"Our men were forced to hunt and gather building materials for Tupaca to send to his native village with the crops. Our once sufficient paradise quickly diminished. When the men were not hunting or collecting, they worked—sometimes to death—building unnecessary structures for the tyrant's vanity.

"One of those structures was a massive stone tower that stood higher than the trees. Tupaca lived comfortably at the top, proudly looking down on those who were barely given enough scraps and rest to survive. After the first years, most of the elders

Tupaca spared had either died or were dying from simple disease and famine."

Dajhri approached the skeleton. "Then a day came when my young king had enough; enough of watching his village fall apart, enough of watching his people die. Mothers unable to feed their babies! He had enough of watching everyone he loved—brothers and sisters, mothers and fathers, husbands and wives—all losing their livelihoods in the name of greed and mad hierarchy.

"After returning home from a hunt, exhausted and covered in llama blood, Sami faced a fork in his path. Nearby, a young village girl, only nine years old, was fighting for her life. Two of the tyrant's guards had gone from harassing to beating her and trying to force themselves inside her. It was nothing new. They had their way with the women and girls whenever they wanted. Everyone was too scared to resist. Not Sami, though. Never again."

"He was not even five feet tall or one hundred pounds at the time, but when blessed with the power of fate, Sami's size meant nothing. Without thought, reason, or any logical explanation of impulse, his spear skewered both guards' heads in one swift blow. Their bodies went limp, and Sami violently retracted his weapon, slinging their cold blood everywhere and alerting other guards on standby.

"Sami's sudden declaration of morality started something he knew only he could finish. As the other guards approached with their weapons drawn, he stood at the ready. He was ready to slay them all, ready to take his fight all the way to the top of the tower, and even ready to die if he had to.

"He knew there was no turning back. With his blood-soaked spear held high above his head, Sami wailed, 'For all!' in our native tongue of *Quechua*. One after another, the guards came running, but Sami was far too fast and agile. He killed them all, inspiring others who dared to ever pick up a weapon in defense again to do just that!

"He and a few other brave men stormed the tower. From the ground below, I watched Tupaca's mutilated, bloody corpse tumble and then land at my feet—completely unrecognizable as anything close to human. Tupaca never was a human. He was a beast, and my king slayed it. From that day forward, our village was ours. After everyone heard of Sami's strength and courage, we were never attacked again." Following a pleasant smile, she added. "I was the young girl that Sami not only saved, but who gave him the inspiration to save us all and become who he was born to be."

Otherwise amazed by the queen's story, all Julian could manage was Sami's war cry: "'For all.'"

"Yes, for all of us. When I grew into a young woman, he chose me to be his queen. We married and ruled the village as equals who never let anyone suffer again."

"Did you and Sami ever have children?"

"No, we did not," she somberly moaned. "We tried, but it wasn't our fate. When I was twenty-nine and he was thirty-one, we discovered our destiny, and I became what I am."

"How did it happen?"

"I was bitten by a snake—a *bothrops insularis*—or as it is commonly known: the golden lancehead." Dajhri snickered. "Imagine the humor. my husband saved me with a copper spearhead, and it all ended with a golden lancehead."

"Is it venomous?"

"It is. Thanks to modern medicine, the survival rate is much higher than it was before the common era. However, I was bitten five hundred years before Christ walked the earth. Even then, I had only a seven percent chance of death, but then my kidneys ruptured."

"—my God!"

"Love and fate saved my life. Within the first few days, Sami had reached out to every shaman he could find, all doing their absolute best to keep me comfortable and free of pain, but still I suffered. I knew I was dying. I was not afraid of death. I was afraid of losing my king. After the fifth day on my deathbed, my greatest fear came true when I awoke, too weak to speak, and discovered Sami had left my side. The shamans were there, but the one person I wanted was not. I thought he had abandoned me."

"Where did he go?"

"The shamans who cared for me in Sami's absence told me he went to the Temple of El Paraiso, north of modern Lima. I did not believe them, but they told me rumors made their way to Sami of an ancient female spirit inhabiting the temple. They said she could heal anyone, and they would live forever."

Almost eagerly, Julian blurted, "Was it Lilith?"

Dajhri nodded. "Seven more days passed with no signs of Sami's return. My condition worsened each day. In my dreams, I saw him calling my name in the dark, searching for me. No matter how loud I said his name back, he never saw or heard me. I knew what the dreams meant. I knew I was closing in on death. On the thirteenth day, the shamans prayed over me, preparing to send my spirit to Inti. Then Sami returned. He was not alone. A woman with dark hair and darker eyes came too. Her skin was just a shade or two darker than mine."

"And she made you a vampire?"

"She did. She stayed with Sami and I the entire time. Once I healed, Lilith told me her will to remain in this world had long grown thin. She said I was the first vampire she had made in at least six thousand years. She could not be certain because she had long since forgotten the concept of time, something which would likely become meaningless to anyone at that age. People only knew of her powers because she told them, trying to find me after dreaming about saving the barren wife of a chieftain, dying from a snakebite."

"She was that specific?"

"She was. The mother of all our kind told me many came seeking her power, but she turned them away."

"But why not help them too?"

"You may or may not know this, but when we share our blood, we relinquish a piece of our soul. Lilith gave so many pieces of herself over the course of many millennia, so much of herself, she had so little left. Many ancient kingdoms rose and fell for her blood. She said she could not explain why, but her visions of me were so moving, she waited, knowing one day she would find me. Once she did, she taught me her secrets before disappearing. No one has seen her since. I choose to believe wherever her soul might be, she is at peace."

"It is so weird you say that, about her seeing you in her dreams."

Returning to her big round pot and stirring the contents, Dajhri asked, "How so?"

"Violet started having dreams about me the day I was born. She knew I had an eye condition and even that my hair is long and brown. I read about it in her diary. She often questioned her sanity, but she kept her own faith, following her heart and the synchronicities as they presented themselves. Then, we found each other."

Her bold green eyes leading the way, the shaman slowly looked up from the brew. "What do you see in your dreams?"

"I see *her*. She comes to me in her wedding dress, but her face is always hidden beneath her hair, or she's a shadow. Pana said it might be because she knows she is dead, and she feels ashamed, like I won't accept her. I do accept her, though. I've told her that. We've tried to make love twice—since we never got to before. Every time, my dream is disrupted, and it never happens. The dreams are so real, as if I were awake." Their eyes still locked, he added, "You have no idea how badly I want her. I love and miss her so much."

"You have blockages, dear one. You have faced many trials as of late and you have suffered greatly." She smudged her middle and index fingers against his forehead. "Your third eye is open, but your vision is cloudy. The third eye is where the pineal gland is located. They say our pineal gland produces our body's own natural dimethyltryptamine: the psychoactive in *Ayahuasca*. The pineal gland is said to be where our souls reside. I told you last night, vampires cannot drink *Ayahuasca*. Only humans can. Normal food would rupture our stomachs. Imagine what something as acidic and aggressive on the digestive system as *Aya* would do to us."

She snickered while Julian nodded and quivered at the idea. "We cannot drink that medicine, but others can be smoked. Tell me, Julian, do you know what *bufo alvarius* is?"

"Five-MEO-DMT?"

"Yes, the extracted, dried venom of the *bufo alvarius* or the Colorado River Toad."

"I read a little about it back when I was researching *Ayahuasca*."

"Make no mistake. Though DMT is in the name, it is nothing like the dimethyltryptamine in *Aya* or our bodies. It is a substance all its own. We call DMT the 'spirit molecule.' We call *Bufo* the 'God molecule.'"

"Does it cause a psychedelic trip?"

"A 'trip?' For humans, no. When humans partake, they experience the death fade—the feeling of losing all ego and consciousness, like with *Ayahuasca*. Some say they see a white light. Others say they see nothing but lost consciousness while experiencing themselves condensed to their purest abstract form: spirit energy and at one with all."

"And when vampires smoke it?"

"I can only speak for myself, but I see things that have already happened, currently are happening elsewhere, or have not yet but will happen. I have my strongest visions with *Bufo*. Do you know what the Akashic Records are?"

"No."

"It is the collection of all universal knowledge: past, present, and future. Think of everything you will ever know as having already occurred. From an outside source, we are looking in and taking part in the universe at various points in history. Think of it as an archive—a gateway to all life, time, and space as we know it. This collection is the Akashic Records.

"For me, the venom of the *bufo alvarius* allows me to access this 'archive' and not only see what I am meant to see, but remember what I saw when I awaken after the medicine runs its course. The records are always present. It is likely you accessed them during your previous ceremonies, but as a human, you would not remember."

"And you want me to smoke this?"

"The decision is yours. I would never force anyone to engage in such an act unless they knew they were ready. I simply wanted to open the door for you. I believe the toad medicine will not just show you what you need to see. It will remove the blockages in your third eye chakra, and your crown, heart, and other important points of energy preventing you from embracing your love the way you and she so desire."

"If I do this, it will bring me closer to Violet?"

She nodded. "It will, and it will be every bit as real and magical as you desire."

"Does it help you communicate with Sami?"

"It does not, but I do not desire it to."

"Why wouldn't you? He saved your life twice. He loved you and you loved him."

"Loved? I still love him, and I always will, but nothing is meant to last forever. I imagine even the most perfect concept of 'perfect' would become torture in the never-ending idea of eternity."

"I want to be with Violet for never-ending eternity," Julian said without hesitation.

"That is your right and prerogative, but for me, the five hundred years I gave to Sami grew tiring. It is not that I didn't love him. I just loved him so long, this human notion of romance we all come to know—merely from ego—always fades; at least for me— with him—it did."

"You are very wise. Perhaps I could learn a lot from you." Dajhri smiled. "But even after everything—fighting tooth and nail like a son of a bitch; I still believe in a fairytale romance, and how with the right person, it can last forever. I have that love with Violet. We are apart now, but she once told me, 'Now is not forever.'"

"You are right, but with all due respect, you have not experienced what I have. When facing forever with anyone but yourself, it is much to consider. I've taken other lovers since Sami, some lasting only days, and even one whom I gave six hundred years of myself to. Each lost their luster, just like Sami. Ultimately, each failed me, just like Sami."

"Did you make Sami a vampire?"

"I did, but unlike the circumstances of my transformation, he was neither sick nor dying. He lived a full human life first. I never left his side. In his elder years, he offered himself to me forever."

"Forever," Julian snickered. "At least you got to spend five hundred years together, even if the romance didn't last."

"After his transformation, our love eventually grew sour. Not even one hundred years later, he came to regret it. He spent nearly four hundred years in misery, but he still loved me and did all he could for me. After my visions of Taltosia, he even built this temple for me with the other vampires we made together. That is how my once great empire arose.

"For a time, life was good. When we made love, it was heavenly. Though he wore the body of an old man, that brave, strong, agile boy who saved my life and our village was the Sami in control of that body. Life itself was our Garden, until finally he could no longer hide his pain. For decades, he begged me to kill him. I did not want to. I prayed to Lilith day and night to bring him the same happiness I still had, but it never manifested. Then the day finally came when I found him in this room. He had cut open both of his wrists and his throat. By the time I found him, he had been gone for hours."

"Jesus Christ! … I couldn't imagine what that was like."

"To discover the love of your life that way, knowing they did it to themselves? It hurt. It hurt tremendously. Even now, two thousand years later, it still hurts. If he had never done that to himself, my feelings of romantic love might be different. I wish they were different, but in all my time in this universe, the only one I have ever been able to truly depend on beyond everything is myself. I am self-sufficient and self-serving."

"But as a shaman, you serve others too."

"I give and take as I wish. I do what I do because there must be balance. I feed upon and kill living beings. To make up for that the best way I can, I try to help those in need by opening their doors of perception so they might become who they were meant to be. Unfortunately, in this new world, I often find my efforts meaningless."

"How so?"

"You see the darkness in this world. Some light does exist, but very little. Earth needs to be cleansed of its wickedness. Though more people live in this world now than when I discovered Lilith, bringing modern advancements, time was simpler then, even with vicious tyrants like Tupaca lording it. He received the justice he deserved. Now, the tyrants only thrive and produce more in their wake; like ticks and leeches. I told you chaos and order are two sides of the same coin."

Julian said, "I often wonder what the world would be like if it suddenly went back to the way it was before things like the internet, television, media, and other negative influences began shaping us into the furthest thing from our ancestors' intentions possible."

"For me and other vampires who lived in that simpler time, it would be paradise once again, but for those who lived through the more common era, it is hard to say. Even you were conditioned to be accustomed to modern conveniences. However, unlike many other young vampires, your thinking is rational. I see your mind and soul as far superior to many vampires who are hundreds of years older than you."

"Everyone keeps telling me I am wise, but I feel weak."

"You are sensitive and lack confidence in areas, but your mind, heart, and will to survive are what make you a man." Dajhri rested her palm over Julian's heart, adding, "Be proud of the man you are. You are not the physical warrior my king once was, but you are just as cunning and every bit as brave."

Julian blushed. He said, "Thanks. That makes me happy to hear someone as gracious, wise, and experienced in life as you are to say."

Dajhri smiled, pulled away, and returned to the cauldron. "I think the medicine is ready now. Would you like to help me collect it?"

"Sure."

"Then we can go to Pacha, and the ceremony can begin." They spent the next several minutes clearing all the plant material from the cauldron. The scalding hot mess having no effect on him, Julian used his hands to collect the bulk, paying no mind to Dajhri, beside him, doing the same. Then, they bottled what muddy brown water remained. After changing from her robe into a loose white gown and collecting everything she needed for the evening, Dajhri called for Serene and her four cloaked guards, all wearing white.

Once everyone met at the top of the stairs, they left the temple and took to the amethyst sky. Julian rode on Dajhri's back, his stomach full of butterflies, his head buzzing with anxiety and wonder for the night to come. *Soon, my flower. Soon, we can have our wedding night. I swear. Soon.*

Chapter Forty

Not even a minute passed before everyone landed on the Peruvian jungle floor, less than a half-dozen miles from the volcano. On Dajhri's left, Julian observed low light in the distance, exposing the silhouettes of dense trees and bushes in the forefront. On her queen's right, Serene carried a white cloth bag with the image of a yellow sun embroidered into the fabric.

Her four cloaked guards looming behind, Dajhri took Julian's hand. "Follow me and watch your step," she said. "The grass is thick and tall." Along his short walk towards the village of Pacha, Julian's ears succumbed to the chirps and squawks of the surrounding wilderness, many of which he recalled serenading him and the queen as they bathed, the night before. At the center of the performance, a distinctly calm, elongated whistle came tooting from somewhere close, zigzagging in and out like a child having fun with a volume dial.

After a short walk, the dense forest opened on a sizable field of cut green grass. Nearby, Julian spotted a high domed pavilion with several lit torches surrounding its outer white pillars and four more circling the inside. The weathered wooden structure stood roughly thirty-five feet in diameter. Two slender, almond-skinned men, both dressed in white, stood at the wide entrance.

When everyone drew close enough for the men to see, one called out, "*Allianchu*, Dajhri!" The man spoke with a strong accent.

"*Allianchu*," the queen repeated, offering a pleasant bow. Her hooded guards kept watch near the doorway and the two men in white moved aside, allowing Dajhri, Julian, and Serene entry to the ceremonial space. Inside, a dozen other people were gathering, all wearing white.

Julian panned the area, counting six yoga mats—some orange and some blue—arranged around the cement floor. Three lay on each side, with plenty of space between them. Beside every mat sat a small, blue, plastic bucket for vomiting, a folded brown hand towel for wiping mouths and faces, and bottles of water for hydration. At the opposite end of the pavilion from the entrance sat a small round table where Dajhri and Serene were removing items from the embroidered sun bag.

To the left of the table lay a short stack of extra mats. On the right, another small table sat with a pair of green and red maracas and a dual set of brown tribal drums with a shoulder strap attached. Julian admired such authenticity, remembering the shamanic music at his ceremonies was all pre-recorded and played from a cellphone instead of the traditional way with live shamanic *icaros*. He also appreciated how spacious the area was in comparison to the cramped cabin room he'd shared with nine others.

He observed all the faces of those who were gathered. Most of their skin was various shades of brown, some as fair as Dajhri's, and others darker. Two pasty young blonde women with northeastern American accents laughed and joked between themselves. Other men and women Julian assumed were more native to the area sat silently on their mats, their eyes all closed, and focused on their slow, deep breathing. After checking everything out, he joined Dajhri and Serene. Watching the queen place a large decorative glass bottle full of *Ayahuasca* on the table, he asked, "Is there anything I can do?"

"Right now, we are setting up," she said. "First, I am going to distribute the *Aya* to those partaking. Later, I will administer the *Bufo* to you and two others who are here for it. In the meantime, you may take one of those spare mats and get comfortable, if you like. When we begin, you can listen and observe."

Julian retrieved a blue mat from the top of the pile and set it near the table where Dajhri was placing empty cups for the *Ayahuasca*. Beside the cups sat a tiny glass canister, half full of a white, grainy substance, labeled, *5-MeO-DMT*. Next to it lay a portable hand torch and two transparent glass spoon pipes.

Still giggling, the two blondes moved their mats closer to one another while everyone else remained quiet and reserved. Two young darkly tanned men—both wearing white—entered the pavilion and took their own mats from the stack, placing them on Julian's right and then sitting. He forced a smile and said, "Hello."

They both smiled back. One nodded and the other said, "*Hola.*"

Everyone was now inside, including an older man and woman near the table of instruments and the two men in the doorway. Dajhri approached the center of the room, holding the capped bottle in her hands. Smiling at everyone, she said, "Welcome to our ceremony on this new moon. Most of you, I have seen before, but for the rest, I am Dajhri. I made the sacred plant medicine you will be drinking tonight from the *ayahuasca* vine and leaves from the *chacruna*. To keep with tradition, those who have never drunk before shall drink first. We begin each ceremony with the participant speaking their intentions into the open bottle—what you hope to gain from the experience. We finish by blowing into the bottle, sending your intentions to the plant spirit: *Mama Ayahuasca*."

Dajhri walked to the blond closest to the entrance and handed her the bottle. The young woman untwisted the lid, still giggling under her breath. She cleared her throat and straightened her composure. At first, Julian did not see her lips move, but he heard, "What the hell is this going to do?" Then her lips moved, and everyone heard, "I want to be successful with my new job and meet a good man who will take good care of me." She closed the bottle and started to hand it to her friend.

"You must blow your intentions into the medicine first," Dajhri said.

"Oh!" The bubbly young woman snickered, her thoughts saying, "Like that's even going to matter, you dumb hippie," to

Julian's vampire ears. While certain Dajhri also heard the snide thoughts, he watched the woman unscrew the white lid again and almost sarcastically blow a quick hard breath into it before putting the lid back on and passing the bottle to her right. "There … satisfied?"

Fucking bitch.

In a softer, more sincere tone, the other blonde nervously mumbled, "Mother, I ask you to show me how to release the trauma from my past that is holding me back from my present and future. I ask that you show me how I can forgive those who hurt me and learn how to love myself again." She untwisted the cap and blew slowly inside it.

While she passed the bottle to a stocky man with short dark hair and tan skin, her friend's thoughts spoke to Julian once more. "Really, Trish? You really think this dumb shit's going to erase what she did to you, like a magic spell? Why did I ever let you drag me down to this shithole? We could've just dropped acid back home." So badly, Julian wanted to say something, but he knew it was neither his place nor logical to even try.

The man now holding the bottle removed the lid. In a deep accent Julian had not heard before, he said, "*Madre*, I thank you for allowing me to return to your embrace once again. I offer you my mind, body, and soul, and I pray you guide me and show me what lessons I have yet to learn. I thank you for this night."

He blew into the bottle before closing it and handing it back to Dajhri. The other three on the opposite side—two men and one woman—all spoke Spanish. Though Julian could not understand them, he watched each blow into the bottle after speaking from their hearts. When all six participants said their piece, Dajhri stood between them, opening the bottle and declaring her own objective.

"*Mama Ayahuasca*, I ask for your guidance and permission to lead these brave souls to your teachings. I ask for your blessing to guide not just them but all who are lost. May you light my way as you light theirs." Like the others, she too blew into the bottle. Then, she returned to the table where Serene waited. With her eyes on everyone, the shaman asked, "Who here has never drunk?" The two blondes were the only ones who raised their hands. Dajhri pointed towards the one seated closest to the entrance. "Come," she said.

The woman hopped from her mat and approached the table where Dajhri poured roughly a shot glass worth of the brown substance into one of the clear cups. Taking it, the woman stared at the small amount with an air of bewilderment. "Will I get more if this doesn't work?"

"In two hours, everyone will be given the opportunity to have a second cup if they wish," Dajhri said. The woman drank it all in one gulp and horrendously scowled on her way back to her mat, showing signs of instant regret in her bulging brown eyes. After Dajhri poured the same amount into a clean cup, the more sincere blonde came forward, drinking with no questions asked. Like her friend, she also displayed her discontentment with the foul-flavored sacrament.

One by one, the other four came to the table and drank. Then the two musicians and two facilitators who previously stood outside the entrance all sipped a micro dose in comparison; allowing them access to the energies needed to assist everyone along their journeys but not incapacitate them from doing so. Before they could all drink, both blondes' faces were already buried in their buckets, heaving and vomiting loudly. Julian bit his lip to keep from laughing, remembering all too well how quick the medicine had also hit him.

Once drinking her dose, an elderly salt-and-pepper-haired woman picked up the set of green and red maracas from the table of instruments. Heading to the center of the room while shaking them in a rhythm, she chanted a native shamanic tune. By the time a balding man joined her with the drums strapped over his shoulders—beating along to the *icaro*—everyone on the floor who'd drunk were either vomiting or gasping and spitting between heaves.

From the round table, Dajhri said, "Remember to breathe and take a drink of water every time you remember it is there. May each of you have a peaceful journey. … *Aho*, brave spirits."

Julian observed the blondes, vomiting far more violently than the others. He took it as a sign of neglecting the strict diet leading up to the ceremony to avoid such horrendous amounts of purging. The brutal upchucking—not just from the women but everyone else included—were overwhelming to his ears. Thirty minutes passed before everyone's agony had ended.

Now confined to their mats, some unconsciously wallowed while others lay motionless. The musicians continued playing and singing as Dajhri, Serene, and the two male facilitators kept a close eye on everyone, aiding those who needed it, making sure they were all comfortable and free of distress. At one point, the more sincere blond, "Trish," as her friend called her, started to cry. "Please don't leave me, Mommy!" Dajhri gently cradled and rocked her in her thin, empathetic arms until the woman eventually relaxed enough to be left alone again.

From his mat, Julian watched the entire scene. Having also been held and rocked during his ceremony after tapping into unhealed wounds regarding his own abuse and neglect, he identified with the woman's pain. His mother hurt him, too. He wanted to approach and assist but refrained. Instead, he silently waited with the other two men who came for the *bufo alvarius*, knowing there was nothing he could do that the queen and her more experienced helpers couldn't do better.

Nearly two hours passed before Dajhri announced, "Anyone who would like a second cup, you may come now." The stocky man to the right of the blondes staggered to the table first. Dajhri poured him a little more than his first dose. He drank it and returned to his mat. One of the Spanish-speaking men on the other side of the room came next, also receiving a larger dose. Finally, Trish approached for another cup. Her friend was out cold. Moments later, those who drank were vomiting in their buckets again.

Aside from Trish's outpour and all the harsh purging, the ceremony had gone smoothly. Even the musicians were still playing and singing. After nearly another hour passed, and with most of the participants out for the night, Dajhri finally approached Julian and asked, "Are you ready?"

He had been calm up to that point, but when reality set in, his heartbeat increased. "I am nervous," he said. "I feel like after everything else, I shouldn't feel this way at all, but I do."

Dajhri knelt to his level and whispered, "How many times have you died or almost died now? This will make you feel like you're dying, yet you are not. With this, you shall feel, heal, and step closer toward your power, divine purpose, and the one you love."

Julian took a deep breath and nodded. "I am ready," he said.

Dajhri returned to the table where Serene was removing the lid from the tiny glass container with *5-MeO-DMT* written in black. Holding the torch and one of the clear glass pipes, on her way back to him, she said, "Stretch your legs out in front of you, Julian. Now, take deep breaths through your nose and release them from your mouth. Focus on your intentions." He nodded, relaxing his body as the doctor ordered. Then, he pictured only Violet's precious face. Her perfect depiction appeared before him, plain as day: her brown almond eyes, her soft cheeks, and full, pillowed lips—every detail—even her flowing, thick auburn strands and her unmistakable starlet shape and satin-draped frame.

With Serene by her side, Dajhri knelt over Julian's legs and said, "Once I heat this pipe, Serene will drop the dose inside. I will place it upon your lips. You will inhale as hard as you can for ten seconds, until I tell you to stop. After that, you will hold it in for ten seconds. Once I tell you to exhale, blow it out and we will lay you back. Shut your eyes and let the medicine take you."

His heart beating madly, Julian swallowed a lump and muttered, "Okay."

"Once you have exhaled, I will inhale a small amount, so I can properly guide you." Dajhri pulled the trigger on the torch and aimed the scorching blue flame at the pipe's thick glass bowl.

You can do this, he told himself. *You can do this. You're a vampire who's experienced death on many levels. This is nothing. You've got this! I am so close, my flower.* When Dajhri pulled away the flame, Serene leaned forward with a fat crumb of the grainy substance on a tiny scoop and dropped it into the scalding hot bowl. Pale gray smoke arose and Dajhri gently placed the mouthpiece to Julian's lips.

"Breathe," she commanded. "Breathe as much and as hard as you can. Keep going … keep going … almost." Julian vacuumed with all the might his pectoralis had, tasting the toad's venom, and randomly placing the flavor with burnt corn chips. Finally, after he had no room left in his lungs, Dajhri pulled the glass piece away. "Hold it in. … hold it … only a couple more seconds … and release slowly."

Julian exhaled and watched Dajhri take two small puffs from the smoldering remains. She and Serene gently laid him back. Overhead, the dancing orange flicker of a nearby torch kept his attention until the distinction of life slipping away and the void closing in dawned such a dread. *What the fuck am I doing?!* In a panic, Julian started to rise, moaning, "I can't do this," trying to fight it off.

The queen put her hand over his chest. Softly, she said, "Yes, you can. Don't fight it."

Julian lay back again, focused on the ceiling's wavy torchlight patterns. Any other visuals quickly began to dissolve from inside a growing black hole of nothingness, pulling him further and further from life as he knew it. Every other time he had experienced the cold whisper approach, he panicked. In this instance, the panic ended with his ego, leaving a calm sense of peace and tranquility. Just as he'd accomplished before blacking out in the catacombs, he smiled. Then, the final glimmer of light faded to black when his eyelids closed on their own.

A vibrant luminosity emerged, overcoming all with an absolute intensity. Julian was not just viewing white light; he had become it—stretched for true eternity in every direction, merging all time, space, and matter into one never-ending frame of self-creation. Such exquisite glory seemed far too intense for any sentient mind to conceive. Julian Frost—the man, the physical form, the notion—no longer existed; unending energy and the divine relativity of an all-knowing God did. After what only could have been seconds or millennia of this everlasting infinity, God's divine light withdrew, giving way to new abstract forms and concepts.

A vulgar display of crimson transpired, accompanied by the unmistakable smell of blood. It was like Julian was the blood until the metallic essence revealed itself as dried red streaks on white fabric. While the miniscule form he'd become floated in midair as a shimmering ruby particle, Julian's field of vision expanded as the soiled white fabric's nature took shape, revealing itself as a shirt. Wearing that shirt was Bernard, brandishing the king's dagger above his head—the sharp end forward.

The king's face said it all. He smirked with pride, his bewitched eyes glowing with the unsettling rage of a vengeful murderer, taking sick, erotic pleasure from committing such an atrocity. Bernard succulently licked his lips, his dark grimace festering with the onset of a raging wildfire detonating behind him. Like the wrath of a once sleeping dragon having woken prematurely, the flames grew rapidly until engulfing his entire body, leaving no trace of the monarch assassin.

From the epic inferno, a dark silhouette emerged in the shape of Violet. Then as if separating from his own point of view, Julian watched himself, naked in the fire with the shadow—also naked. Both he and his love laughed together like overly fortunate hyenas, admiring such sparkling beauty in the flames, destroying all living things in the way.

Their bodies unnaturally intertwined like mating snakes. Their coming together brought forth the conception of a new world: their world. All that remained was either them or theirs, as the new gods; the absolute balance a disease-ridden world so desperately needed. He had her and she had him. To Julian, nothing else would ever matter again, only *her* and the beautiful reign of fire she brought with her.

The unnatural red blaze grew higher and brighter, illuminating them both. When her face became clear for the first time since the dungeon, their eyes met. His was lovestruck; her brown almonds wide and panicked. Noting her distress, Julian asked, "What is it?!" Rather than English or words, a series of high-volume tones slipped through his lips. "What the hell?!" Again, high-pitched beeps replaced his words.

Now trembling with dread, Violet opened her mouth, releasing her own ear-piercing cryptography. "Beep-beep-beep beep---beep---beep … beep--beep--beep."

Immediately, Julian recognized the pattern. It was the same she'd used when squeezing his heart, telling him she loved him in threes. "I love you!" he cried, but the intense shrieking that came out was not the same he heard from Violet.

Her face melting in desperation, she repeated herself. "Beep-beep-beep … beep---beep---beep … beep--beep--beep."

"But Violet, I—I don't understand!" Julian scrambled, trying to think of a way to communicate. "What are you trying to say? Talk to me. This sounds kind of like morse co---" It was then he remembered reading something in her diary about Eric once teaching her morse code. "I—I don't know any morse code." He kept speaking but still only heard beeps. "The only phrase I've ever even heard before is S.O.S." Though it was English in his head, "Beep-beep-beep … beep---beep---beep … beep—beep--beep," is what came out of his mouth.

Violet's eyes lit like firecrackers and her head shook rapidly. "S.O.S?" Julian repeated. She reached out and took hold of him, the sheer terror weathering her restless face was enough to know something wasn't right. It was like she'd been trying to tell him all along. She appeared lost, distressed, cold, alone, and above all, hopeless.

"—Julian!" From a million miles away, Dajhri's disheartening squall withdrew him from his lover's arms once again, and directly back into the Hell he longed to escape. Every relaxed muscle in his body at one with absolute balance, he couldn't open his eyes if his life depended on it. He could just breathe and listen. While a fierce vigor engulfed his body whole, occasional pops, cracks and the final screams of men and women overlapped the continuous roar from all directions.

Heavily under the toad medicine's influence, he was beyond comprehension, but he knew someone had swiped him up and was carrying him through the immense threshold. Somewhere along the way, his blinders were jarred open, exposing the real-life horror show he could only witness. The entire pavilion was a freakish dome blaze. Whether mounds of human remains lay roasting over their melted yoga mats or elsewhere on the floor, no other signs of animate life appeared except the hooded guards, rushing in to guide their queen to safety. After making it out, one of them frantically yelled, "Where is Serene?!"

"She's still in there!" Dajhri shouted. As the man charged into the flames, she commanded, "Jorge, no!" but he was already gone.

Slightly more cognizant of reality and able to gain a better view of himself and Dajhri, Julian was astounded to find both their bodies had been fully baptized in the fire. Neither a single hair nor stitch of clothing remained between them. Now able to move more freely, he scanned the area, discovering nobody else outside the golden cataclysm but the queen and her three remaining guards. He then focused on the entrance to the pavilion, hoping others would escape such a horrific fate, but only seconds after Jorge ran inside, the flaming roof and supporting pillars collapsed, along with any hope that might have emerged.

Even in his inebriated state, Julian knew such an anomaly should not have occurred or created such rapid damage as to prevent anyone else from escaping. With the little sobriety he had, he whispered, "What happened?" Nobody answered him.

One of the other guards, his face bleak as death itself, turned to everyone and said, "We must go." Scowling like she could cry, the hairless, soot-tattered queen nodded and tightened her grip on Julian. With three surviving guards, they took to the sky, heading towards the volcano, leaving the devastating grave and monument in their wake.

Chapter Forty-One

E ven with the *bufo alvarius* still altering his perception, Julian was well-oriented enough to know something ungodly and cataclysmic had occurred. As the group landed outside the gate of Taltosia, he groaned, "What just happened down there?" The remaining three guards all glared, but they said nothing.

Dajhri unlocked the bronze door with the key she had dangling from a chain around her neck. Once everyone entered the temple, she locked the door, and the guards lowered their white hoods. The tallest of the three—bald, with a thin, tawny mustache—shot another look of disgust at Julian. "You did this!" he growled.

Dajhri stepped between them. Facing the guard, she said, "Raimi, please. It was not Julian's fault."

"The hell it wasn't!" a chocolate-haired guard interjected. "We saw what happened! Just after his ritual began, the flames on all those torches grew and grew until they exploded! Fire does not do that!"

Dajhri consoled the guard, laying her open palm over his rapidly pumping chest. Softly, she repeated, "It was not his fault, Suri. I cannot explain what happened. Julian has a great power in him ... a power even I do not possess."

Suri's light-blue eyes widened upon the queen's words. "And that makes it okay to just burn Serene and twelve humans alive? Even Jorge died! What about our people?!"

"And I shall mourn their losses," Dajhri said, maintaining her composure. "Jorge was a good man and Serene was the most loyal servant I ever knew. But how many human lives have you taken, Suri?" She skimmed the other guards. "... or any of you? All three of you have killed thousands."

"That was for food!" Raimi insisted.

"Whether it be for food, accidental or intentional homicide, or even duty, how is killing for one reason any more or less unlawful than another?"

Raimi grunted and shrugged his broad shoulders. "You would defend an outsider who murdered two of our own? Why? What if someone comes looking for us now?"

"They won't, my sweet Raimi."

"But how do you know this?"

"Because I have seen it."

He snarled, "Bah! Just because you see things does not mean they are going to happen or in the way you want them to. You are not an all-knowing goddess."

For the first time since the argument began, Dajhri's piercing green eyes flashed a mild shade of animus red with discontentment. "In the two-thousand-plus years that you—" she looked at the other two guards. "—all of you have served me, you have never once questioned my abilities, my intentions, or my motives. Why now? I am still your queen, am I not? And I have always given my all for this kingdom and those who mean something to me. If any of you wish to leave Taltosia," she pointed at the door, "then, you may leave. But do not dare defy me!"

While scolding her subjects, Julian watched the queen's thick, mahogany hair, brows, and lashes all grow back from nothing before his eyes. As if in reflex, he touched his head, feeling his own shoulder-length hair had also regrown. By then, the guards had all backed down as if reminded of their position. Julian understood why they were upset, but his emotions remained askew. Unsure how to respond to such devastation, all he could manage was, "I...I'm sorry. I never meant to hurt anyone, especially friends."

Dajhri said, "It was an accident." As if they'd heard enough, the guards all turned away, grunting under their breath while stomping down the stairs. Suri entered a hall near the top. Raimi and the other guard's hall stood just one floor above the bottom. Left standing naked and alone, Dajhri said to Julian, "We need clothes."

On their way down the stairs, a short, thin, shirtless man with a dark crew-cut and light-gold skin appeared from the same hallway as Julian's room. A black-haired woman standing just inches taller than him poked her head out from behind. Both flinched with looks of confusion when spotting the queen's and Julian's nude bodies. The man said, "We heard yelling. Is everything okay?"

"No, it is not, Rodolfo. We lost Jorge and Serene," Dajhri said.

The woman asked, "What happened?"

"There was a fire. Serene burned alive and Jorge died trying to save her. Go back to your room, my loves. Pray their souls find their way to peace."

The Taltosian's faces each crumbled in heartbreak. Rodolfo took the young woman's hand and said, "Come on, Cristina," and they both moped away.

Continuing down the steps, attempting to refocus his guilty conscience, Julian mumbled "I was starting to think there wasn't anyone else here."

"At one time there were more. There are not many of us left. We have roughly as many as Raz Ahrim. Everyone mostly keeps to themselves. That is why they are scarcely seen."

At the bottom, she led Julian to a green blanket-covered doorway on the right. Inside, wooden shelves stacked high with folded white clothing, sheets, and towels, lined the walls. To the left of the door sat a small blue plastic bin full of shoes and sandals of assorted colors and sizes. Dajhri left him alone to get dressed while she went to do the same.

Nauseated and trembling, Julian tried to ignore it. First, he checked to make sure his wedding band and ankh were still there. He sighed joyfully, finding they were, but then he gasped. His labradorite bracelet was gone. He whimpered, remembering what

Pana told him about it: how connecting with Violet and Xavier in his dreams would come more easily as his powers balanced and potentially weakened. Though Dajhri claimed the *Bufo* would also assist with thinning the veil, losing the certainty he already had with the gifted talisman was devastating nonetheless.

Knowing there was nothing he could do about it, Julian took a fitted pair of white cotton pants and a matching shirt from the shelves and put them on. He searched the blue bin until he found an appropriate pair of brown leather shoes to replace the black sneakers he lost in the fire. The whole time, he had fought the urge to crumble, tried to ignore the dozen-plus lives he didn't even try to end, but once fully dressed and at a standstill, he could no longer resist. Between his shrill wails, he squalled, "How the hell did this happen?! Why do I keep fucking everything up?!"

He tried to imagine where it had all gone wrong. He thought back to the beginning of the ceremony, how he had focused on the torch above his head while fading out. He closed his eyes, recalling his and Violet's naked silhouettes, the flames engulfing them both. He even remembered her startled face, the beeping tones, but he still didn't understand what it all really meant. *With your mind, you set your house on fire. Did you pass that power on to me? If so, why would my vision make me do that? Why have you been telling me S.O.S? What is it, my flower?*

His eyes closed. The menacing sneer plastered over Bernard's face and the dried red streaks on his shirt cut through Julian's desperate vision with the king-slaying dagger held above his head. His inner-tension rising, he wondered, *Could that have been what caused it, seeing him?* After releasing a deep breath, he opened his eyes and the figment evaporated, but the hardened reality remained. His unforgivable act only added kindling to the embers of self-reproach he already held for Winter-Fae and Avice. *'Never forget that.'* "So many lives have been lost now because of me," he murmured. "I am a monster and I deserve to die."

"You do not," Dajhri said, her silky, venomous voice slithering in from outside the hanging green barrier. "You are only who you are meant to be."

"And who is that exactly? All those deaths on New Year's Eve, including Violet's and Xavier's, were partially my fault. Winter-Fae and Avice died trying to save me. Tonight, I killed thirteen people, and another died because of me."

Dajhri pulled the blanket aside, revealing herself in another white dress and her hair restyled into a new beehive. Her deep, vibrant emeralds instantly chased and captured Julian's depleted baby blues, forcing them to submission. "You must not blame yourself for any of those deaths. You forced nothing on New Year's. You did not force Bernard's hand, nor did you force the princesses to help you escape. It was tragic indeed, but not your fault. Tonight, you had no control either."

"But didn't you tell one of your guards you had already seen it happen? Did you know I would do this?"

"I was unaware of the events tonight, but I knew I would find someone who is not only inflammable like I am, but who can form and manipulate fire with their mind. I have waited ages for this night."

"Violet could do that."

"But Violet was neither fireproof nor a man. In one of my visions, she created that man."

"Violet did not make me. She made Daryl."

"That is what intrigued me. Violet did not make you, but you were still healing from your transition when you swallowed her blood, meaning you absorbed her essence as you would have if she made you herself. Her blood was strong, having never shared it before. You absorbed the strongest of her powers. Ingesting

Xavier's blood only days before, it has given you the essence of both."

"So, what about your visions? What do they mean?"

"Are you sure you want to know?" she asked, an undeniable air of sincerity in her eyes.

"Yes."

"I had the first vision over two-thousand years ago, shortly before Sami expired. Since, I have had more, little by little. In my vision, I saw the fire. I learned the world shall be destroyed. Most of humanity will perish, as will all but two of our own."

"I saw something similar, but in mine I was with Violet."

"Violet is gone from this world."

"Not mine," he said. "Who was in your vision?"

"Until recently, I could only see his eyes. That night I saw you in L'abisme, I saw those eyes for the first time with my own. Though my vision tonight was not as enduring as yours, I too took something from the toad's venom. I saw not just your eyes, but the rest of you. We were in the fire together. Then the vision manifested reality."

"What are you saying … that we are supposed to be the last two vampires?"

"Yes."

"But why?"

"Because nobody can escape fate, Julian. The story of the universe is written. We are only here to see it through."

"Is that why you saved me in the catacombs?"

"Yes."

"But I don't want this. I don't want to live to see the end of the world, unless it's just mine."

"You wanted nothing to happen to Violet either, but it did. We cannot change or control what already is. We can only endure and accept it."

"So, you're saying I have no free will or control of my own life? When the sun comes up, I can't make the conscious decision to walk out into it and be done with this madness now?"

"I am saying if you were meant to die another way, that drug overdose would have killed you. New Year's Eve would have killed you. Tonight would have killed you. Yet here you are."

Wishing for nothing more than a gun to blow the brains out the back of his skull, ending it all at once: the guilt, the shame, the sad sack he'd become, Julian knew he had little choice but to accept what he heard. "So, how does it happen?"

Before Dajhri could answer, her stomach growled, setting off a chain reaction. "We still have time before daylight. Let's feed."

"Would there be any point in saying I don't want to?"

Trying not to laugh, she said, "You don't want to starve, do you?"

"According to you, 'the prophet,' I can't die yet, remember?"

She squinted in annoyance, her lips melting almost sarcastically. but then she smiled. "You have been through much. You must relax. I am only offering help and the peace you deserve."

Julian laughed. "You call this peace? I can't imagine Hell being any worse than this!"

Ignoring him, Dajhri took his hand and said, "Come. Once the *Bufo* has depleted and you've fed, you will feel better, I promise." She gently tugged on his hand. Feeling there was no need to resist, he followed her up the steps and back outside before flying shotgun into the Peruvian sky to kill someone else. *After fourteen tonight, what's one more going to hurt?*

Barely two minutes had passed when they landed somewhere smaller than the likes of Rio de Janeiro. Even with his superhuman vampiric abilities, Julian sensed an uncomfortable change in the mountainous air. The oxygen was thin, and he found taking a full breath more difficult than before. From the desolate back alley where they both stood near a small collection of shiny metal trash cans, all stacked to the top with full black bags, he asked, "Where are we?"

"Cusco—not far from Machu Picchu."

"Why is the air so thin?"

"Because we are over eleven thousand feet above sea level. I would have taken us elsewhere, but it will be daylight in only two hours."

"So, where are we going? Being so late, won't it be hard to find someone?"

Dajhri curled her finger at him. "Come with me."

Julian obeyed, following her down a paved alley, observing the backs of various brown and gray stone buildings. Each boasted medieval European architecture and glowed in the outdoor lighting. Despite Julian's mood, he enjoyed his surroundings, welcoming them as a convenient distraction. After walking a few hundred feet, the faint, muffled beat of a bass drum tapered from nothing. A little further ahead, an accompanying melody joined the rhythm from inside a large brick building on their left.

"Is that a nightclub?"

"It is," Dajhri said. "I have not been here in four years. I always wait at least two before returning somewhere I previously hunted. The last time I came here, I went inside. They call it the Crystal Temple. If things haven't changed, it should still be popular for prostitutes, drug dealers, and young tourists."

"So, why are we back here instead of inside?"

"Just wait. Sex and drug deals often occur back here. It is easier when they come to us."

They waited in the shadows with their eyes stuck on a closed red door beneath a bright white light. With nothing else to do, Julian's mind wandered; returning to the fire, the lives it took, and all the prior deaths he considered himself responsible for. Beyond the guilt, there stood Violet, her dark silhouette at the forefront of the hellfire and brimstone surrounding her perfect form. She danced in slow motion amidst such disaster.

She waited there for him. Even if it meant burning the entire world to the ground, he would gladly send every last man, woman, and child on Earth to whatever god they would like in exchange for one more kiss of his precious flower's lips. He knew he was a sinner. To him, the darkness no longer mattered. Come Hell or high water, he was damned if he did and damned if he didn't.

If such a Hell existed, like all the greedy Bible thumpers said it did—preaching damnation to add to their collection plates and bring them one dollar closer to another bottle—he'd be the first in line to go. He knew if he was ever to survive such a life, he must cut the cord binding him to the laws and morality of man: the last piece of humanity he so desperately tried to keep. For his own sanity, it was better that way. He mourned those he cared about who'd lost their lives, but for all the others—the innocent victims in New York and the *Ayahuasca* ceremony alike—he had no room left in his cold dark heart to mourn.

Having spent minutes in silence, he finally asked, "Can't we just go inside and lure someone out?"

"I suppose, but—" Dajhri cut herself off when the red door opened. Lurking in the shadows, she and Julian remained hidden out of sight. From the doorway, Lady Gaga's "Bad Romance" blared until two thin, pasty young men exited, letting the door close behind them, the music fading back to a muffled bass beat. The taller of the two, a short-haired bleach-blond wearing blue jeans and a white shirt spoke first.

In what Julian thought was an Australian accent, he said, "You sure this is some good shrub, mate?"

In the same accent, the shorter man, wearing black, with rusted, ginger hair and a face covered in freckles said, "Yeah, I don't think they'd rip us off."

Dajhri put her lips to Julian's ear and whispered, "I will break both their necks and we can take them off somewhere dark. Wait here, okay?" Julian nodded. The blond lit and puffed on a thick, rolled joint while the other eagerly awaited his turn.

From nowhere, Dajhri emerged. Both men jumped in surprise. "Hey boys, you mind if I join you?" she asked, batting her eyelashes seductively.

At first, the men appeared confused, but then the taller one smiled and took another drag from the fat cigarette. He held up the unlit end, saying, "Certainly, baby doll."

When she got close enough, she reached out and said, "Thank you," but she did not take the cigarette. Instead, she took hold of the blond's head with both hands in such a fast motion, no eyes could follow. One violent twist and snap later, he fell dead. The frightened ginger shrieked before turning to run in Julian's direction. He only made it three steps before Dajhri pounced on his back, sending them both tumbling forward to the ground at Julian's feet.

The man's desperate cries crescendoed as he thrashed for his life. Dajhri also struggled, trying to get a grip on the squirming head. Fearing the noise would alert someone, Julian instinctively delivered a vicious stomp to the back of the man's head. Another followed, then two more: each bringing him more unwarranted pleasure than the last. *What's one more?* Once finished, he found that the man's head was not completely crushed, but too broken for him to have survived, and certainly too grotesque for whomever might have to identify the body.

From atop the corpse, Dajhri looked up, her eyes meeting his and emitting a provocative spark he'd not seen from her thus far. The intensity in her stare reminded him of Violet's, but deeper. Thinking nothing of it, he offered the queen his hand. Back on her feet, she said, "Thanks."

"Don't mention it."

She returned to the bleach-blond's body, taking it while Julian hoisted the redhead over his shoulder with ease. Together, they carried them to a pitch-black section of the alley. There, Dajhri showed Julian the best places on the neck and wrist to bite for a steady stream he could easily drink from with no mess or trouble. She even showed him places on the hands where he could feed in small amounts and not seriously injure his donor, if he needed.

Unlike the obese man in Rio, whose blood tasted like corn oil, Julian found the younger, more physically fit ginger's blood sweet. With each having their own body, instead of sharing like before, he drank more than he ever had in one feeding. While having his fill, a warm, tingling sensation washed over his body. The stimulation was not as intense as from other feedings, but the energizing response was more than enough to remind him he could still feel.

Once finished, they returned to the temple. They passed through the gate and approached the bronze door. Before the queen unlocked it, she flashed Julian the same alluring gaze as before. The two only inches apart, she said, "I am proud of you."

"Why?"

"Because you're beginning to understand what it means to be a vampire—not one of the pretentious, who believe we can live by the laws of modern man—but a real vampire: living by the laws of nature. Tonight, everything changed. Tonight, my greatest prophecy became a reality. Tonight, I discovered the truth."

"What truth?"

"That you are the one I thought you were and the one I have been waiting for." Her soft, warm lips connected with Julian's. His eyes bugged as Dajhri's sweet kiss broke his entire body out in goosebumps. Physically, the declaration was electric passion, a welcoming home, and even somehow familiar, but it was not Violet. Thus, he withdrew. Though she said nothing, the queen's immortal eyes remained on his.

"I am flattered," Julian admitted. "Believe me, Dajhri, I am. I find you so beautiful, wise, and nurturing." He took a deep breath. "But I am in love with Violet. I will not betray her. I am grateful for everything you have done for me, and I feel like I owe you my life, but my heart belongs to her."

Dajhri's teardrop face melted in dismay. She slowly closed her eyes, muttering, "I understand why you feel the way you do." Her eyes then opened like optimistic butterfly wings. "However, Violet is gone, and she is never coming back. You want her to, and you hope she will be waiting for you when you die. We desire madly, but as enlightenment teaches, we know nothing more than the here and now. We should always embrace each moment as it is."

"You are right. That's why I choose to embrace faith. I have faith that when I die, she will be there waiting for me." Still staring, Dajhri finally bowed her head, somberly appearing to accept the widower's decision. With nothing else to say, she unlocked the door and opened it. He followed her down the stairs until reaching his hallway. He then separated from the queen and headed towards his room, Dajhri's eyes, voice, and now a romantic declaration burrowing deep inside his brain.

Chapter Forty-Two

Dajhri's electric kiss, overshadowing the unforgettable sight and steaky smell of burning bodies, fluttered Julian's conscience like overzealous moths until his grandma Gin intervened. *'It is okay to let go, Julian. Nobody will hold it against you, and everyone will understand.'* She first delivered this decree at his own *Ayahuasca* ceremony. It stuck ever since, but he never knew why.

Too disturbed to sleep, he closed his eyes, scouring his evil self for a release, a way to extinguish the liable guilt. He held nothing for the victims he never knew personally, but for Fae and Avice, he would always hold vigil and certainly *"Never forget that."* He didn't deserve to forget. Following a restless yawn, he saw flashes of Violet next, and what he'd kept safe in his jacket: his sanctuary and only other reason to persist. He'd carried so much, so far, and for so long. He had nothing else to prove. So close to the end, he knew it was time to finish the story; it was time to "let go." Nobody would hold it against him. Everyone would understand. *It'll be daylight soon.*

He retrieved a lit torch from the hall and returned to his room, setting fire to the logs in the pit. After returning it, he was ready. Having already read Violet's entry from the diner about killing Chloe when he was still in Virginia, he skipped it. The next was headlined with the same date. Knowing everything left to read was all written after they met, he cleared his throat and muttered, "I love you, my flower. Here's to us."

1/13/19

Dear Diary

Oh my God! It is him! I just now got out of my new psychology class, and I haven't even left the parking lot yet. He was there—the man from the café this morning! I shit you not! I sat behind him in class. His name is Julian Frost. I can't believe this! I have spent almost forty years questioning if he is real or not, but now I know he is! Oh my fucking God! Is this real? I am absolutely bawling my eyes out right now! His voice is so soft, pure, and sweet—like warm caramel. I love it! It is the same voice from my dreams. He even told me he is visually impaired! I knew it! I hate that for him, but that just confirms it even more.

Now, I will be counting down the days until I can see him again, next Friday. I didn't know what to say to him after class. He tripped and fell down the stairs, but I caught him. Next week, I think I will offer him a ride home—not just to make sure he is safe, but to see what happens. Thank you, universe! Thank you, synchronicity! Thank you, dreams!

Violet

1/15/19
Dear Diary

Oh boy, what a weekend, Diary! I have a lot to fill you in on. Not even five minutes after writing that last page, I found Julian in the street, in front of the bus stop. Someone accidentally knocked him off the sidewalk when a bicyclist passed. He landed right in front of my car! I would have hit him if I hadn't been paying attention or slammed on my brakes. Poor thing!

Since I had just written about giving him a ride the next week, I offered him one then and he took it. Did I somehow manifest that? It wasn't just a ride. I was still so torn up over Chloe, I wanted to do something fun, so we went and shot a game of pool. Then I took him to the top of the Stratosphere. Normally you have to buy tickets or be a guest at the hotel to go to the top, but Charlie from the Las Vegas Parliament taught me a trick to get up there for free. The observation deck overlooks the entire city and valley. What a view! NYC is beautiful from the sky at night, and bigger, but Vegas is far more colorful. We circled the top, having this deep conversation about his life. That poor man has been through quite a lot, but he is a survivor! Now I understand why he was crying in my dreams so much. His childhood was horrific enough, but his adult life hasn't been any easier.

I couldn't believe what he told me. His ex-girlfriend of eleven years—"Faith" of all things is her name—cheated on him with some deadbeat, jailbird, white supremacist. To beat it all, he's her own brother! Now, they have two kids together. That sick whore already had a baby before that with a sperm bank donor.

Julian is legally blind and slowly going completely blind. His condition is called Retinitis Pigmentosa. It is hereditary. Faith, having her own hereditary bone and muscle disease, didn't want Julian's baby because apparently her problems, along with whatever else incest does, are okay to pass on. Still, it hurt Julian so much, he actually tried to kill himself when he found out what she did to him.

Later, when I took him back to his apartment, he invited me inside. At first, I didn't want to. It was getting close to sunrise, and I would have barely had enough time to get back to the Parliament. I figured if Julian really was the man I thought he was, everything would be fine if I stayed. In doing so, I scared the hell out of him. To me, I guess I was testing him and myself, but I immediately felt horrible about it. I think I was trying too hard. I was so scared I'd fucked it all up.

I hid in his bathroom when the sun started coming up. I also told him I could read his mind, trying to keep him from calling the cops. I know I shouldn't have been so chaotic and cruel, but all things considered, especially after Chloe, I followed my heart and threw it all on the line.

I am back home in New York now. Don't freak out, but I brought him with me! I had a surprise for him. As if hiding in his bathroom and the way I scared him by reading his mind wasn't enough, I just had to take it one step further and jump off the side of the Parliament to show him I could fly. What the hell is the matter with me? I feel like such a bitch. Julian is so sensitive and timid. I am surprised I didn't traumatize him. I'm not trying to self-sabotage this, am I? Since Chloe, I've been far too spontaneous for my own good, and perhaps even Julian's. I guess that's what happens when you murder someone you considered a friend.

As soon as we got here last night, I introduced Julian to Anna. Eric made him a cheeseburger when I came upstairs to tell Dad about him. I was so excited to tell him I finally found the man of my dreams. He told me not to tell him about the dreams or to encourage him. He wouldn't tell me why, though.

He was also a little upset with me for revealing so much so soon, especially after the way Chloe reacted. Dad said he didn't want me to scare him worse by throwing myself at him. I would never do that, not after what I did to Eric, but I understand why he felt that way. Dad didn't like Chloe but apparently killing her has upset him worse than it did me. Wow! After writing that, I wonder, how heartless am I? Neither of us want Julian to meet a similar fate.

Although I showed him I could read his mind and fly, I never actually told him I was a vampire. By the time I went back downstairs, Bernard had done it for me. Julian took it better than I thought he would. After that, he met Dad, and they hit it off so well. Dad really likes him! Everyone seems to like Julian, except Bernard.

Last night, Dad introduced him to Bishop and the rest of the band. I didn't even have to tell him what my surprise was for Julian. He heard my mind loud and clear. Like me, Julian is a music lover. I wanted him to experience what I did on my 100th birthday, so he got to sing a song in front of everyone too!

He is a writer, a good one from what I can tell. He sang something he'd written a long time ago, called "Mystic Woman." I *know he wrote it about Faith, but since he was put on the spot and so nervous, I don't mind. He was even sipping a glass of tequila or something when he first got on stage. Eventually he got into it and totally rocked, though!*

I had no idea Dad was going to do this, but he tested Julian. When he introduced him to the crowd before the song, he told all the women that Julian was single and good in bed. Once he got back to our table, I was about ready to give him a mouthful for that, but some Navy Seal asshole named Christopher Cauldwell came in. He was yelling at Dad and saying he killed his daughter. Dad and Eric kicked him out.

After that, I watched Julian dance with two goth girls. Not only was he dancing with them, but Black Casket was playing Velvet Underground's "Venus in Furs!" They learned that song for me, goddamn it! Apparently, Dad gave him the key to one of the empty apartments and encouraged him to take the girls there.

They walked right by me. I tried to be supportive. I even gave him a thumbs up and forced myself to smile. I wanted him to be happy. Truthfully, I also wanted to leap over the table and run after them like I was Jackie Joyner-Kersee and fuck those two bitches up. Then, I'd take him up there and wear his ass out myself. But I couldn't, so I played nicely.

Dad assured me if Julian really is who I already know he is, he would do nothing with those gutter sluts. I held faith in that. And guess what: he didn't go through with it! As soon as I saw him this morning, I knew he'd refused them. I am so happy! So, does this mean he is mine forever now? He is currently sleeping on my couch while I am in my bedroom, writing this because I am too anxious and excited to sleep. Earlier this morning, Dad called a meeting over the incident with Christopher Cauldwell. When he was here, he said he would be back tonight with others. If he comes, he's going to have a world of hurt waiting for him.

One more thing I wanted to add, Diary; despite the meeting, something wonderful happened this morning. William came to visit Dad for the first time in years! They played chess while discussing a serial killer who's been mutilating people around the city lately. Apparently, that is who killed Christopher Cauldwell's daughter. Before William left, Dad encouraged him to talk to Eric. He did!

I spoke to Eric earlier and he said William told him he loved him, and he regretted the way he treated him after Autumn died. Eric said he told William he loved him, too, and he forgave him. For the first time since William was still a child, they shared a hug. I am so happy for them! They both deserve peace. Maybe now they can begin making up for all the time they lost. I will keep you posted, Diary!

Violet

1/17/19

Dear Diary

I hurt more now than I ever have in all my years in this world. Eric is dead. My best friend, my brother, and the first love of my life is gone. He was murdered. Those Navy Seal motherfuckers cut his head off and left him laying in the middle of the chapel. We don't even know what they did with his head. They came back to the club two nights ago and started shooting. They didn't hit anyone, and they got arrested after it happened, but there had to be more of them. When the shooting started, everyone scattered. Dad and Julian followed me back to Las Vegas. Eric had gone to William's apartment. I still don't know where Anna and Bernard went. All I know is they are safe.

When we got to Vegas, Dad sold his shares back to the Parliament for seventeen million dollars. He gave seven of it to Julian, to buy this big house in the middle of nowhere. That is where I am now, hidden in the Appalachian Mountains of Virginia. Last night, Dad flew back to New York while I went to pick Julian up at his apartment in Vegas.

I had taken him there the night before so he could pack some things and talk to his aunt and uncle about the house. After that, we flew to New York. Because he first went to the police station, wanting to cooperate with the Cauldwell investigation, Dad and I got back home at the same time. That is when we found Eric. I've never seen something so horrible! My poor, sweet, beautiful Eric's body was destroyed.

Dad gave us the money and said he wasn't coming. I didn't know what to think. When he first offered the money, it was so Julian could buy his aunt and uncle's old house. There, we could have a place to lie low for a while, but none of us expected anything to happen to Eric. At first, I think Dad was planning on coming with us, but since Eric's killer is still out there, and he wants to keep us safe, I don't know where he went.

Last night, Julian and I stayed at a hotel on the Jersey side of the Hudson until it got dark again. Earlier tonight, we flew to Richmond, where Julian's aunt and uncle live. They were nice but mostly just eager to sell the house. Still, they treated us both with kindness. I tried to put on a happy face and make a good impression, but it took all I had to keep from breaking down in front of everyone. I even tried to hold my tears back from Julian, but I could not. He has been so sweet to me during all this. I already knew he would be, though.

Now, he is asleep on the couch upstairs in the living room while I am in a guest bedroom in the windowless basement. This house is huge and beautiful. It is well worth the million it cost to buy, but right now I can't be as happy about it as I feel like I should be. The only peace I have found since discovering Eric has been focusing my thoughts on this entry. I don't know what to do, Diary. I have been crying since we got here, and I know Julian could hear me earlier. In only a few days' time, my life went from cracking, to feeling complete, to completely cracking into pieces. God, if you are up there, please help me.

Violet

When we met, your life was flipped upside down, just like mine. Julian turned the page. The next was from Valentine's Day. The flimsy paper card he'd made for Violet—folded three times—rested comfortably between the pages. Paying no mind to the card, he flipped to the next page, dated *4/21/19*. Violet was in Alaska, plotting her brave journey south. One night earlier, Christopher Cauldwell had gone on television and said everyone's names, triggering Julian's drunken outburst and arrest. Again, he turned the page, finding a new entry he'd not read.

5/2/19
Dear Diary

Interesting. I swore I had left you in my bag, but I just found you beside it, on the floor. For fuck sake, I am losing my mind! The last thing I need is to fuck around and lose you too. Anyway, I made it to Peru. I was so nervous to fly this far on my own. I've only been here once—when Dad brought Bernard the first time. I have been here for about a week and a half now. Dad was here, but he left only a few days before I arrived. Dajhri has not told me much, but she did say he was here for a few months.

Unless he went to Paris, Virginia, or he is looking for Cauldwell, I have no clue where he could be now. Dajhri said he was grieving horribly, and she wanted him to stay until the biggest part of it passed. Before now, I had not seen the queen since Anna and Bernard's wedding, but from the moment she first saw me, she knew I was also grieving. Just like Dad, she wants me to stay too.

She's a little weird, but so far, she has been supportive. I told her all about Julian and my dreams. She seems happy for me in those regards. I told her I made him a promise. I said if I had not come back by July 4th, I would be there then to watch the fireworks with him. I told her I won't break my promise. Other than telling me to follow my heart, and even suggesting I make him a vampire myself, she had nothing else to say about it. Julian and I never even got to share our first kiss. He wanted it bad, but I want it more! The moment I see him, I intend to change that. He is my soulmate and, without any doubt, the man of my dreams.

Violet

7/5/19

Dear Diary

 Oh my God, did I fuck up when I left him! I literally saved Julian at the last second. His own cousin and two of his cousin's friends were going to rob and kill him if I hadn't shown up when I did. I killed all three of them. Don't worry. Julian is safe now. Aside from Chloe, they are the only people I have ever purposely killed. Unlike Chloe, I have no remorse for what I've done. I feel nothing for them.

 One of them, I killed fast. The others, I made suffer. I enjoyed it. They bled all over Julian's living room before I took them both into the woods behind the house. The one who I believe instigated it—I ripped his chin off before I broke his neck. I was mad! I wanted him to feel my anger. I wanted to get off on his pain. As for Julian's cousin, he shit all over himself and begged me to let him go home before I broke his neck and shut him up.

 After I took advantage and fed on the one not covered in shit, I found Julian waiting for me in the yard. Just like me, he was doused in blood, but unlike me, it was his own. They had cut and beat him for the combination to his and Dad's safe, but even that wasn't enough to break my man's spirit! His first words to me were, "Hi," followed by the most adorable thing. He said, "I bought you a guitar." I practically lunged at him and became putty in his arms after that, kissing him and feeling such a tingling sensation. It was the same kind I always heard about when two people who are meant to be together kiss for the first time. It was magical and like I never left. There were even fireworks going off in the sky! It was perfect!

The guitar Julian was talking about completely blew my mind! I shit you not, but it is a purple Fender Stratocaster, autographed by Jimi Hendrix himself! I was nearly floored when I first saw it. At the time, I was having my way with his cousin and the other guy, and it wasn't exactly the right time to say anything, but once he said he bought it for me, I was speechless. I never got to see Hendrix like I got to see Janis. I never really told Julian just how much that bummed me out, but thanks to synchronicity, I got something else, a physical piece of true music history! Wow! Writing that just made me realize Woodstock was fifty years ago. Where did the time go? I feel so old, yet I don't.

Anyway, I just spent the night bandaging Julian's cuts, cleaning the blood from his living room, covering a window I had broken, and getting rid of the bodies and their car. I drove it about an hour and a half into Kentucky and ditched it on a dirt mountain road. All three of them were druggies anyway, so I doubt there will be much of a fuss.

Everybody knows Julian is legally blind and can't drive. Whenever they are found, he will be the last person anyone suspects. Phew! What a night! There is still so much more I want to say, like how wonderful it feels to be home where I now know I belong. However, after flying so far and everything else I did once I got here, I am exhausted and need a nap. I will check back soon!

Violet

Remembering the night clearly, Julian whispered, "Like a goddamn superhero." He turned the page and read the next.

8/4/19

Dear Diary

    I have been home with Jul a month now, and it is almost as if I never left. I do hold some resentment towards myself for leaving. Sometimes, when I fly up to Alaska to get more blood, I know it scares him. He already had abandonment issues. I know he worries I won't come back. I hate that he feels that way, but I can understand why. I mentioned it before, but with everything else going on, I didn't elaborate. Julian holds his own guilt for doing something similar to Faith.

    From what he has told me and what I've seen in his thoughts, Faith was terrible to him. He loved her and did everything he could for her. He even neglected his own dying grandmother for her. That has haunted him for six years now. In hindsight, he knows they were never right for each other. They were lost and too stupid to know any better. On top of that, Faith is a narcissist. They only know how to love themselves.

    After the sperm bank baby was born, things changed. Faith got addicted to something called Xanax. From what I gather, they are like valium. When she wasn't a monster, she was a zombie. For the longest time, she was only mentally abusive, but then she became violent with him. In addition to his abandonment issues, Jul also had PTSD from what his parents and his mother's boyfriend, Bill, did to him, but he gave a third of his life to Faith. She only made his trauma worse.

    Because of his disability, Jul collects social security. Faith was taking his check every month and after paying their bills, she'd blow the rest. When she got sick from her weight-loss surgery and took her baby and moved in with her grandma, Jul was left alone. They still saw each other almost every day, but from then on, her behavior got worse. He said there were so many times things got so bad that the day he'd get his check, he would take a taxi to the bus station and go back home without even telling her. He knew it was wrong, despite anything she did, but it was the only way he could get away from her before she would show up to take his money again.

The first few times he did it, within a few days, she talked him into coming back. She would drive four hours from Staley to Gunnar and take him back, until the next time, he felt like he had no other option but run. Nobody else would ever help him. Of course, to Faith, it was never about why Jul wanted to leave in the first place. It was only ever about how it made Faith feel. Narcissism is a mental illness. They literally only know how to love themselves.

Half a dozen times later, they were apart three months. That is when she apparently got pregnant by her half-brother, Travis. Jul was already suspicious of the two before leaving her one of the final times. Whether she was already fucking Travis while she was still with Jul or not, the way she put another man over his medical needs and well-being was a blatant emotional affair, which is just as bad. There were times he'd have a doctor appointment, she'd promised to take him to. Instead, she would take Travis out to eat somewhere. She would even ditch Jul when he needed to go to the grocery store. What kind of evil fuck does that to anyone who treated them as good as Jul did?

As if that wasn't enough, one of her half-sisters—because all four of her step siblings have a different mother or father—had Jul put in jail for two weeks, claiming it was internet harassment. They got him riled up when he was drunk one night. Jul sent Faith's sister a text message, just trying to ask about that damn kid that was supposed to be his. She told him to forget about him. Jul freaked out, calling her any terrible thing he could think of. Even though the woman claimed she was a Christian, so she forgave him, she took him to court and cried for the judge anyway. In what world does that even make sense? Is everybody in that family mentally ill?

They absolutely wanted him to have no part in the boy's life, even though he took care of it for two years while its mother was too goddamn inadequate to be anything but an abusive, inbreeding, racist and homophobic drug addict. The most fucked-up part is, even as sick and twisted as this bitch is, she still has an entire family of equally fucked-up people who would do anything for her, because she's family, while Jul—who is not a bad person at all—has nobody in his family he can depend on, just me and Dad, wherever he is. How is that fair?

The day he got out of jail, that fucking cunt manipulated him into going back one last time. By then, Travis was already back in jail again for something incredibly stupid—the kind of thing only a trailer-trash brother-fucker would find sexy enough to leave someone like Jul for. And unknowing to Jul, Faith was using his money to pay that skinhead's lawyer fees while claiming she was the one in trouble. He was only trying to help her, but I guess that was the point. It's not like she could make money the honest way, though I am sure incest porn has mainstream appeal somewhere.

He'd told me most of this already, but not the parts about him taking off and leaving her like he did. From Faith's point of view, he knows that is what drove her away, but ... that bitch is crazy! I told him if the relationship was worth something and he just decided to walk out on his family, it would've been terrible, but I honestly believe the worst thing he did was keep going back. When he finally opened up and told me, I told him I already knew, but I wouldn't judge nor was it my place to bring it up first. He hugged me and told me he loved me. We kissed and that was that. Her loss is my gain.

I have still not heard anything from or about Dad. I know in my heart he is okay, but my God, I am worried sick about him. I pray every night that he will return to me safely. This year alone I've had enough death to last a lifetime. I don't need more. I've been so anxious and stressed I have burned through so many of your pages. I am sorry. I just want my daddy back.

Thankfully, I at least have the love of my life by my side. He even wants to become a vampire. I am considering taking Dajhri's advice and turning him. I want to marry him, but it is still too soon to ask. I also want to tell him about my dreams. I know it sounds crazy, but Dad was stern about not telling him. I don't know why though. Should it even matter? Compared to everything else, I know it shouldn't scare him, but it took all these years for me to find him. I did it by following my intuition. I will not stray now. I will tell him when the time is right.

Violet

9/25/19

Dear Diary

It is after midnight now, but yesterday was Jul's thirty-eighth birthday. I knew September 24ᵗʰ, 1981, was a significant date. It was the day he was born! How wild! Aside from Dad's wishes, I think I've refrained from telling Jul about my dreams because I subconsciously tried to convince myself the fabled storybook romance did not exist. Perhaps I felt like I was unworthy of it. There are too many factors now that have proven my theory wrong. I am glad I am wrong.

Tonight was so amazing! While I was away, he bought a jukebox and filled it with both of our favorite songs. We danced through the air to the Moody Blues' "Nights in White Satin." Before that, I tried to bake him a German chocolate cake. It is his favorite. I was never good at baking. I can't even remember the last time I tried to bake something. I guess it was that first Thanksgiving at the Grants'. I had helped Dad fix dinner. He did the biggest part of it, though. On my own, I wasn't so successful.

I burned the cake, but Jul didn't mind. Instead, he asked for a drink from my IV bag. He hated the taste, but I must admit, I was so turned on when he tried it. I want him, Diary. I want him bad!

For his birthday, I gave him the silver ankh necklace Eric gave me on the day he was born. I just felt like it was the right thing to do. He loves it!

Then what I had been dreading all along finally happened. After I gave Jul the necklace, we kissed, but he moved to my neck. I loved it, but I had to stop him. I didn't want to—not at all—but I was not about to let things get out of hand.

I was too embarrassed to say what happened or that it was with Eric. I even laughed at a dark joke he made about it out of context, but I did tell him I once hurt a human I tried to have sex with. My urge to be intimate with Jul is much stronger than it was with Eric. Jul has this certain softness about him. There's something I've always found attractive about sensitive men who are a little more in touch with their feminine side. I want him so bad I can taste it, but not enough to hurt or risk killing him. I hate it, but I can wait. The worst part of all is I feel like I lied to him. I don't want to start things off the same way Anna and Bernard did. I have been thinking about that a lot lately. I wish Anna was here. She'd know what to say. She always does. I hope she is okay. I miss her so much.

At this point, I know Jul wants the gift. I want to give it to him. I have no clue when or if Dad will ever come back. Nothing like this has ever happened before, at least not to me. Jul is strong-willed but he is blind and certainly not the physical type. Even if he was, as a human, he could never defend himself against potential threats like Christopher Cauldwell or worse. Besides, if I gave him my blood, we would be together forever, even in our dreams and beyond. I have yet to offer it, but as each day passes, I find it harder not to. I know he would say yes if I did.

I have never made a vampire before, and after everything Dad told me about the vampires he made before me, I would be scared I'd kill him. Aside from knowing Dad is safe and back in my life, that's another reason why I wish he would come home. I don't want to do it alone, but for the greatest love I've ever known, I will do what I must.

Violet

9/25/19

Dear Diary

     Guess what, Diary! Only about fifteen minutes after writing my last entry, Dad came home! I knew he would. More synchronicity! He had horrible news, though. I am in shock. It was not Christopher Cauldwell or his men who killed Eric or William. It was Bishop! It is so bizarre, but apparently his mind was being controlled by the Raja Kahiji. I really don't know what to think about all this. If it is true, I fear what it might do to the truce. Dad always said neither L'abisme nor Taltosia alone could defeat Raz Ahrim if it comes to a war. Dajhri once prophesied this would happen. If that is true, and Jul is going to be in my life, he must be turned. As a human, he just won't be safe.

     Dad forbids me from giving him the gift since we are lovers. He is worried about us sharing our blood because if something happens to one, it will drive the other insane until we are both dead. Dad is going to turn Jul. He has given him until Christmas to get all his affairs in order. One thing he wants him to do is confront his family and unburden himself, once and for all. Jul said they won't ever listen to him, so we are going to make them listen.

     Dad thinks Jul is a ticking time bomb and seems a little apprehensive, but he knows how much we love each other. Dad just doesn't want him taking all that pain with him when he crosses over and doesn't want him to do something like what I did to my parents. So, Jul is going to confront his family at his grandpa Johnny's house on Christmas Eve. Then on Christmas Day, which is only three months from today, he will be turned.

So, I have this idea. We are almost at the end of the decade. Tonight, Jul asked Dad if being turned would also cure his eyes. He said it will. What would be a better way to kick off 2020, the year of perfect vision, than by getting married at midnight on New Year's Eve?! I know Christmas Eve will be hard for him, but once he's said everything to his family he's always tried to say, I am going to pop the question. I want him to be mine forever!

Hopefully, that will also help with softening the blow afterwards. I already told Dad, and he is so happy for me. I am still a little angry at him for staying away so long, but that will pass. With any luck, all of this will, in time. Jul and I deserve happiness. Once he is turned and we are married, it will be smooth sailing from there!

Violet

10/28/19

Dear Diary

Dad has been back just over a month now. We both agree, it's not the same without the rest of our family. Jul is our family now, too, and he is treating us so well. He holds our lives in his hands, but he's more than earned our trust. Though Dad won't say it, he admires Jul. They bond over history and boardgames. Dad's always loved chess, but Jul taught us both how to play Clue. That's his favorite. Otherwise, he loves hearing Dad tell stories about his past.

As for Jul and I, we bond over music and movies. Would you believe his favorite band is Tool? I told him about the time I saw them open for Henry Rollins at CBGB. He called me a "Lucky asshole." I stuck my tongue out at him and said my asshole isn't lucky but magical, and I fart rainbows and shit unicorns. I don't know where that came from, but he laughed so hard, and then I laughed. He's goofy, and he's bringing out my inner-goofy, too!

He's seen Tool three times. He saw them twice on the "Lateralus" tour and once on the "10,000 Days" tour. After thirteen years, they finally released a new album in August. They are about to tour it soon. Maybe for a late wedding gift, I can brave the big arena crowd and we can go see them together. I am sure Jul would love that. I know I would! That band has come so far since I saw them on their very first tour. Jul and I agree, Danny Carey is the greatest drummer of all time. And don't tell him I said this, but Maynard James Keenan's voice still drives me wild—woo, smokey!

Despite his pain otherwise. Julian took a moment to laugh, reflect, and then wipe away the few tears he'd collected along the way. Following a deep breath, he continued.

... That fucker wants to talk about lucky ... his first concert was Carlos Santana! He was at Woodstock, but I didn't get to see him because his performance was during the day. Jul said it wasn't even a year before his father died, and only a few days after Stevie Ray Vaughan died. Jul said he remembered the plane crash being talked about on the news, and then Santana dedicating his performance to him. We got curious and looked it up on the internet. The concert was at the Fox Theater, in St. Louis, on August 31st, 1990, less than a month before Jul's ninth birthday.

Sadly, Jul remembers his parents fighting that night more vividly than the concert itself. At least they did expose him to lots of great music before things all went to shit. His dad, Arthur, liked Rush, Van Halen, and Pink Floyd. Jul said his love for Pink Floyd was the only good thing his father ever gave him. His mother, Marcie, liked Elton John, Supertramp, and the Rolling Stones.

Back in the '80s, when radio stations still played music worth listening to, Jul and his parents were big fans of St. Louis's KSHE-95. Jul even got to meet all his favorite DJs at a charity softball game that Marcie put together, as the vice president of the St. Louis chapter of the RP Foundation. It's an organization to raise awareness for Jul's eye condition.

For a while, Marcie was heavily involved. It was a big deal to her. She organized several charity events, and sometimes spent hours preparing newsletters to mail out, but Jul said nobody in his family ever gave her credit for any of that. From the way he talks about her, Marcie made tons of bad choices, and she could have been a much better mother, but at least she tried before Arthur ruined her completely.

Arthur played baseball. According to Jul, he wasn't great, but he still liked to play with his friends on a team in some sort of unofficial minor league. It was Arthur's team who played against the KSHE-95 DJs. Jul said they had dunk-booths and all sorts of fun activities. He said that day was one of the last happy memories he had of being with both parents before their divorce. Shortly afterwards, Arthur fucked everything up.

That man was a monster. He came home drunk and high one night, and would you believe he raped Jul's young, teenage babysitter?! By the way, it took me a while, but I told him what my own father did. Jul's father did much worse than mine. He never touched Jul, but he almost killed Marcie more than once.

Jul said, there was this one time when he was only six, Arthur shoved her down right in front of him. He did it with such violent force, she quit breathing and almost died. At least Arthur had the decency to call 911—probably only because Jul saw everything. He said he remembers an EMT saying "We're losing her."

Arthur's parents blamed Marcie. All she did was put too much pepper on her eggs for Arthur's liking. They were both fucked up to death and had Jul out at a Denny's in the middle of St. Louis at 1 a.m. Arthur didn't like Marcie's free will, so he called her a *cunt—his favorite name for her—until they got home and he could do what it took for him to feel like a man.*

I couldn't believe it, but according to Jul, this "man's" parents blamed Marcie for every bad thing their son ever did. Jul doesn't talk about them much. He said they've had barely anything to do with him since Arthur's death. At least he is dead and burning in Hell now, though. That's the only place shit like that belongs. Jul doesn't even know if Arthur's death was murder or suicide.

Apparently, he was a cocaine dealer, and he tried to bury some dirty cops for a lighter prison sentence after he raped Jul's babysitter. His parents think he was murdered and it was elaborately staged to look like a suicide. It sounds ridiculous and like something any grieving parent would probably rather believe, but nothing is impossible. Who knows? Better yet, who honestly cares if some wife-beating, pedophile rapist maggot got what they deserved for a change? Toe-may-toe—toe-mah-toe. He's dead, and the world is now a better place for it.

Before any of that, Jul said some of his best memories from his time with both of his parents was riding in his dad's Toyota, singing along to his favorite songs on the radio. He gave me a good laugh. He knows I adore Lou Reed, so he was telling me by the time he was five, he knew "Walk on the Wild Side" word for word. He'd sing along every time it came on the radio without even knowing what he was singing or what the song was about. He still didn't know who it was about until I told him. He loves my stories about New York and a much simpler time. I wish he could have been there with me. He would have loved it.

It turns out, Jul's seen a lot of great concerts over the years, and not just Tool. Most of them were at big venues with old friends. With so many people thinking so many things at once, Woodstock was overwhelming. I tried ignoring it, but it was still a bit much. After that, I was always too scared to go to any other big shows.

Jul's been to several outdoor concerts, but none of them were as big as Woodstock.

He's attended two Ozzfests. One of them was in 2006, with that bitch, Faith. They went to a lot of shows together. Ozzy wasn't even scheduled for that date, but Faith only wanted to see System Of A Down, and use Jul's money to buy $600 tickets, so they could be in the 4ᵗʰ row. That's fucking crazy! He said he would have given anything to be that close at literally any other concert he'd been to but that one. He said, aside from Lacuna Coil playing "Heaven's A Lie," and Faith, the "Christian," getting so worked up and pissed off at him foe dancing to a song she thought was blasphemous because of the title, everything else was underwhelming and overpriced. He said no matter how hard he tried explaining to her the meaning of that song, it never mattered. She'd freak out on him, but not her other family members, just for saying, "Goddamn," too. I'm not the Christian I was long ago, but my fucking God!

He said that Ozzfest was nothing like the one he attended with some old friends in 2001. That year, it was headlined by Black Sabbath. He had a blast that day. In addition to Sabbath, he also got to see Marilyn Manson, Slipknot, Disturbed, Linkin Park, Drowning Pool with Dave Williams, and so many others. At the main stage, he was in the 38ᵗʰ row. His ticket was only $40, not $300. You should have seen how he smiled and lit up while talking about it. From everything he told me, that was one of the best days of his life.

Jul's parents saw Ozzy on the "Bark at the Moon" tour, but he was still too young to go with them. He'd always wanted to see the man himself, but to also see the original Black Sabbath was a huge bonus. That day was also Geezer Butler's 52ⁿᵈ birthday, and Jul said Ozzy led everyone in singing him "Happy Birthday." It was at that same amphitheater, in Charlotte, North Carolina, where he first saw Tool a couple of months later. He said of all the concerts he'd ever attended, that first Tool show was his favorite. He said something awoke in him at that concert. I told him "Tool is love."

That little shit even got to see A Perfect Circle perform almost all their first two albums in Nashville. He said after the show, James Iha, who also plays guitar for Smashing Pumpkins, started playing the opening riff to "Zero." Jul said Maynard had already left the stage, but all the others started playing along. Marilyn Manson's old bassist, Twiggy Ramirez was with them too. A few years later, Jul saw him again, playing bass for Nine Inch Nails in Richmond. He said that was probably his second favorite concert.

Speaking of Marilyn Manson, Jul even got to see them three times in 2000 and 2001, while they toured "Holywood." The first of those three, he saw with his mother. He said she was drunk the entire time, even the three and a half hours she drove to and from Greensboro, but it was still the most fun the two ever had together. As if all that was not enough, he also got to see Roger Waters perform his two favorite Pink Floyd albums: "Dark Side of the Moon" and "The Wall" in their entirety. He's seen all that plus more, and he thinks I'm the lucky one. I say, fuck you, buddy!

Julian laughed, unable to imagine his love keeping a straight face as she wrote it. "Fuck you too, 'Woodstock,'" he snickered before moving on.

... We watch movies together all the time. He has quite a nice collection of classics and more current DVDs. He's got a few hundred of them. He keeps them in a big CD binder. A few of his favorites are "Monty Python and The Holy Grail," "Pulp Fiction," and "The Crow." All three are fantastic!

Jul said he was first exposed to "Holy Grail" in his 11th grade history class. He said his teacher showed the best movies, to not just teach but to keep teenagers entertained. It was a good approach. Jul loves history because of "Mr. Smith." Jul's mother later bought him the DVD and his first DVD player for Christmas. It was also the first DVD he ever owned. He still has it, and it plays perfectly. He often falls asleep on the sofa while watching it. It's a silly movie, so I think it makes him feel safe.

Thanks to his grandpa Johnny, he got to watch his other two favorites in the theatre when he was just a young teenager. Jul said growing up, there wasn't much to do here besides go to the movies. For his age, he watched a lot of dark and obscure stuff that most young teens didn't understand, weren't interested in, or just weren't allowed to watch. At only thirteen years old, I can imagine he got some weird looks while watching something as out there as "Pulp Fiction," in a cinema by himself.

Being underage, he couldn't buy tickets for R-rated movies. Johnny would often buy the ticket for him. There was one time in particular Jul said he will never forget. The local theatre in Gunnar is small. It only features three cinemas. They often show more than one movie in a cinema at a time. When "The Crow" was playing, it was only shown for one week, and at 9 p.m. Being so late and on a school night, Jul was terrified to ask Johnny to take him, but not only did he say yes, he also went in and watched it with him. Not long before this, his mother had abandoned him. She took off and went to Myrtle Beach with Bill, leaving him with her own parents. To Jul, his grandpa's kind gesture meant everything, especially since he knew Johnny probably hated the movie but sat through it for him anyway.

Sadly, he and Johnny don't get along. I haven't met Johnny yet, but from what Jul says, he was hurt badly by not just him but others in his family. There's a lot of pain and resentment, but those emotions come from a place of love. Jul loves his grandpa, but his heart aches for closure, and every time he tries to get it, he is silenced. They don't care about his feelings or what their actions did to him. That is why Dad and I are going to be there with him when he addresses his family. Jul deserves peace, and he will have it, and

I dare them to even think they can stop him. Let's see how their pride stacks up against ours.

Violet

11/1/19
Dear Diary

It is official. I have the best boyfriend in the world! Diary, you are not going to believe what Jul did last night. First, Dad and I took him to a little cemetery behind his mother's old house. His uncle is buried there. When Jul was a kid, he'd often spend hours at the gravesite, hiding from his mother's abusive boyfriend, Bill. Jul said he hadn't been back in years. Dad and I helped him find the grave. We left him alone for a bit until he was ready to leave. The poor thing tripped over a footstone hiding in the grass. He fell flat on his face but didn't hurt himself. He laughed it off and we went home.

I've been practicing and trying to improve my cooking skills lately, so I'd planned on making Jul something for dinner and then watching a scary movie together, but he sprung the most amazing surprise on me. I know he hates to fly. Almost every time he's been in the air with me, he's thrown up. I've not even asked him to go anywhere else with me since I got him here in January. He caught me completely off guard, telling me he wanted to take me on a surprise Halloween date.

I was a little confused, especially since he said we would have to fly for a good while. Dad knew what Jul was up to, but he wouldn't tell me. I wanted to cheat and try to read his mind, but I trusted Jul and played along. He showed me on his phone where he wanted to go. I saw from the start it was somewhere in Los Angeles, which was interesting enough, but not as exciting as what I found when we landed. The directions he gave me were for the Hollywood Forever Cemetery.

Again, I was a little confused. I had no clue why he wanted to visit another graveyard until we walked in through the front. Then I saw the projector screen and people gathering around it. I never knew cemeteries showed movies, but this one showed the 1922 classic, "Nosferatu." I was just a little girl when that was made. At first, I thought it was a little weird, and maybe even a little disrespectful, but once the movie began, I had a blast, and so did Jul!

That alone was unique, sweet, and something I will never forget. For me, the movie wasn't the best part though. I didn't know this, but Johnny and Dee Dee Ramone are both buried there. Jul knew, and after the movie, he took me looking for them. Well, it was more like I held his hand and we took each other looking. Johnny has a statue, but not Dee Dee. I'm not sure why. Still, it was a touching moment for me. Only Jul could make a graveyard romantic. By next Halloween he should be able to fly, so we'll have to go look for the other two Ramones, Joey and Tommy, together.

By the time we got back to Virginia, it was almost 4 a.m. In addition to being so turned on by all he did, I am also proud of Jul. Traveling both ways, he didn't throw up once. As much as he hated flying with me before, I still can't believe he did this. I can't believe how happy I am. With Dad back home, and Jul and I getting closer every day now, this whole idea of eternity doesn't sound so bad anymore. Right now is the happiest I have ever been in my life. As long as Jul's part of it, I think I could get used to this.

Violet

For a second, Julian thought he was going to cry. That night was just as meaningful to him as it was to her. It was when he saw the same movie shown in the catacombs he nearly fell apart, wishing with all he had that he could return to their only Halloween together—cuddling on the grass, their lips and fingers locked like guiltless high schoolers on a Friday night out. For a time so

448

sentimental, the memory cut deep. Before it could slice any further, he turned the page and moved on.

11/28/19

Dear Diary

I only have a few more pages left now, so I've been trying to wait until I have something important to say. Today was Thanksgiving. This time, with Dad's help, we made a big turkey feast for Jul, just like that one we once made for Eric, William, and Autumn. This one being his last, we wanted it to be special.

Dad and I had a blast working in the kitchen together again. It wasn't just that one Thanksgiving dinner; we cooked for the Grants often, but after Eric's transition and his mom and brother moved out, we had nobody else to cook for. I tried to make another German chocolate cake since I wanted Jul to have his favorite dessert one last time. I didn't burn it! He had a big piece and said it was delicious! That made my day!

Jul's been a little down lately. He has told me all about his best friend, Daryl. In their childhood, it sounds like he and his parents were really good to him. Daryl even took up for him at school. Because kids are assholes, Jul was bullied horribly all through school. Before he moved away and they lost touch, Daryl got into many fights over him. Jul said he's always been really strong, tough, and meaner than a rattlesnake if you push him the right way.

Jul had invited Daryl, his wife, and their daughters to come join us for dinner, but he declined. It being such a holiday, we both understand why, but I still think it hurt Jul's feelings. Daryl keeps telling him they can go out and do something together when he is off work, but instead he keeps going out and doing things with his other friends and ignores Jul. It's upsetting him because he doesn't have much time left in the light. He wants to take advantage while he can, but he's also unsure how he will handle eventually having to tell him the truth when that day inevitably comes.

He's been trying to introduce us all, but he hasn't even seen Daryl since July 4th. He thinks he might have scared him by telling him some of the things he saw in New York. He also thinks the years apart might have changed them too much, and Daryl just doesn't think about what he says before making empty promises.

Even if nobody else was here, that's okay. We had fun on our own. I had forgotten how much I missed Thanksgiving. At one point Jul broke down and cried. He said he'd never felt so loved before. I am happy I make him feel this way. He knows I feel the same. In less than a month, he will be one of us. I am so excited, but nervous too. I know I am probably just paranoid, but I feel like I have come so far and if anything goes wrong at this point, it will break my heart. I am keeping the faith, though. We love each other, and they say that is all we need.

With that said, Dad finally confessed something to me. I always wondered why Lusa never came back, after Anna and Bernard's wedding. Dad said something about Dajhri made her incredibly uncomfortable, but he wouldn't elaborate. She wrote him a letter, not long after. Apparently, I am not the only one who's had dreams about Jul. Dad claims he lost the letter somewhere over the years, but he said one of Dajhri's prophecies was wrong, and it will change everything. He said we must show Jul all the love and comfort we can or else the fate of our kind and even the world itself could be at stake.

Barely, Julian whispered, "What the fuck?"

... I don't know what that means, but I don't want to keep even more secrets from my future husband. Dad has always been weird about keeping secrets. I trust him, and I even trust Lusa, but that was a little morbid. After Eric, William, learning about Bishop,

450

and everything else that's happened, I don't trust the world right now. Being so close to getting what I want, I refuse to let anything ruin it. Jul and I are fated, and nothing is going to stop us!

Violet

12/24/19
Dear Diary

Jul said yes! I asked him to marry me, and he said yes! He raised some hell at his grandfather's house earlier. He felt so guilty, he had a breakdown outside in the snow when we first got back home. Like all those times he held me, I held him while he cried. He said some dark things to Johnny, his uncle Craig, and aunt Bobbi-Jo. They said some dark things back.

Jul was so brave to go through with it. I know it hurt him badly, but he finally let it all out. They tried to shut him up so many times, but neither Dad nor I would let them. Even I showed my ass a little. I regret it and I don't. I think I angered Dad a little, but I don't care. They deserved it. They deserved everything. Even Dad intentionally scared them.

After seeing it all unfold with my own eyes, and even reading Johnny's thoughts, I know he loves Jul. He knows he made a lot of mistakes. It doesn't change anything, though. It might be cruel to think this of my fiancé's family, especially now that it's all about moving forward, but I hope tonight haunts them to the end. Long after that, Jul and I will still be here, loving life and each other. After tomorrow, and then New Year's Eve, our new lives begin as husband and wife, 'til death do us part.

Violet

Two salty beads rolled down Julian's cheek upon finding only three pages remained. Two had entries. The last was empty. *Soon*, he thought, remembering when they returned, he never saw

Dajhri lock the bronze door behind them. *The sun's risen by now.* After taking a moment to dry his tears and nod at his choice, Julian refocused on the diary and continued until the end.

12/26/19
Dear Diary

Jul's transformation was a success! Thank you, God. Thank you, Christ. At first, he wasn't swallowing the blood from Dad's wrist. We thought he was going to die, but finally, it was like a lightbulb clicked on inside him and he drank. He has since vomited everything out of his stomach and evacuated anything left in his bowels. I cleaned and dressed him.

Earlier, Dad and I moved his bed down to my room in the basement, next to my hammock, where I am now. Jul is sleeping, but I swore to stay by his side the whole time, and I plan on keeping my word. Now, the hard part is over. All he has left to do is heal. After that, we have the rest of time and space to spend together. It is only a matter of time now before my dreams become a reality. 2020, here we come!

Violet

12/31/19
Dear Diary

The clock says it is 4:44 a.m. Jul's healing has gone much better than Dad or I could have imagined. He was easily walking up and down the stairs only two days after his transformation. Right now, he is asleep in our basement bedroom while I am in the library. I am tired, but far too nervous to sleep. I am not just jittery because tonight is my wedding night, but because Dad took off again. A few nights ago, after he knew Jul was safe enough to be left alone in my care, he departed. He said he had some surprises he wanted to collect for the wedding, but he would be back in time. He is the one who is going to marry us, after all.

We were hoping to get married at midnight, but Jul wanted Daryl to be his best man. Daryl is going with his wife and daughters to a New Year's party, though. He said he would do it if we had the wedding early. I was annoyed and didn't want to do it before midnight, but I want Jul to have at least one person here, since I am going to have my dad. Oh well, I guess we can't have everything we want, but as long as I have the man of my dreams, the time we say, "I do" shouldn't matter, should it?

Even while healing, Jul has been hard at work. All this time, since we first met, he had been writing the story of his life on his laptop computer. He put his absolute all into that book. He even wrote about me and Dad, but he passed it all off as fiction. He calls it "Through Dead Eyes." I read all of it but the last chapter, which is what he just put the finishing touches on. He told me I could read it before he sends the whole thing to a bunch of publishers, later before the wedding. Since his lucky number is 44, he said that's how many emails he is going to send.

I am so proud of him! He says he doesn't want to be famous. He just wants his story to be told. He wants to show others, who have walked a similar path to his, that they are not alone. Jul has been through some of the strangest things—almost fictional, in a way—but he survived it all. He is my superhero!

It was his idea for us to write our wedding vows. I have been so scatter-brained, trying to figure out what to write. He definitely has me beat when it comes to that. Perhaps I will just say what I feel, rather than writing something beforehand. I do want to try to remember to throw something in there about him being the man of my dreams.

I've waited so long now to tell him. In the beginning, Dad told me not to, so I wouldn't scare him off, but as for all this other shit about that letter from Lusa and my past with Eric, I feel dishonest for keeping it to myself. I will tell him later tonight. It is only fair that he knows everything. Then our future shall begin. Come Hell or high water, this marriage will start off right, even if for some reason you should have to tell him all this for me. You know me better than anyone, after all.

Oh, Diary, all I know is: I, Violet Cordelia Troúton, love Julian Malcolm Frost with all my heart and soul. Well, that, and after the wedding tonight, we are going to destroy our bedroom! I am going to drag that beautiful brown-haired man across the walls and ceiling. After that, I'm going to take him outside and fuck him all over this mountain. I might even take him up into the sky! I have waited so long for this, and I know he has too.

I don't mean to sound so crude, but I have longed for so many years to make love to the right man. For so long, I hated myself for what happened to Eric, and it will always be my fault, but maybe now I can finally move on. I'll never forget him, but life isn't about looking back. It is about moving forward.

I only have one final page left before I must say good-bye to you, Diary. I will save it for after the wedding—maybe our one-year anniversary. That way, I can give you an update on how things are going. It has been one hell of a ride! You have helped me get through so much, just by letting me write about it and getting it off my chest. My sweet, innocent mother, Edith, bought you for me when I was just a little girl. Who knew by the time I reached the end, so many years and so many difficulties would have filled all these pages? I sure didn't, but what is life without surprises? Thank you for keeping my secrets. Thank you for everything, Diary!

Violet Frost

Julian closed the book, his eyes and cheeks now soaked in tears he couldn't stop from flowing. "We almost made it, my flower. We almost had our happily ever after. It might not have happened in this world, but I swear it will in the next." He laid the diary on his jacket, strewn on the floor beside the bed. His eyes fixed on the hanging green blanket over his doorway. He trembled when he stood, knowing where his feet were heading. *'You are the medicine, brother, and you manifest reality in your favor.'*

Beyond the door and down the hall, he reached the stairs. First, he looked left. Finding no one, he turned right and cautiously inched his way up to the top. He faced the closed bronze door, knowing the hot summer daylight waited on the other side. His heart raced. His eyes only flirted with the large knob above the keyhole. His hands were more eager; gripping the round lever and daring himself to turn it. *'What are you avoiding?'*

Julian swallowed a lump and closed his eyes, having no intentions of failing a third time. All he had to do was just let go. He released a breath. *To all time and space. Here I come, my love.* To his dismay, the knob wouldn't budge. *Goddamn it! Why?! Fucking why?!* With no choice but to turn back, he faced the stairs again, startled off balance when finding he was not alone. Unhooded near the bottom, standing still as a statue, his dead, dark eyes projecting directly into Julian's, Raimi glared from beneath his transparent mask of unkempt hatred.

Julian broke eye contact immediately. He said nothing on his way back to his hallway and room. He wasn't sure what the guard might say or do, but he wanted no part of it either way. Thinking, *There's always tomorrow,* he climbed into bed and stretched out on his side. Yearning to at least see his love one last time before ending it all, in hopes that Hell was just a fantasy, he yawned, closed his eyes, and whispered, "Come to me, Violet. Dajhri said it'll be easier now. Come to me, please." Soon enough, he was asleep.

Chapter Forty-Three

Julian slept through most of the daylight hours. When awake, he thought of Violet: her sweet tenderness and her blunt savagery, so passionate and territorial; the fire. He sulked over just how madly she'd longed for him as he had for her. Having lain in bed with his eyes shut for hours, he grasped onto the hope of awakening in his flower's arms.

His carnivorous desires snarling so intently, like a ravenous wolf who'd longed for days, he swore he could smell her "cheap vanilla bean" in the air. He rolled over and opened his eyes, expecting to see the inert green blanket, flickering in the remaining dim light. Instead, his heart cooed, finding himself not where he'd fallen asleep but somewhere else—somewhere dark, damp, and far from unknown.

"Violet?" he muttered, sensing her poised overtop him.

Offering no verbal response, a soft hand took his and pulled him from the hard floor. He'd waited so long for the moment they would come together in the cave again. With the opportunity so lucid and imminent, he refused to give anything else a chance to ruin it. As the silhouette led him towards the exit, he stopped in the middle of the path.

When she turned to face him, Julian closed his eyes and took a step forward. Their lips met sweetly at the flesh. A magical rejuvenation washed him over during the glorious exchange. Shivers rained down upon him just like the first time they had embraced as one. Next, their shy tongues reacquainted at the tips. Though Julian assumed his arousal was obvious, he wondered about hers. It was not until the same two erect nipples, she'd brushed against him in previous dreams, gently pushed into his torso from behind her thick hair that he not only discovered she was already unclothed, but her own fervency was every bit as rich as his.

Their lips separated just long enough for Violet to remove Julian's white tuxedo jacket and shirt. She also took his pants, boxers, and shoes off. Both fully nude, their eager bodies rejoined. His eyes still closed, Julian's mouth moved to Violet's neck, grazing her soft earlobe with the side of his tongue. She gasped suddenly. In response, he said, "I love you."

"I love you, Julian." Like the rare occasion in Paris when she whispered in his ear, he quivered then too. She wrapped her arms over his shoulders while his lips ventured towards her breasts. Hard breathing became soft moans as Julian's tongue circled her areola while periodically squeezing her thick nipple between his moist lips. After showing ample attention to one, he moved to the other, offering the same courtesy before returning to her mouth.

Violet wandered to Julian's neck, kissing it like he had hers. Then she reached his ear and bit the bottom half of his lobe, escalating the arousal. She took notice. Her hand moved south until gently gripping her lover's upright penis. Her lips broke away from his ear and she dropped to her bare knees. With the intimate encounter going further than ever, all Julian could think was, *Please, don't let me wake up yet. Please, don't take this from us.*

Still holding it in her hand, Violet kissed the snake on its head before allowing it full access. Her warm pillowy lips narrowed on the shaft and her moist tongue slithered in all the right places. She took in more while Julian gasped. He watched vague motions of her head bobbing in the shadows until all of him entered her precious mouth. Having never known such exquisite stimulation, Julian moaned, "My God!" But it wasn't God. It was Violet. The fellatio lasted for several minutes until she pulled away and got back to her feet. He asked, "Is everything okay?" She took his hand and led him onward, beyond the exit and into the arctic wilderness.

From the stratosphere, the eerie green mist of the Aurora frolicked for its hosts, leading the way to their own garden. Though the viridescent phantom engulfed all from above, below, Julian could only make out occasional shapes, shadows, and reflections in the otherwise murky silva.

Along their walk to the inevitable, his anxious heart slammed his insides. He knew what was coming. Even in a dream, the idea of living up to Violet's expectations terrified him. He remembered everything she had written in her diary about how she wanted to be made love to—how she wanted to make love to him. Passing several trees, he imagined how she might react if he were to push her up against one and have his way with her like the man and woman in the alleyway, whom she'd confessed to watching and wanting for herself.

Without giving himself time to reconsider, he gripped the naked shadow by its hips. Offering him no resistance, he mindfully shoved her upper half against a sturdy trunk. Thick enough to withstand the upheaval but thin enough to hold on tight, Julian firmly wedged his unbreakable flower between himself and the frozen spruce.

Violet arched her back, offering permission to enter. Still erect, Julian carefully advanced until the lovers intertwined. Together, they released a moan. His trembling lips pressed firmly against the back of her ear—her sweet aroma filling his nostrils; Julian began to thrust. He was slow at first, but once tightening his arms around her and the trunk, he picked up momentum. Every passionate collision dropped a white dusting on their backs from the caked branches. Both ignored it as the intensity grew. The mini quakes lasted over a minute before Julian had to stop.

Both panting, their backs dripping with melted snow and gathering sweat, Violet slipped loose from Julian's grip and took his hand again. After leading him farther into the forest, they reached the natural spring. Even with the Northern Lights reflecting onto the water from above, the rocky pool only emitted enough light to border the hourglass figure standing between it and the man of her dreams.

Now just feet apart, Julian grew weak in the knees when looking upon his one true love. Violet's thick, darkened locks veiled her divine face like always. As he approached, she stepped back, her bare feet entering first. Julian followed until the waterline reached his heart.

The whole time, he'd wondered, *Am I even doing this right? It's been so long. I sure hope so.* Utterly terrified, he took a deep, reassuring breath. Before he could act, Violet intervened. She wrapped her wet hands behind Julian's neck and shoulders. Their lips met again, and his fears melted instantly.

Their kisses enduring, a smooth boulder rising just above the water caught Julian's eye. Struck with an idea, he lifted Violet by her waist again, this time with barely any effort. She squeaked pleasantly when he set her on the rock. She lay back into an inch of water and stretched her legs, making herself comfortable. As if he already knew what she wanted, Julian put a leg over each of his shoulders.

After softly pecking his way back down Violet's body, he reached her inner thighs. He'd softly kiss one and then the other. Back and forth, he worked inward until reaching his flower's holy garden. He exhaled slowly, allowing his warm breath to stimulate and tease her. Otherwise inexperienced, he had no clue where such confident ideas came from, but his drifting thoughts were short lived once his love impatiently pulled the back of his head forward. Grinding his face, she gave him a mouthful of her fruit; so sweet, juicy, and forbidden to all mouths but his.

Julian's kiss was deep. Violet's vocal display of satisfaction was loud. Her hands firmly planted against his head; her thighs often quivering and tightening over his ears. He rapidly licked the alphabet around her small hidden clitoris while creating a suction with his puckered lips. Using his middle and index fingers, he aggressively rubbed against her upper wall in a circular motion. Violet's huffing intensified. Her thighs wavered madly. She howled, and her fingernails dug into the back of Julian's scalp. He knew she was close to climax. That's when she murmured, "Stop."

He pulled away and asked, "What's wrong?"

After catching her breath, she slid back into the water and reached between Julian's legs. Charming the snake once more, she sandwiched him between herself and a tall boulder, intending to have her way now. Before Julian could even wonder what she had planned, Violet's arms hugged his neck. She pushed her knees and shins against the rock on each side of Julian's abdomen. Hovering at the perfect position, she inched forward, becoming weightless, and granting the snake its deepest entry yet.

Julian's eyes bugged out from such a mind-bending sensation. Barely anything happened yet, and it was already the best gratification he'd ever received. Violet kissed his lips while gyrating her pelvis. Like Julian, she began slowly, but she was much quicker to pick up the pace. It didn't take long before he thought he was going to explode.

"Slow down!" he groaned, not wanting it to end so soon. Violet complied. She remained locked in place, but the grinding ended. They stayed in that position while they returned to kissing like adolescents again.

Once Julian had a moment to rest, Violet whispered, "Hold me."

He gulped, "What?" but she blasted to the sky. Her arms remained tightly wrapped over his neck and shoulders. Hugging his waist with her legs, her pistil protected his stamen. Holding on for dear life, he fearfully clenched his eyelids shut. Both their bodies dripping wet, Violet tightened her clutches before she returned to thrusting.

Again, she started slow, but shortly after, went wild, riding him hard like a bucking bronco. Julian begged for the bravery to open his eyes, especially so close to orgasm. When Violet's legs shook intensely and she screamed, he knew she was having hers. *Fuck it,* he thought. *If I slip and fall, the worst that will happen is I wake up.*

His own powerful surge rushing to the surface, he unsealed his lids, finding them both coupled in midair, anointed by the surrounding aura. Just as she wailed, so did he. Once they both finished and caught their breath, Julian kissed her lips one more time and said, "I love you so much, Violet."

Her thick drapes still concealing her face, she said, "And I love you, Julian." Up until then, she'd whispered everything she'd said. Violet whispered in his ear so rarely and so long ago, he'd paid little attention to it before. It was the same timbre that entered his bed in Paris, and the same body from his other dreams in the cave. But when spoken at a normal volume, it was not Violet's sweet, southern drawl he recognized. It was a silky, venomous voice. His gut about to rupture, he cautiously brushed the dark shape's hair aside, praying to find Violet's brown almonds, but it was two beady green eyes attached to the teardrop face of a queen he saw staring back.

"What the—" Julian choked on his own words. His entire body shook with an equal amount of unlawful shock and disgust. He gasped and gagged. Already slippery and wet—not just from the spring water but each other's fluids, he slid right out of Dajhri's arms. Two hundred feet separated him from the solid ground below. He twirled uncontrollably, catching flashes of black and green along the way. Acting on instinct, he sealed his eyes and braced for impact. *What if this isn't a dream? What if it's real?! Oh shit! I don't want to die! I'm not ...*

His heart pounding, Julian opened his eyes, finding himself lying on a hard stone surface. Smooth and gray, the slab flickered orange. Looking in each direction, he searched the bare floor, finding nothing but empty space. When he tried to stand, he nearly toppled over his own weight. That is when he looked up. Either his eyes were playing tricks on him or the now apparent fire burning in the pit, his bed, and the makeshift blanket door all appeared upside down.

"What the fuck?" he mumbled. He looked down at his feet, only then discovering they weren't touching anything—but suspended inches from the ceiling. Curious and astounded, he imagined his body spinning to an upright position. As he did, all the items in the room followed, losing their abstraction. Completely stuck in the surreal moment, Julian trembled. He was floating like a bird while his mind and body dripped with the gooey wet byproduct of a sinner's deception.

He looked down, finding the intended floor only a foot below. As he imagined a soft landing, there came a distant series of bangs, echoing throughout the temple like a battered gong. The sudden clamor startled Julian. Before he could safely plant his feet, he crashed hard. … *Bang … bang … bang …* "Open the door!" *Bang … bang … bang …* "In the name of King Caanis: open the door!"

Chapter forty-four

From his room, Julian's intrigue had momentarily overshadowed his 'protector's' unwarranted assault and resulting effects. The recent commotion from upstairs led him into the hallway and towards the vacant flight. It was only minutes earlier the belligerent man arrived, desperately begging for an audience. Julian never saw his face or who let him in, but their low, incoherent voices came from the bottom floor.

He believed it was Dajhri, speaking to the man he presumed was from L'abisme. He took his time, descending the steps, the conversation growing louder with every tiptoe. Preferring to avoid detection, he stopped just short of the bottom. His left ear pressed firmly against the wall, he listened to the man stutter his motives in a broken Mediterranean accent.

"… I found forty-four—all dead! I—I had been away for two weeks. I—I was visiting my homeland. When I returned, I f—found them all massacred and scattered throughout the cavern. Some were crushed and beheaded. Several had even been shot with guns. Many of them had been eaten by the rats." The man cried. "I—I ha—have never seen anything so sick and grotesque in all my life as I did down there. … Jesus!"

Calmly, Dajhri said, "You only found forty-four?"

"I did."

"Where are the others?"

"I—I don't know. When I left, everyone but Queen Annabel was there. Shortly after yours and the Ahrims' departure, and Caanis' assassination, rumors spread of the Ahrims having quarreled with the outsider king, Bernard. According to him, they were but only rumors."

"And was the new king or his queen among the bodies you found?"

"They were not, but the kingdom's two most loyal and longest standing guards: Paul Mecklenbury and Teddy von Wolkenstein were. I imagine they died trying to protect our people."

Dajhri sighed. "And you believe it was the Ahrims who did this, Vincent?"

The Ahrims use guns? He said some had been shot. That doesn't sound right.

"I do!" the man yelped. "It was after Caanis' murder; I heard whispers. They said the Raja Kahiji was insulted by the treatment and mockery his translator had received. To resolve the matter, Bernard intended to barter with the Ahrims—giving them Caanis' accused assassin in exchange for restoring the truce.

"According to Bernard, before the deal could be made, the princesses—Winter-Fae, and Avice—betrayed us and freed the accused. He said Caanis' daughters were both killed by the Ahrims while trying to escape, but the other, Julian Frost, died somewhere in the catacombs. This angered the Raja Kahiji. He felt cheated. That is why I believe those I found must have faced his wrath."

"And how do you feel about this?" Dajhri asked, still offering no hint of empathy in her voice.

"Your highness?!"

"A man whom neither you nor anyone else in L'abisme— other than Winter-Fae, Paul, and Teddy—had met before shows up and becomes the king, mere hours after he is named the heir. He blamed a grieving new vampire for murdering 'the great King Caanis.' Then Bernard used that man as leverage to undermine what the former king and I had done to save that man's life. So, I will ask you again, Vincent Calo of Istanbul. How do you feel about that?"

"All right! I cannot speak for the others, but I never once believed Bernard. We'd heard Julian Frost had gotten into some trouble a few nights before Caanis died. I know it angered him.

After just losing his son, he feared Frost might have exposed us. Queen Dajhri, you know Caanis had a temper, and I couldn't imagine he let Frost off easy, but I know it didn't contribute to his death. We all knew the kid was innocent. That is partially why I left to begin with. Just as I assumed Bernard lied about who killed Caanis, I also thought he was lying about the Ahrims."

"I assumed Bernard was using the barter as an excuse to cover his own crime. I took it as him attempting to save face with L'abisme—knowing most of us did not support him—while also trying to reunite with Raz Ahrim. At first, I wanted nothing to do with 'Bernard's L'abisme,' but soon after I left, I found Turkey was not the same home I'd left behind. There was nothing there for me, so I returned to Paris."

"And that is when you found the bodies?"

"Yes, my queen."

"If you had to guess, how long would you say the bodies had been there before you found them?"

"I could not say for certain. Their blood had been long congealed, and it appeared they'd been dead for days."

Still listening from the steps, Julian nearly leapt off balance when the shrill squeak of the heavy bronze door startled him. His anxious eyes immediately shifted to the top of the stairs. There, Raimi was passing through and lowering his brown hood. Torchlight reflecting off his bald head, he groaned, "Why is this unlocked?"

To avoid him, Julian started up towards his hall as the guard headed down. Near the middle, their eyes finally met. Though he said nothing, the scowl Raimi forced on Julian after he'd first glanced back at the unlocked door, screamed, *"Fuck off!"* By the time he reached his room, the idea had become his church. *The door is unlocked, huh? Can I still fly? I will gladly "fuck off."*

He took a breath and shivered, ignoring the nausea for a more pleasant thought: Violet's perfect face. Fighting the guilt of something beyond his control, he imagined himself floating a foot off the ground, his flower there to catch him should he fall. Once again, his thoughts became reality as his movements mocked his desires. *Check!*

Back on the ground, Violet's old blue diary lying atop his jacket caught his eye next. He instantly erupted, unable to hold back his warm, salty anguish any longer. "Please, forgive me," he sobbed while placing the hardback in its usual spot. Examining his moist crotch, he knew the infidelity wasn't his fault, but that was not the point. He was supposed to be with *her*—nobody else.

He took his wallet from another pocket, ensuring all the money he'd taken from his and Xavier's safe was still there. *Check!* Having not tried his phone since he got there, he held in the power button, praying it would turn on. A couple of seconds later, the device vibrated, and the screen lit up. *Oh, thank God!* The time and date read: *11:11 p.m. PET. Feb 20, 2020.* The battery only read *4%*, but that was more than enough for what he needed.

He slid his arms through the sleeves of his black leather jacket with embroidered skulls before passing through the covered doorway, heading down the hall with a purpose. All the way, he thought of Violet. She tried to warn him. In Virginia, so did Daryl. He told Julian Violet couldn't find him, but he never listened. He let his lust and obsession become his own dagger, and his heart, the king.

At the top of the stairs, he turned to look back down, finding no one in view. Out of anger, disgust, and the utmost prejudice, he raised his middle finger towards the bottom, mouthing, "Fuck you!" If he could spit, piss, or shit on the queen's ancient steps, he would. If he could push her into the sunlight, he'd do it with bells on. His rage burrowed so deeply that he swore, if only for a couple of seconds, the ground actually shook beneath his feet. Moving on, he slowly pulled the bronze door open and made his way to the gate.

Outside, he checked his phone again, finding he not only had a signal, but a new text message coming through. Despite everything, he instantly shivered with a sparkle of hope when the name *Daryl Stillwater* appeared. He'd not only read the text message Julian sent the previous month, but he also sent one back. The date read *Jan 5, 2020*: four days after Daryl's transformation. Julian wasted no time opening it. Hearing his own heartbeat ringing, he read to himself: *help me, bro.*

All along he'd been torn over where to go next. In Alaska, he would be safe until learning how to control his powers and live fruitfully as a vampire. It wasn't until hearing his oldest and closest living friend call out for help, he knew with absolute certainty where his journey was taking him next.

The phone battery having already dropped to 2%, Julian quickly pulled up a compass to find which way was north. All he needed now was a city—just a cluster of lights with a hotel inside it. There, he could charge his phone, call Daryl, and have a much safer chance of finding his way back home. Aside from his wedding band and silver ankh pendant, everything else was either in his pockets, head, or heart.

He had no more concern for the queen, her prophecies and wishes, or any world-ending war. If she wanted to find and punish him for leaving, so be it. She'd already taken the most she could from him. All he had left now was his life, and as far as he was concerned, taking that would be doing him a service. According to the man from L'abisme, everyone else already thought he was dead anyway.

Facing north, Julian put his phone in the same jacket pocket as his charger before zipping it and all the others with something inside them. He pulled his collar up while inhaling a slow, deep breath of fresh Peruvian air. Just thinking about it, he shot-off abruptly like a fizzling bottle rocket. Hitting the brakes, his body froze in place, a slight jolt shaking his insides. What he saw nearly took his breath away. Even his sorrow couldn't ruin the natural beauty or surrealism he encountered when panning the black velvet sky and intricate valleys below. He was in control: *'Adapting,'* as Violet would say.

"I wish you were here," is what Julian said. but *I am so sorry, my flower. Please, forgive me* was still all he thought. Nevertheless, he wobbled in place for a moment until catching his balance. Then, he extended both hands and eyes forward, fixed on what was to come. After one final breath of hesitation, he threw himself and caution to the wind—blasting off, and doing what he'd always done best when life got too hard: disappear.

Thank you for reading!

Please follow me on social media.

Facebook: @darrenfreyauthor
Instagram: @darrenfreyauthor
YouTube: @darrenfreyauthor

Stay tuned. The best is yet to come!

Printed in Great Britain
by Amazon